Salvaged Love
A Historic Novel of Key West
1828-1829

SUSAN BLACKMON

With the exception of historical figures, all characters in this novel are fictitious. Any resemblance to living persons, present or past, is coincidental.

Excerpt from "The Young Wrecker on the Florida Reef" used by permission of The Ketch & Yawl Press.

This book contains an excerpt from the forthcoming book *Love Again* by Susan Blackmon. This excerpt has been set for this edition only and may not reflect the final content of the forthcoming edition.

Dream Publishing
Lawrenceville, GA

ISBN: 0988664801
ISBN-13: 978-0988664807

http://susanblackmonauthor.weebly.com

Cover illustration: John (Jack) H. Morse III

Printed in the United States of America

DEDICATION

To my wonderful and supportive family, first my husband for his encouragement and sacrifice so I could write and for providing the male point of view. Second to my fan club for reading the drafts, offering advice and cheering me on: Mom, Dad, Aunt Annette, Uncle Ronnie, Jennifer, Anne-Marie, Linda, Tiffany, & Christy. And third, to my Dad and brother for the gift of their time and talent in creating the beautiful cover.

Thanks to my editor, MaryKay Harman, for taking on my project and to the crew of the schooner Western Union, especially Sabrina for her nautical advice of wooden ship sailing in Key West waters.

Last and most important, I thank God for my many blessings.

Author's Note

I find my purpose in writing this book to be the same as Richard Meade Bache. To quote from his forward in *The Young Wrecker on the Florida Reef,* "The author has endeavored, in the following story, to deviate as little as possible from fact, so as to combine instruction with amusement." Although my story is definitely fiction it was inspired by the original inhabitants and true history of the island and as such I did my best to play true to the facts as I was able to find them. I also chose not to change the names of those who played such important roles in the building of Key West.

So take yourself back to the Golden Age of Sail when man depended on wind and water to guide their ships and horse or train to travel across land. When the world was on the cusp of new discoveries like the telegraph and stethoscope. When handwritten mail was the only means of communication and gas lights were just beginning to replace candles in the home. America celebrated her half-century and recently fought the War of 1812 against her former oppressor, England. The country was full of optimism and opportunity. Young pioneers were spilling out across the newly opened Mississippi and Ohio River valleys and a few made their way to a tiny island lured by the adventure of facing pirates and making money from the wreckage of ships.

There was a Presidential Election in 1828. Andrew Jackson defeated incumbent, John Quincy Adams, to become our seventh President. There were only twenty-four states at the time. Florida was still a territory and did not participate in the election although there would have been great interest as many of the island's inhabitants were originally from New England.

Blending fact and fiction my story is set against a backdrop of American history. All of my main characters are fictional but some of the people they interact with were true inhabitants of Key West. If you enjoy history, here's a guide to who's who and what's what in 1828 Key West. If not move on to chapter one and I hope you enjoy the story.

Like most of Florida and much of the United States, Key West was originally inhabited by Indians. Claimed by Spain (1565-1763), England gained control in 1763 until the end of the Revolutionary War in 1783 when all of Florida reverted back to Spain. In July, 1821, at a formal ceremony in Pensacola, presided over by Andrew Jackson, Florida was transferred to the United States. Key West was then called *Cayo Hueso* ('kajo 'weso), meaning 'Bone Key', but we American's manipulated the pronunciation and dubbed it 'Key West'.

A man named Juan Salas received the island as a gift from the Spanish governor of Cuba for services rendered and as the story goes he sold it twice. Salas sold it to John Simonton for roughly 2,000 pesos in 1821. He also made a second conditional sale to John Strong for a sloop valued at $575. Strong met up with George Murray and traded the land for a letter of credit. Murray then 'sold' the island to General John Geddes, presumably with a fake document. A court battle ensued before John Simonton was declared the legal owner in

1825.

Simonton had learned of the island from his friend, John Whitehead, who had discovered it a few years earlier, by way of a detour, after being rescued from a shipwreck in the Bahamas. Whitehead saw the island's potential and with the transfer of Florida to the U.S. opportunity was at hand. The two men tracked down Salas. John Simonton funded the purchase and then sold off three quarters of the island ironically to four men named John. One quarter was sold to John Whitehead, another to his friend John Flemming and one quarter was shared by John Mountain and former Consul John Warner. Mountain and Warner later sold their share to Pardon C. Greene.

Simonton went to Washington to persuade Congress of the benefits of setting up naval operations in Key West and declaring it a port of customs. Meanwhile Whitehead, Mountain and Warner prepared their settlement for a bright future focused on commerce, customs and national defense. They industriously cleared home sites, stockpiled cut stove wood and imported sheep and hogs with the expectation of selling meat and milk.

Their plans seemed to be working. Shortly after their arrival Navy Lt. Commandant Matthew C. Perry sailed into Key West on the U.S. Schooner *Shark*. Sent by Congress to assess the island's potential, Perry sent back a glowing report for its excellent harbor and key location in the Caribbean. It was an ideal halfway point for ships sailing between the Southern and Eastern coasts of the continent. During his visit he officially claimed Key West for the United States, its ownership being somewhat hazily claimed by Spain and England by extension of Cuba and the Bahamas, respectively. He also dubbed it Thompson's Island wanting to earn points with the Navy secretary Smith Thompson and named the harbor Port Rodgers for the President of the naval board.

Piracy was an escalating problem in the Caribbean. In 1820 Congress established the West India Squadron known as the anti-piracy squadron. Initially it had little success. After Perry's glowing remarks, in a case of 'careful what you wish for', the Navy ordered Captain David Porter to take over the squadron and establish a base in Key West. Because of his command of eleven hundred men Porter had the courtesy title of Commodore. He was a hero of the War of 1812 and he took on his new role with enthusiasm and cunning strategy. Using a fleet of small ships able to ferret out the enemy, he successfully eradicated the pirates and illegal privateers.

For the proprietors of Key West this came at a great cost. Upon his arrival Porter declared Martial Law on the town and taking advantage of the dispute in ownership declared the entire island property of the United States. He referred to the island as Allentown in honor of the commander of the *Alligator*, Lt. William H. Allen, who died valiantly in battle against the pirates a few months prior to Porter's arrival. Porter used the harvested wood and took any unpenned livestock without offering compensation to the owners. He built storehouses, workshops and barracks on prime waterfront lots designated for the owners while at the same time forbidding them to build unless he approved. Worse, he inflicted harsh punishment on those caught breaking his rules.

Yellow fever spread across the island the summer of 1823 and again in 1824. Porter was a victim both times retreating to Washington, without permission, to recover. He continued to rule the island through his second in command, Lt. Frederick Varnum. The secretary of the Navy ordered Porter to return in both cases and Porter, passionately hating Key West, asked to resign his post after the second instance. He was relieved by Captain Warrington in February 1825. The citizens rejoiced over his departure but it was short lived. Porter's negative reports and a third outbreak of yellow fever in the fall led the Navy to move their base to Pensacola. Disappointing news for the proprietors but it was only the beginning of Key West's long history with the military.

Unfortunately, it was not the last they would see of Porter. He was court-martialed for insulting the Spanish government at Foxardo and for insubordination and conduct unbecoming an officer. Porter resigned from the U.S. Navy and accepted a commission as commander of the Mexican Navy. On Christmas day 1826, fleeing from Spanish frigates under cover of a storm, Porter took shelter in Key West harbor taking advantage of U.S. neutrality. The Spanish set up a blockade but familiar with the Keys from his anti-piracy campaign Porter successfully evaded them. He used Key West as a base of operations for nine months while he coordinated raids against Spanish shipping. It was a blatant violation of U.S. neutrality (The first and only recorded violation of an American neutral position.) and there was no one in Key West to protest. The Navy had moved to Pensacola and the only civil authority was custom collector, William Pinckney. A friend of Porter's, Pinckney defended him.

When funds from the Mexican government dried up, Porter started selling goods from the captured Spanish ships to pay his troops, hurting the local wrecking business. Fearful of losing trade with Cuba, a vital source of goods and trade for the island, newspaper editors appealed to Congress to get Porter out of Key West. Porter refused to leave until he was ordered to do so or the Spanish blockade left. End of August 1827, both of these happened.

Porter, who later returned to the United States, touted Key West's advantages in a letter to the secretary of the Navy probably influencing the eventual return of a permanent naval base.

Since my story takes place from 1828-1829 the history lesson ends here. My hope is to write future books to take you through more of the history of this unique island all the way to current day.

Why did I choose 1828, you may ask? I was writing my story around ship salvaging and looked for a pivotal point in its beginning. Key West was declared the U.S. Port of Entry in 1822 but salvage claims were either settled by arbitration or had to be taken to court in St. Augustine. This being such an inconvenience most cases were arbitrated. The system became so corrupt that even the salvagers signed the petition to establish a court in Key West. Court was opened November 1828 exponentially increasing the wealth of the city over the next forty years and for a brief moment in time giving Key West the enviable status of wealthiest city in America.

You may notice some discrepancies of location compared to the Key West of today. A lot of places were moved around on the island by man and by nature. For example, there once was a large tidal pond in the center of old town and the lighthouse and cemetery were both originally located on the coast until the hurricane of 1846 destroyed them. They were resituated where you find them today. Men with whatever means they had at the time literally lifted houses and buildings and moved them as needed. For example, the current Oldest House and Le Pepe's restaurant still exist but not in their original locations. In the case of Sloppy Joe's Bar, the inhabitants moved but that's a story for another book. You may also notice the island dimensions are smaller in my story. Over the last century man has expanded the island to suit his purposes.

For the record, in my book, Flamingo Key is a fictional place.

<u>Historical figures - these people really visited/lived in Key West</u>
John W. Simonton (d.1854) - founder of Key West, led the island's development and lobbied Congress to establish a naval base on the island, both to take advantage of the island's strategic location and to bring law and order to the town.
John Whitehead (d.1862) - a friend of John Simonton he advised him to buy the island after discovering Key West by way of being a shipwreck victim. A quarter owner, he lived in Key West for only eight years. He left in 1832 returning once in 1861, during the Civil War.
John W.C. Flemming (1781-1832) - another friend of Simonton and quarter owner. He spent a few months on the island in 1822. He returned ten years later to start salt manufacturing from the salt ponds. He died the same year.
John Mountain and former **Consul John Warner** - received a quarter share of the island from Simonton but transferred it to P.C. Greene.
Pardon C. Greene (1781-1838) - only one of the four founders to live on the island until his death. A prominent merchant, he also served briefly as mayor.
Fielding A. Browne (1791?-1851) - merchant and Mayor of Key West.
William Adee Whitehead (1810-1884) - John Whitehead's younger brother, he developed the land plat still referenced on deeds today. Later he became the custom collector and ran for mayor. Early Key West history comes from his custom records, letters and newspaper articles. He had the forethought to send Key West newspapers to the Monroe County clerk for

preservation. He left the island in 1838 frustrated by the Mayoral election results.

Commodore David Porter (1780-1843) - commanded the Anti-Piracy campaign based in Key West from 1823-1825. He was court-martialed for an unsanctioned invasion of Puerto Rico to avenge an officer of his fleet. He resigned from the American Navy and then became Commander-in-Chief of the Mexican Navy in 1826.

Ellen Mallory (1792-1855) - known as the First Lady of Key West, when she arrived with her husband, Charles, and two sons in 1822 she was the only woman on the island. After her husband and oldest son died, she ran the only boardinghouse.

Stephen Russell Mallory (1812-1873) - Ellen's second son was a future Florida senator and later Secretary of the Confederate Navy. He attended the Moravian academy in Nazareth, PA during the timeframe of my story.

Judge James Webb - first judge assigned to Key West, served 1828-1838.

Clerk Joel Yancey - assigned as first collector of customs in1822, Judge Webb selected him as the first clerk of the court.

Marshal Henry Wilson

Michael Mabrity (d.1832) - Key West's first lightkeeper, member of the town council.

Barbara Mabrity (1782-1867) - took over the light after her husband died and served until 1864. {Look for more of her history in future books.}

Dr. Henry S. Waterhouse (d.1835) - a prominent NY surgeon, he resigned his position to move to Key West with his son. He was the first Postmaster for the island and later served on the town council and as town treasurer.

Mr. Barnum - assisted William Whitehead in surveying the island.

Captain John Jackson - captain of the Revenue Marine Cutter *Marion*
Captain Charles Hawkins - Mexican Navy
William A McRea - US District Attorney

True stories (or at least written history)
Spermo 1827
USS Alligator 1822
Guerrero 1827
Hawkins and McRea Duel 1829

Chapter 1

August, 1828 Midanbury, England - a small hamlet outside Southampton

"Would you like to accompany me to the Caribbean?" Richard Bennington asked from behind his morning paper. Abigail stopped buttering her toast to look at her father across the expanse of the dining room table. *What was he up to?* In all her nineteen years, he had never once taken her on one of his trips. *Did he know about her latest folly? Surely Miss Winterfeldt had not had a chance to tell him yet.*

Richard did indeed know of yesterday's ride through the park - unescorted. Miss Winterfeldt, the nanny he hired when Abby was a toddler, had left him a note requesting he again speak to Abby of her behaviour. It was not the first time his daughter had acted inappropriately and probably not the last either. But her indiscretion was not his reason for wanting to get her out of England. He had noticed she was restless of late and thought a change of place would be good for her but more importantly it was the visit he received from the Duke of Rothebury's son, Lord Jason Malwbry, which concerned him.

Most men in his position would be thrilled to have a duke's son ask to court his daughter but Richard was not a man to be impressed by a title alone. He wanted his daughter to know love like he and his precious wife Anna had shared. Lord Malwbry gave Richard the impression it was money he was more interested in pursuing. Since Jason didn't seem to have any real feelings for his Abigail, Richard was left to wonder if the family coffers were in need of new funds and hence, the offer for his daughter who was clearly beneath Jason's social standing. Still you couldn't outright refuse a request of this nature without some fear of reprisal so Richard decided the best course of action would be to simply remove his daughter from Jason's realm. Although, he left Jason with the impression he could court Abigail without actually saying so.

Richard Bennington looked the part of a wealthy middle aged genteel gentleman with well-trimmed whiskers, clean shaven face and tailored clothes. His hair was not as thick as it once was and his temples were greying but he had a pleasing appearance found to be attractive with the ladies of several generations much to the envy of his peers. Though he was considered the wealthiest man in the area he was not the most powerful. The Duke of Rothebury, Jason's father, ultimately controlled the livelihood of all the inhabitants of Midanbury and the surrounding area.

Richard built his fortune in shipping. He and his younger brother James had worked together to build a thriving merchant fleet. After the War of 1812 his brother acquired a cotton plantation near Montgomery, Alabama. The cotton was exported to England on their ships making them both wealthy. The trade winds had also taken him to other markets, such as tea and spices from the East, greatly expanding his commerce. This trip to Jamaica was a chance to get a firsthand account of his West Indies trade with a visit to his manager on the island, Josiah Landis.

Aside from his business, Abigail was his life. This unusual closeness was due to losing his wife, Anna, to a fever a year after Abigail was born. He almost lost his daughter as well. After nearly a week of sleepless nights holding her tiny hand and soothing her brow, the fever finally broke. The near loss left Richard with little heart for discipline. He knew he was too softhearted towards Abby and everyone said she had him wrapped around her finger, but he just couldn't help it. Thankfully Miss Winterfeldt handled most of the discipline very efficiently, until recently. Without the strictures most parents impose Abby was becoming reckless. The last few years had been trying for Miss Winterfeldt and now she was turning to him to guide Abby at a time when he was even more out of his depth. He was ill equipped to handle a child much less a young lady, especially when the young lady so resembled his late wife with her auburn hair, dainty nose and enchanting smile. If not for having his stubborn chin and grey eyes instead of her mother's green the resemblance would have been too much for Richard to bear. He was as yet still undecided if her personality being more like his than her mother's was a blessing or a curse.

Unlike most of his peers, Richard wanted his daughter to be educated and able to think for herself but she should also defer to her husband. He was coming to realize she was too headstrong and needed more discipline if she was going to make a good wife. And she needed it before she found herself in more trouble than just an embarrassing situation. He made a resolution to start being more firm with her; although he had a feeling it may be too little too late.

Abigail couldn't help but show her surprise with a hint of pique, "To what do I owe the honour of this invitation?"

Richard felt the sting in her question. He had sailed often for business and had never before taken her along. It had been for her own safety but now the tides were turned and danger to her welfare lay on land instead of sea. "The builders have just finished my new ship and I thought we could take her maiden voyage together. I have some business in Jamaica and then we could sail onto Alabama and spend Christmas with your uncle's family on his plantation."

Abigail liked the idea of going away, especially with Lord Jason trying to stake a claim on her. She had hoped riding alone in the park with one of his friends might have deterred his pursuit but leaving England was certainly a more sensible idea. She also was eager to travel the world and to meet her uncle's family. She had only seen her uncle twice in her life and had never met her Aunt Virginia nor her cousins.

"You have had new ships before, why take me this time?" Realizing her tone was belligerent, she softened it with a smile. It wouldn't solve her problem for her father to think she didn't want to go.

"It's safer now. Pirating in the Caribbean has almost been eliminated, finally, and I was thinking you could use a change of scenery....broaden your world, so to speak. Could you be ready to sail in a fortnight?"

"Father! So soon? I will need traveling clothes and Madame Rousseau does not like to be pressured. Remember the hideous green dress she made for Elizabeth in a rush for the Holdsworth's engagement party?"

"So how long?" *Firm, be firm,* Richard reminded himself.

"At least a month for decent day dresses, plus holiday dresses, plus traveling clothes and..."

"Now dear, you can wear this summer's dresses in the islands and for goodness sake's no one in America has ever seen you so you can certainly wear last year's season again...."

"But father...."

Richard pleaded in a firm voice, "Abigail be reasonable."

"Father, I would not be comfortable meeting Aunt Virginia for the first time wearing last season's styles."

Richard smiled and tried for a placating tone. "Dearest, you have no need to fear on that account; the colonies are usually more than a season behind in fashion. Your wardrobe will do quite nicely."

"Well at least one new dress for the holidays and whatever I need for traveling."

"You may have whatever Madame can complete within the fortnight. We are sailing the first of September."

"Yes Poppa. I will go to see her after breakfast."

Richard looked heavenward at the endearment only used when Abby felt she was indulging his wishes. Now with his sailing plans in place it was time to act a bit more fatherly. "Abigail, there is something else I wish to speak of; your actions of yesterday have come to my attention." At this Abigail paused from stirring her tea and quickly looked to him with some concern. "I expect you to behave with more regard for your reputation. Riding alone with a gentleman, even if he has been a longtime friend, is not acceptable as you well know. It will not happen again."

Abigail, surprised by the unexpected parental admonishment, was instantly contrite. "No father."

"Very well." Richard secretly congratulated himself as he pretended to return his attention to his paper.

Abigail felt the dismissal in his action and was more than agreeable to take her leave.

Richard discretely watched his daughter rise gracefully from the table, polish off the last of her toast in a dainty bite, wipe the crumbs from her mouth with her napkin and head his way to give him a kiss on the forehead. *Oh well, at least he had mostly held to his resolution. Rome wasn't built in a day.*

Abby and Miss Winterfeldt left the house just over an hour later in her father's most recent acquisition - a well sprung carriage. Her frugal father bought it used from a broker. They speculated the original owner may have been the Duke of Rothebury judging from the outline of the recently removed crest. Abby sank back into the comfort of the leather upholstery after instructing the driver. She decided to recruit her lifelong friend Elizabeth Kendall to help at the dressmakers. Elizabeth and her husband, Avery, had taken a trip to the tropics for their honeymoon just over a year ago so her advice would be valuable, especially with such limited time to prepare. A mere quarter hour later they stopped in front of Elizabeth's stately Tudor manor.

The door was opened by Molly, the downstairs maid. She led Abby and Miss Winterfeldt to the morning room. Abby barely had time to wonder why they had been ushered in by Molly rather than Alfred, the butler, when Elizabeth rounded the corner. She greeted Abby with a bright smile and a hug then nodded to Miss Winterfeldt and suggested she might like to visit her friend and Elizabeth's cook, Anestia, in the kitchen. As Miss Winterfeldt departed Elizabeth turned back to Abby, "Dear, it is so good to see you. It has been ages. I have wanted to visit but something seems to always keep me from getting out. Today, Alfred twisted his ankle. He had to be tended to while the doctor was summoned and then the household chores reassigned. I just finished settling a dispute in the kitchen and then...." Elizabeth realized she was probably being rude to her guest. "Oh Abby, I apologize. I should not burden you with my domestic trials."

Abby smiled at her longtime friend. Elizabeth's open and giving nature made it easy for her to make friends and keep them. She was beautiful in a quiet, unpretentious way. Her face was round and always smiling, her hair blond and styled artfully to frame her face. She always looked calm and collected even with this morning's trials. Actually, Abby noticed underneath it all Elizabeth appeared joyful. Marriage was certainly agreeing with her. "You sound as if you need to get away for a while and I have just the antidote for your situation. Come spend the afternoon with me. I need your help with Madame Rousseau and then we can have lunch while you tell me all about being married."

Elizabeth frowned, "Abby, I could not leave the house at a time like this. Besides I still have to approve the menus and make out the shopping list."

Abby gave her a quizzical look, "The doctor has been to see Alfred?"

"Yes."

"Nothing to be done except for him to rest his ankle?"

"Yes, that is true but..."

"The chores have been reassigned. Unless you have an event coming up the menu can be dispensed with quickly and I will help with the shopping list. Oh Bethy, please say yes. My father has asked me to travel with him to the Caribbean and the States. We leave the first of September and we will not return until next year. It will be ever so long before we have a chance to visit again."

Abby's declaration took the wind right out of Elizabeth's sails. Suddenly, she had nothing more important to do than join her friend for the day. "Oh my goodness. Oh my... and you leave in a fortnight? How can you ever be ready so soon? Oh, Madame is not going to be happy. Never mind Madame, I am not happy. I know we have not seen each other often but at least we could. You will be gone six months, at least. A lot can happen while you are away."

"I tried to tell Father I needed to give Madame more time but he insisted with more firmness than I have ever heard before so I guess there is an important reason for leaving the first of September. Maybe it has to do with the tides or the weather."

Elizabeth took Abigail's arm and turned her towards the back of the house to find Miss Winterfeldt. "Never mind my house work. I will spend the day with you. I am sure Molly and Mrs. Danbury can manage without me for the day. They were able to do so before I married Avery."

Abby, Elizabeth and Miss Winterfeldt disembarked from the carriage to the walkway in front of Madame Rousseau's dress shop located in the heart of Southampton next to a bakery. The aroma of this morning's fresh baked bread still lingered in the air. The dress shop had a bay window beside the door displaying a dress of the latest fashion - a blue silk gown with lower waist, fuller sleeves, and wider skirt. Abby couldn't help but admire it. The three ladies entered the shop and were ushered to the sitting room to wait for Madame to greet them. The room had a fireplace with a banked fire in anticipation of the warmth of the day; an ornately carved wooden mantle with a painting of Queen Anne at her coronation hung above the hearth. A sideboard occupied the opposite wall next to the doorway from which the maid offered tea for refreshment and above the sideboard was a large gilded mirror. A settee and two wingback chairs filled the rest of the room and were upholstered in burgundy patterned brocade.

Elizabeth turned to Abby sitting next to her on the settee and said for the third time, "Madame is not going to be happy."

"Shh, please stop reminding me. I am nervous enough as it is," whispered Abby. "Besides, that is why I brought you. You can help me decide what is important and help calm her down. You have such a charming way of getting people to do as you ask."

Elizabeth gave Abby a doubtful look. Just then Madame gracefully appeared and smiled at her customers. She was a tall woman with dark eyes, olive skin and a flair for the dramatic.

Madame Rousseau greeted her clients with a kiss on each cheek and her heavy French accent "Lady Kendall, Miss Bennington what a pleasure to see you." The ladies were long time clients but were by no means important ones. From their station, they could not begin to compete with the members of *le bon ton* whose patronage she had been cultivating for years. Nevertheless, they were among her favourite. Lady Kendall's figure was not as tall as Miss Bennington's but she had a grace about her that made a dress flow beautifully while her blond hair made a striking contrast to the bold colours favoured by Madame. Miss Bennington, on the other hand, with her darker hair and slender form carried off designs with an elegance few could match. They both had agreeable dispositions, something most of the *ton* lacked, which is why as she rose in fame and had discarded her less prestigious clientele she still serviced these friends.

Abby gave Madame a beseeching look. "Madame Rousseau, I have come to beg a favour of you. I am in need of some additions to my wardrobe and I must have them quickly." Abby held her breath. She knew she hadn't presented her case with the finesse it required but couldn't think of anything else to say.

Madame frowned and her French accent deepened. "We will see what I can do for you. Tell me more."

Abby and Elizabeth had worked out a list of essentials and a few hopeful items to present to Madame. After looking over the list Madame asked, "When do you need them?"

Abby replied, "A fortnight."

Madame's response was a flow of French. Abby understood enough to know she was not happy, as expected.

Thankfully Elizabeth came to the rescue. "Madame Rousseau, you are the best seamstress in all of Southampton and London. Abigail will be wearing your creations around the world and you know she will draw attention. The ladies will have to know where to get gowns such as hers. I also know you have worked wonders to get orders done during the season. This small order would hardly be a challenge for your excellent staff."

Madame smiled and relented. She could easily take care of the whole order but in her business fame was achieved by being in demand and it would not do for her to give in without a fuss. "We will do what we can to complete the whole order but it would be best to know which can be forgone if we are unable to finish in time."

"Thank you Madame, you are most kind," said Abigail.

From there the ladies settled in to decide on fabrics and styles.

As fate would have it the Duchess of Rothebury arrived for her fitting before Abigail and Elizabeth had completed their business. Madame hurried to greet the Duchess and usher her to the fitting room. Her Grace held back to speak to Abigail. "Miss Bennington. Lady Kendall."

"Your Grace," they replied with deep curtsies.

"Miss Bennington, my son has expressed to the Duke his interests in you. I would think someone of your status would have an appreciation for the honour of his notice." Her Grace started with a mild tone that turned frosty and domineering as she finished her speech. "Your behaviour yesterday would suggest otherwise. Since Jason has chosen to disregard this obvious lack of breeding by continuing his pursuit, and considering your lack of a mother's influence, I am taking it upon myself to instruct you how to comport yourself in future, whether in his company or not, in a manner befitting a young lady of class. Furthermore, you will not put yourself in any further situations which could cause embarrassment to our title. I will suggest to Jason he take you riding in the park tomorrow. You will take the opportunity to apologize for your lapse in judgment." Not expecting anything less than absolute obedience the Duchess abruptly ended her speech with, "Good day ladies." She turned and followed Madame out of the room without allowing Abby a chance to say a word in her defense, not that she had a defense to present.

Miss Winterfeldt took offense of the Duchess' treatment of her charge but was helpless to do anything about it. Elizabeth had grasped Abby's arm halfway through the tirade to offer her support. She now turned to Abby to ask "When did you start courting Lord Jason and what in heaven's name did you do to earn such a reprimand?"

Thankfully Madame returned quickly to complete their order while the Duchess was changing saving Abigail from Elizabeth's questions - for now. The Duchess had shocked her with the directness of her assault but as she recovered her wits her temper flared at the Duchess' assumption if Lord Jason wanted her he would have her.

Back in the carriage, Elizabeth turned to her expectantly. With a pointed look towards Miss Winterfeldt who was settling her skirts, Abby refrained from answering Elizabeth's questioning look. The girls had shared many a confidence growing up. Elizabeth knew from Abby's look she would not get the full story until they had more privacy so she settled back against the seat and looked out the side of the carriage.

Elizabeth smiled to herself thinking back to the days before her marriage when she and Abby spent a great deal of time discussing their beaus and their futures. She loved her husband and enjoyed being mistress of her own home so it wasn't until this moment she realized she missed the closeness she and Abby used to share. Although, she didn't miss being involved in Abby's entanglements or the drama of an unattached debutante's world. There was something to be said for being settled. She looked forward to Abby getting married so they would again have the same interests to keep them connected. Realizing the chasm growing between them saddened Elizabeth but she hoped it would be temporary. *I wonder how serious this relationship is with Lord Jason.*

Miss Winterfeldt straightened from arranging her skirt and faced the two ladies across from her. Starchily though not unkindly she said, "It was too much to hope your actions had gone unnoticed."

Elizabeth's presence was not a concern to Miss Winterfeldt as she opened the subject of the Duchess' chastisement. Quite often she had watched over Elizabeth during childhood when her nanny had a day off and so she treated

Elizabeth more like a sister to Abby than an outsider of the family. Hence the reason, she didn't feel the need to wait any longer to discuss Abby's situation. However, these days she was more aware of her position in the household as a servant rather than Abigail's surrogate mother. So she tempered what would have been chastisement into guidance. "In future you really should consider the consequences more carefully if you hope to marry as well as Elizabeth. Your reputation is everything. Your dowry will only permit indiscretions to a point and I believe you have reached that point. If we were in London the Almack ladies would not be so tolerant. Your actions would have seen you cut from society."

Abby answered out of habit, "Yes, ma'am." She really did not want to discuss her situation with Miss Winterfeldt. Certainly, her nanny was too old and had been a spinster for too long to understand Abby's position. She would probably support Lord Jason's cause as any match would be better than none.

Sensing Abigail's withdrawal Miss Winterfeldt said no more. She was at a loss on how to help when Abigail would not confide in her. Hopefully Elizabeth's perspective would help guide Abby. The ladies passed the rest of the ride in silence listening to the clip clop of the horse's shoes on the cobblestone street and the creaking of the leather springs of the carriage.

They presently arrived back at Elizabeth's home where Miss Winterfeldt excused herself returning to the kitchen to order lunch and continue her earlier visit with Anestia. The girls settled themselves in the sitting room. Molly brought them tea at Miss Winterfeldt's direction. Abby didn't give it a thought but Elizabeth was impressed by the thoughtfulness and assumed correctly it was Miss Winterfeldt's doing. Now that she was managing a household and servants of her own she was more aware of good help knowing how hard it was to find and to train them. Her servants did their jobs well enough but someone like Miss Winterfeldt was exceptional.

While Elizabeth poured tea, Abigail looked around the room taking note of the small feminine touches Elizabeth had recently added. The furniture was the same but was now adorned with delicately embroidered throw pillows. Soft watercolour landscapes hung on the wall and fresh flowers were on the pianoforte in a vase given to Elizabeth by her great aunt on her sixteenth birthday.

While most girls would wish to have a home of their own to decorate it only made Abby feel tied down and restless. She wanted to have some adventure before settling down herself. Avery may adore Elizabeth but to Abby he seemed quite dull and too content with the routine of business and home life. It was the kind of life suited to Elizabeth. Maybe love would make settling down more acceptable to her. Maybe the right man would make the difference. She doubted it. Somehow she knew she would always want to be more than just a wife and mother. Meanwhile, she was becoming more enthused for her upcoming trip by the hour. She was going to have her adventure.

Handing Abby her teacup, Elizabeth looked at her expectantly. Abby took a sip of her tea and started her story of how she had become involved with Lord Jason. "About four weeks ago Father and I were invited to the Waverly's for a dinner party."

Elizabeth's brow creased. "That seems odd. Lady Waverly is famous for snubbing the working class. It does not matter how much wealth your father amassed she would hardly invite you to a ball much less a private dinner party."

"I know. I was quite surprised and considered not accepting but father was keen on the chance to socialize with Lord Waverly. I was expecting a boring evening. Instead it was in turns tortuous and amusing.

"You remember the Waverly's son Robert is good friends with Lord Jason so he was present along with his parents. Robert's fiancée Bridgette Channing and a spinster my father's age - I don't remember her name - were also guests. Jason and I were seated next to each other and across from Robert and Bridgette. Robert only had eyes for Bridgette. You should have seen how he was behaving! He ignored every other guest and spent the entire meal having whispered conversations with her. I am not even sure Robert knew there were others in the room. It was disgraceful. After dinner, instead of retreating with the men, Robert joined the ladies to admire Bridgette playing the piano. Jason followed him. The older ladies had the couches so I was standing by one of the columns as far from her inept noise-making as I could get when Jason came to stand next to me. He told me he had observed my amusement during dinner at his friend's expense. I told him I had noticed his smirk as well. We carried on with pleasant banter for the rest of the evening with poor Bridgette and Robert being the main source of amusement.

"The next day, Lord Jason asked my father for permission to take me for a drive in the park with Robert and Bridgette. My father agreed and off I go for what turned out to be the most uncomfortable hour of my life. Robert kept touching Bridgette in the most inappropriate way. I know my cheeks were flushed the whole time I was so mortified. Jason stared out his side of the carriage and hardly responded to any attempts at conversation. At least Jason had the hood up on his landau, as it looked to rain that afternoon, so few people were able to witness the uncomfortable scene.

"A whole week went by without word from him so I thought it was the end of it...until Friday when I attended the Westwood's Ball. Imagine the surprise when Lord Jason arrives. He so rarely attends a ball that every debutante made a try for his attention. There were more than a few sending me hateful looks when he singled me out for a waltz and left shortly afterwards. You can imagine how flattered I was and every time I saw my father he had such a proud look on his face. Jason apologized beautifully for the ride in the park but said little else. It was as if he had a purpose and once fulfilled he was passing time until he could leave.

"He did the same thing the following week at the Brighten's ball. A single dance and then he was gone. By now, I figure all of the gossips have us engaged. Last week he took us to an opera. He was courteous but he barely said three words the entire evening. There was no emotional connection, either. Then this week he asked my father for permission to formally court me and Father agreed... without consulting me."

Elizabeth said "You expected your father to consult you? Come now Abby, your father is not that progressive."

"Pish-posh. Well at any rate I had hoped he would ask how I felt before giving his consent. Jason treats me kindly but I am not at all prepared to consider a marriage of silence. Plus he is a future Duke! What do I know of being a duchess? And let us not forget having the Duchess for a mother-in-law. I panicked at the idea of being part of his family so I took the first opportunity presented to put some distance to the relationship."

"What did you do?"

"You remember my friend Sir Marcus Danvers?" Marc and Abby were childhood playmates and Marc was also one of Lord Jason's friends.

Elizabeth gave a nod, "Of course."

"He has returned from Sussex and we happened to meet in the park. I suddenly had this foolish idea of how to discourage Lord Jason. You know how impulsive I can be..." Elizabeth grimaced at the reminder of being caught up in some of Abby's more untoward impulses during their childhood. Abby continued "...without considering the consequences I talked Marc into a carriage ride in the park... without a chaperone."

Abby made a wry smile at Elizabeth's gasp of surprise. "Was it an open or closed carriage? Oh, not that it matters, either way you are compromised if anyone saw you."

Abby couldn't help her sheepish grin. "Open and yes, we were seen. I knew I could extricate myself from anything with Marc but I hoped the brief scandal would discourage Jason."

"According to the duchess, your plan failed."

Abby nodded in agreement. "Leaving the country will hopefully solve the problem if I can just avoid getting in any deeper before I leave."

Elizabeth felt obliged to offer direction. "Abby, you may not like this advice, I know confrontations are not easy, but it would be best if you face Jason and make a clean break with him."

"Oh Bethy, I do not have your gift for words and I am terrified if I anger him his father will retaliate against my father's business. If father couldn't decline his intentions than how could I?"

"You are in a precarious situation. I wish there was something I could do to help." Elizabeth noticed Abby's eyes widen and quickly quelled the idea she was forming. "I will not talk to him for you but if it would make you feel better I will accompany you tomorrow."

"Thank you Bethy. Your presence would be a comfort to me. If I make a mess of it I know you will be there to smooth it out."

"I am sure you will do fine, Abby. You underestimate yourself and your ability to charm people to do your bidding."

Abby smiled to hear her earlier words to Elizabeth repeated back to her.

Elizabeth looked down at her teacup and sighed then raised her eyes back to Abby. "I still cannot believe you will be leaving England."

"It is not forever, not even a whole year."

"Still a lot can happen while you are away. Plus, you will miss the beginning of the next season of balls and you will be another year older when you return."

"You make it sound as if I will be on the shelf when I return. I am not that old. Besides what could happen that I would care about missing?" asked Abby nonchalantly.

"Becoming a godmother?" queried Elizabeth with a demure smile.

Abby replayed the afternoon in her mind before falling asleep that night. Elizabeth's announcement was bothering her. She realized for the first time in her life she was jealous of her friend. She had of course congratulated Elizabeth and they talked of nothing else while lunch was served and eaten. Abby had delighted in her friend's wedding, had helped plan every detail. Although she had felt a little left behind as Elizabeth had moved into womanhood and wedded bliss without her, Abby had not been jealous of her. There was plenty of time for Abby to find a beau of her own. She was really looking forward to her bit of adventure before settling down but somehow Elizabeth's announcement had thrown a pall on the idea. She didn't like to miss seeing Elizabeth increasing and most likely the birth of her firstborn. Abby discovered this afternoon that while she had not been keen on a home of her own she really wanted a child of her own. Maybe it had something to do with not having her mother that she had such a strong desire to become a mother. For a moment she contemplated accepting Jason but - no - a child was a desire that could wait not a need worth sacrificing herself to a loveless marriage; therefore, Jason was not an option. Maybe it was best she would be putting some distance between her and Elizabeth. It would keep her from doing something foolish she would spend a lifetime regretting.

Moving on to more pleasant thoughts of her upcoming voyage, Abby finally fell asleep to dreams of stepping off a ship into a new exotic world, hers to explore.

Morning sun streamed through the gap in the pale blue sateen curtains of Abby's window and across the large ivory plush rug under her four poster bed with a matching blue coverlet trimmed in ivory. Ivory patterned wallpaper with tiny blue flowers graced the walls giving the room a luxuriously light and airy feel. Birds chirped a chorus in greeting to the new day outside her window rousing Abigail from her slumber.

She awoke in cheerful spirits feeling refreshed from a night of peaceful sleep. She was sitting up and stretching her arms overhead with feline grace when Miss Winterfeldt entered the room in her usual brisk manner. "Good morning dear, did you sleep well?" She crossed to the window and pushed the curtains open allowing the full radiance of morning to brighten the bedchamber. She then went to the wardrobe to gather stockings, pantelettes, chemise and corset in preparation of helping Abby dress.

"Yes, thank you," replied Abby. Miss Winterfeldt laid the clothes across the bed then reached into her freshly starched apron pocket to hand Abby the calling card delivered this morning.

> ### Lord Jason Albert Duncan Malwbry
>
> *Will arrive at 3 o'clock to take you riding.*

Abigail's buoyant smile dropped at the reminder of the disagreeable task set before her today. Abby wasn't sure if she wanted to laugh or scream. The message certainly didn't surprise her. The Duchess had said she would suggest it to her son. What was amusing was how Jason fell in with his mother's planning. Would a wife be able to manipulate him as easily? Abby wasn't sure. Hopefully riding fell in line with his plans so he went along with her decree. The curtness of his message certainly indicated he did not anticipate any dissension from her which was the annoying element. Apparently neither Jason nor his mother would be able to accept she did not want to be the next duchess. Well, really, it shouldn't surprise her. How many girls in their right mind would turn away from the chance to gain a title? Just another reminder she was not like most debutantes.

Placing the card on the nightstand Abby said, "Thank you Miss Winterfeldt. Would you please send a message to Elizabeth to come over before three."

"Abigail... what are you girls planning? Surely you are not thinking of leaving the house to avoid Lord Jason? You have better manners than that. You need to talk to him. You are of an age to put aside girlhood games and seriously consider marriage. This is an opportunity not likely to come around again. He would make a good match."

Abby had planned to set Miss Winterfeldt straight as to her intentions but the reiteration of Abby's own thoughts gave her pause. Was she wrong to turn away from Jason? "What about love? Should I put that aside for a title?" asked Abby in all seriousness.

"You should not expect to find the foolish love espoused in those novels you like to read. It is not reality. Real life is taking advantage of a good opportunity when it presents itself. A bird in hand is worth two in the bush. Waiting for something better may find you with nothing except memories to keep you warm at night. Besides, many have grown to love their spouse after marriage."

The earnestness in which Miss Winterfeldt spoke clued Abby into the truth of her past. "Is that what happened to you?" she gently asked.

Miss Winterfeldt coloured in embarrassment having realized how much she had revealed.

"Please tell me your story," pleaded Abby. "It may help me make my decision."

After a moments consideration Miss Winterfeldt decided to oblige. She seated herself on the bed adjacent to Abby and started her story with a wistful tone. "I was your age when my parents introduced me to the new vicar's son, Randolph Lewton. He was tall and thin to the point of being gangly but otherwise he was an average sort of fellow. He spoke well but you could tell he was very shy. Our parents wanted us to marry and Randolph was agreeable but I couldn't accept him. I had affections for the boy next door. His name was Thomas. He was such a fine looking lad with sandy hair, an infectious grin and an easy laugh. We played together as children. As we got older we would occasionally take walks together, go berry picking and usually sit together in church on Sundays. I thought he really cared for me so I turned down Randolph to wait for Thomas to ask for my hand. My parents were disappointed especially since I would not explain why I would not marry Randolph. Thomas was sent away for schooling shortly afterwards. He later married a girl he met near the school. I had to start working to help support the family and another opportunity to marry never presented itself."

"What happened to Randolph?"

"After I turned him down he asked another girl in a neighboring village. The same week if I remember correctly. Very strange."

"Why were you so sure Thomas would propose?"

"I don't remember now. I think I may have been so infatuated with Thomas I couldn't even consider Randolph. The point is I wouldn't want you to make the same mistake of disregarding a good match because it does not live up to your ideal. But I also would not wish to see you end up in a miserable relationship. All I can do is advise you. You must make the decision that is best for you." Abruptly Miss Winterfeldt stood up and smoothed her skirt getting back to the business of the morning routine. "Come child, let's get you dressed and off to break your fast."

Abby let Miss Winterfeldt fuss with her clothing as she contemplated all she had learned. She dutifully put her arms through the sleeves of her morning dress of soft green muslin while she tried to picture what Miss Winterfeldt - Mildred, she remembered was her given name - would have been like as a young lady. Her musings were interrupted by the present day Mildred.

"Your father told me of your upcoming voyage." Miss Winterfeldt finished tying the sash of her dress and turned her around to critically eye the results. "He asked me to go with you." She brought her gaze to Abby's and therein

Abby saw the sadness and knew. Her heart grew heavy.

"You will not be joining us."

"No child. I have no wish to set sail at this stage of my life. Besides my sister is getting frail and in need of my assistance. I couldn't leave her for such a long time." For the first time in her life Abby saw Miss Winterfeldt get teary. "I will miss you dear. If I had been blessed with a daughter I would have wanted her to be like you."

All of this left Abby speechless. Within twenty-four hours her world had turned upside down. Tears were welling in her eyes too and her chest was tightening in a way she hadn't felt in a long time - if ever. Seeking the remembered comfort in the arms of her nanny she held on tight as Miss Winterfeldt wrapped her in her embrace. All too soon Miss Winterfeldt returned to her efficient self and set Abby away leaving her feeling a little bereft. "Don't you worry. Your father has promised to find you a suitable lady's maid." Abby could only nod not trusting herself to speak just yet. "Now off with you. I am sure your father is waiting for you to join him."

Downstairs Abby entered the breakfast room. Her father was already there reading his paper. She stopped to give him a kiss on the cheek in greeting before moving on to her seat. Richard looked up and noticed the drawn look on her face. "Is something the matter, sweetheart?"

"Miss Winterfeldt told me she is staying in England. I am going to miss her, probably more than I as yet realize."

"That is only natural. She has been as much a surrogate mother to you as she has been a governess. If we are not able to find a suitable lady's maid before leaving England I am positive we will be able to find one in Jamaica."

Abby was too preoccupied with other thoughts to have much interest in hiring a new servant. She was brought her usual toast, fruit and tea. After the butler exited Abby asked her father, "You really loved my mother, didn't you?"

The question caught Richard by surprise. Sensing the seriousness in her demeanor he laid down his paper before replying, "Yes, I did and I still do. Why do you ask?" He suspected it had something to do with Lord Jason.

"How did you meet? How did you know you loved her and she you?"

Richard couldn't help the nostalgic smile remembering how his Anna had made him feel. He contemplated where to start. He would leave most of the war details out for his daughter's sake. He settled back in his chair and looked towards the window. Yes, the day was much too pretty for thoughts of war. He would keep it to their relationship. He let his mind drift back five and one score years to the day they met. "I was returning to Southampton by horseback on a blustery fall afternoon when I came upon a two-wheel chaise headed towards London on the side of the road with one side precariously stuck in a bog. The horse was an old nag worn out from the effort of trying to free the chaise and the driver was an elderly gentleman holding the mare's harness and trying to add his limited strength to the battle. Standing in the road watching them was a young lady. As I approached she looked towards me.... I think she captured my heart right then and there." He remembered her green eyes were so intense and trusting. Her figure willowy and graceful. Her hair the same dark red as Abby's... although he couldn't tell just then covered as it was by her cloak. He didn't remember getting down off his horse and walking towards her but he certainly remembered how hard it had been to force himself to stop short of touching her and direct his attention towards her companion. "The gentleman she was with turned out to be her grandfather."

Richard paused long enough for Abby to interrupt as she moved from the far end of the table to the chair next to her father. "What was he like, my great grandfather?"

"At that moment - a bit forbidding. He gave me a steely look that had me taking a few steps away from Anna. He was a strict man when it came to what was proper but he was also a fair man. He would lay down his life for his family and Anna was the apple of his eye. She took it really hard when he died." Richard paused again at the sorrowful memory then continued his story. "I helped them get back on the road and watched them drive away. I thought of her often the next few weeks and eventually I got back to London and made discreet inquiries until I knew enough to work my way into a gathering where I could be properly introduced. Over the next few months, and with her family's approval, we saw each other as often as possible and wrote frequent letters. England declared war on Bonaparte before I made the commitment to ask for her hand. With all the excitement and ideology of youth, I enlisted as a deckhand in the Royal Navy."

"How old were you?"

"Two and twenty. The next two years we wrote letters to each other and I was able to see her a few times on leave. My squadron was assigned to do what we could to disrupt the French trade, until the Battle of Trafalgar during the Third Coalition. We defeated the French fleet and as a reward we were granted extended shore leave. I returned to London and married your mother in November.

"The first two years of our marriage I wasn't home much. I was still in the service as second in command of a frigate. September 1807, we were ordered to capture the Danish fleet to keep it from becoming part of the French alliance. With our success I was rewarded again. This time I was allowed to take a post managing the supplying of the ships in Southampton and Portsmouth. We finally got to start our wedded life together. I started building the merchant business on the side and another year later I was a proud poppa."

"And sadly, another year later you were a widower... so little time together," whispered Abby.

"Yes it was too short but better to have had what time we did than to have not had any at all. And I have had you to comfort me. Now tell me daughter what is the meaning of all this questioning? Does it have anything to do with the recent attentions of Lord Jason?"

Abby nodded, "Yes... it does. His intentions are of a serious nature, are they not?"

"I believe so. How do you feel about him?"

"I do not feel anything for him. Certainly not love but Miss Winterfeldt has suggested I should reconsider. She said I should not be so hasty in turning him aside. She also mentioned some couples grow to love each other."

"That is true and possible. But I am not convinced it is the same kind of love. That it would have the same depth and passion as a relationship which starts with a deep and immediate attraction. I want first and foremost for you to be happy."

Abby paused as she considered her feelings for Jason and Richard patiently waited realizing she was trying to collect her thoughts. "I was flattered at the Waverly's to receive his attention and he did seem charming but I have not seen that side of him since then. He has been cold and uncommunicative and a bit demanding."

Richard had to smile at the thought of anyone trying to dictate to his daughter. "Would you feel differently if he had remained charming?"

Abby tried to imagine how she would feel if Jason had continued as he had begun. "Perhaps. I imagine I would be more willing to consider his courtship."

When Abby did not continue Richard said, "And if he were to turn his attentions to another it would not bother you?"

Abby did not even hesitate in her reply. "Not at all."

"If Jason is not the one to make you happy then you should turn him away. You are in a unique position of having enough funds of your own along with a dowry large enough to attract any man. You do not have to marry if it is not your wish. You have the luxury to be particular."

Abby laid her hand atop his and squeezed. "Poppa, I am grateful to you for the liberty and generosity you have bestowed on me. I have also been concerned if I anger Jason his father will retaliate against your business. The Duke can stop you from bringing goods into England, can he not?"

Richard squeezed her hand in turn and offered his reassurance. "You only need to treat Lord Jason respectfully.... let me worry about his father."

Chapter 2

Jason walked through the foyer of his family's ancestral estate after a brisk morning ride on his favourite chestnut stallion, Shelton. The mid-summer morning had proved too beautiful to resist and he had immensely enjoyed the exercise. The day looked to be one worth inspiring poems and paintings, not that he was the prosaic type. Upon hearing the raised voices of his parents coming from the study he resigned himself to leaving the beauty of the day outside. Within these walls were heartache and strife. His mother was lecturing his father again about his gambling at the dog tracks. Jason had just started up the stairs when his mother stepped into the foyer and called for him to join them. With a resigned sense of the inevitable he turned from the stairs and walked towards her. He paused at the door indicating for his mother to precede him then he shut the door behind him. No sense subjecting the servants to more than they had already heard.

The Duchess launched into her questioning without delay. "How are you progressing with Abigail Bennington?"

"Fine," answered Jason.

"Then why was she seen riding alone with Marcus Danvers in the park yesterday?" She didn't wait for Jason to answer, which was just as well since he didn't have one. He couldn't pretend to understand any female, much less one as unconventional as Abigail. "Do you know how much trouble I went through to get her and her father invited to Lady Waverly's dinner party so you two could be introduced? If not for his money and a favour she owed me, she would never have agreed to invite someone from the working class to one of her dinners. You told me you had Abigail in hand. I assumed the matter was settled when you visited her father. That being the case I set her straight on how a future duchess should behave."

"Say again?" asked an astonished Jason.

"I saw Abigail at the modiste's yesterday. I made her aware of her improper behaviour and told her to expect to see you today to apologize."

Jason was at first dismayed then angry and if truth be told embarrassed by his mother's behaviour. He had sent a note to Abby this morning before he went riding. His intention was to gauge her feelings for Marc since he already knew his friend's affections lay elsewhere. Now Abby would believe the note was his mother's doing and he was nothing more than a puppet. "Mother, you are not helping. I will see Miss Bennington today as you wish but if you dare to interfere again, I am done."

"No you are not done. You do not have the luxury of being done. She is only one of a few ladies with a dowry sizeable enough to cover your father's gambling debts. You do not want to see him go to debtors' prison, do you?"

Jason lost his temper and answered back without thought. "Stop exaggerating, Mother. You are simply not ready to give up your pricy luxuries or worse for your friends to find out you cannot control your husband."

"Why you ungrateful..." His mother was so angry she couldn't even finish her expletive.

With Jason's last comment striking hard at his pride, his portly father finally spoke. "Now see here son that will be enough!"

"You are right, Father. I have had enough." Jason turned on his heel and quickly quit the room and the house as both his parents sputtered their displeasure at his retreating back.

He strode quickly to the stables and stopped the groomsman from leading Shelton to his stall. Jason, too impatient to wait on the stable hand, returned the saddle to the horse's back and cinched it. He then grabbed the reins and leapt unaided onto Shelton's back. Turning him sharply towards the exit, he kicked him into a full gallop down the drive, shocking all who witnessed his uncharacteristic behaviour. With the house out of sight Jason was able to regain control of his emotions. He slowed Shelton to a trot trying to decide where to go. His thoughts were too dark and heavy to stand the beauty of the day so he headed for the nearest pub. It was too early for most to be there so he would be undisturbed. The dark and dingy room complimented his thoughts. He chose a table in the far interior corner away from the light and waved off the barkeep as he approached.

He was used to his parents arguing but he was not used to being dragged into the vortex of anger with them. He was not proud of his reaction this morning. The best he could attribute it to was a built up resentment resulting from courting a woman of his mother's choosing.

What was he getting himself into? Would he end up in a marriage like theirs? No. The bloodline would end with him before he accepted such a fate. He sat there considering his next course of action until it was time to meet Miss Bennington.

At half past two Elizabeth was shown into the comfortably spacious drawing room of the Bennington's town home. Abby arose from the settee to welcome her. "Thank you for coming. How is Alfred's ankle today?"

"Better, he is hobbling around. I instructed him to rest another day but his pride would not let him. He insists on doing his duties while trying hard not to show the pain he is in." Elizabeth took a seat on the settee while Abby remained standing.

Feeling just a little anxious Abby got straight to business. "Elizabeth, how do I end this with Jason? I do not believe he is overwhelmed by my charming personality so I rather think it is my dowry that had him visiting my father so quickly. Father did not mention it to me so I do not believe he has asked for marriage... yet." Abby's jaw dropped with sudden insight. "So that is why father insisted on leaving in two weeks, or at least part of the reason. He figures to leave the country before it does become an offer of marriage. And if I do not get Jason to go looking elsewhere an offer may be likely."

Elizabeth was inspired "That is it!" Abby looked at her expectantly. "You convince Jason to look elsewhere, you are not the right choice for him and it would be even better if somehow he believes this conclusion was his idea."

"If it is money he is interested in it will not be easy. Maybe time is of the essence in which case the six month holiday I will be taking with my father may help. I am not willing to forego the trip so he will be forced to find another dowry."

They were interrupted by the butler announcing Lord Malwbry who was following directly behind him. *Drat, of course he would be early,* thought Abigail.

Jason's purposeful stride into the drawing room faltered at the sight of Elizabeth. Abby hid her smile at what she was sure was a blasphemous word muttered under his breath. She should be ashamed it felt this good to thwart his plans but having attempted to order her around she felt it served him right. Abigail greeted Jason with a small curtsey and gestured to the chair across from the settee. "Good afternoon, Lord Malwbry. Please join us." She resumed her seat next to Elizabeth as she introduced her. "You, of course, remember my good friend Lady Avery Kendall."

Jason bowed to Elizabeth before taking his seat. "Yes, of course. How are you Lady Kendall?"

"I am well, Lord Malwbry, thank you for asking," replied Elizabeth.

"I am here to take Miss Bennington riding. Would you care to join us?"

Abby intervened, "Milord, would you mind postponing our ride? I wish to discuss something with you." She waited for his reaction.

He looked relieved and surprised at her directness. "As do I but..." He was obviously uncomfortable continuing in Elizabeth's presence. Elizabeth took pity on Jason and excused herself. She smiled encouragingly at Abby then moved to the far side of the room.

"May I ask why you are directing your attentions towards me?" *Goodness that came out direct and to the point. Good thing Father only said to be respectful. Tact is a talent I appear to be lacking.*

Ignoring her question Jason asked, "What is your relationship with Marc?"

"We have been friends since childhood. You did not think it was more, did you? He is almost engaged."

"I am aware of that fact, I was not sure you were."

"Why are you interested in me? Your mother does not seem to approve."

"On the contrary, you are at the top of her very short list."

Abby's jaw dropped. "Why?"

"She may believe she can mold you into the daughter-in-law she desires."

Abby was sure her dowry was the main reason but of course Jason was too much of a gentleman to refer to money. "Obviously she does not know much about me or I would be at the bottom of her list. She should set her sights on one of those simpering young debutantes without a thought of their own."

Jason studied her for a moment as if deciding what to say or maybe not say. "I think she was looking for someone like herself and maybe, unconsciously, I was too but I do not want the same angry and bitter relationship my parents have."

"What, or should I say whom, do you want?"

"I really have not given it much consideration until this morning. I have avoided the marriage mart for the better part of a decade. At this point, I am so out of touch I hardly know any of the girls or their families. Other than my mother's list of choices I do not have much to go on."

"I could help you, if you like?" offered Abby.

"How?"

"Attend the next assembly room dance. I will save the first dance for you. I can point out some of the more favourable candidates and with Marc's help we could introduce you to the ones you find appealing."

Jason picked up Abby's hand and kissed the back of it. "I appreciate and sincerely thank you for your generous offer mademoiselle. I will look forward to the next dance."

Abby was not only startled by his bold and forthright action but also by the rakish and very charming smile as he thanked her. *Where was this side of his character the last few weeks?* She would not have been so quick to turn aside his attentions if he had shown her more of this behaviour. Another thought nettled her pride. What if his change in attitude was the result of escaping a courtship with her?

Jason arose from his seat to take his leave and Abby followed suit. "Ladies," he bowed to Elizabeth and Abby in turn. "I bid you *adieu*. Enjoy your afternoon."

Elizabeth moved back to Abby's side. "He is leaving in jovial spirits. I would say well done Abby."

Abby turned to her smiling. "Much better than expected. How about a game of whist before you return home, for the sake of old times? Who knows maybe Lady Luck is smiling on me today and I may actually win this time."

Elizabeth could not resist the challenge. "As long as we play outside. The day is much too pretty to be indoors."

A few nights later Richard escorted his daughter to the assembly room ball. As they made their entrance into the ballroom Richard reminded her, "Make the most of tonight, Abby dear. It will be a few months before you are able to attend another dance."

Abby scanned the simple gathering room noting the high attendance that would prove helpful for Jason's quest. "Do you think the balls in Montgomery will suffer in comparison to ours?"

"Your uncle has not mentioned it so I would not know, but it would stand to reason they would."

"I see Elizabeth and Avery." Abby gave her father's cheek a brush of her lips. "I will find you again later. Enjoy yourself Poppa. Be careful you do not cause the desperate spinsters and smitten widows to fight over you."

Richard smiled as he watched his daughter glide across the candle lit ballroom to join her friends. He most likely would not have her company again until the ride home.

Abby had no sooner finished greeting Elizabeth and Avery when a hush fell across the room followed by a wave of whispered conversations ripe with gossip. She looked to the entrance and saw Jason pause in the doorway to scan the crowd searching for her. She could tell the attention he was receiving made him uncomfortable but he appeared determined to bear it as he headed her way.

Marc made his way from further in the room to their group at the same time. Greetings were shared all around before the gentlemen broke off to their own conversation while waiting for the dancing to start.

Elizabeth fanned herself gently and whispered to Abby, "Are you ready for this?"

"I hope so. I have been looking around the room for suitable candidates. The Stalworth sisters are a possibility and Lady Torrington. Louisa Tristan may be older than Jason but she has a charming disposition."

"What about the Earl of Ashby's daughter?"

"A suitable match for his personality but alas she does not have much of a dowry."

They continued working on the list of ladies until it was time to line up for the dance. By then Abby was feeling confident Jason would have his head turned before the end of the evening.

As the movements of the dance brought Jason and Abby together she would point out the various ladies on her list. Jason nodded after each one but showed no interest. He was more focused on the dance. Abby's hopes were growing thin. To lighten the mood she directed his attention towards Robert and Bridgette standing by the refreshments. "At least they are behaving this evening." That earned her a brief smile.

As the dance ended and they moved to the side of the room Jason whispered a confession, "I am sorry I was so distracted. My dancing is a bit rusty. It was all I could do not to make a fool of myself. Tell me again the name of the tall blond by the balcony doors."

Abby's mood brightened considerably. "That would be Lady Jane Torrington. Her father has an estate south of here. Good connections and she has a pleasant demeanor. Would you like me to introduce you?"

Jason offered his arm in response and they walked towards Lady Jane and her father. Abby made the introductions and was pleased to see the becoming blush on Jane's cheeks. The conversation was flowing smoothly and after an appropriate amount of time she excused herself on the pretext of greeting another acquaintance.

She found Marc just as the next dance, a Cotillion, was starting. He gave her a mock bow and asked her to dance. She curtsied and let him lead her to the floor. It was a treat to dance with Marc as he was an excellent partner and together they could temporarily drop the burden of conversation and flirtation. Simply enjoy the music and the joy of dancing. She wished the orchestra would play on and on but alas, every good thing must end and when the last note faded they moved to the refreshment table, joining Lord Jason and Lady Jane.

Marc handed Abby a glass of punch. "I hear you are planning to quit our fair country for distant shores."

Jason could not hide his surprise. "What is this you say?"

Abby replied with enthusiasm, "My father and I will set sail on the first for the Caribbean and then onto my uncle's plantation in the States for the holidays."

Marc teased Abby, "You have no remorse for the spot you have put me in. Mary returns next month. She will hear the gossip of our carriage ride and that you have suddenly left the country and she will think the worst."

"I have no doubt your sweet charm will persuade your fiancée of your innocence. In fact, I believe you can even take on the repercussions of a second dance with me." Abby deposited her emptied glass. "Please excuse us Lord Jason, Lady Jane." She grabbed Marc's hand and pulled him towards the couples lining up for the next Quadrille. "Come Marc, I leave in less than a week, and you are the best dance partner a lady could ask for."

Marc threw an apologetic smile towards Lord Jason and Lady Jane as he was forced to follow the hand in Abby's grasp. Once in line on the dance floor he leaned towards her to whisper in her ear, "That was poorly done, old girl."

Abby whispered back, "For some reason I seem to behave rashly when trying to remove myself from his presence."

Much to Abby's relief Marc appeared to let the subject drop as the dance began. At the end of the dance set Marc gave her a bow and said, "I will leave you with your next dance partner." He nodded over her left shoulder towards the approaching gentleman. "I hope your endeavours of this evening are successful and my services for the purpose of running interference will no longer be required."

"Thank you Marc for indulging me with your company and for your aid in my schemes. I know I can be a hardship at times."

Back to his teasing self, "Not a hardship, just a handful. Heaven help the gentleman who really falls for you and even more so for the one you yourself fall for. But in all seriousness, if we do not meet again I do wish you a safe journey Abigail." He kissed her hand then turned her to greet Lord Alton for the next dance.

Abby danced the rest of the dances with other gentlemen of her acquaintance and even one with her father. At the end of the ball she found a very weary Elizabeth in the ladies salon. They gathered their wraps and paused a moment, out of the way of the other ladies, before quitting the room.

Elizabeth reported to Abby in a hushed voice, "I saw Lord Jason escort Lady Jane to her parents upon their departure a while ago and then take his leave. It would seem as if the evening was a success in redirecting his attentions."

In a melancholy tone Abby replied, "It would seem so."

Shocked Elizabeth asked, "Goodness, you have not changed your mind, have you?"

"Oh no....No, not about him...It is just the evening is over and I was not ready for it to end. I know it is the end of the season anyway but the day we sail is growing near and the reality of all I am leaving behind is sinking in....not that I do not want to go...I still do, very much...it is just a little daunting is all."

"I am not surprised you feel that way. I have enjoyed our time together this past week and I am sure we will see each other again before you depart. I will be sure to come see you off the morning you leave. Friday, is it not?"

"Yes, Friday. I would like that Bethy. You are a good friend."

They gave each other a quick hug before quitting the room, Elizabeth to join Avery and Abby her father as they waited for their respective carriages.

Once settled in the carriage, Abby realized she was exhausted. She rested her head against the cushion and closed her eyes letting her mind wander over the events of the evening. A moment later she was disturbed by her father. "Judging from the Cheshire grin on your face you enjoyed yourself."

Abby opened her eyes to look at her father sitting across from her. "Yes I did." The darkness of the late hour made it impossible to distinguish his features. There was only enough light from the moon and the carriage lamps to see his outline. But light was not required to picture in her mind his handsome visage. Though his age was showing in the wrinkles at the corners of his eyes and the brackets around his mouth along with his greying hair he could still turn a woman's head as was the case tonight. She had seen him dancing often and when he wasn't he seemed to always be the center of attention with the older unattached ladies.

In a light tone her father said, "You and Marc dance well together. Two dances created quite a stir amongst the old hens. Thank you for not waltzing as well. I would have spent all my time defending you rather than enjoying a dance or two myself."

"I would have loved to have waltzed with him, but alas, I could not in good conscience cause him any more grief with his fiancée or you with the old guard."

"Again, my thanks. Did I not see you introducing Lord Malwbry to Lady Torrington? And did they not, after said introduction, spend a great deal of the evening in each other's company?"

"I believe we have come to an agreeable understanding. I do not expect for

31

Jason to continue courting me."

"Well done, daughter. I believe you would make a very fine business woman with that kind of negotiating skill."

Abby smiled at his compliment. "Everything is business with you, Father. I believe it was required of you to become successful and has now turned into a habit."

"You are probably right. Would you like for me to change my ways?" he said in jest.

Abby returned his banter. "Of course not. I have grown too used to the finer things in life to give them up now."

"Well then, daughter, you will just have to overlook my poor character flaws so that you may continue your fine lifestyle."

The carriage pulled to the front of their townhouse. The butler held the door open for them to enter. Abby wished her father good night and retired to her room for a much needed slumber.

Wednesday morning brought the delivery of Abigail's order from Madame Rousseau. Abby had been anxiously waiting for it ever since her final fitting on Monday. The boxes were taken up to her room and Miss Winterfeldt joined her there to assist with packing her trunks for departure two days hence. Her trunks had been brought down from the attic, four in all, and given a good cleaning and airing. Now Miss Winterfeldt was busy sorting her clothing according to summer or winter wear as she would be visiting such varying climates.

Abby began unwrapping her new items to join the growing piles. The third box she opened was the one she was most excited about. Beneath the layers of tissue was an exquisite rose gown of the same modern style as the blue gown in Madame's display window. Abby pulled it from the box and held it to her moving towards the full length dressing mirror. The rose satin gown had a dropped shoulder neck line with a wide ribbon of a darker hue around the middle of her torso. It had short puffed undersleeves finished with a sheer overdress with full sleeves giving the gown a gossamer effect. It was the most beautiful dress she had ever owned.

"Oh my!" Abby turned at Miss Winterfeldt's breathy exclamation.

"Madame surprised me with this at my fitting Tuesday. Due to something Elizabeth said about wearing her fashions around the world she made this dress special for me and only charged the cost of the fabric."

Miss Winterfeldt came to stand beside her. "Would you try it on for me, dear?" Abby was pleased to oblige. Returning to the mirror her reflection showed her a more sophisticated lady than she felt herself to be. "You are all grown up Miss Abigail and if I may say so you are even more beautiful than the downstairs portrait of your dear mother. The colour is absolutely perfect for you."

Abby studied her image in the mirror, mentally comparing it to her mother's portrait. Her features were similar but she thought her mother was more graceful and serene than she felt herself to be.

She resolved to save the dress for a special occasion. She changed back into her day dress and they carefully repacked the new gown in the tissue and box and then placed it in the last trunk along with her mother's jewelry chest she insisted on taking with her. Miss Winterfeldt had tried to talk her out of taking the bulky piece but she wanted a part of her mother with her on her journey even if she had to carry it herself.

Her father had warned her she would only have enough room for one trunk in her cabin so they packed two warm weather dresses and one other cold weather dress to have in addition to the one she would wear at departure along with other articles of necessity. She tied a scrap of material to the handle of the trunk so the crew would know which one was to be taken to her cabin.

The sight of the packed trunks increased the excitement building in her chest. In less than forty-eight hours they would be boarding the ship. She wondered how she would be able to stand the wait.

Friday morning was overcast with a light breeze. The servants bustled about loading the last of the luggage on the cart to be taken to the dock and preparing the house to be closed up. Elizabeth arrived shortly after breaking her fast to offer her assistance with the last minute details, although the ever efficient Miss Winterfeldt appeared to have it all in hand.

When all had been loaded the four of them - Richard, Abby, Elizabeth and Miss Winterfeldt - stood beside the carriage to say their final good-byes.

Richard shook Miss Winterfeldt's hand thanking her for her years of loyal service. He also handed her an envelope from his coat pocket with a hefty severance pay and a letter of recommendation. He bowed to Elizabeth and then moved to the door of the carriage to await Abby.

Miss Winterfeldt apologized to Abby. "I am sorry we were not able to find you a proper ladies maid in time. Your father assures me he will find someone suitable promptly."

"Do not fret Miss Winterfeldt I will see that he does. Thank you for all you have done for me." Abby did her best to hold back the tears.

Miss Winterfeldt handed her a package wrapped in brown paper. "Just a small going away gift. I wish you a pleasant journey and will pray you find the adventure you are searching for in safety. Take care, dear." Miss Winterfeldt pulled out her handkerchief and turned away to hide her tears.

Abby's watery eyes lingered on Miss Winterfeldt for a moment longer before turning to face Elizabeth. "You will write often, won't you? And take care of yourself and your precious gift. Be sure to send me word of his arrival."

"Of course. *Bon voyage, mon amie...* sounds more cheerful than 'goodbye, my friend' does it not? Now go, have your adventure for both of us. I expect long letters telling me all about it."

The girls hugged each other in earnest then Elizabeth nudged Abby in

Richard's direction. Her father helped her into the carriage before following himself and shutting the door. He rapped on the roof signaling the driver to start.

Abby leaned out the window to wave one last goodbye to her lifelong friend and the person closest to a mother she had ever known. Elizabeth and Miss Winterfeldt both waved back while simultaneously wiping away tears. It was a moment of the most mixed emotions Abby had ever felt.

She reseated herself in the carriage and gave her father a watery smile. He returned a look of understanding. "What is in your package?"

Abby looked down at the package in surprise having momentarily forgotten it. She tore off the brown paper with unsteady hands to reveal a bleached leather journal with an embossed cover of a gazebo with blooming vines winding up the posts. She opened the cover revealing a message from her beloved nanny. *Enjoy the adventures in life - both the grand and the small. You will always be in my heart. With love, Miss Mildred Winterfeldt*

To get her mind off what she was leaving behind and focused instead on what lay ahead her father started telling her amusing stories of some of his previous voyages and in no time at all they arrived at the Southampton docks.

Chapter 3

First of September, 1828 Southampton, England

The dock was unusually quiet the morning of their departure much to Abigail's disappointment. The fishing smacks had already left for their fishing grounds in the early morning hours and the few arriving vessels were already discharged. Theirs appeared to be the only ship in the area making ready to leave with the late morning tide. She would have liked to have seen the hustle and bustle of such a large seaport; watched the people come and go whose lives were so different from her own. Abby had accompanied her father to the port a few times in the past but had never sailed.

The carriage continued down the wharf past rows of ships of varying size gently undulating on the water, masts pointed towards the sky. As they approached their destination she noticed her father's growing excitement. He held onto her hand after helping her out of the carriage and with a gentle squeeze said with glowing pride, "Look at her Abby. The newest member of the fleet, the *Abigail Rose*."

Abby dutifully turned her attention to the three-masted barque with furled sails standing tall against the sky. *So that was the reason for his excitement.* She could smell the paint and tar of the newly completed hull. The lettering of her namesake was crisp and the sparkling glass of her stern and port windows faithfully reflected the grey sky. "She is amazing Father."

"Just as you are, sweetheart."

Abby squeezed her father's arm in response. She noticed the men lined up facing the ship and the chaplain walking past them up the gangplank and on up to the quarterdeck before dropping to his knee to pray.

Richard handed his daughter a bottle of wine she had not noticed he was holding. "I held off the christening ceremony in order for you to perform the honours. After the chaplain has blessed the ship you will break the bottle across the bow."

Abby felt humbled to have a ship named after her and was anxious to perform her task well. She took the bottle from her father and waited for her queue. When the moment came she walked up to the hull and holding the bottle with both hands swung with all her might praying it would break on the first try. It shattered completely from the neck down with a satisfying splatter of wine across the hull. The men behind her all gave a loud cheer before disbanding to resume their assigned duties. Her father handed her his handkerchief to wipe her hands then thanked the chaplain for his services.

Richard guided Abby towards the gangplank. She walked up first as there was only room for one at a time. At the top the first mate offered his assistance as she stepped to the ship's deck. She smiled her thanks without really looking at him but Richard noticed and frowned as he watched Samuel Carter's hopeful smile fade away in vain expectation as Abigail moved off towards the railing. Mr. Carter's disappointment was too much. It seemed to Richard as if his feelings were for more than not being noticed by a passing female but deeper as if plans were thwarted. He would have to keep a close watch on any further interactions Mr. Carter might have with his daughter.

Richard had recently interviewed Samuel Carter when he was recommended for promotion to first mate. Mr. Carter had worked for Bennington Transport as a crewman the last two years and although he had satisfactorily answered all of Richard's questions there was something about the man's demeanor that rang false. Not having a solid reason to deny the request, Richard approved the promotion hoping his suspicions were the result of prejudice against the man's long face, cleft chin and oiled mustache that nearly reached his sideburns. In and of themselves there was nothing wrong with these features but as a whole Richard found them offensive. Putting aside his personal opinion, he had decided if Captain Andrews deemed the man worthy of the post he did not have a good reason to deny the request. The way Mr. Carter reacted to Abigail caused Richard to again question the man's character. He hoped he would not come to regret his decision to promote him.

Standing at the rail, with the wind blowing her skirt and whipping the loose tendrils of reddish brown hair across her face, Abby was admiring the masts and sails of her namesake. A passerby would notice the willowy female and not help but take a moment to admire her grace and form while her spirited personality naturally drew people to her. Large grey-green eyes and full lips were her most appealing features although Abby considered her face to be common.

Richard walked up to his daughter. He had just finished overseeing the loading of cargo bound for the islands and their own personal belongings. He hoped their weeks at sea would be smooth sailing. At least he felt safe with the captain, his longtime friend and confidante, Captain Matthew Andrews. "Abby dear, what do you think of her?" Richard's gesture encompassed the whole ship.

"She is a grand vessel, worthy of her name and ready to set sail. You can feel the anticipation of letting go of the mooring lines, the sails filling with the wind and heading out to open water," replied Abby with all the eagerness she had just attributed to the ship.

Richard could not help smiling at her imagery. He patted her hand. "I agree." A moment later he left her to join the captain on the quarterdeck.

Abby observed the two very distinguished looking men as they conferred with each other. Both had grey hair, average build and commanding demeanor. Her father's bearing declared him to be the ship's owner while the slightly taller captain had the weather worn face of a lifetime seaman.

The crew in their matching striped shirts went about the preparations for setting sail. Abby stood clear and watched in awe as the men pulled on the lines in perfect unison rapidly releasing the large square sails. Finally, the mooring lines were cast off and they sailed away from the dock. She felt like waving goodbye and since there was no one watching from shore she waved goodbye to England. It was a silly gesture but it made her feel better as the ship moved away from her homeland.

Abby could not be persuaded to leave the ship's railing, not even to eat. She was entranced with the passing shorelines of places she had read about and seen on her father's maps. She crossed the deck back and forth weaving between the working crew to watch as the next town of thatch roofed houses slid past followed by pastures and forests. Some of the coastline was marshland while cliffs lined other banks. The variety of scenery fascinated her.

They came to the end of the Southampton Water. Abby crossed to starboard to watch as they slipped past Calshot Castle standing guard at the mouth of the passage. It occupied the end of a sandpit extending out into the water from the mainland. The castle was a single, round structure built with large grey brick and surrounded by a moat and outer crenelated wall. The mood on the ship became tense. The crew worked the lines rapidly paying close attention to orders being issued by the Captain and the First mate. Abby sought her father's side. She felt his tension as well. "Is there something wrong?"

Richard intentionally lightened his demeanor when he turned to Abby. "Not at all. We are crossing into the Solent. It is a difficult area with a strong current and a narrow channel but once we pass through it will be smooth sailing. I am only more concerned than usual because it is a new ship and there have been changes in the crew."

Abby nodded her head in understanding. The ship headed west following the passage between the English coast and the Isle of Wight. Tension eased some after the change of course but the crew was still vigilant. Abby resumed watching the coasts on both sides and much to her delight the sky brightened as the sun broke through the clouds. Sometime later Abby was studying the towering chalk cliffs of the Isle of Wight on their port side when her father appeared to suggest she move starboard for a look at Hurst Castle guarding the western entrance of the Solent.

It was built similar to Calshot Castle on a spit of land extending from Milford on Sea but it also included other buildings, a tower and a lighthouse. They sailed close enough she was able to see a company of men doing field exercises on the grounds and several soldiers standing guard on the parapets.

Once past the fort and through the opening of the Solent into the English Channel tensions eased on the ship with the crewman now exchanging lighthearted banter with each other as they went about their duties. The order was given to add more sails greatly increasing their speed.

Abby and Richard once again crossed to the port side of the ship. The western edge of the Isle of Wight brought a sudden end to the white cliffs with stacks of chalk like so many broken pieces falling into the sea. Richard pointed to the formations. "Those are called the Needles."

Abby nodded. "I have read about them. There are three now but there used to be a fourth called *Lot's Wife* supposedly shaped more like a needle and hence the name. A storm destroyed it nearly four scores ago."

Richard smiled at his daughter. "That is correct. We are now in the Channel. Tomorrow we will cross the Celtic Sea and if all is fair we should reach the Atlantic Ocean by nightfall. You will not see land again for nearly a fortnight."

As the Isle of Wight slowly disappeared Abby turned to face the wind from the bow ready for new adventures in foreign countries on the other side of the ocean.

Samuel Carter was called to relieve the Captain at the helm as soon as they crossed into the English Channel. He checked their position then let his gaze drift to Mr. and Miss Bennington standing at the bulwarks of the lower deck watching the last of the land fade from sight. Truth be told he had been covertly watching her all day. He was attracted to her the moment she set foot on the ship. A bonus for the plan he had formulated when he first learned she would be sailing with her father. If he could woo Miss Bennington and secure her hand in marriage he could inherit Bennington Transport and secure his future. Growing up in an orphanage with too little of everything he planned to make sure the rest of his life was filled with plenty and standing before him was the key to making it happen.

Completely lost in his thoughts he was not aware of the approach of the second mate, Mr. McCray, until he heard him say in his Scottish brogue, "You're dreamin' mon. Mr. Bennington will never allow a sod like you near his daughter."

Irritated at having been caught and his motives so easily discerned he boldly declared, "Watch and see. I'll make her my wife."

Mr. McCray snorted in derision. "You'll be lucky ye have a job you mess with the likes of her."

Not wanting any more of his antagonizing Mr. Carter snapped, "Get back to work."

Mr. McCray laughed as he walked away.

Abby spent as much of the day as she could on deck soaking in all that was life at sea. She automatically adjusted her stance in response to the rolling deck and her balance improved with each passing hour. She was surprised how quickly the hours had passed. As the day faded into dusk she watched the sun drop towards the western horizon. She had seen sunsets before, of course, but it always disappeared behind the trees. Here there was nothing to block the view as it slid ever closer to the water; the distance from the orange orb to the horizon shrinking while the colours in the sky bloomed in pinks and purples and melons. It seemed as if only moments later the sun was touching the water and the hues deepened to orange and purple, with a red halo around the sphere. As she watched, it continued to sink below the waterline seemingly faster and faster turning the sky dark red before fading into black. When the last of the colour had disappeared it became so dark she could no longer distinguish the line between water and sky.

The call to supper finally made Abby aware of her hunger. She stopped by her cabin to remove her hat and brush her wind tossed hair. Checking her reflection in the hand mirror she ruefully noticed her wind burned cheeks and the new dusting of freckles across her nose. She would have to take care the rest of the voyage to prevent further damage to her milky skin.

Richard escorted Abby to the Captain's cabin. They would be joining Captain Andrews and the officers for their shipboard meals at the Captain's long table. This being the first night of the voyage rations were good and plentiful. Fresh bread and a hearty stew served with wine. Abby enjoyed every bite well aware the next weeks would see a slow deterioration in diet. The only blemish to the evening was Mr. Carter. His bold glances during dinner made her uncomfortable. For the remainder of the voyage she made a point of avoiding his presence whenever possible and to stand or sit out of his line of sight whenever it was not.

One week into the trip her spirits were still riding high even though she was beginning to tire of the monotony of smooth water, the ships movements, reading and the laborious attempts to write legibly in her journal. She had brought her tatting shuttle and thread but quickly gave up on that occupation the first day having little enough patience for the tedious knots on land. Boredom was leading her to a love/hate relationship with sailing.

Late the second week they crossed paths with a British merchant ship returning home. Captain Andrews hailed her. Both ships came to halt. Captain Andrews and four crewmen sailed over to the other ship in the longboat to speak with her captain. Abby stayed close to her father in the hopes of overhearing what news Captain Andrews had learned.

Upon his return Captain Andrews sought out her father, his face grim. "It is as we feared; civil war in the Azores has broken out in earnest. It would be unwise to stop for supplies. It is fortunate you anticipated this problem. We will cut rations immediately and pray for fair winds." The captain left them to speak to the first mate.

Turning Richard was confronted with the concerned look on his daughter's face. "Not to worry. We loaded extra food and water. All will be well, perhaps a bit unpleasant, but we will be fine."

The end of the third week she was bored to tears of perfect weather, calm seas, always the same food and nothing to do but stay out of the way. She had already gone through all of her reading material - twice - and had walked the deck of the ship so many times she felt she had seen every nail in every board. She was tired of writing in her journal, tired of knitting and tired of trying to avoid Mr. Carter.

By the fourth week, she just knew nothing exciting would ever happen. The tea and sugar were long gone and they were running low on treacle. Coffee, hardtack, beans and salt pork were still plentiful and the weather was fair. The captain and her father rejoiced over this every evening at dinner. Goodness, she couldn't stand listening to it anymore. Then one evening Captain Andrews mentioned to her father they were headed into a storm. He suggested they secure their belongings as soon as they finished their meal.

Abby took a moment to go on deck after dinner wanting to see the storm. The dark jagged clouds appeared more ominous than she had expected not having the buffer of trees and buildings for shelter. Here on the water there was only their small ship and the gathering tempest that overwhelmed everything.

The crew was engaged in battening down the hatches and furling some of the sail. The wind whipped her hair and she could feel the power of the churning seas as the dark leaden clouds moved closer. Suddenly a strong flash of lighting broke the sky causing her to flinch followed closely by a roaring thunder. Mr. McCray approached her from the bow. "Miss, you really should go below deck now." Having come to the same conclusion Abby simply nodded to the second mate and made her way to her cabin.

An hour later, Abby was wishing for perfect weather. Being tossed around in one's berth willy nilly was not the kind of excitement she had had in mind. The storm dissipated in the early morning hours and she was finally able to sleep. She awoke lethargic and bruised in body. Despite his former career in the Royal Navy her father suffered a mild case of seasickness. He attributed it to being confined below decks instead of standing watch. He had little more than coffee for breakfast. Abby found her appetite was unaffected. She enjoyed her breakfast and later a stroll on the deck in the sunshine that was considerably warmer than when they left England. As Captain Andrews walked by he mentioned they should reach Kingston in a few days if the weather held and the winds were fair. She gazed out at the water as if she might be able to see the island now if she just looked hard enough.

Four interminably long days later, Abby awoke to the sound of birds flying outside her port window and deck hands scurrying about in preparation of landfall. A few days ago they had seen a distant glimpse of land as they sailed between the islands of Puerto Rico and Haití Español passing into the Caribbean Sea. The tantalizing view of land had only served to heighten her anticipation of finally making landfall this morning. She rushed through her morning toiletries in her excitement to get on deck.

She nearly broke into a run down the passageway and quickly climbed up the stairs. As she emerged from the companionway the first thing she saw was the dark green and blue of a majestic mountain rising into the sky. Upon gaining the deck, she realized they were still some distance outside the harbour. She walked across the deck, taking care to stay out of the way of the crew, making her way to the railing.

After leaving the grey of London and the endless days of blue sky and darker blue ocean, Abby was overwhelmed by the colours of the island; the clear aqua-blue water, the pure white sand, and the rich green foliage. Many species of birds could be seen. Some even came close to the ship as if escorting the new arrivals.

The mountainous island was more enlivened than she had imagined a place could be. Her nerve endings sizzled with anticipation of exploring this exotic world. The trees and plants were different than those in England. So many varieties of what she assumed were palms. Some in tree form and others were plants. The contrast between this colourful island and her native island of England could not have been more striking, at least not for her. England was so somber in comparison. At the moment she didn't care if she ever saw her homeland again.

Abby watched the birds fly over the foliage and then out over the water and back again. They appeared to be chasing each other. *I wonder if that is a courtship ritual.* Her thoughts turned inward. She had escaped a dull marriage with Lord Jason. What options were open to her now? At nineteen she assumed she could still be choosy but what about when she returned next year and was twenty? There were not any gentlemen in her circles she cared to encourage. Most were committed to drink, cards and other immoral behaviour a lady dare not contemplate instead of marriage and family. The few honourable men searching for a wife were stuffy and boring, too old or too young and disagreeable. Would she need to consider settling for less than she desired in a husband? Turning back to the island, she wondered if there could be someone here for her or maybe she would find someone in America. Exciting possibilities. Tiring of her thoughts she allowed the beauty of the day to chase off the serious turn her mind had taken. Today she was still young and everything would be a new experience.

She felt the gentle salty breeze blow across her cheek, disturbing the tendrils of her hair and realized she had come to love the sea. She loved the sway of the ship and the power of the water; the vastness of the ocean and the thrill of returning to land. Her sense of adventure made her impatient to debark and explore the island but she knew she would also look forward to returning to the sea.

On the upper deck, Mr. Carter supervised the deck hands who were securing the ship in preparation for shore leave. His gaze kept straying to the willowy figure at the railing. So far his pursuit of her had been unfruitful. She was always in the presence of her father or the Captain and refused to show any interest in his overtures. If he could prove his worth to her father on this voyage perhaps he could soon earn a promotion to captain so he would be in an acceptable position to request permission to court her. His imagination was rife with ideas of compromising her but he was held at bay by the very likely result of ending his service with Bennington Transport. His plans of becoming a captain and taking Miss Bennington as his wife required patience and opportunity.

Richard approached his daughter standing at the railing gazing at the island and for a moment he saw, not his daughter, but his wife in her profile. The pain in his chest was sharp and unexpected. Her loss still made him ache despite the spanning years since her passing. *Oh Anna, look how our little girl has grown. I have done the best I can for her. I hope we both have made you proud.*

Reaching her side, Richard laid his hand atop hers resting on the railing and gently squeezed. "Good morning sweetheart. You look well rested." He followed her gaze towards the island. "I wish I could have brought your mother here. I think she would have loved to travel abroad, especially the tropics."

"Why do you think she would have liked the tropics?" Abby was excited to learn something new about her mother.

"She loved colourful flowers and she would have been charmed by the warm-hearted island people, always smiling with generosity despite their subjugation."

"Subjugation?" Abby frowned. "Are you referring to slavery? But I thought England abolished slavery."

"The trading of slaves was made unlawful but owning slaves...that is another matter altogether and a difficult one as it takes many people to run the plantations."

Abby had never given slavery much thought before; not having direct contact with any. Taking a moment now to consider the matter, she decided she was against it. The idea of controlling every aspect of another person's life seemed very unfair. She had heard stories of cruelty to slaves, which of course was abhorrent, but it was so far removed from her life she had never stopped to contemplate the reality of slavery and all its aspects from the slaves' point of view.

They were standing on the starboard side of the ship as it passed through the narrow harbour opening. Richard pointed to the inland side of a sand spit protecting the harbour. "They call that area the Palisadoes. Well over a hundred years ago it was the location of Port Royal before a devastating earthquake caused it to slip beneath the sea. Look there." Richard pointed towards some ruined buildings. "You can see some of the remains of the city.

The brick wall behind them is Fort Charles and beyond it is the Naval Hospital built a few years ago. My ships delivered some of the cast iron sections from England used to build it."

"Port Royal was a famous pirate city, was it not?"

"Pirates have infested much of the Caribbean in the past. However, the last few years have been much improved; otherwise I would not have brought you with me."

"Is that why you have never let me sail with you before? It was to protect me...I thought it was because I would be in the way."

Richard smiled. "Well, that too."

Abby grinned in response to her father's teasing.

They were now in the midst of the harbour surrounded by hundreds of ships. Between the spanning masts and sails Abby could see the buildings of Kingston fanning out from the harbour to nestle against the base of the Blue Mountains. It created a very picturesque view. Eventually the *Abigail Rose* gently bumped into the dock under the expert guidance of Captain Andrews. The crew secured the mooring lines and then scurried below decks to prepare for the unloading of cargo.

Abby watched the dark skinned porter load their trunks on the back of a surrey with a bright yellow fringe decorating the roof line. The chestnut horses twitched their heads and pawed the ground impatient at being made to stand still for so long. They seemed to be as anxious as she was to get moving.

Richard interrupted her thoughts to ask, "What do you think of the tropics?"

"It is so rich and colourful and.... alive!" She turned to look at her father, "Am I making any sense?" He gave her a questioning look. "The birds and the flowers and the people; they all seem so..." she struggled for a word to express herself "alive" was all she could come up with.

Her father didn't understand. "Sweetheart, England has birds, flowers and people too. More actually." Abby looked back to the island and shrugged. She could not explain how she felt. Everything about the tropics made England seem so dreary and lifeless to her.

Uncomfortable with her feminine sentiments, Richard turned to the business at hand. "We will check into the inn and freshen up. Then pay a visit to Mr. Josiah Landis. He has promised a dinner party at his home in our honour."

"How long do you expect our stay to last?" inquired Abby.

"As long as it takes to load the ship, usually a couple of weeks. Are you ready?"

"As soon as I retrieve my parasol and reticule from the cabin."

Captain Andrews approached Richard's side following Abby's departure. "When do you plan to tell her?"

Richard's expression showed his irritation at being reminded of the painful truth he had yet to share with his daughter. "Not today."

43

Chapter 4

Midanbury, England End of September 1828

It was two months to the day after the ball when Jason last saw Abigail Bennington. He was slumped in a leather chair at his gentlemen's club smoking a hand rolled Cuban cigar, a half empty brandy bottle and an empty crystal tumbler on the table beside him. His surroundings, while not as ornate and lavish as the well-known London clubs, was comfortable enough for a gentleman of his station. Rich leather sofas and chairs were scattered about the room with highly polished dark rose wood furniture. The walls were covered in dark damask paper and stained wood wainscoting. Large floor to ceiling windows allowed for enough light during the day and a vast array of oil lamps and candle sconces lit the dim recesses at night. The establishment was clean with enough of the amenities to make one comfortable and most important offered a quiet place for a man to take stock of his life. Jason was doing just that, contemplating the events of the last few months leading to his current situation.

The whole marriage hunt had started with his mother's push to replenish the family funds. When she had arranged for him to meet Miss Bennington he had decided to go along not having any strong feelings either way. His life had become dull with so many of his friends having recently wed that he was willing to take a small step into the marriage mart. He had enjoyed the first evening with Abigail. She had a quick wit and an impertinent attitude to match his mood that evening. The venue he chose for their next meeting turned out to be a disaster. He was so embarrassed by his friend Robert's brash and inappropriate behaviour with Bridgette during the carriage ride he couldn't face Abigail. He had kept his gaze focused outside the carriage for fear of blushing himself. Next, he found himself attending balls at his mother's insistence. He only stayed long enough at each one to accomplish his mission of dancing with Abigail before making good his escape from all the matchmaking mothers and debutantes vying for his attention.

He still was not sure how it happened but his mother convinced him that since *the ton* was already speculating on their upcoming marriage he should speak with her father, which he had done. Mr. Bennington had agreed to his courtship but Jason had the impression he was not as thrilled with the prospect as one would expect. Jason had never dealt with anyone not in awe of his family titles and who didn't treat him like royalty but instead judged him for himself... and dared to consider him inferior. He wondered what it was Mr.

Bennington found lacking in his character. It was bothering Jason more than he would care to admit.

Then he heard the tales at the club of Abigail being seen alone with Marc Danvers. He knew where Marc's interests lay but what of Abigail's? He had decided to find out by arranging to meet with her in a more private setting. He sent a message for her to go riding with him. He was embarrassed and angry when he learned his mother had told Abigail he would request a meeting. It made him appear as if he was his mother's puppet and not his own man. Her continued interference had finally pushed him to his limit and he lashed back at both his parents before going off to a bar to ponder if Abigail was really the one for him or if maybe he should look around at his other options. Abigail made his decision easier that same afternoon by suggesting the same thing and offering to assist him.

As agreed he met her at the next dance where she introduced him to Lady Jane Torrington. Lady Jane was certainly pleasant enough but he kept finding himself distracted whenever Abigail would dance by on the arm of Marc looking so radiantly happy. Jason acknowledged to himself he was a little jealous of Marc's ability to be at ease with her.

In between dances he had learned of Abigail's pending departure. He was quite shocked she had neglected to mention it to him before then. That she had so little regard for him was yet another reason he should focus on other prospective ladies. But as she swept away from him, again with Marc, and he was faced with Lady Jane, he couldn't help but feel his enthusiasm for the evening had vanished. He had been relieved to send Lady Jane home with her parents so he could depart as well. He considered the evening to have been a failure along with all the others he had allowed Marc to talk him into since then.

As if materializing from his thoughts, Jason noted Marc's entrance in the arched wood paneled foyer of the club. Marc scanned the room as he removed his leather riding gloves, saw him and headed his way. He rose to greet his friend before slumping back in his chair and signaling the barkeep for more libations.

Receiving their drinks, Marc raised his glass in a silent salute and downed a large swallow before commenting on Jason's demeanor. "What's wrong old chum? Never seen you look so serious, as if your future depended on this very moment's decision."

Jason returned a wry grimace. "As a matter of fact that is exactly what I am contemplating; my future and my future bride."

"Your bride? I had no idea you had made a decision. Pray tell, who is to be the next Duchess of Rothebury?" teased Marc.

"That is just it. I do not know. But it is time to figure it out. Time to produce the heir and all that."

Marc nodded in understanding. "Which of our fine lasses are you considering? I have introduced you to several these last few weeks."

"Lady Jane Torrington would be top choice of those here in England but there is one not on this soil who still holds my attention."

Contemplating but a moment Marc's eyes widened as he realized to whom Jason was referring. "No! You are not seriously still considering Abby are you?"

"Why? Is there some reason I should not?"

"Besides the fact she risked all sorts of scandal to remove herself from your presence, no."

Jason grimaced, "I came across that poorly, eh?"

"I would say so. You used to be so charming with the ladies during our school years. Did you know we dubbed you 'Prince Charming'? Combine charm with your title and the rest of us did not stand a chance. Have to say I was a little surprised Abby was not enamored with you. I figured maybe she was running scared."

Reflecting back Jason realized his mistake. "Charm was the one thing I did not show her. I was letting my mother control my actions. Abigail was her choice and I was only going through the motions rather than committing to the idea. I did not put any effort into courting her and now I realize I am left with simpering spoiled debutantes when what I want is Abigail's spirit. She probably was running scared from my boorish behaviour. And now it is too late."

"Why would it be? If you are really serious about her why not follow her? What lady could resist the idea she is unforgettable? Show her how charming you can be."

Jason brightened at the idea. It could work and it had more appeal than his other choices. "Do you know where she is headed?"

Marc grinned at the hope lighting Jason's expression. "I do. Her uncle, James Bennington, has a plantation near Montgomery, Alabama. Abby and her father plan to visit with them until spring."

Having a new goal and being one of his own choosing, Jason was now in a hurry to put it in motion. He stood up and moved next to Marc's chair to lay a hand on his friend's shoulder. "Hope you do not mind if I take my leave. I believe I will head to the docks and see when the next ship is leaving for America." Jason didn't even wait for a reply but hastily headed towards the door; a new fervor lengthening his stride.

Marc wondered if he had done the right thing in telling Jason to pursue Abby. He felt Jason's change of heart was sincere and there really was no reason he would not be a good husband to Abby. He couldn't say the same about Abby being a good wife for Jason. He just couldn't picture her as a duchess but then stranger things had happened. He wondered how Abby would handle Jason showing up on her doorstep after all her maneuvering to get away from him. If he didn't have his own wedding to attend he probably would have volunteered to go with Jason so he could witness their reunion. It was sure to be entertaining.

Kingston, Jamaica Middle of October 1828

With the trunks loaded in the surrey, Richard waved aside the driver and offered his assistance to Abby then climbed aboard himself. The driver climbed up in the front seat where a little boy of about seven years of age waited patiently. The pair of them had the darkest skin Abby had ever seen, reminding her of melted dark chocolate. The driver clucked to the spirited chestnut mare. She pricked her ears and eagerly obeyed the command to move. They briskly rode through the neatly laid out white sand streets of Kingston, passing drays conveying goods from the wharves to the stores and women carrying their burdens in baskets on their heads. The neat and tidy wooden houses lining the streets seemed flimsy compared to the predominately brick and stone structures of England, although Abby liked the bright consistency of the whitewashed facades.

The little boy in the front seat was chattering away, pointing out landmarks in the hopes of earning a good tip from the English visitors.

"Dat a mi bredda. Di wola dem a me fambly."

"Coodeh, yuh see de big bud eena de tree?"

"A wan irie likkle place."

Abby was having a hard time comprehending the unique island language but his antics had a universal understanding and she found herself quite amused by him. She even noticed her father grinning on occasion.

She was thankful when they arrived in front of the inn. It was late morning but the day was already gaining heat that Abby was not accustomed to and she was more than ready to enter the relatively cooler inn. As was typical in the tropics, doors and windows were located opposite from each other to allow the breeze to pass through the interior of the buildings.

After checking in, she and her father retired to their rooms to settle in and freshen up before having a light lunch of bread and fruit provided by the innkeeper in the dining room. The freshly baked bread tasted heavenly to Abby after weeks of mostly hardtack, beans and salt pork aboard ship. The fruit was new to both of them, bananas and sliced mango. The innkeeper kindly demonstrated how to peel the skin from the banana and bite into the exposed fruit. Both Abby and Richard were uncomfortable with such a casual eating style and so transferred the fruit to their plate to be eaten with fork and knife in a proper English fashion much to the innkeeper's amusement. Abby enjoyed both fruits so much she wished she could have asked for seconds.

Richard's business partner, Mr. Josiah Landis, arrived shortly after their lunch. Richard welcomed him into the sitting room of their suite and introduced him to Abby. He was a man of small stature with a balding head and a very businesslike manner which was one of the things her father probably found appealing about him.

Mr. Landis politely bowed in her direction. "It is a pleasure to make your acquaintance Miss Bennington. How was your voyage? Hopefully uneventful."

Abby curtsied to their host. "A pleasure to meet you Mr. Landis. Other than what I am assured was a mild storm a few days from here, our voyage was quite pleasant."

"You were most fortunate not to have arrived sooner. A severe hurricane crossed your path a fortnight ago. I would not be surprised if you encountered the tail end of it."

Abby was not sure if she felt relief or disappointment. She would have liked to have seen a hurricane albeit preferably from a safe distance. "Most fortunate indeed, sir. My father tells me you are the reason his business runs so smoothly in the West Indies."

Mr. Landis demurred. "Thank you, Miss, but I assure you our success owes more to his skills than mine." Turning to his employer, Mr. Landis inquired, "Would you prefer to go over the cargo details now or after dinner?"

"Now, I believe."

Mr. Landis and her father launched into the details of business while Abby perused an old copy of *Ladies Journal* loaned to her by the innkeeper's wife. She didn't pay much attention as they discussed the details of the furniture and textiles brought from England and how much coffee, sugar and rum could be loaded to take to the states and back to England but when she heard her father mention buying a slave girl to serve as her ladies maid she impolitely and inappropriately entered into the conversation.

"Father, I must protest. I could not possibly conscience having a slave for my maid."

Richard gave Mr. Landis an apologetic look before responding to Abby. "Abigail, while there are some free negroes in the mountains they are mostly a rebellious lot. If it will make you feel better you can grant the girl her freedom." This statement elicited a gasp from Mr. Landis and understanding his concerns Richard added, "however, you will have to wait till we have left the island to do so for such an act could upset the tenuous balance between owners and slaves."

"Very well Father, if that is what you think is best. I only insist the girl is agreeable to leaving her family and the island. I would not want to take someone against their will."

"As you wish. Mr. Landis, could you arrange for us to find such a girl?"

After considering a moment Mr. Landis suggested his son should drive them to a plantation owned by one of his friends the next afternoon as they would likely have several slave girls available.

It was now approaching early evening and with their business settled for the day, Mr. Landis offered to wait while they dressed for dinner and he would drive them to his home. He had an extra chaise they could use to return to the inn at the end of the evening and retain for their use during their stay on the island.

48

The innkeeper's wife graciously acted as lady's maid for Abby and as it turned out she had a knack for styling hair. Abby chose one of Madame Rousseau's lightweight gowns to wear and three quarters of an hour later she felt grand enough to meet the Queen. As she entered the sitting room, her father and Mr. Landis rose to greet her reappearance. Abby could see the pride reflected in her father's eye and it made her feel special.

Mr. Landis had a nicely sprung carriage allowing them to travel in relative comfort as they journeyed to his home higher up into the heights of Liguanea following a single dirt lane under a canopy of gracile foliage. The air turned perceptively cooler as they made their way into the mountains. Abby was grateful she had picked up her shawl at the last moment before departing her room. She would probably need it on the way home.

The Landis home was a whitewashed two-story structure with green trim, green shutters and a piazza across the front. The carriage stopped and two servants immediately appeared to help them disembark before taking the carriage to the stable. A lush and well cared for tropical garden banked the pathway to the front door. It was filled with all kinds of brightly coloured flowers Abby had never seen before. She was trying to take it all in when she was captivated by the sound of splashing water. Following the path to her right revealed a three tiered sculpted fountain in the center of the gardens. As she watched the cascading waters she noticed two birds seemingly at play on the rim of the middle tier. Mr. Landis paused a moment to let them enjoy the scene before leading the way into the house and a lavishly decorated parlour where they were introduced to his son, Isaac.

Isaac appeared to be close in age to Abby with a charismatic face, tousled sandy blonde hair, cleft chin and a charming smile. Abby was instantly at ease with him. A butler appeared in the doorway to announce dinner was ready whenever they cared to be served. Mr. Landis gave a nod to the butler and led the way to a large dining room. Judging from the size of the room the table could accommodate more than a dozen guests but had been reduced to seat six comfortably. It was set for four. Mr. Landis directed her father to take the seat on his left and Abby on his right. Isaac sat at the foot of the table. Once they were settled the first course was served. Mr. Landis called it fish tea - a light soup broth with fish and vegetables. Richard took a cautious taste before deciding it was good. Abby was not so hesitant, more than ready to try something else new.

Mr. Landis gestured to their dishes. "I hope you enjoy the soup. I had the cook prepare some island dishes I thought you might like: brown stewed chicken with rice and peas, curried mutton, roasted pork, steamed vegetables, fried bammy..." Richard and Abby's questioning look prompted Mr. Landis to elaborate. "It is fried cassava root...very tasty...with plantain tarts and cocoanut drops for dessert."

During the main course Mr. Landis and her father discussed business and local events. Abby gave up following the conversation when they began discussing politics. She turned to Isaac to start a more pleasant topic. "The food is very tasty, not as bland as our English food. I especially like the curry mutton."

Isaac eagerly picked up the change in subject. "Curry is good but the true island flavor is in the jerk seasoning, spicy with a hint of sweetness. You must try some during your visit."

"I will be sure to do so. How far will we travel to the plantation tomorrow?"

"Not terribly far, Mr. Dracner's plantation is only a few miles from here, just past Half Way Tree."

"Half Way Tree? Sounds like a huge tree marking the half-way point."

"Very true. It is a huge cotton tree that due to its size and location is now a major meeting point for travelers and traders from Kingston, Spanish Town, St. Thomas and St. Mary. It has become quite the gathering place with pubs and vendors."

They both fell silent and while Abby was trying to think of another topic she overheard her father mention pirates so she turned her attention to his conversation. To her disappointment they were only discussing the end of piracy. Inspired she asked Isaac about Jamaican pirate history. His stories of Henry Morgan and Port Royal kept her entertained through the remainder of the evening.

The evening ended after dinner. She and her father departed after making their plans to meet with Isaac the following morning.

Mr. Landis introduced them to their driver. "This is one of my most trusted servants. He will be your driver while you are here. You tell Dutty where you want to go and he will see you arrive safely."

Richard shook his manager's hand. "Thank you for hospitality, Mr. Landis. You have been most generous."

The next morning following breakfast, Abby and Richard met Isaac in the lobby of the hotel. Isaac drove them to Mr. Dracner's plantation. Abby was duly impressed by the size of the cotton tree at Half Way Point but played it off as nothing much just to tease Isaac. "I do not see what all the fuss is about. It does not seem any bigger than our English trees." She watched in amusement as Isaac gathered himself to explain the tree's significance yet again to the English chit and the moment when he realized from her grin she had been teasing him. They both smiled at her joke.

Isaac pointed to the buildings and tents lining the road. "As you can see, there are many merchants and vendors. Our destination is just around the next bend."

It was late morning when they arrived. Mr. Dracner and his wife welcomed them from the front stoop and ushered them into the cool shade of the piazza and served them refreshments. They were a pleasant couple and agreeable to selling one of their slave girls. Mrs. Dracner proved helpful in narrowing down the qualities that would be required; such as language. The whole idea of owning another person and actually buying a maid was distressing to Abby but she did her best to keep her feelings to herself.

Mr. Dracner made a list of girls to be summoned. While they were waiting a man approached on horseback riding up the drive. Mr. Dracner went to greet him. Mrs. Dracner explained he was their neighbor from a nearby plantation. The two men moved away from the house so their conversation could not be overheard. Mrs. Dracner did her best to act natural but it was clear her neighbor's appearance was of some concern to her. Considered impolite to inquire in their business, Abby and Richard feigned ignorance.

The slave girls were brought to the side yard and lined up. Mrs. Dracner ushered Abby and Richard over to meet them. Isaac chose to stay behind on the veranda. There were nearly thirty in all ranging in age, she guessed, from about ten to forty. Abby was unsure how to go about the process of choosing a slave but Mrs. Dracner seemed to understand. She had each girl step forward to give her name and age and she occasionally added other information such as where they were born and current position.

"...the last two are mother and daughter recently purchased from another plantation owner." Mrs. Dracner turned to Abby expectantly. "Well, Miss Bennington, is there one you like in particular?"

Abby decided to follow her heart. She drew a deep breath and then calmly addressed the girls. "If you are willing to leave this island, perhaps forever, to be my lady's maid please step forward."

Her announcement surprised Mrs. Dracner but she raised no objection. Six stepped forward of their own. The mother turned the daughter towards her for a whispered conversation. As Abby watched the daughter kept shaking her head but the mother was insistent nudging her daughter to move forward. With a final look at her mother, she accepted this and faced forward. Abby couldn't tell from her face or her posture how she felt but doubted this girl would fill the bill. Mrs. Dracner dismissed the others to return to their duties and directed the seven candidates to move to the corner of the veranda. She then escorted Abby back to the table with the recommendation she speak to each candidate individually to help make her decision.

Abby thought it was a sensible idea but was concerned since she hadn't understood most of the girls as they were giving their names. The interviews proved tedious. The girls were chosen because they understood English. Speaking it was another matter. It wasn't just the heavy island accent, the words and phrases they used were so unique, Abby wasn't able to interpret their answers. Isaac was the first to realize her problem and offered to help interpret for her.

She worked her way down the line trying to learn something from each girl and feeling hopelessly disconnected from all of them until she reached the daughter. Abby had doubts about accepting her. Her name was Maria and she was a house servant eighteen years of age with long silky black hair, a pleasing oval face with dark almond shaped eyes, gently flared nostrils, full lips and rounded chin. Abby could tell she was making an attempt to speak so she would be understood. Her accent was still heavy but Abby was able to understand her words. Abby nodded to Isaac to leave them.

Once Isaac had dismissed the others and moved away so the two of them could have a somewhat private conversation Abby asked Maria again if she was willing to leave the island. "It seemed to me your mother had to convince you to step forward. Are you sure you are willing to sail away? I do not want an unwilling maid."

"I am willing to go wherever ma'amselle wishes," said Maria with a detached tone. It was a statement of fact spoken without emotion.

Abby was at a loss. "Have you ever been a lady's maid?"

"No."

"Do you know what the job requires?"

Maria answered with stilted speech. "Fetching things, hair dressing, putting on de clothes."

"You are correct and also to serve as a companion. Have you ever left the island before?"

"No." Still no indication of her feelings.

"Do you want to see other parts of the world?" asked Abby.

"It does not matter to me. It is as ma'amselle wishes."

Abby gave up trying to learn more from Maria. She was the best choice of the seven. Abby decided to consult her father instead. "Excuse me for a moment, Maria." She moved to her father's side and waited for him to break away from his conversation with Mrs. Dracner. They moved away from the others and Abby explained Maria was the best choice but she had reservations about her willingness. Her father understood her concerns but felt from his observations Maria would overcome her reluctance. She understood how her world worked and if her mother was encouraging her to go it would all work out in the end. They agreed to take Maria and rejoined Isaac and Mrs. Dracner to work out the details. Meanwhile, Mr. Dracner had returned looking very grim.

Abby and Mrs. Dracner went to Maria to tell her the news. She showed little emotion, a bare widening of her eyes which Abby took for surprise. Mrs. Dracner dismissed her to pack her belongings and to say goodbye to her mother. She was expected to return in two hours. Again, Abby was dismayed at the reality of what it meant to be a slave. Something as monumental as leaving one's family was not a choice Maria was allowed to make. It helped to know she would be giving Maria her freedom once they left the island. Abby hoped she had made a good decision.

Returning to the men Abby and Mrs. Dracner noticed all three of them now had a grim expression. Abby looked to her father questioningly.

Mrs. Dracner asked her husband, "Since it is obviously not a secret to be kept from our guests, what was it that brought Mr. Hagley over today?"

"There are rumors of a slave revolt spreading around Spanish Town and Kingston."

"We've heard rumors before," said Mrs. Dracner in a dismissive tone.

"Yes, but this time it is more widespread and there is a date - the next full moon. I have noticed a restlessness among some of our own slaves so I am taking this one very seriously."

Mrs. Dracner's hand flew to her chest. "Dear Lord why that is just over a week away. You think it will really happen this time?"

Mr. Dracner simply nodded and noticing an approaching butler changed the subject. "Richard we will work as hard as we can to have your order of sugar and rum ready to be loaded in the next few days. I believe we can have you under sail in less than a week. Let me take you down to the distillery to see the inventory we have ready now."

Richard and Mr. Dracner left for the distillery while Mrs. Dracner suggested a stroll in the gardens to Abby and Isaac. She had a bird of paradise in bloom she thought Abby would find interesting. The unique orange and blue blossoms intrigued Abby. They looked like brightly coloured sails above a long narrow boat.

There were so many strange and exotic plants that she found herself ahead of the others eager to see what lay around the next bend. She was suddenly brought up short and could not call back the near screech that leapt uncontrolled from her lips at the discovery of a reptilian creature in her pathway. It was the size of a large house cat and looked anything but friendly. The long, thick tail twitched and the split tongue flicked but otherwise he calmly stood facing her.

Isaac peered over her shoulder and laughed, "It's just an iguana."

Even Mrs. Dracner was amused. "I remember the first time I saw one. Reacted much the same as you did dear. Dreadful looking aren't they? But relatively harmless unless it is cornered."

Abby gingerly moved around the little green monster and continued onward in a more cautious manner. Returning to the house she was glad to see her father waiting and Maria approaching from the other side. She was ready to return to the hotel and could tell by her father's expression he was too. They politely thanked their hosts and loaded up for the return trip. Maria's presence kept them from discussing the morning's news and so the ride back to the hotel was mostly silent, each lost in their own thoughts.

Chapter 5

Abby sat on an overturned crate on the deck of the *Abigail Rose* writing in the journal Miss Winterfeldt had given her. They sailed from Kingston a few days ago after loading all the rum Mr. Landis could locate on such short notice. The rest of the hold was filled with barrels of sugar, molasses and cocoa. They also had a good supply of pineapples and bananas to last their voyage and hopefully some to share with her uncle's family if they didn't spoil before they reached Montgomery.

Talk of a slave revolt had grown rapidly after the morning they visited the Dracners. Abby's father had insisted she remain in the hotel room the rest of their stay while he spent most of his time with Mr. Landis and Captain Andrews overseeing the loading of cargo. This left Abby and Maria on their own, except for the occasional visit from Isaac, which helped relieve Abby's boredom. Her relationship with Maria, although congenial, was still strained. Maria did her duties well but kept to herself.

Looking up at the sea birds swirling, feeling the sea breeze across her face, and admiring the puffy clouds in the sapphire sky Abby was grateful to no longer be cooped up in the hotel. She wished they could have had time to explore the island. There was much that intrigued her besides the food.

She smiled inwardly remembering her father's reaction to their last Jamaican meal of ackee and saltfish. His face screwed up as if he had taken a mouthful of salt. He pushed his plate away mumbling something about being sick of strange foods and requested porridge instead. The ackee was so similar to scrambled eggs that Abby had no idea why he had such a strong reaction. Of course this happened the morning after they had Jerk chicken for dinner. Her father suffered through it as they were dining with Josiah and Isaac Landis and he did not wish to offend his hosts but she could tell it was an ordeal for him. Personally, Abby thought the dish was wonderful, more flavorful than spicy hot.

The first day of her sequester in the hotel Isaac brought a chess set that helped the afternoon hours, the hottest part of the day, pass quickly. Isaac was not a very strategic player suffering the disgrace of Abby repeatedly trouncing him. He left the game with Abby and she tried to teach Maria how to play but alas, Maria did not have much interest forcing Abby to abandon the idea of gaining another opponent. It was too bad as Maria seemed to have the intelligence for it.

The day before they were to leave, she and Isaac had just finished a game of chess in which Isaac had finally managed a victory. Maria had left the room for a moment to put something away. Taking advantage of the one and only brief moment they had ever been alone, Isaac, suddenly half standing, leaned over the chess board and quickly kissed her full on the lips! Abby was caught completely by surprise not just by his audacity but also surprised at receiving her first kiss from a man who wasn't her father in such a manner. He had given her no indication of any feelings other than friendship. She wasn't sure how to react. Had he kissed her in his excitement of winning? She had won all of their matches until then. Or was there some romantic interest he was trying to express before it was too late? Even now, several days later she still wasn't sure. Maria's return to the room precluded any discussion. He had blushed and kept his eyes averted from her while he packed up the chess set. She had the impression he was going to gift her with the game but her father's entrance into the room seemed to change his mind. Instead Isaac tucked the game under his arm and made a hasty retreat out the door. It was the last time she saw him. He was not with his father to see them off as they boarded the ship to leave in the predawn hours of the following morning.

They sailed away from Kingston under cover of darkness since there were rumors the harbour would be closed to prevent slaves from escaping by sea. As for the kiss itself, she didn't know what all the fuss was about kisses. It was mushy! She didn't really care for someone else's wet lips all over hers and it certainly wasn't the head spinning dizziness Elizabeth had described. She overheard her father tell Mr. Landis they might make a return visit on their way home. Part of her wanted to have more time to explore the island but another part was not looking forward to the inevitable embarrassing encounter with Isaac.

Returning her thoughts to the present, Abby watched Captain Andrews speak with Mr. Carter and then head to his cabin below the quarterdeck, leaving the first mate in charge of the ship. It was the normal routine of the ship. The first mate had the day watch and the captain took the night watch retiring to his cabin in the late morning hours. She would have thought it to be the other way around but her father said Captain Andrews did not trust anyone else to navigate around these islands at night.

Deciding to stretch her legs she left the crate to stand at the bow railing. The ship was sailing at a good clip, faster than she had ever noticed before. Clutching her journal to her chest and tightly holding the ink bottle with the same hand she grasped the railing with her other hand to keep from being blown by the stiff wind. Her long skirt was plastered to her legs and streamed out behind pulling her backwards. She glanced up at the taught sails full of wind propelling them quickly across the water.

Looking straight ahead with nothing in front of her but sky and water, the sensation, she imagined, was akin to flying. A movement in the water caught her attention. She focused on the bow cutting through the deep blue ocean and finally she saw it again - a fish broke through the surface in a graceful arc. *No, not a fish, what was it they were called? Porpoises.* She had forgotten until now her father had once told her about seeing them on one of his voyages a long time ago. It was just as magical as he had described. She kept waiting and watching - hoping for another glimpse - there - another leapt from the waves and now there were two. A moment later it was a group of several, racing ahead of the bow and breaching the surface; like children at play. Abby was so mesmerized she didn't know Richard had approached until he stepped up to the rail next to her.

"Oh, Father, you startled me. Look.... do you see them?"

"Yes."

They stood together in silence a moment watching the mammals moving gracefully through the waves.

Abby leaned close to him to be heard over the wind. "Did you miss being at sea when you became stationed in Southampton? I already love it so. I think if I had been in your position I would have had a hard time adjusting to life on shore."

Richard smiled inwardly realizing how much his daughter was like him. "The sacrifice was made easy having Anna to come home to every evening. Besides you have yet to see the ocean at its worst. It can be quite fearsome in a real storm."

"Perhaps." She doubted even the worst storm would change her mind. "Is it my imagination or are we sailing more swiftly than usual?"

"We are probably in the gulf current flowing between Mexico and the Caribbean islands circling the west and north sides of Cuba and then out to the Atlantic. The ship will eventually have to break from the current to head north into the Gulf and up to Mobile. It is a strong current and could account for our speed."

"How much longer will it take for us to reach the port of Mobile?"

"Maybe a week, depending on our sailing conditions."

"And from there, how long will the journey take to Montgomery?"

"A few days by stagecoach and another half-day by rented buggy to reach James' plantation."

The sun was climbing to its zenith and Abby became aware of the building heat. She had been without her hat for far too long. She turned to head into the limited shadows of the quarterdeck, pulling an empty crate along with her for a seat, as she was loath to return to the stifling confines of her cabin. Here it was midway through October and she was trying to keep from roasting. If she were home in England she would be pulling out her warmest clothes getting ready for the onset of winter. It was a wonder how her life had taken such a divergence in so short a time. Soon tiring of her journal she went to her cabin to retrieve her hat and the book she had purchased in Jamaica.

Abby was disturbed from the novel she had been reading for the last several hours by Mr. Carter suddenly calling out frantic orders to the crew. There was panic in his voice.

"Back the sails... Now! I say...Heave to."

The sailors scrambled across the deck rushing to their tasks.

She stood up trying to find the source of the problem. Over the last hour or so the sky had grown overcast. The towering layers of grey turned the water opaque, dark and forbidding. Scanning the horizon she spotted a speck of land some distance from them, more a pile of sand really than land. The sails were dropped and the ship's momentum was greatly reduced but they were still moving forward much to the first mate's dismay. Panicked he ordered, "Drop anchor."

It was too late.

The ship shuddered as the hull struck the underwater ridge coming to a stop with a sudden jerk. The force of their landing vibrated throughout the ship. Abby was tossed to the deck by the impact. She involuntarily screamed when one of the young sailors fell from the rigging landing near her. He must not have fallen far for he quickly scrambled to his feet. Seeing her still on her knees he held out his hand to help her stand before running off in another direction. She was vaguely aware of orders being issued and men arguing. She steadied herself then backed up against the stairs leading to the quarterdeck trying to get out of the way of the frantic deck hands.

The captain and the rest of the crew came pouring from the companionway and scattered across the deck. Captain Andrews' made a beeline for the helm. As he passed by her, Abby noticed a look of murderous rage directed towards the first mate. To her surprise he didn't dress down the mate as expected but excused him from his duty with a furious look before turning to the deckhands with orders.

"Take soundings...mind you do it 'round the whole ship," he directed one group. Nodding at two other men, "Check the hull for any damage. Report back immediately. The rest of ye prepare the skiff and spare anchor to haul the ship aft to deeper water."

Richard stood next to Abby waiting until Captain Andrew was able to spare a moment to confer with him. He had been in his cabin when the ship struck the reef. The sound and feel of it was not something he would soon forget and there was sure to be damage. Shipwrecked with a hold full of valuable perishable cargo was a potentially costly plight in lives and money. That she was his newest ship on her maiden voyage only added to Richard's distress. He had raced to the deck along with all the other hands to find darkening skies and little idea of where they were positioned. Without the sun he couldn't even determine in which direction they had been headed. He hoped Captain Andrews would be able to ascertain their location and even more important be able to get them out of this predicament.

Chapter 6

Max Eatonton considered himself a congenial fellow but recent events were wearily testing him. Clear skies meant little work for him and his five crewmen. His crew should have numbered eight but he had not yet gotten around to replacing the three brothers that had recently returned to New England. Slack fishing lines meant little food and drying water barrels meant little water. Having three less souls on board was a momentary blessing. Two of his crew had turned to liqueur to pass the time and were now making a nuisance of themselves on the deck of the *Mystic*, his two-masted Baltimore clipper.

Max was deep in thought contemplating staying out another day or two or heading into town for supplies when Billy, the youngest of his crew, caught his attention. He was pointing towards the darkening western sky some miles distant from their anchorage. Hope of a good storm brought life to his crew and answered Max's question. They would be staying out. Max called out orders. "Raise the sails! Weigh anchor!" Bless them, experienced deck hands that they were, despite the rum, his ship was under way cutting the waves in no time. He ordered his first mate, Mr. Jonathon Keats, to relieve him at the helm so he could climb the rigging in order to have a better vantage point to look for any ships in need of assistance.

The *Mystic* was one of a dozen or so ships operating out of Key West as wreckers; the locals pronounced it 'wrackers'. It was a job well suited to Max. He was one of a fortunate few who owned his own ship. He loved to sail, had no ties to land and didn't care much for fishing. He enjoyed the challenges of fighting storm and sea and the satisfaction of saving a ship caught on the reefs. There were downsides but overall it was a good life for him.

A typical day for a wrecker was spent cruising their favoured section of reef every morning in the hopes of finding a ship stranded overnight and then spend the afternoons doing ship work followed by pursuits of pleasure such as there were to be found anchored on a reef, unless a storm came up in which case a wrecker would seek out ships in need of piloting or rescue.

The wreckers of Florida patrolled the chain of coral reefs and islands, called keys, stretching in a slight arc from the southeastern tip of the Florida peninsula westward towards the Gulf ending at the uninhabited islands of the Dry Tortugas. They formed the northern boundary of the Florida Strait which linked the Gulf of Mexico to the Atlantic Ocean. The reefs were located three to five miles south and east of the keys with treacherous underwater topography. The depth rapidly decreased from three hundred feet in the Strait to the shallow waters of the reefs most of which were uncharted. The currents of the Strait could be fickle and strong making the reefs even more hazardous for those unfamiliar with its waters. Lighthouses and lightships were few and far between. The ones on Sand Key and Key West were built recently.

Knowledge of the reefs was only half the battle. Wooden sail ships depended on wind, currents and sails for propulsion. They were difficult to control. Changes in direction required sailors to make correct and often rapid sail changes with ample area to maneuver. Merchant ships were often overloaded further encumbering their maneuverability. Ships could only communicate with other ships when in sight of each other. They were unable to share warnings of changing conditions. A captain depended on his knowledge of the world around him and the few tools he had at his disposal; a compass, a sextant, a sounding line and perhaps a dipsey for measuring depth and a log line for measuring speed.

The sounding line was a rope marked off in fathoms, roughly the distance between a man's outstretched hands or about six feet, with a weight on the end. It was dropped into the water until the weight touched bottom. Markings on the rope gave the seaman the depth. A dipsey was a heavier deep sea lead used to measure depth in deeper waters. The log line was a triangle chip of wood with a light line attached at each of its corners. When dropped in the water, it would dig into the current and the line would be allowed to play out for a set amount of time. A half-minute sand glass was used to determine the length of time passed and knots tied at specific points on the line were counted to determine the sea knots-per-hour. A sextant was used to measure the altitude of the sun at local high noon which could then be used in a mathematical calculation to determine latitude. Longitude could also be figured but the calculation was so complex very few mariners bothered to use it. On the open ocean careful chart keeping was critical to know a ship's position.

All of these limitations led to a number of wrecks piling up on the reefs. Some were simply grounded while the more unfortunate would have their hulls ripped open. The wreckers offered them knowledge of the area, the extra man power and special equipment to get a ship free or if taking on water, the needed equipment to save the ship and cargo. If the ship sank then the wreckers had divers, often Bahamians referred to as 'Conchs', to retrieve the cargo and valuable ship parts such as anchors and sails from a lost ship.

It was an industry of mixed emotions. Those that were wrecked often thought of the wreckers as saviours while those with money invested more often thought of them as thieves or worse - akin to pirates – for holding the cargo for payment of services. Ship owners and insurance agents believed they took unfair advantage of the situation. With the closest Maritime Court located in St. Augustine most claims were settled by arbitration to avoid the expense and delay of taking it to court. Arbitration was determined by a selected five man jury. As it was impossible to find anyone in Key West uninvolved in the industry, claims tended to be high. In general the wreckers were a respectable lot of men. Only a few were giving the industry a bad name. Most of the wreckers wanted a fair system of awards and went so far as to petition

Congress to install a court in Key West to eliminate the 'good old boy' arbitrations. Their appeal was heard and answered with the news a court would be opened by the end of year. They were now waiting for the judge to arrive.

Max turned his ship towards the storm passing over the Dry Tortugas, a small group of islands owing its name to the abundance of turtles in the area and the lack of fresh water on land. Just over an hour later, out of the corner of his eye he caught a movement in the distance. He pulled out his spyglass. Scanning the horizon before putting the glass to his eye he spotted it again. It was a ship. Looking through the glass he trained it on the hull. Not just any ship, it was the *Sinistral*. Captain Talmage was under full sail headed southwest towards the Dry Tortugas. That could only mean one thing....

Max leaned out from the mast, cupped a hand around his mouth and hollered down to the crew, "Wreak ashore!" He dropped down to the deck and the crew gathered round to find out what he had seen. Max had to yell to be heard over the wind, "Talmage - headed to Dry Tortuga - sails full - has to be a wreck. Can't beat him to it, he's too far ahead. But we can beat his cronies to second. Mr. Keats, take the watch and guide us in."

Max reached the English barque, stranded on Loggerhead Reef, just as Talmage boarded the vessel. Anchoring close to the *Sinistral*, he waited to see if Talmage would get permission for wrecking. Through his spyglass, he watched two men move across the deck to greet Talmage. Max noticed a female passenger standing a short distance away observing the men. Even from this distance where he could make out little more than the blue of her dress and the reddish gold of her hair he felt pulled to her. As if she felt it too she suddenly scanned the decks of both ships halting her gaze in his direction. Feeling uncomfortable, as if he had been caught doing something wrong, he turned his attention back to the men who were now having a heated discussion.

Obviously they chose not to accept Talmage's assistance so he returned to his longboat and paddled back to his ship to wait. Max would also wait. Having seen this play out many times, Max knew the captain of the stranded ship would attempt to get off the reef on his own to avoid the salvage fees. If unsuccessful, he would be forced to accept the assistance of the wrecking crew.

The ship was riding low in the water, hopefully an indication of a full hold of cargo and not seawater. A full cargo meant it would be likely Talmage would need assistance if the ship must be off loaded. If the hold was already full of water, their assistance would be a foregone conclusion but it also increased the danger the ship was in and made their job more difficult.

Sometime later after several attempts to haul the ship off the reef by dropping anchor and pulling, a procedure known as kedging, Max knew the captain would be frustrated. Shortly after he sent two crewmen below for a third time presumably to check for damage. It was apparently bad news. They were taking on water. Max had noticed the ship starting to list to starboard. To add to their difficulties the wind had picked up and the waves were increasing.

The captain and the other gentleman on deck appeared to discuss their lack of options and then the captain sent the gentleman below decks and the lady followed him. Max frowned. It was probably becoming unsafe below decks; he hoped they were not intending to stay down there for long.

The captain finally signaled Talmage to come aboard. This was the moment Max had been anticipating. He dropped quickly by rope from the deck to his waiting row boat. Pulling hard on the oars he headed towards the floundering vessel. Max was rowing in a forward position while Talmage was facing rear allowing him to see Max in pursuit and for Max to see he was not pleased about it, as expected. Talmage would rather share the reward with his cronies, that is, if he wasn't able to keep it all to himself. Being younger and stronger Max caught up with him and was able to board the ship right behind Talmage.

As soon as they reached the deck Talmage turned on Max forcing him to stop in his tracks. "You wait here," said Talmage pointing to the spot Max now occupied. He then pivoted around and continued towards the captain.

"The hell I will," muttered Max. He continued to follow a few steps behind Talmage across the deck. He stopped just close enough behind Talmage to hear the conversation.

Talmage strode up to the captain with confidence. "Change your mind, Captain Andrews?"

Captain Andrews' face was grim. "Captain Talmage, I am forced to accept your assistance but your terms are unacceptable. I must insist that you submit to arbitration of the reward."

Max could only imagine what exorbitant amount Talmage had requested. He had heard the man was greedy and at times underhanded. It was very smart of the *Abigail Rose's* captain to ask for arbitration. Max had seen many other captains accept a wrecking captain's terms without question believing it to be their only option. The wreckers were getting rich but also earning a bad reputation. Public opinion of them was low and men like Talmage were the reason. He hoped the courts would help bring some equality of justice to the business.

"It is at my price or I leave you here to flounder. Do we have an accord?" countered Talmage.

Max could not believe the audacity of Captain Talmage.

Captain Andrews knew he had no leverage to negotiate and with the hold rapidly filling with water it was important to unload quickly to save both the cargo and the ship. Something that could not be done without the aid of these two men, their ships and their crews so he shook Captain Talmage's outstretched hand, albeit grudgingly. "Aye."

The gentleman returned from below deck and handed the captain papers he had brought with him. Max wondered what his role was on this ship since he obviously wasn't a deck hand and seemed to be more than just a passenger.

Captain Andrews nodded to the gentlemen then addressed Captain Talmage. "Here is the manifest...."

Talmage interrupted him, "Give me that."

Captain Andrews was clearly getting angry now. "No sir, I will not give you this, the only evidence I will have of my claim. I will tell you that we have on board rum, sugar, molasses, cocoa and some fruit in the hold. We also have the personal possessions of Mr. and Miss Bennington as well as the crew not to be considered part of the salvage."

"I am well aware of the salvage guidelines," grumbled Talmage.

"Just so we have an understanding. I do not want you and your crew," at this he nodded in Max's direction, "taking undue advantage."

Max took offense at the assumption he was part of Talmage's outfit but said nothing. Talmage only grunted and turned to signal his crew to prepare to board the ship.

Max moved to stand in front of Talmage. "This ship is carrying a heavy load and you will need help. My crew is ready."

"Get out of the way, maggot, you're not wanted."

"Do it the hard way, then. You could have this whole ship unloaded and be back in port before the storm worsens," Max indicated the dark clouds to the southwest of them, "but if you prefer working in the rolling waves whom am I to dissuade you."

Talmage scanned the horizon all around and not seeing any other sails headed their way he realized the whelp was right. "Fine. Start with the passengers and their luggage and then you can help with the cargo."

Max wasn't surprised by Talmage's decree. The passengers and their belongings were not included in the claim and there was no reward for their rescue although it was expected that the wreckers' first priority was to rescue people. Talmage was hoping to keep Max out of the way until other help arrived. He would have to hurry if he was going to have any chance at a share of the reward. Max signaled his crew they had work to do and returned to Captain Andrews just as a large wave rolled the ship. The men struggled to maintain their footing. Max noticed the gentleman scanning the deck in search of something before turning to the captain. "Where is my daughter?"

Captain Andrews shared his concern. "I have no idea."

Max said, "I saw a young lady follow you below deck earlier. She has not returned."

The ship rolled again with another wave. They could hear the cargo shifting below them. The gentleman started towards the companionway but Max laid a restraining hand on his arm, "Please, let me, you need to get to safety. My crew will take you to my ship." Max headed down the opening he had seen the girl disappear through earlier. He heard the gentleman following him. Max wished he had stayed on deck but he really couldn't blame the man for wanting to find his daughter.

Max looked over his shoulder, "Where is her cabin?"

The gentleman pointed down the passage. "Two doors down on the left."

The waves continued to buffet the ship so that it was rocking from side to side making it difficult to walk a straight line. When they reached the room it was empty except for a bunk and a single trunk, undisturbed. Max turned to the gentleman, "Sir, where else could she be?"

Before Richard answered they were tossed against the cabin wall by another wave. They heard a woman's frustrated cry come from below. Max, used to dealing with rolling ships, sprinted ahead of Richard and down the next set of stairs leading into the cargo hold. He glanced around to get his bearings. This deck had crates of fruit and dry goods stacked all around. The grate was removed opening up the shallow cargo area in the hull of the ship where he could see barrels of rum and molasses some of which were rolling with the ship.

Max kneeled down to look into the hold underneath him and found the girl, standing in calf deep water, bent over an open trunk. She had pushed another trunk off the one she was currently digging through leaving it in a precarious position. She seemed to have no idea how easily the cargo could shift and crush her.

"Miss, give me your hand!" Max reached down into the hold intending to grab her arm and hoist her up. Instead he had a box thrust into his hand. He brought it up and tossed it to her father standing just behind him. The box opened in mid-flight covering her father in a rosy cloud of fabric.

Max reached down again. "Miss you need to get out of there." Again she tried to hand him something else from her trunk. Max was getting frustrated. He didn't have time for unloading a trunk one piece at a time. Ignoring the small chest she was holding up to him he tried to grab her arm instead. The ship rolled hard to port and he nearly toppled into the hold. The girl fell against the trunks and a rolling barrel just missed going over her foot. Max prostrated himself on the floor above and reached down into the hold again. The girl got back to her feet, flinging one of her arms in the air for balance. Max took advantage of the opportunity and captured her arm. She struggled against his hold still trying to retrieve the small chest she had dropped.

"Leave it," Max demanded.

"I will not," she replied and finally pulling free of his grasp she bent to retrieve the chest.

Using her left hand she grasped the handle of the chest and then climbed atop a small crate and raised her right hand towards her rescuer. Max returned to a crouching position for better leverage and seized her hand. The ship tilted again thankfully starboard this time, the other way would have sent Max pitching headfirst into the hold; instead it caused the young lady to drop the chest and press her free hand to the edge of the opening for support. Max grabbed her other arm just below her wrist and now having both arms was easily able to pull her out of the hold and taking a step back, right into his arms.

Abby found herself flush against the sailor's body with one of her hands resting against his chest where his shirt was parted touching warm bare skin. At first contact he had moved his hands to her waist to steady them both. She was keenly aware of those strong fingers wrapped around her midsection. As she stood there looking up into his vivid blue eyes, her chest constricted and her breath caught. She knew propriety demanded she remove her hand from his chest, step back and break their physical contact but she was becalmed by his gaze.

Richard had finally gained control of the dress and now found his daughter in a tight embrace with the sailor. He cleared his throat but they continued to stare at one another so he took a step forward.

Abby noticed the movement over the sailor's shoulder but it still took a second to clear her head and to realize her father was watching her. The sailor was a bit quicker. He stepped back and turned as if to hand her off to her father. Free from the spell of his embrace she remembered the dropped chest. She bent down to the floor preparing to drop back through the cargo opening when her father's voice and the sailor's grasp on her arm stopped her.

"What are you doing Abigail? He just pulled you out of there."

Abby struggled to free herself. "Mother's chest is still down there. I will not leave it...do not ask it of me."

Max used his most cajoling voice while gently pulling her upright. "Miss?"

Abby stopped struggling for a moment. "Bennington."

"Miss Bennington." The ship rolled with a wave. Abby lost her balance and fell towards him. He promptly set her from him. "You must come with me. My men will be here shortly to retrieve your luggage."

Abby tugged her arm from his grip and tried again to return to the hold. "But the hold will be underwater by then. I have to get it now."

Her father added his voice to the argument. "Abby, it is not safe. You are more important than that box. Come, child."

Max, tiring of the waste of time in a situation where time was so crucial, picked up the contrary female from the floor and tossed her over his shoulder as if she were nothing more than a sack of flour. His long strides had them moving up the stairs of the storage deck and then to the crew's quarters with Miss Bennington pounding on his back the whole way.

Abby took out her frustration on his backside. She wanted to go back for the chest and she was humiliated by his treatment. She hoped he would put her down before they emerged on the main deck for all to witness her disgrace. She couldn't believe her father, trailing behind them, had allowed this man such liberties with her person. She thought her wish was granted when her transport suddenly stopped in the middle of the crew's quarters but he kept a firm hold on her while speaking to someone, presumable one of his fellow crewmen, out of her view.

"Mr. Keats, glad to see you. There are trunks in the hold to be retrieved but see you get the smallest chest first or this lady just might try again to salvage it herself."

"Aye."

Abby was relieved to hear the only item she owned of her mother's wouldn't be lost if the ship went down. She saw the back of Mr. Keats as he continued on to the hold then pleaded with her captor, "Sir, please, put me down. I promise to go above decks now that I know the chest will be secured."

Max moved his hands to her waist and let her slide down his front to her feet. She was sure he inflicted more contact than was necessary creating a weakness in her limbs that caused her to wobble upon reaching the floor. He then continued his hold a few seconds longer than was necessary to steady her. She found herself lost again in his impossibly blue eyes until he removed his hands from her waist and turned her towards the stairs. She had never in her life felt so conscious of her movements as she did while climbing the last set of stairs knowing he was right behind her. Upon reaching the deck he issued orders to some other men crossing the deck towards them before ushering her and her father to his longboat.

Richard climbed down from the ship to the longboat first. He still had her dress box with the rose gown once again inside. Abby descended next followed by the sailor who she now believed to be a captain. His commands clearly bespoke his rank. Abby sat opposite her father in the boat, clutching the garment box her father had transferred to her and trying desperately to keep her gaze from straying to the muscular arms and chest of the captain as he rowed silently across the turquoise water. Abby noticed they were heading to the smaller of two schooners anchored just off the reef. Once there, the captain tied the longboat. He turned to her before taking the ladder.

"Here Miss, let me take the box."

Abby reluctantly handed it to him realizing she couldn't mind her skirts, the box and the ladder. She followed after the captain and at the top accepted his outstretched hand in assistance. She felt a jolt at their touch and brought her eyes to his to see if he felt it too. He wouldn't look at her. He briskly helped her to the deck of his ship, handed her the box and turned to await her father. Out here, anchored off the shoals the waves were more moderate. Looking across the water she could see their ship being tossed as the surf struck the reef and the exposed hull.

Abby looked around the very tidy deck of the *Mystic*. She had noticed the name painted on the hull as they approached. When her father came to stand behind her the captain finally introduced himself, his words were perfunctory but also held a hint of pride and some impatience.

"Welcome to the *Mystic*. I am Captain Max Eatonton."

Abby was finally standing far enough away from him to take notice of more than just his eyes. He was nearly a foot taller than her and of medium build which she already knew to be muscular. He was deeply tanned and his tousled dark blond wavy hair, cropped shorter than the norm these days, barely brushing his collar was lightened from long days in the sun. His face looked to have only a day's growth, leaving her to believe he was usually clean shaven. His white shirt was parted halfway down the front revealing a chest lightly covered with dark blond hair. Abby clenched her fist against the sensory memory of touching his chest and wondered what it would feel like if she could let her fingers trail down the path of his open shirt. Her thoughts brought her up short. *What was wrong with her?* Never had a man affected her so. Her gaze drifted past his tanned chest and snug fitting breeches, down to his well-worn boots and all the way back up again to clash with his piercing blue eyes and a half smile as if he knew what she had been thinking. She couldn't help the blush that stained her cheeks. She broke their eye contact and looked towards her father who blessedly hadn't noticed her blatant perusal.

Richard offered his hand, "Thank you for your service Captain Eatonton. I am grateful to you for the rescue of my daughter. I am Richard Bennington and this is Miss Abigail Bennington." The men shook hands and Captain Eatonton gave her a nod that she returned in kind. She noticed how his eyes widened at the mention of her name and wondered what he was thinking.

The daughter's name assured Max he had guessed correctly. "I take it you are the owner of the *Abigail Rose.*" Richard confirmed his assumption with a nod. "You can take refuge from the storm in my cabin. The water barrel, over there, is nearly dry but help yourselves to what is left."

He led them below deck to his cabin, let them precede him in and then abruptly turned and left. They listened as he crossed the deck in long strides, climbed down the rope, dropped into the longboat and heard the first splashes of the paddles as he pulled away from the ship.

Abby raised her eyebrows at her father in response to Captain Eatonton's hurried departure. "Goodness, his manners are lacking."

"What does he mean depositing us here like luggage while he returns to plunder my ship," grumbled Richard. "I am going up on deck so I can keep an eye on them."

Abby chose not to follow her father. She was curious to learn more of Captain Eatonton and what better place to do so unobserved than alone in his cabin. She made a slow turn surveying the small simple room. It had two open port windows allowing a fresh breeze and light to penetrate. A large neatly made bunk dominated one corner of the room with a wooden chest at the foot. A small writing desk with a hinged top allowing for storage inside was bolted to the floor on the opposite wall and a crate of books was beside it. Neat and tidy, everything in its place. Just as she had noticed the deck was well kept so was this room. The captain ran a taut ship.

She stooped to examine the book titles in the crate. She had been forced to leave so quickly, she didn't have her own book and she had a feeling it was going to be a long afternoon. She was surprised to find a book of poetry mixed in with the books on navigation, admiralty law, and the ships logs. She pulled it from the crate and took a seat in the chair at the desk. Abby quickly turned past a handwritten dedication on the first page. Observing what was open to see was one thing, snooping was quite another and reading a personal note was not the proper thing to do. She tried to start reading the first poem but curiosity was getting the better of her. So far she had not learned much about the man. After reading the same first sentence three times without comprehension she finally gave into the temptation. She turned back to the inscription only to find stark disappointment.

Something to remind you of me on your long voyage.

Your loving wife,

Emma

"Married!" Abby snapped the book shut. She couldn't believe it. *Why was she so attracted to someone who was unavailable? And how dare he act as he did, giving her the impression he was attracted to her too?* The emotional pain was unexpected. *For heaven's sakes she just met the man, why did she feel this way?* No longer having a purpose for being in the room she replaced the book and made her way back to the deck.

Exiting the hatch, the wind hit Abigail full force almost knocking her backward. The storm was certainly building. She carefully made her way to her father's side. He was watching the salvagers through a spyglass. The midafternoon sky grew even darker as the storm moved towards them; with it came stronger wind and waves. Abby wondered how long the crew would be able to continue to unload the ship before the storm reached them.

Chapter 7

Max, returning from depositing Mr. Bennington and his daughter safely on board his ship, swung his leg over the side of the *Abigail Rose* landing on the deck next to a pile of trunks ready to be off loaded to the longboats. Perched atop one of the trunks was an island girl holding a hat and book Max assumed belonged to her mistress. Noticeably absent was the small chest he had instructed Jonathon Keats to retrieve first. Max headed to the hold in search of his first mate to find out why. He passed one of his crewmen on the way. "Billy, see that one of those water barrels is taken to the *Mystic*," directed Max without a break in his stride. He loped down the ladder and could hear his first mate working with Thomas, another one of his crew, to bring another trunk up from the hold.

"Report Mr. Keats?" asked Max in a casual tone.

"This is the last of the luggage from the hold. Captain said there are a couple trunks in the cabins. Should be able to get it all in the two boats and make one trip before pay load."

"Good. What happened to the small chest?"

Mr. Keats confirmed what his frown had already conveyed to Max. "Talmage. He stopped me coming out of the hold. Claimed it was cargo. No one was around to disagree. I tried to argue but he threatened to remove us from the claim so I surrendered it to his goons."

Mr. Keats had done right by them to not risk their stake in the salvage. It was a conversation Max would have to have with Captain Talmage. He wasn't looking forward to the confrontation.

Max continued down the hall to Miss Bennington's cabin to retrieve her trunk having seen on his earlier search for her it was of a size he could manage on his own. He noticed a journal on her bunk. He picked it up and opening her trunk he placed the book on top of her folded undergarments. He took a second to appreciate the neatly packed belongings before closing the lid. He heaved the trunk to his shoulder and made his way to the deck adding the trunk to the pile. His crew headed back to the other cabin for the final trunk. Max turned to find Talmage heading his way.

Talmage started yelling at him while still ten paces away. "Eatonton! What are you doing with that barrel? You're on luggage detail. Trying to sneak in some cargo, are you?"

Max held back what he would really like to say to this man currently in control of his livelihood. "No sir. That's a water barrel to replenish the *Mystic* for the passengers."

Talmage sneered. "Run out of water landlubber?"

Max chose to ignore the barb. Trading insults with Talmage would only get him dismissed from the salvage operation. "My first mate retrieved a small chest belonging to Miss Bennington. He said you mistook it for cargo. Have your man bring it to the deck so I can return it to her."

"You don't give the orders on this ship. Now get that luggage off this deck so we can get to offloadin' some real cargo."

"I must insist you return the chest to Miss Bennington, it's not part of the cargo," countered Max.

"One more word about that damn chest and you're done," threatened Talmage before turning on his heel and storming across the rolling deck.

Max decided it would be best to let arbitration or the new judge deal with the chest. He needed this haul to buy supplies, pay his crew and keep his salvage business afloat. Better to turn away now and fight another day so he directed his crew on loading the trunks in the two longboats along with the water barrel and the maid and returned to his ship.

It was early evening by the time they reached the *Mystic* and started unloading the luggage. The skies threatened to unleash a deluge at any moment and the waves threatened to capsize the longboats. Rowing the short distance between ships had been difficult but his crew had worked through much worse. Now the movement of the boat against the ship and the swaying motion of the hull made climbing the rope ladder a precarious task for his men as they worked to haul the trunks up to the deck, not wanting to use precious time setting up block and tackle. It was even more dangerous for the inexperienced maid. Max breathed a sigh of relief when she cleared the rail. He hadn't relished the idea of rescuing her from a watery landing. He was last to make it on board his ship.

His crew hadn't eaten since breakfast but knowing they would probably work all night they would have to take the time now to grab a quick bite of bread. Their payday wouldn't start until they returned to the *Abigail Rose* and started helping to offload the cargo. He was impatient to get back before Talmage thought of another way to cut him out of the claim so the last thing he was ready to face was the comely Miss Bennington looking anything but happy.

"Captain Eatonton may I have a word with you?"

Her words were polite enough but Max could guess what she wanted. If she had been willing to risk her life in the hold of the ship to retrieve the chest he was a little concerned with how she would react to his failure to secure it. "Certainly, Miss Bennington."

"Where is my chest?"

She crossed her arms under her own chest temporarily distracting him from answering her. He forced himself to meet her eyes only to find them as stormy as the sky over her shoulder. She was even more beautiful angry and he found her English accent intriguing. Swallowing hard he tried again to gather his scattered thoughts. "Captain Talmage loaded it aboard the *Sinistral.*"

"Why didn't your man put it with the items bound for this ship?" demanded Abby.

Thank goodness her father was headed in their direction. Maybe he could keep this scene from getting out of control. "Captain Talmage is wreck master. When he asked Mr. Keats to hand over the chest he didn't have a choice but to defer to his dictates. You will have to make your request to Captain Talmage, Miss."

"I thought you understood how important that chest is to me." She hoped she wasn't coming across as petulant as she sounded to herself.

"Miss, it's not lost. You'll just have to wait awhile to get it back," reasoned Max. "Excuse me, Miss. I still have work to do." He moved away to take care of his men, prepare the ship for the approaching storm and oversee the storage of their luggage as her father returned to her side.

Abby didn't even try to hide her disappointment from her father. "They did not bring the chest."

"What chest?" asked Richard.

"Mother's jewelry chest."

"You mean your mother's heirloom jewelry chest; the one with the satin lining and the angels carved on top? Is that what you were trying to bring up from the hold?"

Abby was gratified to hear the rising anger in her father's voice. He would get the chest back from Captain Talmage. She was caught by surprise when his anger turned on her.

"What in the world were you thinking bringing that chest on a trip like this? Whatever you needed from the chest you should have brought separately. I didn't even know you had the chest. I didn't give it to you. How did you get it?"

Abby couldn't remember her father ever being this angry with her. She tried for a placating tone. "Father do you not remember a few years ago when I asked for something of mother's you told me to take whatever I wanted from her room?" Now she found questions of her own. "Why is it so terrible I brought the chest? It cannot be worth much."

Realizing his agitation was not helping matters he calmed himself. "You are right daughter. The chest alone is not of concern. It is what the chest contains."

"But it's mostly paste jewelry. You know I left mother's expensive pieces in the safe at home."

After looking around the deck to make sure no one was listening, her father lowered his voice. "It is what is hidden inside the chest that is so valuable."

"Hidden? I packed the chest myself. There is nothing hidden in it." Abby might as well have been talking to the wind. Her father abruptly brushed past her headed towards Captain Eatonton.

Abby turned and watched as her father confronted the captain. They squared off against each other of the same height and build. Both were confident men, sure of their place in the world. The biggest difference between them was age. The captain was definitely not of the mama's boy variety that characterized so many of the men of her recent past. Maybe it explained the instant attraction she felt towards him. Recognizing the cause should help her guard against any deepening feelings.

Her father turned away from the captain and even at this distance she could tell he was displeased with the result of their conversation. The darkened skies overhead were no match to the thunderous look on his face. It was very seldom her father was not able to obtain that which he sought.

The wind whipped her skirts between them. Abigail said, "He told you to take your request to Captain Talmage."

Richard's mouth thinned even more. "Worse. He said I would probably have to take the matter to court. He at least offered to stand up on our behalf for whatever his testimony is worth."

The wind made it difficult to converse so they stood there silent with their thoughts as they watched the crew work. The luggage was all stowed away, the ship battened down for the coming storm and one by one the captain and crew returned to the longboats leaving her, her father and Maria alone on the ship.

Maria, afraid of the approaching storm, was huddled in a corner of the deck. Abby was enjoying the power in the air from the gathering tempest. It felt as if it would break loose very soon. She had thought the storm would bring a halt to the salvage crews unloading their ship but it was not to be the case. Her thigh muscles were starting to feel the strain from trying to maintain her balance on the swaying deck. Their stranded ship was being rocked even more violently on the reef. The longboats moved through the frothy waves so high now she would temporarily lose sight of the boats as they went down in the troughs. It must be very dangerous for the men to retrieve the cargo out of the hold when it and the ship were constantly shifting.

A bolt of lightning, seemingly directly overhead, made them both jump. Her father firmly took her elbow and guided her towards the hatch. He signaled to Maria as they passed to join them. She was very quick to do so. They settled in the main room. There was a table in the center with bench seating for four and several hammocks hanging at either end.

Abby made several attempts to start a conversation with Maria and her father but neither one was inclined to talk so she retrieved the book of poems. Purposefully avoiding the dedication, she opened it to the first poem and started reading. As the storm intensified, the light faded to the point she was forced to give up the book after having read only one poem.

Richard stood up. "We should probably locate some light before it grows too dark." The ship was pitching so violently now she was forced to use her hands for support. Her father searched deeper in the ship while Abby was intending to head up to the deck. Just as she reached the stairs the sky opened and a deluge of heavy rain seemed to hit all at once. Abby quickly closed the hatch. Fortunately her father announced he had found a lantern.

Abigail peered out a port hole facing the reef to see if the crew was returning. She was surprised to see lantern lights bobbing in the vicinity of the *Abigail Rose* and moving shadows she assumed to be men. It was hard to be sure but there didn't appear to be any boats headed in their direction. She couldn't believe these men were risking their lives working through this gale just to save some cargo.

Her father turned to her from looking out the other port window. "Looks as if we will be on our own for a while."

"Why would they risk their lives to save your cargo?"

"For money, sweetheart. They are loading all my cargo on their ship to take to shore where it will end up at auction and I will have to buy it back. What I pay will go in their pockets. They will probably tow the ship too and I will be forced to pay whatever fees they demand to get it back. Very nearly blackmail if you ask me."

"What about our crew and Captain Andrews?"

Richard sighed. "Captain Andrews is watching over them looking after our interests. The crew will be helping with the unloading and taking turns manning the pumps."

Abby took a seat at the table. She let her thoughts wander watching the lantern flame until she realized Maria was missing. She rushed to her feet and then had to take a moment to steady herself against the sway of the ship before taking the lantern to check on her maid. Not seeing her in the main room, she called over her shoulder to her father, "I will be right back."

Unsteadily, she crashed through the door of Max's cabin as the ship was tossed by the storm. Transferring the lantern to her other hand so she could rub her bruised shoulder, Abby held the light aloft to find Maria huddled in the corner with her arms crossed over her bent knees and her face hidden behind them trembling in fright. Kneeling down beside her Abby laid a gentle hand on her arms. Maria raised her head and Abby saw terror in her eyes. Abby held her hand out for Maria to get up and follow her but Maria shook her head no. Abby asked, "What is it that frightens you so? Is it the dark or the storm?" Not really expecting to receive an answer Abby tried another tactic. "Come with me, there is a table outside with a secure place to keep the lantern. Maybe we can find something to eat and drink. Please, come, Maria." After another moment's hesitation in which Abby was afraid she wouldn't consent Maria finally took her hand and stood. Abby could feel the tension radiating from her. Something had truly frightened the poor girl. They made their way safely back to the table where her father was patiently waiting.

"Ah Maria, good of you to join us."

Bless her father; sometimes he knew just what to say to put a person at ease. Maria would not sit with her employers especially since, to her mind, they were her master and mistress. Her father understood she needed to be reassured of his acceptance of her at the same table. They seated themselves across from her father. Maria reluctantly let go of Abby's hand and clasped hers together in her lap until the ship rolled again and she instead braced them on the table. The lantern, now swinging from a hook over the table cast eerie shadows about the room.

Abby asked her father, "Do you think it would be alright if we looked for some food and drink?"

"That is an excellent idea." Richard stood up and retrieved a second lantern. After lighting it he told the girls to stay there while he went in search of sustenance. While he was gone Abby tried to get Maria to open up. It took many attempts and much cajoling before she was rewarded with Maria's confidence.

"My old master used to lock me in de cellar to make my mother do what he asked. One time he left me there long time and a big storm came. Cellar filled with water. I had to climb on de crates to stay dry. No one came for me. It was so cold and dark down there." Maria shivered at the memory and Abby put her arm around her. The intensification of Maria's accent gave Abby further indication of how traumatic the experience was for her. Maria continued, "I was there all night and de next day before I was let out. My mother tried to get me out sooner." Maria hesitated and a big tear slid from her eye. She wiped it away impatiently before speaking the last. "She was beaten to death."

Abby drew in a deep breath in horror. "Mr. Dracner beat your mother to death?" Abby was shocked, as the man seemed so nice.

"No, not him. Him's a nice man. This was the master before him. He sold me to Master Dracner the next day. I didn't even get to bury my mother."

Abby felt her story was sincere but there was one detail that didn't make sense. "But Maria, you were with your mother at the Dracner's. I met her."

"I have called her mother for a long time now but she is really my mother's sister. She was sold with me. The Dracner's assumed she was my mother and we didn't tell them any different for fear they would separate us."

Abby kept her arm around Maria's rigid shoulder. "So it was the storm and the dark room and being left alone that brought back the old memories." Maria only nodded yes.

There were so many injustices in the world but slavery had to be one of the cruelest. Abby wanted to do something to help end it. She would ask her father. Maybe he would have some ideas. No one should have to suffer such abuse or the senseless death of a parent not to mention being sold in bondage in the first place.

"I wasn't able to find much." Abby was so lost in her thoughts she was startled by her father's return. "Just some old bread and a bottle of rum. I also brought this cup if you would prefer to fill it with rainwater." He broke the bread handing a piece to each of the girls. Abby took the cup and poured a small amount of rum in it. She took a swallow and felt it burn down her throat. It was all she could do not to cough. She nudged the cup towards Maria. She tried to turn it down but Abby insisted, "It will ease your nerves." Maria drained the cup and then sputtered. Abby took the empty cup to the port hole and opened it to let the rain refill it. It did not take long. She shared the water with Maria.

Her father put out the second lamp and started to reach for the one over the table. "We should probably conserve the oil."

Abby stayed his hand and nodded in Maria's direction. "Please leave it. It is of some comfort to have the light."

Richard did as she asked and they settled again at the table each quiet with their own thoughts. None of them seemed inclined towards conversation. Abby had no idea of the passage of time. She couldn't tell if it was minutes or hours. It was a relief when the rain finally stopped. One didn't realize how deafening the sound was until it had ceased. She listened to the waves hitting the side of the ship. Eventually even the rocking turned into a more gentle motion.

Abby awoke with a start surprised she had fallen asleep sitting at the table. Maria was still sleeping next to her but her father was not in the room. She then realized morning light was coming in through the port holes and she heard men's voices outside. The crew had returned. She got up from the bench as quietly as possible so as not to disturb Maria. She shook out her dress and stretched her back and shoulders and was just about to move towards the porthole to try and judge the lateness of the morning when Captain Eatonton appeared in the hatchway.

Their eyes met across the room and her breath caught in her chest. She was drawn to him in some inexplicable way, even knowing he was married didn't change it. Abby couldn't have stopped it from happening if she had tried. He seemed to feel it too because he paused mid-step before continuing down the steps and into the room. A room that had been perfectly comfortable with her father and Maria now felt entirely too small with his presence. He was filthy and his face showed his tiredness from working all night at such hard physical labor. His clothes clung to his body stiff with salt from the sea water and perspiration. Still she found him attractive. She forced herself to look away. Her father appeared behind the captain and moved around to her side which helped to break the spell. Although not completely. Tendrils of awareness still tied her to him.

Captain Eatonton laid a black drawstring bag he had been holding on the corner of the table. "You must be hungry. I managed to save a few of your bananas. The crews ate the rest of them. I would say I'm sorry but they were a lifesaver. We would have had a hard time continuing to work without them. Especially my crew as we had missed our midday meal. Excuse me while I change into some dry clothes." He went into his cabin and shut the door finally allowing Abby to take a deep breath.

Maria came awake at the sound of the closed door. Richard retrieved the black bag and removed the three bananas, giving the girls theirs. Abby slowly peeled hers open halfway and considered breaking off a bite but one look at her dirty hands she decided to take a more direct, albeit less ladylike, approach. She had just put the end in her mouth when the door reopened. The captain looked straight at her and she froze as she was for a heartbeat before finally taking the bite of banana. She could not control the blush of embarrassment flushing her cheeks. Drat him for making her feel so gauche. He grinned at her in amusement revealing deep cheek dimples. She thought his eyes were something but his smile nearly undid her. Those dimples!

Max turned to her father and advised him, "You should probably move the ladies back into my cabin. My men will be wanting to come change into clean clothes as well once they finish stowing this last load of cargo." He then turned and went back upstairs. Her father muttered a begrudged, "Thank you," to his retreating back.

"Well you heard him ladies, off you go now to the other room and mind you latch the door behind you."

"Are you not coming with us?" asked Abby.

"No. Captain Andrews came aboard with them. I am going up on deck to confer with him."

Abby quickly said, "I am going with you," and brushed past her father headed for the stairs before he had a chance to protest. She was not in the mood to be cooped up in a cabin. Especially not *his* cabin.

Chapter 8

Gaining the deck of the *Mystic*, Abby was momentarily overcome by the bright morning light, the brilliant blue sky, and the fresh air. It was as if the world had been washed clean by yesterday's storm. She felt her father put a hand to the small of her back and guide her in the direction of Captain Andrews who was conversing with his first mate. Upon seeing their approach he curtly dismissed Mr. Carter before greeting them.

"Good morning Mr. Bennington, Miss Bennington."

Richard said, "Good morning Captain Andrews. I trust no harm has come to you or your crew."

"No sir. We are all hale and whole if wretchedly weary. It was a long night working in the storm."

Abby felt a prickling sensation along the back of her neck; she turned her head in the direction of the helm to find Captain Eatonton watching her. She had yet to see him wear any kind of hat allowing the wind to play with his burnished gold wavy hair. It was long enough to catch the breeze but short enough not to reach across his face. She wondered what it would feel like to run her fingers through those curls. Irritated at herself for the way she was drawn to him she rudely ignored his small nod in greeting instead returning her attention to her father and Captain Andrews but her mind could not erase the image of him looking like a statue of Adonis come to life.

Richard nodded in understanding. "What is the report of our ship and cargo?"

"All the perishable cargo from the lower deck has been moved to Captain Talmage's ship. As long as the barrels didn't take in sea water we should have little damages. Talmage sent a diver down last evening to patch the leak. He seemed to have met with some success. The diver went back down this morning to ascertain any further damage. It appears the rudder is broken. He was not able to repair it so Captain Eatonton sent his diver down to have a go at it but the damage is too great. They are planning to tow the ship to Key West for repairs. I will be headed back to the *Abigail Rose* momentarily to prepare her for sail."

Richard's forehead furrowed. "Key West is the closest port?"

"Aye. We're in the Dry Tortugas, about seventy miles west of Key West."

"How did that happen?"

If anyone else had asked Captain Andrews would have simply stated it was a navigational error but Richard Bennington was a good friend as well as the ship's owner so he gave him the courtesy of a full accounting of events. "It was clear skies when I left Mr. Carter on day watch headed north. The most difficult task would be to break from the Caribbean current to move into the Gulf which normally we wouldn't have reached that point till tomorrow... eh, today. When the skies became overcast, rather than disturb me, he tried to navigate by chart. The problem was the current was stronger than he had accounted for and when the lookout spied the lighthouse on Garden Key off the port bow he suddenly realized our position was much further east than he had surmised. He then tried to break from the current and turn back to the correct heading. Not being familiar with these waters he didn't realize he had turned straight into the reef. With the cloud cover darkening the waters he didn't see what was below the surface until it was too late. If you will excuse me now I must head back to *The Rose* to oversee towing her in."

Richard wanted to ask of the first mate's punishment but as it was the Captain's responsibility and not his and furthermore it would be an insult to his friend, he refrained.

Captain Talmage, being wreckmaster, declared his ship would tow the *Abigail Rose* to Key West. Abby and her father took up positions at the railing to watch as tow lines were run from their stranded ship to the *Sinistral* off her bow. The *Mystic* would keep pace just in case further assistance was needed.

Despite efforts to not pay him any attention and much to Abigail's dismay, she was constantly aware of the *Mystic* captain's movements. To distract herself she studied the *Mystic's* other crew members.

She knew there were five besides the captain. Two of them were currently working the capstan to bring up the anchor. Thomas had skin dark as midnight and a manner of speaking that clearly denoted his island heritage. He was the ship's diver, a very important person on a salvage ship. His springy black hair was cropped close to his head so it wouldn't get in the way underwater. He was of average height and well defined physique, not a large man but still he was intimidating until one looked upon his kind face and infectious smile. Working with him was Billy, obviously the youngest member of the crew. Abby guessed him to be about four years her junior. He was shorter than she, but he probably wasn't done growing yet. His youthful exuberance was still apparent in his easy smile, affable nature, and bright green eyes even though she knew he had to be exhausted from moving cargo all night. His light brown hair was the longest of the crew reaching past his shoulders and pulled back in a queue.

Two men were in the rigging preparing the sails. So far she had only heard them referred to as the 'twins' which was puzzling as they obviously weren't identical twins nor did they even look to be related other than both being lanky blonds of Nordic descent.

The fifth man was his first mate, Mr. Keats, standing at the helm with Captain Max. He looked to be close to her height, broad in the chest, with straight dark brown hair. She couldn't determine his age. He was older than the rest of the crewmen, but just starting his third decade at most. It made her wonder about the age of the captain. Her gaze drifted to the man standing with feet braced apart, one hand on the wheel, gaze momentarily turned towards the other ship off their port side, giving her a view of his face in profile. Captain Max, as his crew referred to him, had a long straight nose, strong chin and high forehead. She would guess his age to be more than five-and-twenty but less than thirty. He turned and looked directly at her as if he had felt her gaze. She felt the weight of his look as if it were a physical touch constricting her chest. Realizing she was doing exactly what she had started out trying not to do she turned to face the water while her cheeks cooled and she regained her composure. *Married*, she reminded herself. *He's married.*

Max dragged his gaze away from the lithesome female leaning her back against the bulwark. Having a lady aboard ship was a distraction, not only affecting him but also his crew. It could only lead to mistakes. Max called out more orders trying to keep them and himself busy. It worked well while they were getting underway but once they were sailing smoothly his thoughts returned to her. His hands remembered the size of her waist, his chest remembered the feel of her light touch and he didn't think he would ever forget the flash of surprise that widened her stormy grey eyes when he pulled her from the hold into his arms or the light scent of rose water on her skin. Her creamy complexion made him think of soft rose petals. Everything about her made him think of a delicate English rose like the ones his mother used to grow. Her colouring was even the same as his mother's favourite rose by the front stoop, creamy white with hints of pink. He remembered roses have thorns and he had a feeling she had her share of them, one of them probably being she was spoiled. He would bet his last coin her father had named his ship after her. *I wonder if Rose is her middle name. How fitting.*

He had to forget her. There was no room in his life for an English rose no matter how attracted he was to her. He was trying to build a wrecking business which had him anchored in the reefs more days than naught; not to mention it was a highly dangerous occupation. His kind of life left little room for female companionship of any kind and most definitely not of the English rose variety. Best he turn his mind from her before it wandered into more dangerous thoughts.

Focusing on more practical matters Max checked the angle of the sails. Normally he could traverse the distance from Loggerhead Reef to Key West harbour in a few hours but following Talmage's schooner towing the larger and much slower barque would stretch the trip into a full day ordeal. They were without food but at least the water supply was replenished from the rain. It was approaching noon and his arms were tiring from holding the wheel. He signaled Mr. Keats to relieve him for a spell. After transferring the helm and completely forgetting his earlier decision, he asked, "Have you ever dealt with an English miss before?"

Mr. Keats let his gaze trail to the lady in question. "No, can't say that I have but if they're anything like the daughters of Cuban immigrants ye best be wary." Jonathon Keats was in love with a Cuban girl whose parents were very strict. He was often frustrated with the limitations placed upon her and their relationship.

"Still having problems seeing Miss Sanchez?"

"Aye." Not wanting to discuss his situation Jonathon asked, "Wasn't the old Cap'n's wife English?" referring to the former captain of the *Mystic*.

"Aye, only met her twice. A very proper English lady."

Jonathon said, "How did they meet? Did he ever tell you how he courted her?"

"Nay. You know how he was, kept private matters to himself."

"Aye. Most seamen do."

"Um," Max nodded his head in agreement then left Jonathon to see to the comfort of his passengers, at least it was the excuse he gave himself.

Mr. Bennington and Abigail were still standing at the railing. There was little comfort to be found in the hot stale air below deck. Mr. Bennington was holding onto his hat to keep the strong air current from stealing it. Abigail had her wide brimmed hat firmly tied below her chin. Max noticed faint freckles appearing on the bridge of her nose. She would probably hate them but he thought they were charming.

"Mr. Bennington, Miss Bennington." Max nodded to them in greeting. "I apologize for the lack of comforts aboard the *Mystic*. Is there anything I can do to make you more comfortable?" Even knowing there wasn't anything more he could provide decorum required he make the offer.

Abby disregarded his polite gesture in favour of opening a topic sure to engage him in dialog. "Captain Eatonton..."

"Please, call me Max."

Abby gave him a nod in acknowledgement and started again. "Captain Max, are not your ship and Captain Talmage's both schooners?" As the daughter of a merchant shipline owner she couldn't help but know a little something about sailing vessels.

"Aye," replied Max.

"I was noticing the difference in sails."

Max was surprised she would notice something as functional as sails. Maybe she wasn't completely spoiled. "This ship is a Baltimore Clipper. She carries a square topsail rather than all fore-and-aft and she has a V-shaped hull with a slightly deeper draft which allows us to sail close to the wind giving her a little more speed and maneuverability than the run of the mill schooner."

"I would think a deeper draft to be undesirable for working close to shore."

Max was impressed. She was intelligent and beautiful. "It can be a hindrance but as it is merely a foot or two it is generally of little consequence in that regard."

Abby had noticed the pride behind his words when speaking of his ship. It was easy to see it meant a lot to him. "What does your ship's name mean?"

"Nothing unusual, her former captain hailed from Mystic, Connecticut."

Her father interrupted before she asked another question. "How long do you believe it will take us to reach port?" Her father's tone and posture gave a clear sign he wished for Max to remove himself from their presence

Max took a moment to assess their wind speed before answering. "If the wind remains fair, six to eight hours. Feel free to take refuge below if you wish and be sure to drink plenty of water. This tropical sun will parch you in no time." Heeding Mr. Bennington's unspoken request, Max took his leave.

After her father chased him off, Captain Max did not speak to them for the rest of the, as it turned out, ten hour voyage. Abby preferred the open deck and found a place to sit where she could watch the birds playing on the aft wind and the activity of the crew. Her maid, Maria, sat with her for a while. It didn't take long for Abby to realize Thomas and Maria were attracted to each other. It was certainly more fun to watch them covertly taking notice of each other than dwell on the golden haired man watching her.

She found something else to occupy her time as well. She conversed with her father at great length about slavery in Jamaica and what could be done to bring it to an end. He suggested she write to Elizabeth to encourage Lord Kendall to bring a petition before Parliament. His idea appealed greatly to Abby as she would have a direct hand in helping the cause and knowing something of Avery Kendall's beliefs and Elizabeth's power of persuasion there was some assurance of its success.

With last night's storm having bridged some of the distance between herself and Maria she now felt comfortable enough to gently ask Maria questions about life as a slave, carefully probing the more painful parts. Armed with her new knowledge she set about drafting a letter to her friend. She became so involved in her task she barely acknowledged the dwindling daylight and it was several minutes before she realized the crew's activity indicated they were nearing their destination.

Her first view of Key West was in the soft light of early evening. The sun riding low in the horizon behind them bathed the trees and buildings in a golden glow giving it the appearance of a shimmering jewel within its setting of cerulean water.

A tiny jewel.

The island was certainly lacking the grandeur of Jamaica's Blue Mountain. It was flat and small and though they were nearing port she could still see the shoreline from end to end. The whole of the island looked to be smaller than all of Kingston Harbour.

She couldn't see how many buildings in all; it didn't appear to be a large number. Standing tall above the trees in the distance was a lighthouse, a lone sentinel on the southern point. The town formed on the northwest shore where the harbour was deepest. Near the docks were a couple of warehouses and large towers. She wondered what they were used for as they were too far from the water's edge to be used for unloading cargo from ships. As they drew closer she could tell from the lumber nearly all the buildings had been built in recent years. Most had not been painted. She wondered how it would appear in the clear light of day.

The *Mystic* was brought gently to rest against the wharf and quickly secured testifying to the skill of her captain and crew. Abby was both relieved to have finally made it to port for she was starving and yet saddened her sailing days had come to another temporary halt. Looking around the ramshackle seaside town of Key West she wondered how much adventure there was to be found. Plenty for a gentleman to be sure but what of a gently bred lady?

As it turned out adventure started with a narrow plank placed from the ship to the dock. Abby wondered how she was going to cross the foot wide board without falling in the water. She couldn't see where she placed her feet unless she hiked her skirts to an embarrassing degree. While still contemplating this dilemma she was joined at the head of the gangway first by Maria and her father and then by Captain Max and the 'twins'.

Max spoke first. "Mr. and Miss Bennington, may I present Tim Sudduth and Tim Grantham. I offer you their assistance with your luggage."

The two fun-loving tow-headed crewmen each gave her a deep royal bow complete with one leg extended fully forward and pretend hats flourished to the side. "At your service Miss," they said in unison. The act was done as much in jest as in courtesy. Abby thanked them for their offer while trying to hold a serious composure in response to their performance. Her father thanked Captain Max, politely if not enthusiastically. Her father was holding some kind of grudge against the captain. It was unlike him to do so and being he was a good judge of character she decided it was one more reason for her to ignore her attraction, as if she needed another reason. Married should be sufficient but for some reason her pulse just didn't understand that fact. It still quickened every time he came near.

The "twins" exited the ship first, each carrying one of their trunks, followed by Maria. Abby watched her easily make her way across the narrow board but then her dress was thinner and not held out by layers of underskirts like Abby's. Her father went next then turned to wait for her on the dock. Abby didn't want to appear nervous or weak kneed about crossing a piece of wood so she took a deep breath and stepped on the board. Then took another step and another and then made a mistake.... she looked down into the water below and froze. It wasn't really the height or the narrow board that stopped her. It was the thought of how embarrassing it would be to fall in the water.

Captain Max obviously interpreted her hesitation differently for in two steps he was right behind her. The sudden movement of the board under his weight unsteadied her and she felt his hands come to rest on either side of her waist then he whispered in her ear. "Look straight ahead to your father."

Now what should I do? Should she continue with the pretense of fear and let him escort her the rest of the way or declare her bravery and demand his release. Feeling his warm breath against her nape sent butterflies alight in her midsection. She decided release would be best. Speaking over her shoulder without turning her head, "Captain Max, it was a momentary lapse. I am fine now. Please release me."

"As you wish." He slowly released her as if testing her steadiness. He didn't retreat but rather waited for her to move ahead. This time she kept her eyes on her father and took careful steps forward until she was standing safely on shore. She turned around to politely thank the captain only to find he had returned to his ship. She felt bereft at the loss of his presence and it alarmed her. Her father tugged her arm turning her away from the *Mystic*. She fought the urge to look back over her shoulder.

The *Sinistral* left the *Abigail Rose* safely anchored in the harbour before docking. Her father held a hasty conference with Captain Talmage concerning the transfer of cargo and then they headed inland to the island's only boardinghouse. It was growing dark and difficult to make out the signs on most of the buildings they passed as they followed the unpaved white limestone to reach the hotel on Fitzpatrick Street. It was a very clean and comfortable two-story Bahamian style house run by Ellen Mallory, the widow of Charles Mallory. She was a sweet Irish lady who showed them to two cozy rooms. The 'twins' deposited their trunks with the promise of bringing the rest of their personal belongings tomorrow. It was approaching nine o'clock in the evening and with their last meal, aside from a banana, having been more than twenty-four hours prior they quickly freshened up and went down to the dining room where Mrs. Mallory served them fish stew, bread and fresh cocoanut. It tasted heavenly to Abby and it was all she could do to keep from devouring the food in a most uncivilized manner.

Having satisfied their immediate need of sustenance her father turned to business matters. "Sleep in as long as you like tomorrow. It has been a very long two days. I will be returning to the wharf in the morning to secure repairs for our ship and see to the storage of the cargo. I expect to be gone till late afternoon. If you need to go out for anything be sure to take Maria with you and I will leave word with Mrs. Mallory to provide you with an escort."

Abby wearily nodded her head in consent. After thanking Mrs. Mallory for her hospitality they returned to their rooms. Abby gave her father a goodnight kiss on his cheek, gratefully accepted Maria's assistance undressing with a brief inquiry to confirm she had eaten as well, and slipped into bed hardly noticing anything else of her surroundings other than the soft sweet smelling linens cocooning her tired body. She was instantly asleep.

Abigail slept soundly until well after ten when the sounds from the street below her window woke her. She stretched her limbs and then rose from the bed to freshen her face with water from the china basin. Maria must have heard her stirring for she knocked softly on the door and entered upon Abby's summons.

Maria curtsied apace and with perfect diction said, "Good morning, Miss. I trust you slept well. I have already requested your bath. Which gown would you like to wear today? I will see that it is pressed."

Abby was momentarily speechless. She had expected to have to make her wishes known to Maria. It was a pleasant surprise to have her needs anticipated and taken care of before she could ask. Going to her trunk she lifted the lid.

There were only three gowns in this trunk, one of which was the rose gown rescued from the hold which had been carefully repacked yesterday. The other two were everyday dresses, one yellow striped and the other a blue sprigged muslin. Having worn a blue dress for the last two days she chose the yellow one and handed it off to Maria with a very sincere, "thank you".

Her bath arrived a short time later and she gratefully sank into the warm water. It was a small tub, her knees were pressed to her chest, but it felt heavenly to finally have a real bath. She leaned her head against the rim of the tub and let her hair tumble towards the floor then ran her fingers against her scalp and simple relaxed for a few moments before washing with rose scented soap from her favourite shop in London. She had Maria help wash her hair and later help her dress. Feeling completely refreshed she was ready to face the day.

Maria appeared to be freshly washed too and was wearing one of the two dresses she owned. Both were threadbare and on the small size. Abby resolved to improve Maria's attire as soon as she had something to eat.

After an early lunch in the dining room Abby sought out Mrs. Mallory for the recommendation of a young page for an escort. She called to a neighbour boy outside who was happy to oblige. Abby, Maria and the boy set off to find a dress shop. As they left the porch Abby realized she forgot to ask where to find one but in a town so small how hard could it be? Seeing only houses to the left, she turned right from the boardinghouse and then right on Front Street as again only houses were to be seen to the left. Smaller lanes branched off Front Street, which was the main street of the town running parallel to the harbour, but none were very long being bounded on one side by the harbour and the other by a tidal pond covering a large area behind Front Street. All total she thought there couldn't be more than fifty buildings.

Conveyances were not prevalent and were mostly used for carrying goods, not people, as the town was small enough walking from one end to the other would not take her more than ten minutes, the whole of the street being less than half a mile long. Standing between Fitzpatrick and Duval streets she passed an abandoned navy barracks falling into disrepair, and then a dock she would later learn was called the Fish Market as the fisherman would sell their catch at the end. Beneath the dock was a turtle kraal, a pen built around the piers, where the creatures were held until they were sold for food. Beyond Duval was a cluster of warehouses, ships chandlers, shipwrights, sailmakers, riggers and other skilled craftsmen interspersed with housing and pubs. A dock extended from each warehouse with ships at anchor including the *Mystic* and *Sinistral*. With limited dock space many larger ships were anchored in the harbour including the *Abigail Rose*.

Between the docks and the Fish Market several fishing smacks and smaller boats were anchored offshore. One of the boats was closer to shore with a cart and donkey backed up to it. She could see the men unloading the goods that appeared to be coal and produce. Her page explained that being an island, all goods arrived by ship. This island being formed of limestone was further limited by only being able to produce a few food items. These ships brought in valuable fresh produce and food staples from Cuba, Bahamas and New England. Cattle were a rare commodity, so much so anytime fresh beef or lamb was available word spread fast around the community and it was sold in mere hours.

The other side of Front Street offered a grocer, a mercantile store, a cigar shop, milliner's shop and also interspersed with housing and more ale houses. She was coming to the end of the street without finding a dressmaker.

Abby was used to being noticed by men but walking down the island street she became uncomfortably aware of curious stares from all the men they passed. She also noticed a very marked lack of other females. Added to that was the further disconcerting fact many of the pubs were scandalously busy for such an early hour of the day.

As she was passing the front of one of the bars while reading the merchant shop windows on the opposite side of the street she collided with a sailor reeking of alcohol. Taking a step back and waiting for the man to pass she recognized Mr. Carter, the first mate from their ship. He weaved unsteadily on his feet. "Pardon me, Miss," and then his eyes narrowed as he recognized her, "You!" With more speed than she would have thought a man that far in his cups could muster, he grabbed her shoulders roughly. "It is all your fault. You're the reason I am being left to rot on this island."

The page leading the way had continued skipping on ahead not realizing what had happened behind him. Maria was behind her but Mr. Carter had such a tight grip on her she couldn't turn around to send her maid for help.

He started shaking her. "You owe me and I'm gonna have some fun with you, make up for all this trouble you brought on me."

Abby was becoming alarmed at the look in his eyes and what he meant by 'fun'. She was struggling to free herself when a fist came out of nowhere and connected solidly with his jaw, silently sending the mate crumpling to the ground and pulling Abby down with him before his grip slackened. She rolled away from the inert form of her attacker onto her back and found a very masculine hand ready to assist her to her feet. She allowed her hand to be engulfed in his warm grasp sending a tingle through her whole being before following the arm to the face to find her rescuer was none other than Captain Max Eatonton.

"Are you alright Miss Bennington?"

Quickly recovering her wits she replied, "Yes, I am. Thank you. Where did you come from?" She could see over his shoulder the page had finally realized he had lost his followers and was headed back their way.

"Your maid went into the bar and screamed for help. I was the closest one to the door so the men in the room sort of nominated me." He didn't mention he was already headed her way having seen her pass the window. His tone turned angry. "What are you doing out here alone? Do you know what could have happened if I hadn't been here? You need to understand - this is a small island; probably three hundred souls at most and only a handful are women. The men are a rough and tumble lot who live hard and play hard. It is not safe for a woman to walk alone during the day and even worse after sundown. You should take care to protect yourself. This is a frontier town, not your English countryside."

Affronted by his scolding Abby retorted, "Pardon me, Captain Eatonton, but I was not alone."

Anticipating her argument Max said, "Your maid is not enough for she is in as much danger as you."

"Not that it is any of your concern but I also have a hireling."

"Where is he?"

Even knowing he was going to object to the boy she nevertheless said, "Behind you." Fortunately the boy had made it back to their group or so she thought.

"What happened to him?" The boy asked, kicking Mr. Carter's booted foot. "Is him dead?"

Max was trying to control his growing anger. "So not only are you being escorted by a lad still in knee breeches but he wasn't even around when this happened! Where are you staying?"

Guessing his intentions Abby took a step backwards. "I am not going anywhere with you. I have errands to run and I intend to do so."

Max leaned through the doorway of the bar and yelled something about getting Mr. Carter removed from the sidewalk. Abby picked up her skirts, stepped over the man and continued on her way with her head high expecting Maria and the boy to follow her. Max quickly caught up and fell in stride with her walking along for a few moments in silence. Without the boy in the lead Abby had no idea where she was headed but she didn't want to give Max the satisfaction of learning that fact so she continued as if she knew where she was going until she came to the next corner. She looked in all directions trying to make up her mind which way to go as none of them seemed particularly promising.

Losing patience Max asked, "Where are you trying to go?" When Abby remained silent and finally decided to turn right, Max added, "If you don't tell me I'm going to ask the boy where you are staying, toss you over my shoulder and carry you to the front door."

Abby turned to glare at him, "You wouldn't!" but she knew from experience he would. "Fine. I am trying to find a dressmaker."

"Do you have a recommendation?"

Sheepishly Abby admitted, "I do not."

"Come. I know of a shop back the way you came. It is probably the only one we have anyway." He offered his arm.

Abby hesitated before slipping her hand around his bicep. She immediately felt his muscle flex alighting butterflies in her abdomen. Irritated with herself and him she said, "Do you not have something better to do with your day than walk around town with me?"

Max replied in a very nonchalant manner, "Not really."

"Will not your wife have something to say about this?"

Max looked at her in shock. "Wife? Whatever gave you the idea I had a wife?"

She looked down at the crushed coral street while deciding how honest to be with him. "When you first left us on your ship I was looking for something to pass the time and I found the book of poetry. I tried to skip past the inscription but I could not help seeing it."

Max knew exactly which book she was referring to and didn't fault her for looking for something to read. "It was not my book originally. It belonged to the former captain. Emma was his wife."

Abigail's relief was great. It was a relief to realize she could stop praying for forgiveness for coveting another's spouse. Now she was free to feel and to express those feelings so she allowed the smile to spread across her face and tossed a sideways glance at him just to admire his physic. His shirt was laced up today concealing his skin but it still failed to sufficiently disguise his muscular chest and shoulders. He stood out from the rest of the island men. His dress was more casual than the businessmen and he was definitely more cleanly cut than the other sailors and laborers she had seen thus far. But there was something else more indefinable that made him stand apart. It was more the way he carried himself.

Unfortunately she found not having the slight edge of anger to hold onto she was now even more aware of her attraction to him and she was having a hard time finding a topic of conversation. "Do you like poetry?" asked Abby at the same time he said, "Here we are." They came to a halt in front of a small house with a shingle announcing *Seamstress*.

"Pardon me?" asked Max.

"Never mind. It was nothing. Thank you for your escort and for coming to my rescue earlier." Abby extended her hand intending to shake his. Max instead lifted her gloved fingers to his lips. "It was my pleasure, Miss Bennington. I can wait for you, if you like."

"Thank you Captain but that will not be necessary. I am sure we will be fine." He continued to hold her hand.

Max was forced to accept her dismissal but he took his time in leaving her. "Please take care. I meant what I said earlier. This is not a town for ladies."

After giving herself a brief moment to drown in his blue gaze - he had such mesmerizing eyes - Abby replied with unusual acquiescence, "I will sir," then retrieved her hand from his grasp. "Good day to you." She gathered her skirts and turned to enter the shop. She heard Max whistling as he left. She hoped she was the reason for his happy tune.

Awhile later her party left the friendly and helpful seamstress after ordering several serviceable dresses for Maria. The shop was not as fancy as Madam Rousseau's but Betsy, the dark-haired petite proprietress, proved to be a very charming and helpful widow who was grateful to work on something other than men's shirts. She ushered them through her parlour into her workroom to choose fabric. Various stages of work could be found on every surface in the room. She promised to have two dresses ready by the end of the week. They returned to the boardinghouse without incident where Abby found her father ensconced in a chair perusing some papers.

"How was your day, Father?" Abby gave him a cheerful greeting and kiss on the cheek before taking a seat on the damask sofa opposite him.

"Mostly frustrating. I have been to the chandlers to arrange for the repairs of the ship. If the rudder must be completely replaced it could take several months to obtain another. We may be staying here longer than I first anticipated. The cargo has been commissioned to the warehouse of Mr. Pardon Greene at Captain Eatonton's suggestion since I was not comfortable taking the recommendation of Captain Talmage. Also, I was unable to get Talmage to release the chest and so I sought legal counsel this morning. It seems I will have to demand a court hearing to resolve this just has Captain Eatonton predicted. Fortunately the judge has arrived on the island so it may not take as long as the repairs. You will like this one piece of news. It seems there will be a ball to welcome the new judge Friday evening and we have been invited."

Abby's face brightened. "A ball! How unexpected and interesting since I understand there are very few females. It should certainly prove to be an amusing evening."

"Mr. Martin, the lawyer who invited us, did mention it would be a smaller gathering compared to what we would be used to in England. I would be surprised if you were not the reason we were invited."

"What do you mean? Why would I be the reason for an invitation?"

"As you said, very few females are on the island, I am sure our host was taking advantage of the opportunity to add another with the added coup that you are new to the island. How did you spend your day, sweetheart?"

"I slept late and took Maria shopping for dresses after lunch. Hers are in dire need of replacement."

"Very good dear. You still wish to grant Maria her freedom, do you not?"

"Of course."

Her father handed her a piece of parchment paper. "I had Mr. Martin draw up this document while I was in his office. You may give it to her whenever you wish. What do you feel should be the terms of her employment?"

As Abigail usually managed the household staff she told her father the terms she had already decided upon confident he would have no objections and then left him to go in search of her maid. She found Maria unpacking her other trunks which had arrived while they were out.

"Maria, I have something for you."

Maria finished hanging the dress she was holding and turned to Abby with a questioning expression. "Yes, Miss?"

Abby extended the piece of paper towards her. "Do you know what this is?"

Maria accepted it with a puzzled look and shook her head negatively, "No, Miss, I can't read."

"Would you like to learn?"

Maria nodded her head in the affirmative this time but kept a guarded expression. "Slaves aren't supposed to read."

"This piece of paper means you are no longer a slave."

Maria's expression immediately showed her distress. "You are disappointed with me? You are sending me away? Please don't. I will do better just tell me what to do and I will do it. Please don't send me away."

"No, no Maria. You misunderstand. You have done nothing wrong, in fact you have done a wonderful job and I would not want to lose you but I cannot in good conscience keep you as a slave. You must choose to stay. You have your freedom and as a free person you now have a choice to make. You can continue as my maid and besides meals and a place to stay, you will also earn wages or you can seek other employment on this island. I will offer to teach you to read and write no matter which path you decide upon."

Maria stared at the paper she held with dawning wonder. When she finally lifted her eyes to Abby's they were turning misty with tears. "I choose to stay." Nodding her head she said it again. "Yes, I will stay. Thank you." She clutched the paper to her chest in a protective manner.

"Would you like for me to read to you what it says?"

Maria again nodded her head and handed the paper back to Abby with an unsteady hand.

Chapter 9

Abby made one final check of her reflection in the mirror above her bureau before accepting a light shawl across her shoulders from Maria. She loved the way Maria had pulled her hair up in a cascade of curls and adorned it with island flowers to match her apricot silk dress. She met her father in the sitting room. He looked rather dashing in his freshly pressed waistcoat and breeches. They were going to the ball held in honour of Judge James Webb, first judge appointed to the newly created Admiralty Court. As they prepared to leave the boardinghouse Abby noted the first difference between this ball and previous ones she had attended in England was they would be walking the short distance rather than taking a carriage. The home of Mr. and Mrs. Henry Martin was at the other end of Front Street and it looked to be a very nice evening for a stroll.

They were ushered into the charming Victorian home by a liveried butler and warmly greeted by their host and hostess. Abby found the second difference to be the guests. Aside from the much smaller number, perhaps forty in all, Abby didn't know anyone. Back home she usually knew three quarters of the guests at least by name or reputation and often would know everyone in attendance. She considered herself to be a socially adept person but she soon realized this evening would be a challenge unlike any she had ever encountered. Confronting a sea of strange faces was daunting. Her father squeezed her arm as if he understood her thoughts. She gave him a confident smile as he escorted her further into the room. A mere half hour later she was wishing it had been a smaller gathering; her head was swimming with names and faces. She was terribly afraid when called upon to remember any of these people again she would have them all mixed up.

Abby was standing quietly in a corner sipping some punch and feeling relieved to be alone for a moment to clear her head when a spirited brunette near in age to her approached. She was almost the same height as Abby with large brown friendly eyes that sparkled in the candlelight from the chandelier. She had high cheekbones, a pert nose, and a beautiful smile that seemed to hold some secret amusement. She came to stand next to Abby facing the milling guests then leaned towards Abby and said, "So you're the new girl in town everyone is talking about."

Abby was surprised to find herself the subject of island gossip already, although she probably shouldn't be and if anyone else had said those words it would have been offensive but this girl made it seem like she was happy to finally make her acquaintance. Feeling as if she had just met a kindred spirit and deciding to be just as forthright Abby introduced herself, "I am Abigail

Bennington and you are astonishing. Nice to meet you.....?"

The girl turned and shook Abigail's hand then said with a mixture of awe and amusement in her voice, "Victoria Lambert and it is very nice to make your acquaintance. I saw you yesterday with Max Eatonton outside Betsy's shop. He usually keeps his distance from the ladies but he looked to be quite attached to you. Now tell me, however did you manage to capture the elusive captain, Miss Bennington?"

"Abigail, my friends call me Abby, and I would not say I have captured him. It is more like he has nominated himself as my protector even though I do not need one."

"I don't care much for Vicky or Torie so unless you can come up with an acceptable nickname, please call me Victoria. What has the handsome captain done that's so protective besides escort you around town?"

Abby replied tongue-in-cheek, "Well, let us see... in the last two days he has pulled me out of a hold full of shifting cargo, removed me from a stranded ship, kept me from falling off a plank, rescued me from a drunken sailor and then escorted me around town although I did not require his assistance on any of those occasions."

"No, it doesn't sound like you needed rescuing at all," Victoria replied in kind. "By all means, please give me all the details starting with where you hail from. Your accent sounds English. I myself am Charleston born. My father is a lawyer and he assisted with a case here a few years ago and fell in love with the island. He moved mother and me here as soon as he could get us to pack which was not an easy thing to accomplish as my mother's family has lived in Charleston since its founding. I'm not sure she has adjusted yet."

Abby could not help her grin. Victoria's frank speech was unlike anything she had ever heard. "I am from England, near Southampton. What about you, have you adjusted? Do you like Key West?"

"Some days are exciting but most of the time I find it quite boring. What I wouldn't give to travel and see places like England, not just read about them. What's really sad is it's not a lack of funds keeping me from traveling; it's my father. He will not leave the island and he won't entrust my safety to anyone else. Now you, what brings you to this island?"

Just as Abby started to reply the orchestra started the music for the evening. Victoria held her hand up. "It will have to wait till later. The mob will be descending upon us. No lady on this island is allowed to be a wallflower, we are always severely outnumbered by the men and therefore in great demand. I most likely won't see you again until supper."

Sure enough here came several men racing towards them trying to appear as if they were casually walking in their direction and still be the first to ask for a dance. Abby had a hard time trying to hold back her mirth at such a display. Three of them reached her at the same time and each extended their hand towards her in supplication. Victoria called out, "have fun," as she was swept towards the area cleared for dancing on the arm of a tall, bearded and somewhat gangly gentleman.

Abby wasn't sure how to choose and realized now what a blessing it was that in England a man would not approach without a proper introduction. One of the men was more boy than man. He seemed to have recently hit a growth spurt as his legs and arms extended well past the cuffs of his clothes. The middle one was of middle age, short and portly with a balding pate and the last was a man of indeterminate age with a scraggly beard and beady eyes. There were another half dozen more men waiting behind them. She opted for diplomacy and accepted the middle portly one whom she had met earlier with her father and with whom her father had some business although she couldn't for the life of her remember the nature of their business. "Mr. Barclay, correct?"

"Yes, yes you are correct Miss Bennington. How kind of you to remember a dapper little fellow such as myself." He bowed to her as deeply as his protruding waist would allow. Abby curtsied to him and then placed her hand in the crook of his elbow and tried not to notice she was a head taller than him. They joined the couples already lined up for a cotillion. Mr. Barclay was a surprisingly more graceful dancer than she had expected, easily guiding her through the steps which were slightly different than the way it was danced in England.

When the music ended she had Mr. Barclay escort her to her father's side in the hopes of narrowing down the number of men vying for the next dance. Her father understood her predicament and cast a discouraging scowl towards the horde of swains. One was braver than the rest. He introduced himself to her father and asked if he might dance with his daughter. Permission was of course granted after receiving an agreeable nod from Abby and off she went spinning around the floor.

Thus became the pattern thereafter. The novelty of being new to the island greatly increased the attention she was receiving. Abigail understood America did not have a class system like England but it was still amazing to her the diversity of backgrounds she discovered amongst her dance partners which included the captain of a fishing vessel, a secretary to a prominent businessman, a bank teller and a visiting Viscount from France. Far from offending her, as it might most English ladies, she found all the differences made for very interesting conversations.

Returning to her father after the seventh or was it eighth dance - she'd lost count - Abby was determined to sit the next one out to give her feet a rest until she was introduced to her next partner, William Whitehead. A very nice looking young man who appeared to be very close in age to herself. As they whirled around the dance floor she asked, "Mr. Whitehead, if I may be so bold as to ask, what is your age sir?" She caught him by surprise. It registered on his face and he missed a step in an otherwise perfect dance performance.

He turned the tables on her. "I will answer your question if you will answer mine."

Expecting him to ask her age in return she hesitated but curiosity made her capitulate.

At her nod of agreement Mr. Whitehead said, "I am eighteen years of age. Now you.."

She hated answering even more now that she knew he was younger so rather than wait for the actual question she interrupted him, "Nineteen."

"Indeed. However that was not my question as my mother instructed me never to ask a woman her age."

Really embarrassed now she said, "Then you shall receive two answers for the cost of one. What was your question?"

"It escapes me now. Your beauty has cleared the thought straight from my head."

"Nonsense. You are merely humouring me now." They made a tight turn on the dance floor before Abby continued. "Alright, if you will not ask yours then I will ask another. What is it you do to occupy your time on this island, Mr. Whitehead?"

"Surveying and map making has been my latest occupation. You see my brother owns a quarter share of the island and they have been in need of a good map for dividing lots. Being the only resident with some, albeit minimal, experience in surveying I was recruited for the task. I am proud to say it is nearly complete and very thorough if I may say so myself."

"I am sure you did a wonderful job. How rewarding it must be to have a useful occupation."

"Are you one of those women not content with your lot in life?"

She assessed his meaning and only finding sincerity in the question she answered honestly. "I might be content to be a wife and mother. I do not know not having reached that point but for now the uselessness of a debutante's life I find burdensome."

"You are a very unusual woman, Miss Bennington." He twirled her one more time as the music came to a halt. He gracefully bowed to her and then escorted her back to her father.

Mr. Whitehead bowed again. "Thank you Miss Bennington. I greatly enjoyed your company."

She curtsied. "Thank you Mr. Whitehead. You are a charming partner." Abby liked the young man and the forthrightness of his conversation. He was studious without being boring and good looking without being taken by his good looks. She tried to keep track of him the rest of the evening but other than glimpses here and there their paths did not cross again much to her disappointment.

Just as Victoria predicted she did not have a break from dancing until supper was announced and she was more than ready for a reprieve. Another difference with this ball was not having dance cards and there didn't seem to be organized music sets. The orchestra was much smaller too. She missed the rich sound of a larger ensemble but the less formalized dancing appealed to her spirit of adventure.

She discovered a fourth difference at supper. Not only was the seating less formal, the menu was lighter and made up of favoured dishes of the island. They were served turtle soup, conch fritters, a variety of fish and flamingo all garnished with fruit. Abigail enjoyed every bit of it.

The evening ended with a few dances after dinner one of which for a time had the ladies moving in an inner circle while touching hands in the center like the spokes of a wheel and the gentlemen danced around them in a wider circle. This gave Abby a chance to speak to Victoria. "I believe I have come up with a suitable nickname for you."

Victoria looked interested. "What would that be?"

They turned to circle in the opposite direction. Abigail answered hopefully, "Tria."

Victoria pondered for a moment. "Tria. Light, different." She smiled at Abby. "I like it."

The dance changed pattern returning the dancers to their partners. Abby bore a triumphant smile that left the poor man she returned to quite baffled.

At the end of the evening, Victoria and her parents waited at the door for Abby and Richard to thank their hosts. Mr. Lambert was considering representing their salvage case and invited them for luncheon Monday to discuss the details. Abby and Tria bid each other *adieu* until then as if they were old friends. It was amazing to Abby how close she felt to someone she had met just a few short hours earlier.

She and her father strolled home arm in arm enjoying the starlight and the cool salty breeze. Her father was in jovial spirits and told Abby all about meeting the new judge and after conversing with him at great length found him to be a fair-minded and respectable man giving her father hope for a favourable outcome for their suit against Talmage over her mother's chest.

The home of Mr. and Mrs. Lambert was a two-story laid out in a very traditional manor except for the unusually low roofline which all but obscured the second story windows from the front view of the home. Some called the style an eyebrow house. Mr. Lambert believed the purpose was to keep the upper stories cooler by blocking out the sun and to offer more protection during the harsh tropical storms. With several large palms and a banyan tree also shading the house he couldn't say for sure if it really helped.

Tria and Abby left their parents to adjourn to Tria's room where she immediately began quizzing Abby starting with what her home in England was like before getting to what she really wanted to discuss - all of Abby's encounters with Max. Victoria sensed there was more going on between them than either Max or Abby realized and she was even more convinced after Abby finished her story. She had been very matter of fact when recounting Marc Danvers, Lord Jason Malwbry (Victoria was still amazed Abby knew a future Duke) and Isaac Landis but when it came to Max Eatonton her voice betrayed emotions she probably hadn't acknowledged to herself yet. Added to that fact was Max Eatonton's behaviour towards Abby. He usually steered clear of the female population as a rule but had gone out of his way on several occasions to assist Abby. It was definitely going to be interesting to watch this relationship develop and goodness knows the diversion would be welcome. Entertainment was limited in a small island town.

They rejoined their parents for luncheon of grilled grouper, Cuban rice and beans and a fruit salad. Afterwards Tria suggested a walk to show Abby more of the island. They strolled arm in arm down Caroline Street each carrying a parasol to protect them from the harsh afternoon sun and followed by their maids. They headed towards Front Street and then turned towards the wharf. Tria not only pointed out the sights along the way but kept a running commentary of who lived in the houses and their role in the small island society. To listen to Tria, living on the island was a hardship but what she found to be burdensome Abby found charming, delightful and appealing. The soaring mountains of Jamaica may be majestic and awe inspiring but Abby found the simple vista of this island peaceful. She also liked the bold shapes and colours of the exotic foliage compared to the softer vegetation found in England. She couldn't wait to explore the island's more natural and less developed side. She had heard there were salt ponds on the northern end. She couldn't see Tria willingly traipsing into the wilderness for the sake of exploration so her pursuit would have to wait for another time.

As they approached the wharf Tria's pace seemed to be more purposeful and her commentary less vocal, although she did offer the explanation for the towers Abby had noticed on her arrival. They were used by the wreckers for spotting stranded ships on the nearby reef or returning vessels in need of assistance. There were many ships docked today gently rocking against their mooring lines. Victoria beckoned her onto one of the docks. She said there was something she wanted to show her. Abby recognized the *Mystic* just ahead with her crew at work on the deck. The 'twins' spotted her and waved. Abby called out a greeting to them. She expected they would continue on past going to the end of the dock but Victoria halted in front of the ship. She shaded her eyes and called out, "Permission to board?" Abby was taken by surprise at Tria's bold behaviour even though she had mentioned a few times society restrictions were less formal on the island.

"Permission granted," a voice called back. Abby saw Mr. Keats lean over the rail and wave a greeting. Abby, Tria and their maids took turns crossing the narrow gangplank without incident. The 'twins' waited on the other side to receive them. "Always a pleasure to see such pretty ladies. What brings you down to the docks?" asked Mr. Keats.

Victoria replied, "Just taking an afternoon stroll. Is Captain Eatonton around?"

"He's below deck doing some paperwork."

Victoria gave Mr. Keats a coy smile. "Would you mind calling him for us?"

Mr. Keats turned to do her bidding. Abby gave her a questioning look which she shrugged off. Abby had no idea what Tria was intending, she only hoped it was not so brash as to cause embarrassment. A few moments later two sets of booted feet were heard climbing the stairs. Abby ran her hands down her dress in an unconscious check of her appearance.

"Well good afternoon ladies, a pleasure to see you." Captain Max made a gentlemanly bow and smiled his welcome.

Abby's heart skipped a beat. She had forgotten how handsome he was and his smile set her insides to quivering. She was glad Tria was leading the conversation to give her a chance to recover her senses.

"Captain Max. Good to see you as always. I've come to ask a favour."

"I'll be happy to oblige if I'm able Miss Lambert. What is your request?"

"I would like to take Abby sailing around the island and the nearby keys so she can have a better feel for the area. If the calm weather holds I thought you would have the time and wouldn't mind accommodating us."

"I do believe our fair winds will hold for another day or two. When were you thinking of making this excursion?"

"Would tomorrow morning be reasonable? I'll pack a picnic lunch with some of cook's fried chicken." Victoria knew her cook's fried chicken was legendary on the island. Even if Max didn't favour it she was still sure to get his crew on her side.

As if on cue Max's crew of five simultaneously cheered their encouragement for him to accept Victoria's proposal. "It seems we have an accord Miss Lambert." Max turned his attention to Abby. "It's good to see you again, Miss Bennington. How are the repairs progressing on your ship?"

Abby locked gazes with Max and it took her a moment to gather her wits, again, enough to respond to his question having drowned in the deep blue depths of his irises. "We are waiting on word of the rudder damage to know if it can be repaired or a replacement must be obtained."

"In other words you are waiting to learn how long you will be detained on our charming little piece of paradise."

Abby thought his choice of phrase revealed his attachment to the island. "It would seem so."

"Such a dilemma, that. Where were you headed before your captain found our reef?"

"Actually it was the first mate who made the mistake. You acquainted your fist with his face the other day."

Max's knuckles were still bruised but he didn't regret his action, on the contrary, he was even more satisfied knowing he had also hit the man responsible for putting this woman in harm's way with his inexperienced sailing. "Why did he attack you in the street if he knew you?"

"It seems he is unhappy to find himself without employment and for some reason blames me for his misfortune."

Max could guess why the man felt Abby was to blame but if she didn't understand why he wasn't going to be the one to enlighten her. "You didn't say where you were headed."

"Montgomery, Alabama. My father and I are going to visit my uncle's plantation for the holidays."

"If the rudder must be replaced I'm afraid you will be spending the holidays with us. I'm sure it would be a disappointment for you."

"It may be a given anyway. I believe my father means to take Captain Talmage to court over the jewelry chest he refuses to return."

"If you need me to testify please don't hesitate to ask," Max reminded her.

"That is very generous of you, Captain Max."

"Not at all Miss Bennington. The actions of Captain Talmage are not the accepted practice of this industry and should not go unpunished."

"Please call me Abby."

Max gave her a broad smile and replied, "Miss Abigail," in such a way that Abby's heart seemed to squeeze just a little tighter.

Victoria chose that moment to remind them of her presence. "Captain Max, I'm sure we have been keeping you from your work. We will excuse ourselves and say *adieu* until tomorrow."

"Until tomorrow." Max held his hand out for Abby. She placed her gloved hand in his and he bowed over it placing a gentle kiss on the back then continued to hold her hand as he escorted her to the gangplank. "Do you need assistance to cross the plank?"

Abby was flattered by his attention but a little embarrassed by the reminder of her last attempt at exiting this ship via this same board. "It will not be necessary. I believe I have the trick of it now." Once she reached the dock, Abby turned to wave to Max who returned the gesture. Tria was last to exit the ship after their maids. Abby was a little satisfied to note he merely bowed to Tria, no kiss on the hand for her.

As the girls walked away they could hear Max calling out orders to his crew to get the deck ship shape for tomorrow. Abby felt a little sorry for the extra work they had caused the crew, but not enough to keep her from looking forward to tomorrow. They returned to Tria's home the same way they had come, speaking very little, each deep in her own thoughts. Max was right she would be disappointed to not make it to her uncle's for the holidays but there was the consolation of spending more time on this island with her new friends and to have time to explore starting tomorrow with a sailing excursion. All in all she was as happy as she could be with the situation.

She told her father of the sailing plans on their way back to the boardinghouse from the Lambert's. He objected at first on two grounds: one he still harboured doubts about Captain Max's character and two he thought it unseemly for two ladies to sail about with six young men and only their maids as chaperones. In the end Richard decided it would be best not to disappoint Victoria since the outing was her idea and he was counting on her father's aide so he finally consented as long as he joined them. Abby was not adverse to her father joining them as she believed it would help change her father's opinion of Max and they would probably need Max's help in court. Tomorrow promised to be an exciting adventure.

Chapter 10

The next morning Abby anxiously waited in the foyer for her father to finish one more review of the documents he was taking to Mr. Lambert this morning when they went to meet Victoria. Abby was feeling a lot of nervous energy. She was excited to be getting back out on the water but if she was honest with herself it was the fervor of seeing Max that made her impatient to leave. Just as she decided she was going to check on her father, he appeared at the top of the stairs.

"Are you ready sweetheart?" her father asked as he descended. He paused next to her at the threshold and studied her face for so long she became uncomfortable. "You look radiant this morning," was all he said before opening the door and guiding her ahead of him but she had a feeling he had read something more in her face than she had meant to reveal.

Upon reaching the Lambert's, Victoria greeted them at the door as anxious as Abby to start the day. They waited for their fathers to speak briefly with each other. Both girls struggled to contain their impatience. Abby nearly sighed out loud in relief when her father was finally ready to leave.

It was now mid-morning as they walked along Front Street to the docks. The water was a light turquoise reflecting the bright morning light with sparkling clarity and the birds seemed to be determined to out chorus each other but Abby hardly noticed. Her steps were so buoyant she felt more like she was floating rather than walking and her gaze was fixed ahead on their destination. She missed Tria's knowing and amused smile.

As they approached the *Mystic* they could see a spare sail had been strung on deck as a makeshift shade from the sun. Abby was touched by Captain Max's thoughtfulness. Almost as if drawn by her thoughts the captain appeared at the head of the gangplank to welcome his passengers aboard. He crossed the plank and shook her father's hand. "Welcome Mr. Bennington. It's good to see you again. Here, may I take the basket?" Victoria's cook had fried several chickens to keep her promise to the crew. Richard relinquished the basket to Max and crossed the board.

Max greeted each of the ladies before handing them off to the ship. Abby was the last of his guests to board. She was relieved to find this gangplank was much wider than the previous one she had used from his ship. She placed her gloved hand in the palm of his and felt her heart skip a beat when Max smiled at her. She returned the smile and had the satisfaction of hearing his breath hitch. She liked knowing he was as involved as she in whatever this was between them.

Upon gaining the deck, Max showed his guests to the arrangement of crates they could use for seating under the sail. He handed off the basket of food to one of the Tim's to be stowed away for later. "Miss Victoria, as this outing was your idea do you have a particular course in mind?"

Victoria turned to him with a flirtatious smile. "Why no, Captain Max. I leave it to your auspicious expertise to decide upon the direction of our journey today."

"Well then, I say we sail past the southern tip of the island and see which way the wind blows." Not expecting any dissension he turned on his heel to convey his plan to Jonathon Keats who would have the helm for most of the day leaving Max free to entertain their guests.

Richard mumbled to himself. "That is what he calls a sailing plan?"

Abby settled herself next to Tria on the middle crates to watch as the sails were raised by the crew and billowed with an effervescent sea breeze. Abby's nerve endings hummed with anticipation. The creaking of the wooden ship moving away from the port and out into the current was a pleasant sound, heightening her excitement. She was having a hard time sitting still.

Max rejoined their group taking the crate next to Victoria leaving the one on the other end beside Abby for Richard, who was last to be seated.

They cleared the dock and as the ship was facing north they started out on a northerly course before the crew made a perfect shift in sails and the ship smoothly turned in the water until it was headed in the opposite direction and then another change turning them southeast. Abby could tell the maneuver impressed her father.

Max looked to Mr. Bennington. "Being a seaman yourself I'm sure you noticed our fine harbour - best in all the keys. It is naturally large enough and deep enough for the Navy's largest ships. Protected in all directions from storms except the southwest from which they seldom come and having access from three directions allowing ships to come and go in almost any wind."

Mr. Bennington agreed. "It is most advantageous."

They sailed past the wharfs and warehouses located at the deepest point of the natural harbour. Max pointed out the structures along the coast as they slowly sailed past. She was familiar with most of them from her walk through town but she had neglected to notice one unassuming building.

Max pointed to the tiny structure on the beach. "That is our equivalent of a jail. We call it the 'Sweat Box' as it is mainly used as a sobering place for the excessively soused. The long building next to it is the Navy barracks, now abandoned and the building on stilts beyond it is the Custom House.

"Commodore David Porter had the barracks built for his anti-piracy campaign about five years ago. Porter did an excellent job ridding the Caribbean of pirates but he ruled the island under martial law and took what he wanted claiming it for the government, not just land but anything he could use. He made it clear any livestock not kept in a pen was considered government property. People were forced to build fences and provide feed for animals they had intended to let roam free and be self-sustaining. He also mandated a curfew and dictated any new building. So while thankful for safer waters, we were not sorry to see him leave. The end of the pirates also brought an end to the Navy's presence and our community has suffered for the loss of income they provided. Porter later joined the Mexican Navy and used our harbour as a hideout while he attacked Spanish ships. When payment stopped coming for his troops he started selling goods to pay his men, upsetting our relationship with Cuba and once again threatening our way of life. Why we tolerated his presence for two years I still don't understand. Our country was neutral in their war." Max looked at the others and suddenly realized how aggravated he must have sounded. "I apologize. I will endeavour to speak of more pleasant subjects."

As Max spoke the rest of the buildings slipped by - mostly merchant shops and homes, some with fenced yards. They sailed past the corner of Whitehead and Front Street which marked the end of the settlement. The town was located on the northwest end of the island with a verdant backdrop of undeveloped land beyond. Large shade trees were scarce around the town proper; most were cocoanut palms, the other trees having been used for lumber.

Max pointed to a spot on the coastline between the last home and the lighthouse, "...and there's the cemetery. The rest of the island is currently uninhabited. There are some salt ponds on the other end being developed as an export for the island."

As they sailed past the lighthouse several children raced down to the shoreline to wave to them. Abby counted three, four, six children. "I always thought of lighthouse keepers as old bachelors. You obviously have a family tending to yours. How many children do they have?"

Tria waved in return to the children. "I believe the Mabrity's have altogether eight children."

Max said, "Hard to count. They never stand still and rarely are they found all in one place. There is another lighthouse about seven miles southwest. Sand Key Lighthouse was built last year on the reef opposite of our light so navigation through this point is much safer now."

Once past the lighthouse at the southernmost tip known as Whitehead Point, they were forced to sail away from the coastline as the water was too shallow. After the lighthouse the dwellings ceased and only nature was left to be observed including a lone green turtle swimming past, birds circling the treetops and trailing the ship and a white heron perched on a mangrove root providing a stark contrast against the darker vegetation.

Max continued his narration while nervously monitoring their intentionally slow progress out of the harbour, as he normally would not allow anyone else to guide his ship through this area. "The red mangrove tree grows along the coastline of most of the islands while the interior has a vast array of trees including mahogany, black mangrove, and banyan. The island is not more than a mile wide at its widest point and only four miles long. Many of our citizens are sailors who do not have a land residence."

Richard asked, "What is the current population?"

Max shrugged. "I'm not sure, probably only a few hundred."

They were exiting the harbour and leaving the island behind. Looking back they could see two men working further down the coastline making their way through the twisted mangrove roots.

Victoria murmured, "I wonder what they are doing."

Max picked up his spyglass lying nearby. "I believe it is Mr. Barnum and Will Whitehead, John Whitehead's younger brother."

Abby laid a hand on her father's arm. "We met Mr. William Whitehead at the Martin's ball. He is a very nice gentleman. Do you remember, Father?"

Richard answered, "I believe so."

Max added, "I heard tell he is making a map of the island."

Abby nodded in agreement. "Mr. Whitehead told me he was almost finished. It will be used to divide the island among the founding members."

Max found himself envying William. He and Abby had probably danced together at the ball. "From what I hear his brother John intends to formally layout the city development to go along with the new town charter."

Richard turned to Max in surprise. "New charter? Why? Was there a problem with the old charter?"

"No, sir. This will be the first charter. The island has been held in common by its owners. In January there was an act to incorporate the Island. This will be the first charter for the town. We are currently governed by a mayor and a council of citizens. The town was started only six years ago by John Simonton. Prior to that the island was owned by Spain then granted to Juan Salas for services rendered. Salas sold it to John Simonton in 1821.

"Another man, General Geddes, showed up here with supplies and big plans of his own believing he owned the island. He was turned away by Simonton's group and Lt. Perry, who happened to be here surveying the island on behalf of the Navy. I felt sorry for Geddes. He had to find out in court he had a fraudulent title. Imagine how disappointed he must have been."

Max made a quick visual check of his crew and the ship's location. Finding all was well he continued his narrative.

"The Spanish called the island *Cayo Hueso* which means Bone Key. Rumor is a lot of bones were found on the island both exposed and buried. *Cayo Hueso* turned into 'Key West'. John Simonton sold off three quarters of his interests ironically to several other men named John: John Whitehead, John Flemming, John Warner and John Mountain. They started the development in 1822 and Simonton managed to get the United States Navy involved by '23. Key West has been an official Port of Entry for the United States ever since, although we are not currently one of the states. Florida is still only a territory."

Richard was astounded. "Why I have wine in my cellar more aged than your settlement. I knew the town was not established but I certainly had not realized it was so new either."

Abby said, "It is a bit strange, 'tis it not, when everything in England is measured in generations, to find a place essentially in its infancy." Abby looked to the captain. "So tell me, Captain Max, since you obviously did not grow up here how did you find your way to Key West?"

Max regarded her for a moment while gathering his thoughts. He saw an honest interest in her shimmering irises and responded with more openness than was generally in his nature. "I worked my way up to first mate of this ship under her former captain, Nate Hamilton. During the New England winters, he would fish the Keys for the Cuban markets. One winter, he got too sick to sail. Just before he died he bequeathed me this ship and told me to head south and find my future. When winter was over, I realized there wasn't really anything for me in New England so I decided to stay. The rest of my crew, except for Mr. Keats, headed back north. The two of us continued fishing until we discovered there was better money to be made from salvage."

"Why not choose something more respectable like merchant shipping?" asked Richard.

Max tried not to take offense at the implication in Richard's words. Most people considered what he did to be one step away from piracy and Richard certainly had reasons to think the worst of the industry having experienced it first hand from Captain Talmage. It took some effort but he managed to hold a neutral tone. "Well sir, as a matter of fact my first sail was aboard a merchant ship. I didn't care for the long voyages, the unpredictable crew changes and the poor rations. I found local fishing to be more agreeable. Now instead of hauling in fish, I haul in ships and cargo. I'm providing a valuable service and it's more profitable for my crew." Technically, it was only more profitable when they actually salvaged a wreck and so far those were few and far between but Max kept such knowledge to himself.

Richard wanted to argue the point but as Abby was clearly indicating her wish for him to withhold his comments by look and gesture he refrained from doing so... for now.

The wind increased as they moved further into the Strait. The clipper sailed much faster than the barque. The increase in speed gave Abby a thrill. For the next several hours they headed in a generally northeasterly direction. They passed many tiny islands that were nothing more than bits of exposed coral, some with vegetation, most often red mangrove, the leaves of which reminded Abby of a rhododendron. The mangrove roots were unlike any she had ever seen. They had the appearance of long fingers reaching down to the sand and water holding on for dear life against the tides. Max called them 'land makers' as the debris would settle around the roots and over time expand until a land mass was formed.

They continued on with the occasional trivial conversation and trading the occasional half smile. Abby felt her awareness of Max, already heightened by his nearness, increase again.

Max said, "Your situation is not unique." Abby looked at him questioningly. "Many have found their way to Key West by shipwreck. In fact, this town wouldn't be here if not for the wreck that brought John Whitehead to this island. He recognized its potential and it is because of his encouragement John Simonton purchased the island from Juan Silas."

She had a hard time thinking when he looked at her so intently so her reply was an absentminded, "Is that so."

The ship suddenly leaned to port as they exited the main current and turned back towards the keys. The crew made quick work of shortening the sails as Max excused himself to personally guide his ship through the coral reef and shallows to whatever destination he had in mind. At Mr. Keats' recommendation the ladies and Richard moved towards the side railing to view the wide variety of coral and fish to be seen just below the surface.

They halted offshore from a small island with an elevated center and many trees to offer an inviting cover of shade. Max called for the long boat to be lowered. Abby noticed there was already a load of crates and a barrel aboard the small craft. The crew of four rowed to shore and unloaded the row boat. Three of them stayed behind on the island to move the cargo further inland while one returned to the ship in the boat. Abby was quite curious about these proceedings. She wondered what the cargo contained and what possible purpose could there be for cargo on what she was sure was an uninhabited island. Her father was bold enough to ask but all Captain Max would say was, "you'll see".

Captain Max, Richard, Victoria, Abby and the remaining crew rowed over to the island with the lunch basket. Max led them about two hundred yards inland to where the trees gave way to a small freshwater pond and revealed the mystery of the cargo. The crew had used it to make a dining area; a barrel and large crate lid for a table with four crates set around for seating under the umbrella of palm trees. Abby and Richard were both duly impressed by the extraordinary gesture and creativity of Max and his crew. Victoria removed a checkered table cloth from the basket and spread it over the makeshift table. Then she removed dishes and silverware and proceeded to set the table. Max seated Victoria by offering a supportive hand under her elbow and then gestured for Richard and Abby to take their seats before he seated himself. Victoria served them chicken, biscuits and lemonade from the basket before passing the remaining food to Mr. Keats. The crew gathered around the edge of the pool a short distance away to share their meal.

Abby cast Max a surreptitious glance. She was pretty sure he had gone to all these extra efforts on her behalf and she had to admit she was quite flattered by his attention. Max caught her glance and gave her a boyish grin in return making her heart flutter.

Max was feeling quite proud of how the day was progressing. He even felt like he had made some progress with improving Mr. Bennington's opinion of him. He shook out the napkin and placed it in his lap following everyone else's example then picked up a juicy chicken leg with his hand and took a huge bite...and nearly choked on it thanks to Victoria and her innocent comment.

"Mr. Bennington, I understand you and your brother run a successful merchant ship line."

Mr. Bennington looked up from attempting to cut into his chicken thigh with a fork and knife to smile at Victoria. "Why, yes, that is so."

Max wanted to groan but held the sound in check, recalling his earlier conversation with Mr. Bennington he had said he didn't like being a merchant crewman which was probably just as good as if he had said he didn't like Mr. Bennington's business. Max then noticed the others at the table were all using a knife and fork. He placed the chicken on his plate as discreetly as possible, wiped his hands on his napkin and picked up his silverware feeling as if he had just lost every bit of ground he had gained in his bid to impress the Benningtons.

Victoria asked, "How did you get your start in shipping Mr. Bennington?"

"I served in the Royal Navy during the Finnish War. Towards the end I was in charge of shipping and used what I learned to start building my own shipping interests."

Desperate to regain his ground Max said, "Captain Hamilton often told me stories of the Royal Navy and its strength. How long did you serve?" Max intentionally didn't add that the stories were of the War of 1812 and often ended with the United States' fledgling Navy beating the Royal Navy.

"Seven years from 1803 to 1810," replied Richard.

"How many ships do you employ in your trade, Mr. Bennington?" asked Max.

"I own fourteen and engage another dozen or so trading all around the world." Richard's voice was tinged with more than a hint of pride.

Max grew even more uncomfortable realizing he was in the company of a very wealthy man. Another very good reason to keep his distance from the very tantalizing English rose sitting to his left, although it seemed when dealing with her reason didn't matter.

Seeing Max's discomfort Abby took pity and changed the subject. "Tell me Captain Max, does anyone inhabit this island?"

Max turned to her with what looked to be a smile of relief. "No, it's a bit small. This pool is in the center of the island. It's mostly used by a few wrecking crews as a source of fresh water and a convenient place to anchor in between storms."

"Then there is nothing more of interest worth exploring here," said Abby with regret.

"Not really. There are some other islands of interest further north. If you like we could plan a longer voyage next time."

Next time... Abby liked the sound of that. "I would love to. Does this island have a name?"

Max thought for a moment. "No, not that I aware of, we refer to it as the water hole."

Enthusiastically Tria suggested, "Let's give it a name."

The men didn't offer suggestions of their own but were quick to offer opinions of the ladies' suggestions.

Victoria opened with, "What about Pirate's Cove?"

Max answered, "Already exists - besides we're not pirates."

Abby offered, "How about Wrecker's Island?"

Victoria said, "Wrecker's Key."

Abby said, "Max Key."

Max laughed, "I think the others would take offense."

"No Name Key," retorted Abby.

"I think that one has been taken as well," said Max.

It turned into a game of the ladies trying to outdo each other to find a name the men didn't object to until it was interrupted by a flock of flamingoes flying overhead to settle on the far side of the pool with little concern for the humans on the other side. One of the crew mentioned flamingo for dinner and suddenly a knife was flying across the pond. It missed the birds landing safely in the sand as they took flight. Abby wasn't sure which one of the crew threw the knife but they all got a good laugh as one of the flock seemingly took revenge by dropping a deposit on Billy's shoulder. All, that is, except for Billy who found nothing humorous about his soiled shirt.

"Poop Key," suggested Victoria in between laughing.

"Victoria!" said Abby with mock disapproval.

"Most unladylike, I know," said Victoria without an ounce of regret.

"Flamingo Key," announced Abby with triumph.

"Perfect," agreed Victoria.

None of the others offered a protest so the island was dubbed Flamingo Key.

As they finished eating Richard said, "Miss Lambert, please thank your cook for the lovely lunch. I enjoyed it very much."

"Yes sir, I will."

At the end of their meal Max offered his hand to assist Abby to her feet. He held her hand a fraction longer than necessary and looked in her eyes as if he were trying to see to her soul. They both felt the deepening connection building between them. Max wanted to run his hand down the side of her cheek to see if it was as soft as it looked but Richard's presence standing behind her had him dropping Abby's hand. He turned to assist Victoria who gave him an all too understanding smile momentarily disconcerting him. The ladies followed Max back to the rowboat with Richard taking up the rear guard.

Mr. Keats and the rest of the crew were left to gather up the lunch remains and repack the hamper along with getting all the crates and the barrel back to the boat.

"Good grief, I didn't sign on to be no butler," complained one of the Tim's.

"You sure enough enjoyed that chicken, you must've had 'bout ten pieces," the other Tim retorted.

"What's with the Cap'n, making all this extra work for us?" asked Billy.

Thomas smiled. "That's what happens when man like him gets smitten. Yo' end up makin' tents and hauling empty cargo into the wilderness for tea parties."

Mr. Keats decided they had complained enough. "Stow it men! Twins, you get that barrel filled with water and back to the beach."

They automatically responded in unison, "Aye, sir."

With everyone and everything back on board, the ship was carefully navigated back to the deep water of the Strait. As the ship skimmed across the water towards the afternoon sun and Key West, Abby leaned her back against the railing resting on her elbows and observed Max and her father talking. Richard was sharing his war stories and Max shared Captain Hamilton's stories like how he had won one particularly difficult battle and was allowed to keep the *Mystic* as a reward. Abby observed her father's relaxing attitude towards Max and felt relief. Max was a good man and didn't deserve the harsh opinions her father had thus far been holding against him. Today, he had proved himself to be a very thoughtful and generous man. He handled the ship and his crew well and as for being a wrecker, he seemed to be hard working and honest. All of these were qualities her father could appreciate.

She started thinking what if... What if a relationship developed between them? She found the idea exciting. What if he kissed her? She instinctively knew it would be better than Isaac's kiss and she found that even more exhilarating. What if she continued these thoughts? Someone was bound to notice her expression and wonder what in the world she was contemplating or worse, have a good idea what she was thinking. Time to study cloud formations and get her thoughts under control or maybe she should rejoin Tria under the tent.

Max was trying hard to keep his focus on Mr. Bennington in an effort to further impress him. He didn't want to say the wrong thing and he was trying to emulate Mr. Bennington's more formal speech. Despite his efforts he was embarrassed to discover, when Mr. Bennington cleared his throat, he had been caught staring at his daughter. Max redoubled his efforts to keep his attention centered on her father. She did not make it easy. Her pose strained the bodice of her dress to the point he thought a seam would surely give. Only instead of enjoying the view, something he normally would have done, he wanted to objurgate her for her unladylike stance. It was a proprietary feeling he had no right to feel. She was not his responsibility so why did he care? Realizing he was too distracted to continue their conversation Max excused himself from Mr. Bennington on the pretext of needing to consult with Mr. Keats.

As the island of Key West came into sight, Max joined Abby at the railing but kept a respectable distance. Her pose now decorous as she once again faced the railing. "I hope you had an enjoyable afternoon, Miss Abigail."

"Yes, I did. You were very attentive to the details and a lady cannot help but be impressed with dining *al fresco* in such style. Please be sure to thank the crew on our behalf for their efforts."

"It was my pleasure," replied Max warmly, "but it would probably mean more to them if you thanked them yourself."

"I believe I will."

And so she did, managing to make them all blush with her exuberant praise for their efforts, echoed by Victoria. After bidding the crew of the *Mystic* farewell, Richard, Abby and Victoria made their way back to the Lambert's home.

Richard and Abby arrived back at the boardinghouse in time for one of Mrs. Mallory's wonderful dinners. Afterwards, Abby retreated to her room to record the day in her journal and write a long overdue letter to Elizabeth. She had a lot to share with her friend starting with how she came to be in Key West and found herself in the arms of a golden Adonis. She smiled to herself imagining Elizabeth's reaction when she read her letter.

Chapter 11

The following day brought a rare all day rain to the island keeping them indoors. Mrs. Mallory said it was a blessing as the water was needed to refill the cisterns - excavations in the limestone under or beside the houses in Key West to hold water. It was their main source of drinking water and therefore vital to the island residents. Abby spent most of the day teaching Maria to read which proved to be a very pleasant and easy task since she was excited to learn.

The next morning was beautiful and clear and Abby was more than ready to join her father to visit the Lambert's. She pulled her shawl tighter as they walked the short distance. End of October mornings in Key West may be as warm as late spring in England but when the day's high would be warmer than the hottest summer day back home it made the morning temperature feel quite chilly. She was still trying to get acclimated to the afternoon heat and found herself wore out after the simplest of tasks. Thank goodness they had arrived in fall and not during the summer months. She wondered how long it would take before she was able to cope with the heat and humidity. Mrs. Mallory was constantly reminding her to drink plenty and rest often. But mornings were pleasantly chilly.

Upon arriving at the Lambert's, Tria immediately requested Abby's company. She was running some errands starting with a visit to Betsy's shop. This worked out well for Abby as the seamstress had promised to have Maria's dresses ready today and she wanted to mail her letter to Elizabeth. Abby said goodbye to her father before exiting the front door with Tria, although he barely noticed as he and Mr. Lambert were already deep in their discussions of legal matters.

As they descended the front steps Abby asked Tria, "I have not seen the post office. Where is it located?"

"We, as yet, do not have an official post office building. Dr. Waterhouse collects and distributes the mail. His house is just ahead. If he is not home he leaves a receptacle by his front door."

Max was in a buoyant mood having just picked up payment for piloting a ship during yesterday's storm. He was on his way back to the *Mystic* when he spotted a familiar figure up ahead. What luck to run into her on the street rather than having to invent an excuse to visit the boardinghouse. He had already been thinking along those lines and was having trouble coming up with a plausible reason for seeking her out. He quickened his pace easily catching up with his target.

Max made his best attempt at flirtation. "My, aren't you ladies even lovelier than the island flowers. May I join you and bask in your beauty?" Unfortunately he was very unskilled in the art. The ladies stopped, turning towards each other as they turned around, almost as one unit, like a double gate opening and closing.

Victoria gave him a saucy grin. "Why Max Eatonton, I declare, I thought I would never see the day you were openly flirting in the streets."

Max was uncomfortable with her teasing but chose to bear it out for the sake of keeping company with Abigail. "Miss Lambert there is much you don't know of my personality." Not wanting to give her time to respond he moved the conversation towards his target. "Miss Bennington, how are you finding our city? More congenial, I hope, than when last we met on this street."

Abby continued his banter. "We have only met with pleasant gentlemen such as you this morning. I am in no danger of needing rescue at the moment. Perhaps you should return in an hour or so."

Max said, "Maybe you need rescuing of a different sort. I could enliven your day with more adventurous pursuits; something more exciting than whatever errands you have been employed in up to now."

He definitely had Abby's interest. "What did you have in mind?"

Trying to think of something quick his gaze caught on the structure towering over the treeline in the distance. "We could walk to the lighthouse. The view from the top is excellent. You can see the whole island."

Intrigued Abby asked, "The light keeper would allow us to climb to the top?"

"I'm sure he would. Mr. Mabrity and his wife are very friendly. Besides I helped build it, how could they refuse my request?"

Victoria saw an opportunity to encourage their relationship. "You two go ahead I still have the cobblers and the new milliner shop to visit. Besides, I have no interest in traversing across the island in my new boots, not to mention all the creatures one is bound to run across on the other side of the pond."

Max couldn't resist teasing Victoria. "Afraid of a few toads and insects, are you?"

"Those toads are the size of a small cat!" Victoria held her hands out indicating the size of a large dinner plate. "Thank you very much but no, I have no interest in meeting up with one of them again."

Abby's eyes widened in disbelief. "Really? You must be exaggerating. Toads could not be so large."

"Tell her, Captain Max. Tell her I am not exaggerating."

Not wanting to lose Abby's willingness to spend an hour or so with him, he lied. "Of course they aren't that big. Even if they were, what harm can a toad do? There is nothing to fear, Miss Bennington."

Abby looked to Tria for confirmation she wouldn't mind if Abby went without her. Receiving a nod of encouragement she then looked to Maria. "Do you have any objections to toads?"

"No Miss. I grew up on an island with small creatures."

With Maria to act as chaperone, Abby put aside any reservations about propriety in favour of taking advantage of the small adventure unexpectedly presented to her. "Well then, Captain Max, you shall have your exploring party."

Max grinned, charming all three ladies but none more so than Abby. "Wait right here while I run to the ship. I'll need my machete." He was off before they could even have a chance to protest. They watched him sprint away and return just a few minutes later.

He offered Abby his arm. "Shall we go?"

She trustingly placed her hand in the crook of his arm.

They agreed to rejoin Victoria at the milliner's shop upon their return.

Max led Abby and Maria down Duval Street towards the shallow tidal pond behind the town. At the moment it was nothing more than a soggy bog as the tide was currently out while high tide brought a mere eighteen inches in depth. Spanning the pond was a narrow boardwalk about fifteen feet in length made of planks placed across piles of rock. Max helped Maria to climb the first board and then held Abby's gloved hand while she gained her footing before following behind her.

Abby held her arms out for balance taking a few small careful steps until gaining confidence she dropped her arms and her steps became more sure. "Why does it seem I am always crossing planks when I am with you?" Abby tossed a brief glance and a teasing smile over her shoulder to find Max was much closer than she realized - too close - her nerve endings jumped and she momentarily lost her balance. She instinctively put her arms out and in less than a heartbeat she felt his hands on her waist steading her. He whispered in her ear, "I like keeping you unbalanced," which in turn caused a tingle to run down her spine. She focused ahead and took in deep steadying breaths in an effort to regain her emotional as well as physical balance. Chastising herself for reacting too easily to his nearness she moved ahead pulling away from his grasp. She carefully continued along the boardwalk until she reached the end and safely descended to *terra firma*.

Max stepped off the boardwalk and boldly took Abby's hand placing it in the crook of his arm before moving forward down the wide clear path headed towards the treeline. Maria trailed behind them. The coastline was off to their right but they were taking a more direct route through the trees to the lighthouse situated on Whitehead Point. The sun was climbing towards its zenith and what had started as a pleasant morning was turning into the usual warmth of the day. Abby had forgotten to consider the effects of the heat and now felt perspiration gathering. She looked to the trees anticipating some relief from the shade.

Abby said, "I am disappointed not to see this famous large toad, would it not reside around the pond?" She felt his bicep flex under her hand.

He turned to her with a serious expression. "I told you those toads don't exist."

Looking straight ahead she replied likewise. "And I did not believe you."

Affronted, Max cocked his head back. "What reason would I have to lie?"

Abby let a smile hover on her lips. "I did not say you lied. Perhaps you just have not seen one. Maybe they are elusive creatures looking for a kiss from a maiden to turn them back into a prince."

Max thought if any maiden had the power it would be her. "A believer of fairy tales, are you?"

"The occasional indulgence in fancy relieves the boredom of life, does it not?"

"I'm not much of one for fancy. My thoughts are usually of a mundane nature such as how are you finding our weather? The days are cooling down now that we are leaving the storm season. You are fortunate you were not stranded here in the midst of summer when the sea breeze offers the only relief from the heat."

"If this is cool weather then you are correct. It is plenty warm for my liking." Abby desperately wished she had brought a fan or her parasol with her. At least she had her hat to keep the sun off her face and she was wearing her lightest dress.

She thought it was the distance at first making the trees look small but as they drew near she realized they were about to enter a miniature forest. Max referred to it as a hammock. Many of the trees were hardly more than twice her height. He pointed out a few he knew the names of - black mangrove, buttonwood and seagrape which had leaves larger than a man's hand. Some had funny sounding names like gumbo limbo, tamarind and pigeon plum which offered berries Max claimed made excellent jelly.

The path narrowed forcing them to follow single file behind Max. He pulled his machete from a sheath strapped to his waistband and started cutting away much of the thick underbrush blocking their path. The work kept him quiet. She could hear the rustling of small animals fleeing from their path but never caught site of any of them. Birds chirped in the low canopy and every once and awhile she would see one fly overhead. Max exposed a box turtle nesting in the leaves. Closed up as it was it looked like a soldier's helmet with yellow markings. Abby stood quietly watching until the turtle opened its front and she could see its head. It appeared to be watching her, not opening any further. Not wanting Max to get too far away she left the turtle.

She did her best to keep up with Max but found the trail and humidity were quite taxing on her strength. The heat, instead of lessening, was made more intense by the stagnant moisture in the air under the trees. Feeling the beginnings of a headache she hoped they would be there soon. She glanced back to see how Maria was faring and found her preoccupied with keeping her new dress from getting ruined by the dense vegetation but otherwise seemingly unaffected by their surroundings.

Abby was thankful when the path in front of Max suddenly opened to a clearing with the shore ahead of them. Leaving the hammock the breeze made the air feel better but not her. They stopped for a moment to take in the picturesque view. The whitewashed brick lighthouse topped with a black iron lantern stood on a dune facing the Florida Strait. She guessed the whole structure to be more than four stories tall. The lighthouse keeper's quarters stood nearby. A woman and several children were working in the yard.

Max looked at the light with pride. "It was built a couple of years ago. Many wreckers were against installing the light as it would keep the ships from wrecking on the shoals of this island. Although it is my livelihood I'm not against seeing it brought to an end as it would mean safer passage for all. For now, there are still plenty of wrecks nearby. What do you think of our little lighthouse?" He turned to Abby and noticed she looked very tired and her face was extremely flushed. He was immediately concerned she was suffering from heat sickness. "Miss Bennington, do you feel alright? Can you make it to the cottage? Mrs. Mabrity is sure to have something refreshing to drink."

Abby was feeling very weak but judged the distance of a hundred yards or so to be manageable. She nodded affirmatively to Max and started forward leaning heavily on his arm for support. As they neared the yard Max called out to the keeper's family. "Hello there." The woman stood up from her task of straining whale oil for the lamps to greet them. "Good afternoon Mrs. Mabrity. I brought a friend to marvel at our new light but she seems to have succumbed to the heat on the way. Would you have a cool drink of water for her?"

Mrs. Mabrity reached for Abby urging her towards the house. "Heavens dear, come inside out of the sun and sit down." She led Abby into her tidy home and directed her to a chair near the window to take advantage of the coastal breeze. Abby was intimidated at first by the stern looking woman with spectacles but soon found she was one of those people whose appearance did not match their demeanor. Mrs. Mabrity had a firm hand on her household but she was also a very friendly and sympathetic hostess. "You poor dear." She laid the back of her hand against Abby's cheek, testing the heat of her skin, in much the same way Miss Winterfeldt used to check her for a fever. She then directed one of her daughters to make some lemon water. "Shame on you, Captain Max. You should know better than to expose someone new to the island to such exertion in the heat of the day." After scolding Max she looked her patient over again. "No wonder you suffer so, too much covering. Let's start with removing those gloves. You are still much too warm." Before Abby could so much as lift her hand the efficacious lady was tugging the covering from her fingers. She finished removing the gloves just as her daughter, Nicolosa, brought Abby her lemonade. "Drink it slowly child. Best to sip it or it won't stay down and that would make matters much worse." Turning to the children crowded behind her she shooed them away. "Back to work, all of you, nothing to see here. She's going to be right as rain in a few moments. Captain Max, would you be so good as to help them finish the chores while her maid and I tend this poor soul?"

"Yes, ma'am." Max reluctantly followed her brood back outside.

Once the room was cleared she turned back to her patient. "My name is Barbara Mabrity and you would be?"

"Abigail Bennington and this is Maria. Thank you, ma'am, for your hospitality."

"Nothing to it. Now dear, you are still too flushed. More will have to be removed. Maria, please take a towel from the shelf just behind you and soak it in the bucket there by the table, then wring it out and bring it here."

Maria did as she was asked while Mrs. Mabrity helped remove shoes and stockings and then placed the wet towel on the back of Abby's neck. "This may get your dress wet but it is the quickest way to cool you down short of striping off all your clothes. The next time you go traipsing across the island you may want to consider leaving the corset at home. When did you arrive here? I mean on the island."

"A few days ago. The heat has only slightly bothered me. I certainly did not expect for this to happen."

"It usually does catch newcomers by surprise. What brings you to Key West?"

"Actually, we were headed to Mobile and became shipwrecked near here."

"'Tis the way of it for many of our citizens and the main reason my husband and I do our work carefully and diligently. The light, we hope, will spare many a wreck. We would much rather people visit for pleasurable reasons.

"There now, your cheeks have returned to a more natural colour. Young and healthy as you are, this won't keep you down long. You stay here till you finish your drink and are feeling yourself again. Then put your shoes back on, but leave the gloves off, and come outside to sit a spell in the shade. I'm going to help them finish the chores so my poor husband can get some sleep before dusk." Mrs. Mabrity returned to the yard where she could be heard directing her children and Max in the tasks required to keep a lighthouse in good working order.

After resting another ten minutes, Maria helped Abby put her boots back on and they returned to the yard where Mrs. Mabrity directed her to a ladder-back chair in the shade where Abby waited with a second glass of lemonade in hand until the chores were all completed. Water and whale oil had to be hauled up to the top of the lighthouse to clean and refill the fifteen Argand lamps and then brought down and refilled again as the lamps would have to be cleaned several times during the night. The younger children and Mrs. Mabrity filled the buckets while Max and the older ones took turns working the rope and pulleys to transfer the buckets to the top and down again. Mr. Mabrity and the oldest son unloaded them at the top.

When they finished Max loped across the sandy yard towards Abby. "Are you feeling better?"

She looked up to his face and smiled, pleased by his eagerness to rejoin her. "Yes, I believe I am."

He looked at her hopefully, "Do you think you're well enough to climb the stairs to the top?"

Abby carefully stood up to ascertain how she felt. Max reflexively put out a hand to steady her. Not finding any lingering weakness she decided she could manage it. "I believe so."

Max smiled broadly, his dimples accentuating his boyish enthusiasm. "Come on. You'll love the view at the top. You too, Maria."

They met Mrs. Mabrity at the entrance to the lighthouse. She strongly objected to Abby exerting herself so soon but Max and Abby convinced her it was safe enough so she let them pass as long as Abby promised to rest several times on the way up. Abby had never been more than three stories high in her life and she was too excited by the possibility of seeing over the treetops to heed Mrs. Mabrity's advice. Looking up the center of the lighthouse at the spiral of narrow wooden stairs Abby almost reconsidered but desperately wanting to see the island from the top she tackled the stairs one at a time.

Abby was doing fine; she was even keeping up with Max but after going only a dozen stairs Maria was forced to go back down having discovered a heretofore unknown fear of heights. Max and Abby continued without her. About halfway up they came to a small open window. They stopped for a moment to let her rest in the refreshing breeze and to take turns looking out the window where they could see just over the treetops. Max patiently waited until Abby said she was ready to continue. The short respite and excitement helped propel her up the last of the steps. They reached the service room below the lantern where a spry middle aged man was working.

Max greeted him with a handshake. "Mr. Mabrity. How are you?"

"Good, good. And you Max?"

"Never been better, Mr. Mabrity. May I present Miss Abigail Bennington? She has climbed the stairs to see our island. Miss Bennington, this is Mr. Michael Mabrity, our esteemed light keeper."

"Now son, don't you go giving this old salt airs that don't belong. How do you do Miss? Welcome, welcome. You two go enjoy the view while I finish trimming the wicks on these lamps so they are ready come sunset. It's way past my bedtime."

Concerned Abby said, "Oh sir, forgive us. I apologize if we are keeping you from your chores."

Mr. Mabrity brushed aside her guilt. "Not at all Miss. We were running a bit behind due to the storm last night but Max here helped us out so all is well. You just enjoy yourself. That's a mighty hard climb up those stairs not to make it worth your while."

Abby gave him a smile and a nod. "Thank you and your wife for your kindness and your hospitality Mr. Mabrity."

"Nothing to it, lass. Just being neighbourly."

Max asked, "Do you mind, sir, if I show her the lantern?"

Mr. Mabrity nodded to the stairs leading to the lantern room above. "Go on up but mind your fingerprints. I just cleaned the glass."

Max led the way turning at the top to offer his assistance to Abby. The smell of vinegar used to clean the windows permeated the round glass room. Fifteen Argand lamps with parabolic reflectors occupied the center. The walkway around was very narrow and not wanting to risk ruining Mr. Mabrity's hard work Abby led the way back down after only a quick look. Max then coaxed Abby out to the main gallery, a metal platform surrounding the lighthouse outside the service room, to view the island.

Abby stepped outside first. She leaned over the railing to look straight down. Feeling a wave of vertigo, she quickly returned to an upright position and leaned away from the railing. "Oh my goodness... and we are on solid ground. How do sailors climb the mast of a moving ship?" Abby's gaze skimmed the treetops automatically seeking the horizon. Instantly she felt better.

Max said in matter-of-fact manner, "The first time is the worst. After... you become accustomed to the height or you find another occupation."

Testing his words Abby cautiously leaned over again. Max was right. A moment more was all it took for her to grow comfortable looking towards the ground. Proud of her accomplishment she shared a smile of pleasure with him. Nothing had ever given Max as much pleasure as pleasing Abby.

They looked in silence for a few moments enjoying the vista. The town was off to their left, the undeveloped eastern side to their right and the ocean at their back. From this vantage, she could nearly count all the roofs in town. It was easy to locate Mrs. Mallory's boardinghouse and the Lambert's home.

The breeze was stronger at this height and it worked to loosen the hair from Abby's braids. She tucked the tendrils behind her ears drawing Max's attention. He wanted to do it for her. Instead, he pointed to a few places of interest including the location of the salt ponds on the eastern side of the island discernible by the lack of trees.

"What is a salt pond?" asked Abby.

"Just as it sounds, a pond filled with salt water from the tides such as the one behind the town. Evaporation causes salt to collect around the edges of the pond. It can be harvested by controlling the tidal flow. There are plans to do so with the ponds on the east end. It is one of the few natural resources we have to export."

"I would like to see them," said Abby, more than a little curious.

"I'll take you someday."

Despite the trial of her walk today, Abby knew she would like to do more exploring with Max. She studied the profile of the man beside her trying to gauge the depth of his feelings for her and for his home. When he turned to her she asked, "What is it about this island that keeps you here? That makes you want to make this your home? I have not traveled much, but I know this certainly is not the grandest island. It is beautiful but it has its downside of being nearly flat and hot, lacking in fresh water and civilized comforts."

Max added half-serious, "Don't forget the mosquitoes and sand flies making it downright miserable in summer and the bouts of yellow fever turning it deadly." He was quiet and thoughtful for a moment. "I originally came here because of familiarity having fished these waters with Captain Hamilton, but I guess I've come to love it because I have no desire to be anywhere else." He turned to her and she had the impression his words meant more than what he said. "I like that this town is just beginning to develop and I can take a part in shaping its history, like helping to build this lighthouse."

She watched as he lovingly ran his hand along the circular brick wall behind them and found herself with a desire to feel those long fingers touching her. Snapping her attention back to the conversation in an effort to control her wayward thoughts she replied, "I can see how it would be appealing to help build something new. In England, everything is old and set, new ideas are hard to come by but this place seems to inspire them."

She looked down at the feel of his hand brushing the back of hers. It was the first time he had touched her intimately since the ship wreck. Her hands had been bare then too but her preoccupation in retrieving the chest had kept her from noticing the feel of his touch. This time all of her senses were focused on the sensation of his work roughened skin against hers and there went her breath again, shallow and tight. *Why was the simple process of breathing, unthought-of before, now difficult because of him?* She had never experienced this before him.

Her eyes flew to his face not sure what she was reading there but feeling undeniably drawn to him as a moth to a flame. Max leaned a little closer to her and her eyes dropped to his lips. She could feel his desire to kiss her, a mirror image of her own. She leaned another degree closer to him. Her head started swimming again but this time had nothing to do with height or with the sun's heat. It was all because of the handsome visage in front of her drawing her ever closer. His lips were a breath away. Anticipation filled her. Until a throat cleared beyond Max's shoulder breaking the spell and startling them apart.

Mr. Mabrity had a knowing look on his face and she felt herself blush all the way to her toes, completely mortified. She turned away to face the beach side of the lighthouse. The ocean breeze helped to cool her burning cheeks. She heard Max and Mr. Mabrity talking behind her but with the wind in her ears she couldn't make out what they were saying. The calm turquoise water beckoned. She walked around the lighthouse until she was facing the sea and the endless expanse of water and sky broken only by the sails of the passing ships. One of the Mabrity boys was playing along the shoreline. He waved when he noticed her. She waved back. He skipped down the beach stopping every now and then to examine whatever the tide had brought in of interest.

Max approached her from the left. She looked to the right expecting to find Mr. Mabrity but the gallery was vacant. She turned back to Max with a questioning look. She hoped they could stay but she was sure Mr. Mabrity had chastised Max and they would not be allowed to be alone for long.

He asked, "Are you ready to leave?" He gestured for her to go to the right towards the stairs.

She walked slowly to the doorway soaking in the view along the way. Mr. Mabrity was waiting in the service room to escort them down.

Abby pondered the depth of her feelings for Max as she descended the depths of the lighthouse. She was attracted to him, there was no doubt he was a handsome man. She liked the way he looked at her. She enjoyed spending time with him. He was kind and thoughtful, courteous and considerate. Not too serious. He had a nice sense of humor. Oh dear, she wasn't finding anything she disliked. And what about his feelings? He had wanted to kiss her. He must want to spend time with her too, he invented this walk to do so, and Tria said he was acting differently with her than any other female. She may not know where these feelings would lead her but she was certain of one thing: she would rather have a lifetime of this breathless anticipation than to never have experienced it at all.

They bid their farewells and offered many thanks to the Mabrity's then headed back to town. Max was silent the whole way back which took longer as he set a much slower pace and checked on her often to assure she was doing fine in the afternoon heat. He chose to take the longer way of walking around the edge of the pond rather than testing her balance across the footbridge again. She appreciated the gesture although it was her feelings for him rather than the heat keeping her unbalanced. She wondered if his silence was to avoid speaking of their almost kiss. Abby hoped he was as disappointed as she was to have been interrupted. She wished she could ask him but she was too shy to broach the subject first.

They were approaching the houses on Whitehead Street when Max asked her, "Where would you like me to take you?"

"I'm not sure. How long do you think we have been gone?"

"More than two hours."

"I guess to the milliner's as we planned." Abby didn't want to think how awkward the situation could be if Tria had returned home without her.

"I agree."

They walked side by side down Front Street without talking or touching, followed by Maria. Max finally broke his silence. "What is your home like in England?"

She wasn't sure if he asked from sincere interest or if he was simply making an attempt at a neutral conversation. "It's colder. The trees would be nearly bare now and the winds would have a winter bite to them. Only the hearty winter birds would remain and they are much quieter. It is colourful for a while. Everything will have turned to shades of orange, gold and yellow except for the sky which seems to remain a perpetual shade of grey after summer. Then everything goes drab until it is covered with snow."

"It is much the same in New England and not very appealing."

"No, I suppose not. But that is winter. Spring brings flower blossoms in many colours, new green growth everywhere and all the birds are singing their mating songs. Summer has a much brighter colour palette and our warmest days may not compete with yours but they are very pleasant."

"That is something the island is lacking. Here there are only two...." Max stopped speaking mid-sentence as Captain Talmage's first mate, Santos, suddenly blocked their path.

He was looking for a fight.

Chapter 12

Santos was a bad-tempered Spaniard, short and wiry, with an inferiority complex. He faced Max with a challenging attitude while six of his crewmen fanned out behind him in support. A seventh man, uncomfortable with the developing situation, lingered behind. Feeling confident in his attack Santos said, "Blaggard, you been harrasin' one of my men and now yer gonna answer for it."

Max not only held his ground he feigned impassivity. "What are you yammerin' about Santos?"

The men gathered closer in a more threatening manner. Santos continued, "Amos here says you been giving him what for, tellin' him what he needs say to the law or else."

Max noticed Amos, coward that he was, standing furthest away trying to blend into the bushes. Amos had been in the hold when Max rescued Abby, probably assigned by Talmage to guard Max and his crew in case they did more than rescue passengers. When Max had discovered him alone in a bar last night he took the opportunity to try and appeal to the man's sense of honour and decency. He knew it was probably a wasted effort but he had to try for Abby's sake. Now it appeared not only had he not helped their cause but he had put her in more danger with the current situation.

Maria pulled on Abby's sleeve to bring her behind Max and closer to whisper, "Miss, this doesn't look good. These men be spoiling for a fight. His ship is just ahead, I'm going to get help." Abby nodded her agreement. Maria waited another moment before slipping back the way they had come to circle around behind the building and get to the ship without the other crew taking notice.

Abby refrained from watching Maria's progress not wanting to draw attention to her. She breathed a sigh of relief when she saw Maria cross behind the angry men then start running towards the wharf, her movements unnoticed by the men. Returning her attention to the situation at hand Abby caught the end of Max's response, his voice rising in anger. "...chest was not part of the cargo and the law clearly states luggage is not part of the salvage to be auctioned. It should be returned to its rightful owner and it shouldn't take a judge to make that happen." Max tossed a quick glance over his shoulder to ascertain Abby's position. He had a bad feeling about what was going to happen next.

"Shut up, you bilge rat. Yer not gonna tell me or my crew what to do and as far as I'm concerned that chest is a prize, rightfully salvaged and my friend here is gonna make sure you don't soon forget your place."

Santos stepped aside and the man behind him moved forward to face Max. Abby gasped when she noticed one of the men off to the left had a knife in his hand. She had to warn Max, but how?

Max addressed Santos, "You coward. You send another man in to fight for you." He turned back to the man in front of him just in time to block his punch and then shove him backwards. "Leo, there's no reason we need to fight. Message received loud and clear, just let us pass."

Santos rammed himself into Max's side. Caught unaware while talking to Leo, he stumbled towards Abby. Santos stood over him. "No one calls me a coward."

Max quickly regained his feet and landed a solid punch square on Santo's jaw. "I believe I just did."

Santos was knocked off his feet. He lay on the ground, momentarily stunned. Leo surged towards Max trying to land another blow to his chin. Max ducked and then swung around and punched Leo in the back of his gut sending him sprawling next to Santos. Two more of the crew attacked Max while he was still turned with his back to them. Abby cringed as he took both of their hits.

She desperately looked around for something, anything to use as a weapon and wished for the second time that day she had brought her parasol. It would have been very useful for jabbing or thrashing their attackers. She spotted a small piece of limestone. She picked it up not sure how it was going to help and found Max now being held by two while a third one punched him and Leo was headed into the fray intending to attack him from behind. Fortunately Leo's back was to her. She hurled her weapon as hard as she could at the man and rejoiced to hit her mark on the back of his head just where she had aimed. Rejoiced, that is, until he turned and headed in her direction. She backed up a few steps only to find herself pressed against the rough wooden planks of the building behind her. She looked to her right and left trying to decide which path would lead her to safety when a commotion distracted them all.

It was Max's crew descending on them with makeshift weapons from the ship. Mr. Keats called out, "Six to one ain't no way to fight you scoundrels. Let's see how you handle a real fight." Leo turned from her to face this new threat along with all the others except for the one with the knife who now circled Max holding his knife in one hand and Max's machete in the other. Abby held her breath as he made several swipes at Max and missed but his strikes were so close she would swear at least one had cut his shirt. Max fended off a few more blows and managed to land a blow knocking the machete from his assailant's hand before the other knife sliced his arm. Abby screamed at the same time he winced from the sting of the blade. She had no idea how Max managed to land another punch across the man's face forcing him to step backwards and causing his lip to bleed. The pause gave Mr. Keats, who had already dispatched his opponent, a chance to step in and punch the man again before knocking the remaining knife from his hand. When the man regained his ground he noticed the rest of Talmage's crew was leaving and he decided to join them, post-haste, leaving his knife behind. Mr. Keats picked it up, cleaned it on his pants and tucked it under his belt. Max retrieved his machete.

Abby rushed to Max's side. She lifted the hem of her dress and ripped a piece of her underskirt to wrap around his upper arm to stop the bleeding, his shirt was already soaked past the elbow, while Max verified the safety of his crew. The others only sported a few minor bruises. She tied off the temporary bandage and looked around for her maid. Not finding her she started to fear the worst. "Where's Maria?"

Mr. Keats answered, "She's safe. Thomas made her stay with him on the ship. Wasn't easy. I think he had to bodily keep her from following us to get back to you Miss. Come now gents, let's head back and raise our mugs to those running cowards."

Stunned Abby asked, "You are not going to press charges against them?"

"What for?" asked Mr. Keats, clearly puzzled.

"For attacking us with weapons and without cause."

"Generally speaking, these kinds of fights happen all the time and nothing's done about it unless one of the combatants is crocked or someone gets hurt. Then they're put in the Sweat Box. You see that old ship cabin over yonder?" Mr. Keats pointed to a small wooden structure not far from where they stood.

"Someone did get hurt," said Abby.

Max protested, "It's just a scratch."

"Scratch, my foot, Captain Eatonton. You have bled all down your shirt and you probably need stitches. You need a doctor and those 'pirates' should be put in your Sweat Box."

"Now Miss Bennington, calm down. I've had enough wounds in my life to know when one is serious and this one isn't. A little cleaning and a good bandage - not that yours is bad - and I'll be fine. Now let's get back to the *Mystic* so we can let Maria know you're all right. She's probably worried sick about you."

Abby didn't believe him about his wound but chose to follow his lead as she was sure he was right about Maria.

Approaching Max's ship they could see Maria pacing the deck. When she spotted them coming up the dock she nearly flew across the gangplank in her rush to get to Abby. "Oh Miss, you're alright. They got there in time. I ran as fast as I could and then Thomas wouldn't let me get back to you. I was so worried they would hurt you. I couldn't live with myself if anything happened to you because I didn't stay."

Abby grasped her hands, "You did right. You saved me by getting help and they did arrive just in time. Thank you for your quick thinking." She turned Maria and together they walked back towards the ship. Max followed behind while his crew headed to their favourite haunt in town for celebratory drinks. Once on deck Abby turned on Max. "Captain, I will see that your wound is properly cleaned and ascertain for myself the necessity for stitches." Max started to protest but Abby stopped him. "No, you will not argue with me. This whole situation is because of my possessions and your attempts to protect them so it is the least I can do to repay you. Maria, would you please bring some water and have Mr. Thomas find whatever medical supplies are aboard this ship. Captain, if you would have a seat on the crate over there I will get to work."

At this point Max decided it would be easiest to do as she asked. He took a seat on the crate and started rolling up his sleeve until he was stopped by her makeshift bandage.

Abby brushed his hand aside and undid the knot, carefully unwrapping his arm. "It would be best if you removed your shirt as the cut is high on your arm."

Max hesitated. Her request was highly improper, even he knew that. Seeing her determined look, he gave in and shrugged out of his shirt with Abby's assistance in gently pulling it away from the dried blood from his wound. The bleeding had stopped. She gingerly touched the edges of the cut testing for depth and how easily it might start bleeding again. She then made a survey of the rest of his upper body looking for any other cuts or bruises in need of tending all the while trying to ignore the hard muscles of his chest and abdomen and the nervous butterflies wreaking havoc in her midsection.

She was now thankful for all the times she had accompanied Miss Winterfeldt to the orphanage. Those children had been in many a fight acquiring all sorts of injuries. Abby had mostly only watched Miss Winterfeldt work but she must have picked up more about nursing than she had realized. Maria and Thomas brought a bowl of water, salve and fresh linen strips setting them down on the crate next to her. She soaked a towel in the water and started cleaning the dried blood from his arm. Maria mumbled something about not liking blood and left them.

Max decided to take advantage of the situation. While Abby was turned away, he gave Thomas a meaningful look, sending him trailing after Maria. Abby finished cleansing his arm and was relieved to see for herself Max was right. The cut was shallow. She gently applied the salve and then bandaged his arm with a fresh strip of linen.

Max's husky voice broke the silence. "You surprise me. I would not have expected a lady such as you to be such a competent nurse."

Abby paused in her task, surprised by his compliment. "This is my first."

"I suppose there is not much call for doctoring gentlemen since they probably don't fight much. How did you come by such knowledge?"

"You are forgetting gentlemen occasionally duel and have hunting accidents."

"Still those are gentlemanly pursuits - not street brawling - and you didn't answer my question."

"My governess insisted I learn, in case it was needed."

"How fortunate for me then to have you nearby."

"It would seem so, Captain Eatonton."

"I suppose a real gentleman would have found a way to walk away from that scene without fighting," said Max in a self-deprecating tone.

Abby immediately defended him. "You are more of a gentleman then you give yourself credit for Captain Eatonton." Abby finished her bandage and smoothed the edges against his arm before stepping back from him. "There, it should heal fine."

"What happened to 'Captain Max' or better yet just 'Max'? Why the return to such formality, especially as we are alone?" Standing, Max stepped closer to her.

"That is precisely why. We are improperly alone."

"How will using my surname keep you from feeling what you do?" Max moved infinitesimally closer to her.

"Sir, a gentleman would keep his distance," said Abby, weakly, as she stared at the wall of his chest.

"But, I am not a gentleman." He lifted her face with the finger and thumb of his right hand on her chin forcing her eyes to meet his, to see the desire burning in their depths. Her pupils dilated and her lips parted slightly. He rubbed his thumb slowly across her petal soft lower lip and felt the increase in her pulse and the hitch in her breath. He also felt her start to tremble. Fearing she might pull away he placed a hand on either side of her head, brushing his thumbs across her cheekbones before tilting it to the perfect angle as he lowered his face to hers.

She watched his lips descend to hers, slowly, as if he thought he might frighten her away. He needn't have worried. It was as if she was tied to him and could not have moved away even if she had tried. Her eyes closed as his lips finally met hers and she released the breath she hadn't known she was holding on a sigh. His lips were soft, yet firm. This feeling was much more than she had ever been told it would be. She felt it everywhere. Her whole body melted. She leaned into Max, clinging to him for support. Her hands braced against the solid wall of his chest. To her disappointment he pulled away. He paused, hovering just above her face. She could feel his breath brush across her sensitized lips. She tried to open her eyelids to see what he intended to do next but they were so heavy. Then to her great relief he brought his lips back to hers for a kiss even more potent than the first. She moved her hands to his shoulders needing all his support as her muscles went lax. His hands drifted from her face, past her shoulders and down to her waist to pull her closer to him.

She was drowning in this kiss. Thoughts were gone, all she knew was the sweet sensation created by the movement of his lips across hers. They infected every portion of her being until he abruptly broke contact, setting her away from him. Her eyes flew open to see him turn away from her. He took a few steps running both his hands through his hair then dropped them to his side but he remained looking out to sea. Meanwhile, bereft of his support and not being steady on her feet, she collapsed onto the crate and waited for her mind and body to return to their normal rhythm.

Now she understood why Elizabeth could not fully explain what a kiss felt like and what she meant by all kisses were not the same even when they were received from the same person. Not being able to see his face she was unable to determine his feelings, and not wanting to make assumptions about the wall he suddenly seemed to have erected between them, she worked on sorting out her own feelings. She knew a kiss from him would be different than Isaac's but she was completely unprepared for the power it had over her senses. *What did that mean? Was she falling in love with him?* It probably shouldn't surprise her as her mother had fallen for a sailor and she herself loved the sea. Maybe that was some of the attraction.

Regaining control of his emotions, Max decided it was time she was returned to her father. He turned back to the ship but avoided looking at her and whatever he might read in her eyes. He headed down to his cabin to retrieve a clean shirt. He was still stunned by how a little teasing flirtation and what he had intended as a simple kiss had turned into an abyss of emotions. Kissing Abigail had been unlike anything he had ever experienced before. He had tumbled his share of wenches without feeling any of this. Maybe it was because she was a lady. That had to be it. She was inexperienced and so he was feeling naturally protective. It was all because she was an English lady. At least that was what he wanted to believe. Deep down he knew this was different for another reason that he wasn't prepared to acknowledge.

When Max returned to the deck he found Abby cleaning the blood from his torn shirt. She looked at him expectantly. Not knowing how to answer the questions in her eyes he said, "Leave it," referring to the shirt. "I'll take care of it later. We need to get you back to Victoria."

Max, Abby and Maria walked silently to the milliner's shop at the end of Front Street. They hadn't really expected to find Victoria still lingering there so they were all quite surprised to be greeted by her at the door.

"My goodness, you sure took your time. I've now ordered twice as many hats as I need and Mr. August, the shopkeeper, must think I'm the most fickle-minded female he has ever met."

Abby hugged her friend not only happy to see her but needing her effervescent personality to lighten the mood after Max's silence. "Thank you for waiting. You are truly a dear friend."

"You would have done the same. Shall we return home then?"

Abby turned to look at Max expecting he would return to his ship. Instead he silently offered an arm to each of them walking between them to Victoria's with both maids trailing behind having their own hushed conversation.

Tria asked, "Did you two enjoy your walk?"

Max and Abby simultaneously answered, "Yes," then looked at each other.

Abby's lips compressed. "Except for the fight."

Tria gasped. "Fight?"

Max spoke up before Abby had a chance. "It was nothing, just some of Captain Talmage's men causing a fuss."

Abby added, "A knife wound is not 'nothing'."

Tria looked Max over. "You have a knife wound?"

"Just a scratch on my other arm and I received very competent care." Max shared a private smile with Abby.

Tria said, "You are fortunate it was not more serious."

Abby looked around Max to Tria, "It nearly was worse."

Reaching the entrance of her home, Tria turned to Max. "Won't you stay for supper, Captain Max?"

"Thank you for the offer Miss Victoria but I must decline. I have duties I have neglected too long already today."

Victoria didn't believe him. He had the look of a man desperate to escape the company of females. She wondered what had happened today and couldn't wait to get Abby alone. "You are always welcome, anytime. Thank you for the escort home." Sensing he wanted to speak to Abby alone, Victoria moved to the front door to give them some space. Their maids had already disappeared inside.

Abby tried to patiently wait for Max to speak first. When it seemed he wasn't going to she said, "Thank you for taking me to the lighthouse."

At the same time Max said, "I apologize if my behaviour was too forward."

This made them both smile and relieved some of the tension.

Abby said, "You needn't apologize."

"I think I do. It won't happen again. Thank you for taking care of my arm. Goodnight Miss Abigail." He turned and was gone, leaving Abby standing there with disappointment churning in her stomach and clearly showing on her face.

Tria returned to her side and linked arms with her. Watching Max's retreating figure she asked, "What won't happen again?"

Abby moved her head side to side and refused to answer. She wasn't ready to discuss her feelings, not even with Victoria.

No one questioned their long absence. In fact both their fathers were still discussing business until they were called to the evening meal. Much to her relief, Victoria didn't press Abby with any more questions. She and her father returned to the boardinghouse after the meal and Abby noticed her father was looking more tired than usual.

"Poppa, are you alright?"

Richard smiled weakly at his daughter. "Yes dear, just tired. Maybe it is the heat draining my energy. I believe I will retire early."

Abby was feeling fatigued herself from the events of her day so she readily accepted the excuse.

"By the way dear, Mr. Lambert has requested a list of all the jewelry in the chest."

"Certainly Poppa. I will do so this evening. Tell me please, what is hidden in the chest? Is it of great value?"

"A very special crown. I will tell you all about it another day. I am not feeling up to it tonight."

"I understand. Goodnight, Father."

They had reached the landing outside their rooms. Richard kissed her forehead, "Goodnight sweetheart," and went to his room.

Abby lay awake remembering the day's events and trying to determine if Max really meant what he had said or was he just saying what he thought she wanted to hear. *It won't happen again.* She finally drifted to sleep in the wee hours of the morning only to dream of sky blue eyes, tender caresses and tantalizing kisses.

Chapter 13

The next week was a long one for Abby but exciting for the town of Key West. Monday morning following the lighthouse escapade dawned bright and clear. Abby and Richard left the boardinghouse early to meet Mr. Lambert at the Custom House turned Court House. Today was Judge Webb's first court session. There were no court cases planned as it would mostly be court business of which Mr. Lambert had a vested interest and her father wanted to witness the making of history. Abby was there having only a passing curiosity and nothing better to do with her day.

They were fortunate they were able to find seating when they arrived at half past nine. Court wouldn't open until ten o'clock and already the room was almost filled to capacity. It was a momentous day for the little island settlement. The "wrecking court" as the islanders were calling it, was expected to bring people and prosperity from around the world to their small corner of it.

The Custom House was a simple wooden structure on the ocean side of Front Street near Clinton Place. It was built on stilts to protect it from storm surges. The room was full to bursting by the time court was called to order and the doors had to be shut against even more who were now gathered outside hoping to gain entry. The windows were opened to allow the breeze to pass through but it did little to alleviate the heat already starting to build with so many excited people seemingly all talking at once.

Abby sat quietly fanning herself and observing the assembly. Many were obviously there for business purposes but there were a lot of people especially towards the rear of the room who were there out of curiosity. Her eyes came to rest on a familiar blond Adonis standing on the side over her right shoulder. She hadn't seen him since the day of their kiss. That was five days ago. He was wearing a coat over his shirt in deference to the occasion and he looked as handsome as ever. He was easily the most well-favoured man in the room and suddenly she realized without a doubt she was falling for him. Max didn't look her way but her father noticed her staring. He turned to see what had caught her gaze. She couldn't tell if he figured out the source of her interest or not and not wanting to reveal too much she turned her attention back to the front of the room making a point to not look in Max's direction again. Occasionally she felt as if his eyes were on her but she refused to allow herself to look his way to confirm it. Of course he would be here. She should not have been surprised given his interest in building the city. He really cared about the growth and development of Key West. Still she had not prepared herself for facing him again.

A sudden hush fell across the room as Judge Webb appeared from one of the two side rooms, presumably his chambers, and a man announced, "All rise." He paused for everyone to stand. "Superior Court for the Southern Judicial District of the Territory of Florida at the Town of Key West in the County of Monroe on the 3rd day of November in the year of our Lord one thousand eight hundred and twenty eight is now in session. Present the honourable Judge James Webb."

They of course had already met Judge Webb at the ball held in his honour over a week ago so Abby was familiar with his person but she had expected to see him dressed for court in a periwig such as was still worn by the barristers in England. His exposed head of thinning dark hair in her mind made him seem less authoritative. Other than that the proceedings were every bit as formal as she could have imagined.

During the course of the morning the judge officially appointed and took sworn oaths from Joel Yancey - the man who had issued the opening speech - as Clerk for the court, Henry Wilson as District Marshal, and Edgar Macon as attorney and counselor for the court. The swearing in was a very serious and formal action, that seemed to take longer than necessary in Abby's opinion. Next the judge ordered the marshal to find thirty good and lawful men to report the next day at eleven o'clock for jury selection.

Judge Webb adjourned court until the following day. Upon the judge's departure, the crowd all stood at once to leave. With the single doorway, they had to wait their turn to pass through. By the time Abby made it to the outside of the building Max was nowhere to be seen. Just as well, it would have been inappropriate for her to seek him out and what could she say to him even if she did. Accusing him of avoiding her certainly wouldn't help matters.

The next day was much the same. Mr. Lambert and some other attorneys took oaths and Charles Wilson was chosen as deputy Marshal and sworn in. A jury was chosen from the thirty men brought in by the Marshal. They would serve for any case requiring a jury during the entire session or term of court. They were sent to the jury room, next to the judge's chambers, to await further instructions. Judge Webb then adjourned the court until Monday.

There were less people present the second day but the Custom House was still filled to capacity. Abby hadn't actually seen him but she had "felt" him behind her. This time when they exited the building she saw Max striding towards the wharf, probably returning to his ship. She was disappointed to have missed another chance to talk to him and frustrated it would most likely be Monday before another opportunity was presented to her.

Mr. Lambert stopped to tell her father he was able to schedule their case third on the docket for Monday. Richard thanked him and then he and Abby returned to the boardinghouse for their midday meal.

Thursday, Abby accompanied her father to the ship's chandler to see what progress had been made on the repairs to their ship. Her father was very pleased to learn the rudder not only was repairable, the repairs were almost complete.

Leaving the chandler's Richard told Abby, "Once this court business is finished we will be able to continue on our journey. Good news, is it not, Abby girl?"

Abby was of two minds on the matter but simply responded, "Yes, Father. Good news indeed," in as lighthearted a manner as she could muster.

Richard wondered at her tone. It had a hollow ring to it which made him curious as to which ties would make her want to stay. He had a growing suspicion it had more to do with a certain captain than with her new found friend. His opinion of the lad had certainly grown in esteem since first they met but he could not yet say he believed him worthy of his daughter's affections. He would have to make a point of learning more of his character starting with the opinions of the other islanders.

On Sunday Abby and her father accompanied Mrs. Mallory to the Custom House to attend the only worship service offered on the island since a church of any kind had yet to be built. Mrs. Mallory was aflutter as a clergyman had 'washed up' on the island this week and had agreed to offer this morning's service. She had rushed them through their breakfast and now set a brisk pace to reach the Custom House early so they would have seats knowing many islanders would be in attendance. Abby listened to her father and Mrs. Mallory discuss the need for a permanent minister and a church building and how the town might go about securing the funds for such an undertaking.

Waiting for the service to start, Abby's gaze swept the room looking for sun-kissed curls. Not finding him, she kept watch of the newcomers only to be disappointed when the service began and he had not appeared. She had seen the *Mystic* at its berth before entering the building and had hoped he would be in attendance. It would be disappointing if he was not a religious man.

The judge's chamber door opened to a very tall kind looking man with greying temples who proceeded to the front of the room. The service was simple with only the preacher's sermon and a few hymns sung without accompaniment led by a local gentleman with a rich tenor voice. Abby was surprised to find more meaning in this simple worship than she had ever gained from the elaborate services of her home Church of England. Here worship was not taken for granted. These islanders pulled together to fulfill their need and appreciated what they had. To them this service was more than just an obligation and the feeling carried through to her. She could never have imagined she would learn the fullness of faith and worship in such a simple place.

During the opening hymn Abby felt as if she was being watched. She discretely turned her head to look behind her. Piercing blue eyes captured her from the back of the room and her heart fluttered. It took a nudge from her father's arm to break the spell. She turned her attention forward with the speed of guilt and did not turn around again but often felt his gaze on her for the rest of the service.

When it was over, he was gone. She felt keenly disappointed having missed yet another opportunity to talk to him. She was sure he felt something for her but without speaking to him she had no idea how deep those feelings were and she was afraid to let her own take hold in case it was all for naught. She wondered again just what his avoidance really signified. How horridly embarrassing if he had determined from one kiss he did not have any feelings for her in much the same way as she had discovered she had no feelings for Isaac Landis. She pondered the distressing thought on the return walk to the boardinghouse but kept returning to the same conclusion. It just wasn't possible he could be disinterested. If that were the case she would not have found him watching her. Which brought her back to why was he avoiding her?

Richard and Abby spent the rest of the afternoon with Mrs. Mallory and another guest of the boardinghouse reading in the parlour. Abby finally gave up the pretense around four, finding herself too distracted by her thoughts. She retreated to her room to write another letter to Elizabeth in the hopes that maybe putting her thoughts to paper would help her find some peace.

It was late afternoon, Monday, November 10th, when the clerk finally called their case much to Abby's relief having grown exceedingly tired of following the proceedings of the two previous claims, or maybe, her irritation had more to do with the lack of appearance by Captain Eatonton. She had thought he would be here today, of all days, as he would offer testimony on their behalf. Apparently the proceedings of the court had lost their charm for many. Returning from the afternoon break there were now numerous empty chairs, including two to her right. She and her father were sitting two rows back from the claimants' tables.

Captain Talmage and his lawyer, Mr. Williams, took their places in front of the judge at a table on the left while Mr. Lambert and Captain Andrews were on the right. Since theirs was an admiralty suit for theft at sea, technically called a *causa spoln civils et maritima*, there would not be a jury.

Judge Webb asked Mr. Lambert to present his case to the court. Focused on the proceedings, Abby was startled by a presence slipping into the seat next to her. Turning to see who had entered so late she found herself face to face with Captain Eatonton and the now familiar reaction he created in her. Next to him was his first mate, Jonathon Keats. Sitting up a little straighter, she returned her attention to Mr. Lambert who had started his opening remarks.

"The evening of the 20th of October, the *Abigail Rose* became stranded on Loggerhead Reef. Captain Andrews agreed to a set amount for the assistance of Captain Talmage and his crew to remove the passengers, personal belongings and cargo and to release the *Abigail Rose* from the reef. Captain Andrews reminded Captain Talmage the salvage prize did not include the passenger luggage to which Captain Talmage agreed. Captain Talmage violated the agreement by taking into his possession as part of the salvage a small jewelry chest belonging to Miss Bennington."

Captain Talmage suddenly stood and declared, "I did not take any such chest!"

Mr. Williams tugged on his sleeve trying to pull Talmage back to his seat. Judge Webb rapped his gavel on the table. "Sir, sit down. You are out of turn. Is that not your lawyer next to you?"

"Aye," replied Talmage.

Judge Webb frowned in displeasure at his less than respectful response. "Then it is his duty to defend your claim at the proper time. I suggest you let him. Another outburst from you and I will declare you in contempt of court."

Talmage returned to his seat and Mr. Lambert continued where he had left off. "Captain Eatonton requested the chest be returned to him for transport to Miss Bennington and was denied by Captain Talmage. Furthermore, the location of the missing chest is unknown at present as it is not in storage with the rest of the ship's cargo. My client, Mr. Bennington, is filing a claim for the return of the chest and all of its contents."

Judge Webb then addressed Talmage's lawyer. "Mr. Williams, your opening statement please."

Mr. Williams stood and addressed the judge. "Captain Talmage did not take nor does he have possession of said chest from the *Abigail Rose*. All cargo is in storage at the warehouse of Mr. Greene. He is of the opinion Captain Eatonton's crew has misplaced the missing trunk."

Mr. Williams returned to his seat and all was quiet for a moment except for the scratching of Judge Webb's pen as he finished his notes before starting his questioning.

"Mr. Lambert, who removed the chest from the hold?"

Mr. Lambert stood to reply. "That would be Mr. Keats sir. He is the first mate of the *Mystic*."

"Is he present?"

Mr. Keats stood to answer for himself. "Aye, sir."

The clerk hurried forward with Bible in hand instructing Mr. Keats to raise his right hand and place his left on the Bible. Mr. Yancey said, "Sir, do you solemnly swear to tell the truth, the whole truth, and nothing but the truth, so help you God?"

Mr. Keats replied, "I swear."

This scene was repeated for each new witness called. Mr. Yancey retreated and Judge Webb began his questioning. "Where was the chest located, Mr. Keats?"

"It was dropped by Miss Bennington as she was being rescued from the hold. I retrieved it from the top of a barrel and brought it up first at Captain Eatonton's request."

"If it was on top of a barrel why did you believe it to be her personal property?"

"It did not look to be cargo and her trunks had been stacked nearby, one of which was opened."

"Did you see her remove it from her trunk?"

"No sir but I'm sure Captain Eatonton did."

"Is Captain Eatonton present?"

Max stood up next to Jonathon, "Yes sir."

"Did you see her remove the chest in question from her trunk?"

Max hesitated. He looked down at Abby as if in apology before replying to the judge. "No sir, I did not." Judge Webb considered this and when it seemed no other question was forthcoming Max and Jonathon returned to their seats.

Abby leaned towards Max and said in a whisper louder than she had intended, "What do you mean you didn't see me? Of course you did." At this Max, Mr. Lambert and her father all hissed at her to be quiet.

The judge heard her. "You must be Miss Bennington."

Abby reluctantly got to her feet and meekly replied, "Yes sir."

"Pray tell young lady, what were you doing in the hold of a wrecked ship?"

"I was retrieving a jewelry chest that belonged to my dearly departed mother."

"And you believed this chest to be worth more than your life?"

"To be honest sir, at the time, I did not feel my life was in danger. That may have been naive of me but it is the truth of it."

"I agree, it was naive. Please sit down Miss Bennington. Mr. Lambert, have your client provide a description of this chest before you leave here today."

"I have one ready for you sir." Mr. Lambert approached the bench to hand Judge Webb the paper. "It also includes a list of articles inside the chest." Mr. Lambert then leaned over to whisper to Judge Webb so no one else in the court could overhear. "Please note it is believed the Bennington's are the only ones who know of the last item and Mr. Bennington is the only one who has laid eyes on it as it is in a well hidden compartment."

"I see," acknowledged Judge Webb and motioned him to return to his seat.

"Mr. Lambert, did anyone from Captain Talmage's crew witness the removal of Miss Bennington or the chest from the hold?"

"Mr. Amos Hardy, crewman of the *Sinistral*, was present in the hold according to Captain Eatonton."

"Is Mr. Hardy present?"

Mr. Williams replied, "No sir. Captain Talmage was unable to locate him."

Judge Webb addressed the clerk. "Mr. Yancey, you will issue a summons for Mr. Hardy to appear in this court at 10 o'clock sharp tomorrow morning so he may be questioned."

Mr. Yancey nodded, "Yes sir."

Max did not care for the look that passed between Leo and Talmage. It did not bode well for the case or for Amos and maybe both.

Judge Webb then asked Mr. Lambert, "What evidence is there that Captain Talmage has possession of said chest?"

Mr. Lambert replied, "Mr. Keats emerged from the hold with the chest at which point Captain Talmage demanded he hand it over to his crew."

Addressing Mr. Keats directly, Judge Webb asked, "Is this true?"

Standing quickly, Mr. Keats answered, "Aye, sir," returning to his seat just as quick, reminding Abby of a rabbit peeking out of its burrow. It was all she could do to hide her grin behind her gloved hand.

Looking towards Talmage the judge asked, "Did you order your men to take the chest from Mr. Keats?"

Mr. Williams nudged Talmage, reminding him to stand before responding. "No. He handed it to them when I asked what he was carrying, as if he was guilty."

Max laid a restraining hand on Jonathon's arm to keep him from protesting Talmage's lie.

The judge asked Talmage, "Which *Sinistral* crewmember took the chest?"

Talmage shrugged his shoulders. Irritated with the man, Judge Webb looked to Mr. Lambert for an answer.

Mr. Lambert reviewed his notes. "Mr. Keats said he handed the chest to Mr. Santos, the *Sinistral's* first mate, who passed it to a crewman they call 'Fish'. I don't have his given name."

"Are either of them present?"

Mr. Santos, seated behind Talmage, stood and replied, "Aye. I'm Santos."

"Mr. Santos, did you take the chest aboard the *Sinistral?*"

"No."

"Did the other crewman you call 'Fish' take it aboard then?"

"Don't know if he did."

Addressing the court in general Judge Webb asked, "Is 'Fish' present?"

Mr. Santos quickly answered, "No."

"Mr. Yancey, please issue a summons for 'Fish' as well." Pushing forward, Judge Webb tried another tactic with Mr. Santos. "Did Captain Talmage order 'Fish' to take the chest?"

"No, he did not."

"What did 'Fish' do with the chest?"

"I don't know."

"Mr. Santos, are you not the first mate of the *Sinistral?*"

"Aye."

"Then shouldn't you know where 'Fish' took the chest?"

"I did not follow him."

"Where did you instruct him to take the cargo of the *Abigail Rose?*"

"To the hold."

"Which hold?" Judge Webb firmly asked.

"The *Sinistral's.*"

"Is that where he took the chest?"

"I did not see where he took the chest."

"Are you saying 'Fish' took the chest for himself?"

"I wouldn't know. I did not follow him to see where he took the chest."

"Please be seated Mr. Santos."

Abby had the impression Judge Webb was irritated at getting the same answer and had given up with Mr. Santos.

"Mr. Keats, was anyone else present at this exchange other than Captain Talmage, Mr. Santos and 'Fish' to support your claim?"

Rising Mr. Keats reluctantly replied, "No sir, none that I can recollect."

Judge Webb opened his timepiece and then snapped it shut. "Mr. Williams, I charge you with the appearance of Mr. Hardy and the crewman known as 'Fish' at court opening. If they fail to answer the summons, warrants will be issued." He banged his gavel, causing Abby to involuntarily jump. "Court is adjourned until 10 o'clock tomorrow morning."

As soon as the judge quit the room, Max turned to Abby. "Please forgive me Miss Bennington. I had to tell the truth."

Quietly Abby said, "I would never ask you to lie. I was only surprised you hadn't seen me."

"You handed me the dress box, remember? And I turned to pass it to your father when you were removing the chest so although I'm reasonably sure I know where the chest was located originally I didn't actually see it."

Abby wanted to ask why he had avoided her last week but how did one broach such a subject when there was nothing more than a simple kiss between them, putting aside the fact that emotionally the kiss was anything but simple. It certainly wasn't just a kiss for her and she was willing to stake her reputation it hadn't been for him either. Whatever had happened between them she felt sure had caught him by surprise. Which she supposed was the answer to her question. He was avoiding his feelings for her. So instead of questioning him she continued the conversation at hand preferring it to none at all. "Of course, you were right to answer as you did. I would never expect you to tell a falsehood."

"That is pirating!"

Her father's sudden outburst brought Max and Abby's attention to her father's conversation with Mr. Lambert and Captain Andrews.

"He as much as stole the chest. There has got to be a way to prove it." Feeling a pain in his chest Richard tried to calm down. "Mr. Lambert, this doesn't seem to be going well. We cannot prove Abby pulled the chest from the trunk. We have no way to prove Captain Talmage or his crew has the chest since they will surely protect each other. What happens when the testimonies of both his crewmen tomorrow leave us exactly where we are right now? How can the judge rule in our favour?"

Mr. Lambert tried to reassure them. "On testimony alone he would not be able to but I think the description and list we presented will help balance the scale in our favour."

"Are you sure of this?" questioned Richard.

"Of course not but you said yourself you judged him to be a reasonable man with an intelligent mind," said Mr. Lambert.

"So we are to pray it is enough?" Richard continued, "It is bad enough I have to sell my goods at auction to pay for the salvage and the court costs but to deal with such underhanded 'pirating' is more than I can stand."

The conversation was starting to make Max uncomfortable. He had a part in the salvage expenditure and although he had nothing to feel guilty about he still felt guilty all the same. "Mr. Bennington, Mr. Lambert, Captain Andrews, Miss Bennington, I believe I will bid you good evening." He bowed his head to each of them and as he received their return greetings he noticed Mr. Bennington turn a ghostly white just before collapsing. Acting quickly he caught the elder gentleman before he slipped to the ground.

Abby cried out in distress, "Father!" She rushed to his side, waving her fan in his face pleading, "Father, please open your eyes." He didn't which brought Abby to a near panic. She looked from Captain Eatonton to Captain Andrews to Mr. Lambert silently pleading with them to help. Help her father, do something, she knew not what, just do - something. It seemed like long minutes passed before Mr. Lambert mentioned a cart close by they could borrow but it had probably only been seconds. Another eternity passed as she watched her father's face for any signs of regaining consciousness.

The cart arrived. Max still held her father by his shoulders. Someone else picked up his feet and he was moved to the cart. Abby placed her reticule under his head wishing she had something softer. Max shrugged out of his coat, balled it up and handed it to her. He then carefully lifted her father's head so she could exchange 'pillows'. They started the walk to the boardinghouse. She was aware of the men around her, of the occasional murmured words of reassurance but she was entirely focused on her father. One strange thought occurred during the ghastly trip to the boardinghouse; she wondered if her father would consider it to be more embarrassing to be taken by cart or to be carried.

Once they reached the boardinghouse Mrs. Mallory immediately took charge of the situation, directing the men to take her father to his room and forcing Abby to take a seat on the divan in the parlour. Abby sat there for only a few minutes until the numbness of shock wore off. She gained her feet just as the men returned filing down the stairs. Captain Eatonton and Mr. Lambert quietly nodded as they exited the front doorway. Captain Andrews made his way to her. She didn't like the solemn look on his face.

"Miss Abigail, has your father mentioned he has been ailing for some time now?"

Abby couldn't speak around the lump in her throat so she merely shook her head from side to side.

"I know he planned to tell you soon. It's his heart. The doctors have warned him to take it easy. I suppose the stress of today was too much."

"Has..." her voice failed so she cleared her throat and tried again, "has a doctor been called?"

"Dr. Waterhouse has been sent for although I'm told there is no one better to care for him on the island than Mrs. Mallory."

Abby could see over Captain Andrews' shoulder Mrs. Mallory descending the stairs and rushed around the captain to meet her at the bottom step. Mrs. Mallory brushed back the hair from the side of Abby's head and gently said in her Irish brogue, "He opened his eyes love and tis asking for you."

Abby barely had the presence of mind to say "thank you" before dashing up the stairs. She paused outside her father's room to compose herself for his sake. She then quietly rapped on the door with the back of her hand before entering the room. She was struck first by how small her father looked resting against the pillows. It made her heart wrench. Next she noticed some of his colour had returned and he had a weak smile for her. He lifted his hand towards her and she hurried to his bedside to grasp it, sinking into the chair thoughtfully placed there.

"Oh Abby, I am so sorry you had to find out this way. I knew I should have told you a long time ago but I could not bring myself to burden you. My heart is weak, love. I am afraid I am not long for this earth."

Abby didn't want to hear it. With tears she was hardly aware of quietly streaming down her face she said, "Shh, do not talk like that. You will get better. Is not this climate supposed to be good for one's health? If not, we will go somewhere that is good for you. I am not going to lose you, not yet."

"Abigail, one day you will have to face losing me but I am feeling stronger already so I do not think it will be too soon. I had hoped to see you settled before my time came."

His statement gave Abby pause, "If you wanted to see me settled then why did you not encourage me to marry Lord Malwbry? Why bring me halfway around the world to a place sadly lacking in medical care?" Abby knew she should not be arguing with him at such a time but couldn't seem to keep herself from doing so.

"If you recall, daughter, we were not supposed to be here. We should have been nearing James' plantation by now."

"Who is to say there would be any better medical care for you there?"

Her father continued, "And as for Lord Malwbry, I wanted someone better for you."

Abby was skeptical. "Better than a future duke of the realm?"

"Yes. A title means nothing if there is not love in the heart and all the riches in the world cannot bring joy to the soul as love does. No matter his station in life, if you find love you must grasp it with both hands and never let go. It is the only true thing worth fighting for."

Abby was left speechless by her father's declarations. She knew it was how he felt but he had never stated it so clearly before. She kissed his hand.

"Now dearest, dry your eyes and leave me. I need to get some rest. Do not look so worried. I will be good and well in the morning."

Abby didn't believe him but did as he requested. She kissed his cheek before leaving. Quietly she shut the door and retreated to her room to wash her face with a cool cloth before returning downstairs. Finding the parlour and dining room empty, Abby wandered outside with the idea of sitting in one of the comfortable looking rockers to try and clear her worried mind. The house faced southwest and as she pushed open the louvered front doors and stepped onto the porch the vibrant colours of the setting sun to her right arrested her movement. She stood still for a moment absorbing the beauty of it while still holding the doors open. When she brought her attention back to the porch she stepped forward releasing the doors and was startled to find Captain Max sitting in the very chair she had been headed towards. He got to his feet to greet her. "Good evening Miss Bennington. How is your father? I heard he regained consciousness. That is encouraging news."

"Yes it is. I spoke with him a short while ago. He said he was feeling better. Thank you."

Max moved aside and gestured for her to take the chair he had just vacated. Feeling emotionally and physically drained from the day, she gratefully accepted his offer. After she was seated he took the chair next to her.

Max watched the breeze play with a tendril of her hair brushing it across her cheek. He recalled how soft her skin was and found himself jealous of the wind, wishing it was his hand instead brushing her cheek. The growing twilight behind him cast her face in shadow while the sinking sun behind her lit the edges of her hair on fire. She mesmerized him. He noticed her worry her bottom lip between her teeth and not surprising his desire to kiss those lips increased. What was surprising was his desire to know what thought prompted the action.

His fascination with her was getting out of control, actually had been out of his control since they had kissed. That he was still sitting on this front porch was proof. He had no reason to be here or to believe she would leave the house again that evening and yet here she was and she seemed to accept his presence without question. For although she had been caught off guard to find him sitting there she had not questioned that he was there.

Abby grew self-conscience under the scrutiny of his gaze and wondered what he was thinking. To break the spell she asked him, "Do you think we can still win this case? I fear if we lose, my father's health will take a further turn for the worse."

Max had no experience with the laws of the courts and didn't know how their case would turn out. He did have experience with the previous method of arbitration used to solve claim disputes prior to the arrival of Judge Webb and that he knew would not work in her favour. Talmage had many friends on the island and it was not uncommon for several to be on any arbitration committee he faced so the claim was more often than not decided in his favour. Hence the reason, Max, and others like him, had petitioned to have the courts established. So far Judge Webb seemed to be a fair judge and he hoped it would be a favourable verdict so he said the only comforting thing he could think of to ease her worry. "Your father feels Judge Webb is a just man and Mr. Lambert said your evidence was good. Captain Talmage has not been able to provide any other evidence except for the testimony of his paid crewmen to substantiate his side of the claim. To my way of thinking, your side is more credible."

Abby accepted his words without question knowing he said them in an attempt to bolster her spirits. Unfortunately for Max, her spirits were very low. It was going to take a lot to cheer her this evening. "It will break my heart if we are not able to get the chest back. Oh why did I have to bring it? It was a foolish idea."

"If it was so valuable why did you bring it?" asked Max.

"In my silly female way of thinking, it was like bringing my mother along. I wanted to have something of her with me when I was leaving everything I had ever known behind, except of course, for my father."

"You're right, it was silly," Max gently teased before adding, "but I think I understand." He pulled a watch from his pocket; a simple silver pocket watch, not even on a chain. It was scratched but well-polished. Not a bit of tarnish to be seen as if well cared for. "It belonged to my father. My mother gave it to him on their wedding day. This is the only thing I have of theirs after they died."

"If you do not mind my asking, how did they die?"

"Scarlet fever. My father got sick first and my mother sent me to a neighbour's home. I wasn't allowed to see them until they were carried out on stretchers. Dead. They wouldn't let me go near them for fear of spreading the disease. The townspeople burned the house that night. Early the next morning I searched through the ashes and found his watch. It doesn't work but I keep it with me anyway. Like you, I want to keep a part of them close." Max dragged his mind back to the present with effort, surprised he had so willingly shared such a painful memory. Not many knew his story. He was startled by Abby's hand gently squeezing his arm. It broke the somber spell he had been under.

Quietly Abby said, "Thank you." Max gave her a questioning look she was barely able to read in the waning light. "For trusting me with your story."

Max felt the bond between them grow and tighten and looking at the darkened sky over her shoulder decided it was time for him to leave for both reasons. He stood up and her hand fell away. "It's getting late. You should probably go inside now." Not trusting himself near her in his current frame of mind Max quickly exited the porch. He stopped at the bottom of the steps, turned and politely said, "Good night, Miss Abigail."

Abby rose to her feet and walked to the railing. "Good night, Captain Max." She watched him stroll away until he faded from sight, pondering the reason behind his sudden departure.

Chapter 14

The next morning the little boardinghouse was in an uproar. Richard was insisting he would attend the court hearing and Mrs. Mallory and Abby were insisting he remain abed for the day. In the end, Richard won simply because the ladies feared continuing the argument would be even more harmful than allowing him to go.

They arrived at the Custom House the same time as Captain Max and Mr. Keats. After exchanging pleasantries and commenting on Richard's rapid recovery, they found themselves in the same seats as on the previous day.

The clerk dispensed with the court protocol. Judge Webb resumed their case by questioning the now present Mr. Hardy; the *Sinistral* crewman who had been present during Abby's rescue. "Mr. Amos Hardy, please rise."

Amos nervously stood up from his seat behind Mr. Williams, Talmage's lawyer, and was sworn in as a witness.

Judge Webb asked, "Mr. Hardy, were you witness to Captain Eatonton's rescue of Miss Bennington?"

"Yes sir. Captain Talmage sent me to keep an eye on him, cause he might try and cheat on the salvage prize and as my bum leg kept me from being able to haul cargo myself."

"I see and where were you standing Mr. Hardy?"

"Against the bulkhead behind the lady's father."

"From where you stood could you see into the hold?"

"No sir."

"So you could not see from whence the chest was retrieved?"

Amos nervously glanced at Leo before answering timidly, "No sir."

"Did you see Mr. Keats retrieve the chest and carry it topside?"

"Yes sir."

"Did you see where the chest lay when Mr. Keats picked it up?"

Now Amos was nearly shaking but he managed to answer, "No sir."

"Why not?"

"The ship was swaying and I stayed near the bulkhead while Mr. Keats went into the hold."

"Mr. Hardy, were you present when Mr. Keats handed the chest to Mr. Santos?"

Again, a very nervous, "No sir."

"Mr. Hardy, you may be seated."

Amos sat down hard on the wooden chair as if his legs had buckled.

Judge Webb looked through his notes then asked, "Is the crewman 'Fish' present Mr. Williams?"

"His given name is Mr. James Tish, your honour, and yes he is present."

"Mr. Tish, please rise."

Abby and the others turned in their seats to find a very thin tall man with puckish features and large lips stand up at the back of the room. She wondered if he was able to swim too or if it was just his looks that had earned him his nickname. He walked forward to stand, tall and straight, in the center of the isle just behind the lawyers shoulders, facing the judge and was sworn in by the clerk.

Judge Webb started questioning Mr. Tish. "Did Captain Talmage order you to take the small chest in question from Mr. Keats?"

"No sir," answered Mr. Tish in a very forthright manner looking straight at the judge. He then paused and glancing in Captain Talmage's direction added, "…not with words." A collective gasp of surprise was heard in the courtroom at this unexpected statement.

Judge Webb banged his gavel for silence. "What do you mean, sir?"

"I mean I knew he wanted me to take the chest without him actually saying so."

"Where did you take the chest?"

"To the *Sinistral*."

"Where did you leave it on the ship?"

"With the rest of the cargo, sir"

"Was the chest still with the cargo when it was unloaded and put into Mr. Greene's warehouse?"

"I didn't see it."

"Mr. Tish, you may be seated." Mr. Tish returned to his seat at the back of the courtroom past his captain and crewmates who were all watching him with varying degrees of animosity.

"Captain Talmage, may I remind you, you are still under oath. Did you give an unspoken command for Mr. Tish to take the chest from Mr. Keats?"

Captain Talmage stood up with calm composure. "Your honour, I cannot be expected to know the contents of every piece of cargo removed nor from whence it was retrieved. If I knew what the chest looked like I might could remember the situation."

"Mr. Yancey, please show Captain Talmage this drawing, submitted as evidence yesterday, of the chest in question."

Captain Talmage studied the drawing, which included dimensions and colour, as if he had never seen the chest before. In truth he was buying time trying to find a way to turn the situation back in his favour after that darn crewman Fish had betrayed him.

"Captain Talmage?" said Judge Webb with an impatient tone.

"I don't recall seeing this chest."

"Do you recall the incident on your deck where Mr. Tish took a chest from Mr. Keats?"

Begrudgingly Talmage replied, "Yes, sir." He felt like he was being walked into a trap, he just couldn't figure out how it would be sprung.

"Did Captain Eatonton later confront you about a missing chest?"

"Yes."

"Did you give a non-verbal instruction to Mr. Tish to take the chest?"

"I did not." Lying was the only answer he was going to give to that question now.

"Did you instruct both crews to remove the cargo to the *Sinistral*?"

"I did."

"How is it your ship, a clipper, was able to hold all of the cargo from a barque?"

Talmage was thrown off balance by Judge Webb's sudden change in tack. "Not all of the cargo had to be removed in order to float the ship off the reef."

"How much was removed?"

"As much as the *Sinistral* could hold, about a third of the cargo."

"Upon arriving in Key West, your hold was immediately discharged into Mr. Greene's warehouse, correct?"

"Yes sir."

"Your crewman, Mr. Tish, said he placed the chest in your hold. Where is the chest now, Captain Talmage?"

And there it was - the main question. Talmage easily deflected this one...or so he thought. "I am sure I don't know what has happened to it sir. It should be in the warehouse with the rest of the cargo. I did not order otherwise. Captain Eatonton's crew assisted with the unloading; perhaps one of them knows the location of the chest."

"Captain Eatonton, could one of your crew have misplaced the chest?"

Max stood to answer. "No sir, my crew only unloaded the *Mystic*. Mr. Santos insisted our help was not required to unload the *Sinistral*."

Talmage nearly groaned out loud at his mistake. *Damn and double damn. Why didn't he remember telling Santos to keep that cur away from the cargo? He was as good as sunk now.*

"You both may be seated. Is Mr. Greene present?"

The warehouse owner came forward from the back of the room. "Yes, your honour."

"Are you familiar with the crewmen of the *Mystic* and the *Sinistral*?"

"Yes, sir."

"We're you present when the cargo of the *Abigail Rose* was moved into your warehouse?"

"Yes, sir."

"Can you tell me which crews did the off-loading and from which ships?"

"Only cargo from the *Sinistral* was unloaded into my warehouse and only Talmage's crew did the unloading."

"Sir, you may be seated. Marshal Wilson did you and Mr. Greene complete the inventory check of his warehouse I requested last evening."

"Yes, sir."

"Did you find any discrepancies between the salvaged cargo logs and the cargo in his warehouse?"

"No sir," replied Marshal Wilson.

"Was the remaining cargo on the manifest found onboard the *Abigail Rose*?"

Marshal Wilson nodded. "Yes, sir. All cargo is accounted for except of course for the fruit which was consumed."

The judge nodded. "Thank you Marshal Wilson. That will be all."

The courtroom grew very quiet as Judge Webb reviewed his notes. The only sounds in the courtroom were body movements as fans were waved and people tried to find more comfortable seating in the hard chairs. Finally the judge looked up and addressed the courtroom.

"It is the opinion of this court that the chest in question is indeed the personal property of Miss Bennington and was not to be considered cargo." Judge Webb cast a stern look in Talmage's direction as he had started to make a verbal protest. "However, there is insufficient evidence to determine if Captain Talmage ordered the chest to be taken as salvage knowing it was personal property. It is also the opinion of this court that someone from the *Sinistral's* crew does know where the chest resides. Therefore, I am suspending award of the salvage claim until the jewelry chest and all of its contents are returned to this courtroom. Captain Talmage, you have one hour to see the chest is produced. If not, I will charge you with piracy and you will forfeit the *Sinistral's* entire share in the salvage claim." He struck his gavel. "Court is adjourned until one o'clock."

Max looked to see how Captain Talmage was taking the news. His face was red and he was hissing at poor Mr. Williams who looked like he was ready to abandon ship. Talmage then stormed from the room with his men trailing behind. Max would have dearly loved to follow that crowd to see where Captain Talmage had hidden the chest. He chose not to for many reasons, not the least of which was staying by Abby and her father, but mostly it was better not to further antagonize an angry shark like Talmage.

Richard invited Mr. Lambert, Mr. Keats and Captain Max to join them at the boardinghouse for a quick lunch. They were all hopeful the chest would soon be safely returned and talk was mostly of the morning's events and the amazingly brave testimony of Mr. Tish. There were some brief considerations as to what his fate might be as Captain Talmage did not seem to be the forgiving kind.

Mrs. Mallory had a light lunch ready for them and fortunately had made extra. Mr. Bennington had made a request to have dinner provided for all those involved in the case, win or lose, and had provided generous funds for the purchase of ingredients. Learning of the pending victory of the case she immediately decided to head to the grocers to see if there was anything available other than the usual fish and turtle with which to make a celebratory dinner leaving her cook to finish attending to her hostess duties.

Abby noticed Max was deep in thought and asked what was bothering him.

He looked at her with troubled eyes. "It's Mr. Tish. I'm afraid Talmage will not treat him kindly for what would seem to Talmage as a betrayal."

"Kindly? What you really mean to say is you are worried for the man's safety, are you not?"

Max smiled tightly, "Yes. It was smart of him to sit in the back. If I were him I would have left before court was adjourned to get a running head start."

"We have him to thank if we get the chest back and the poor fellow is, at the least, out of his job on our behalf." Abby had a sudden distressing thought. "You don't think his life is in danger, do you?"

"No," replied Max, even though that was exactly what he was thinking. He didn't think Leo would show any mercy once he caught up to Mr. Tish. "Captain Talmage wouldn't go that far."

"Isn't there anything we could do for him?" asked Abby.

"Like what, are you thinking of hiding him behind your skirts?"

"No. I thought you weren't worried about his safety. I was thinking more along the lines of employment."

Max's face lightened. "Good idea." He leaned over to Mr. Keats to whisper instructions resulting in Mr. Keats excusing himself from their company. Abby looked questioningly at Max but all he would say was, "We will see what happens."

They returned to the Custom House three quarters of an hour later and were gathered outside under the shade of some palm trees when Talmage returned with the chest. He started to hand it to Mr. Bennington when Marshal Wilson stepped up. "I'll take it to the judge. Please wait here."

After a few minutes of silence Max said to Talmage, "It didn't take you long to find the chest."

Captain Talmage nearly snarled back, "What are you implying?"

"Only what we all know, you took it and you have had it the whole time."

Talmage started to fly at Max, when the door opened for Marshal Wilson to exit. "Mr. Bennington, the judge would like to see you in his chambers." Mr. Lambert started to go with him but the marshal stopped him, "only Mr. Bennington." Marshal Wilson did not follow Mr. Bennington, either.

Concerned, Richard entered the Custom House. The room was empty so he proceeded to the open door and into Judge Webb's chamber. The judge was sitting behind his desk with the open chest counting the jewelry pieces. He looked up when he was finished. "It appears to all be here except for this last item which you said was hidden. Quite well I must say. I can tell there is space at the bottom which does not seem accessible but I could not find the opening."

"May I?" asked Richard.

Judge Webb gestured openly towards the chest, "By all means."

Richard walked over to the desk and turned the opened chest towards him.

He reached in and released the hidden catch which allowed the cleverly disguised front panel to drop open. He held his breath for a moment and sent a silent prayer heavenward the crown was still there. He then leaned back to look and released his breath with a sigh of thanks. He started to shut the door but the judge stopped him. "May I see it? It's not necessary but I must admit I am curious."

Richard couldn't find any harm in the request so he carefully pulled out the tray and laid it on the judge's desk. He then lifted the midnight blue velvet pouch, opened the drawstring, removed the crown and laid it on the matching tray. The sunshine from the window behind the judge gleamed off the gold and gems with more clarity than any of the other pieces.

Judge Webb was impressed. "My goodness, it is exquisite. A family heirloom, you say? You are extremely fortunate to have this returned to you."

"Yes sir, I know. I am indebted to you for your diligence in your duty."

"Not at all sir. Justice is its own reward. If you are satisfied all is here you may take the chest and we will bring this case to completion."

"Yes sir, I am satisfied."

They returned all the pieces to the chest. Richard carried it with him to the courtroom and placed it on the floor in front of his chair. Judge Webb summoned the clerk from behind the closed door of the second room and sent him to recall everyone from the yard. Max escorted Abby to her seat. Once the room settled down court was called to order.

Mr. Keats slipped into his chair just as they were returning to their seats after standing for the judge's entrance. Abby heard him tell Max, "They've not found him yet." She assumed it was Mr. Tish they had not found but she wasn't sure who all was included in 'they'. Turning to look at the other side of the room she noticed only one of Talmage's crew was present, Mr. Santos, the first mate. She hoped Mr. Tish escaped their search.

Judge Webb spent the next quarter hour questioning both sides about the weather conditions during the salvage operation and the amount of participation from each ship's crew. Talmage described it as worse than it was and devalued the role of the *Mystic's* crew. At one point he even was so bold as to question the Judge as to why it concerned him as a prior agreement had been struck between him and Captain Andrews concerning the salvage award. Judge Webb did not address his grievance and instead told Talmage if he was out of order one more time he would find himself in lockup for the night. Anyone could see Talmage was steamed by this latest set down and it was beyond Mr. William's ability to calm his client down.

Judge Webb returned his final verdict on the case, much to the relief of all the participants. "It is the opinion of this court that having violated the terms of the agreement between Captain Talmage and Captain Andrews by the taking of personal property the salvage award is now subject to the court's decision. Since there is doubt of who actually took the chest and as the chest has been returned intact an award will be rendered in the amount of fifteen percent of the value of the salvaged cargo to be divided evenly between the *Sinistral* and the *Mystic*. Mr. Greene, you are charged with dividing the cargo accordingly." Judge Webb paused before addressing Captain Talmage directly. "Furthermore, Captain Talmage, misconduct will not be tolerated by this court. The next time you or your crew is found to be guilty of any wrongdoing I will revoke your salvage license. Case dismissed."

All those involved in the case rose to leave. On Talmage's side with much belligerence but on the other side with smiles and lightness of step and much relief to be putting this ugly business behind them. The award was significantly less than Talmage's agreement with Captain Andrews but for Max it was a larger award than Talmage had agreed to share with him.

Max offered to carry the chest. Richard hesitated not wanting to relinquish that which had so recently been returned but having learned over the past weeks he could trust the young captain and painfully aware he did not need to tax his strength he passed the chest to Max.

Abby could hear the next case being called up as she followed her father through the door. She was very thankful to be leaving. Four days observing the judicial system was more than she could bear.

At the bottom of the steps her father shook hands with Mr. Lambert. "We cannot thank you enough, sir, for all you have done."

Mr. Lambert demurred. "I didn't help much. It was the good fortune of Mr. Tish's testimony."

"Still, I sincerely thank you. How soon will I be able to load my ship?"

"It will depend on Mr. Greene. He will divide the cargo according to the judge's award and then you will be able to reload your ship."

"I will speak with him tomorrow then. Tonight, we would like to have you and your family join us for dinner this evening. Captain Eatonton, Mr. Keats would you do us the honour of joining us for dinner as well?"

"Certainly sir, we would be glad to accept" replied Max on their behalf.

Max called to an enterprising lad standing nearby, eager to earn a coin, and engaged his services to carry the chest back to the boardinghouse. Max transferred the chest to the youngster along with a coin and after introducing young Timothy to Abby and Richard, he and Mr. Keats said their farewells and retreated to the wharf. Mr. Lambert followed suit, headed home to share the good news with his wife and daughter, not only had they won the case but they would be dining out this evening.

Richard offered his arm to Abby, which she took, and they strolled the short distance to Fitzpatrick Street at a very leisurely pace, enjoying the pleasant afternoon and the comfort of their victory. Timothy would have run off ahead of them but Abby called him back, not wanting to let the chest out of her sight for even a moment.

Upon arriving at the boardinghouse, Abby directed the lad to take the chest up to her room and gave him an extra coin for his effort. She laughed as he raced past her father and down the stairs in a hurry to show his new found wealth to his friends.

Abby beckoned her father into her room. "Will you tell me about the chest now?"

Richard kissed her on the forehead as he passed by and turning her desk chair to face the bed he took a seat in front of the chest where it lay on the bed. Abby sat on the bed across from him and waited to finally learn why her mother's chest was more valuable than she had ever imagined.

"This chest was custom made to hold a family heirloom from your mother's side. A tiara encrusted with diamonds, emeralds and sapphires given to your great-great-grandmother by her betrothed who was bequeathed the crown by King George II as a reward for services rendered. Unfortunately, I don't know any of the details. Perhaps you could find more of its history amongst your mother's journals. I do know your mother and your grandmothers each wore the crown on their wedding day."

"There is a secret compartment your mother once showed me. The release is so well concealed even a person looking for it without knowing exactly where it is would have a hard time finding it." Richard turned the chest so it opened towards Abby and lifted the lid. "Take the trays out and you will see a medallion imbedded in the bottom lining. Lift it with your nail and turn it to the right to reveal a hidden lever. Move the lever to the left."

Abby followed his instructions and when she moved the lever the front of the chest opened. With much anticipated excitement she reached inside for the tray; removing it to her lap. She then carefully removed the crown from its velvet slip and held it with shaking hands. The emotions of the moment overwhelmed her and tears began to fall. Here, in her hands, was not only something of her mother's but also several grandmothers. She gently traced a finger along the gold filigree and across the gemstones, finding them cool to the touch. Abby was awed to have such a priceless family treasure. "Why have you not told me this before?"

"Honestly, I forgot all about the chest. I didn't realize you had taken possession of it or I would have told you." Feeling drained from all the emotions of the day Richard rose from the chair, leaned over to kiss the crown of his lovely daughter's head and headed towards his room. He paused at the door. "Sweetheart, I think I'll lie down until dinner. Will you call me in time to freshen up?"

Abby noted the pallor of his skin, but chose not to comment. "Certainly, Father," and added with the fullness of gratitude, "Thank you." He understood without her saying that she thanked him not only for sharing the story of the chest but for its safe return and on a deeper level she thanked him for being her father.

Dinner at the boardinghouse that evening was a lively affair. Mrs. Mallory had hoped to find some beef but was happy to at least have several hens and potatoes which the cook roasted to perfection. Abby found herself seated between her father and Max with Tria sitting across from her. Every time her arm brushed Max she felt her face heat and would find Tria watching her with a bemused look upon her face.

Richard noticed the way Abby looked at Max; her eyes had that soft look, her mouth that secret smile. The same way his Anna had looked at him. It gave him some comfort to see Max's face was as besotted as his own must have been when he was courting Anna.

The participants in court regaled Mrs. Mallory and her other guests with the day's proceedings. Her father patiently answered most of their questions but Abby noticed her father seemed to be more tired than usual and as soon as the meal was over he bid goodnight to all. It was such unprecedented behaviour Abby grew even more concerned for him.

Richard's departure signaled the other guests to leave and Abby impatiently waited for them all to say their farewells so she could check on him. Closing the door on the last one, Abby raced up the stairs and gently knocked on his door. At his question she announced herself and received permission to enter. She found him already in bed with the lamp turned down. At her entrance he turned the flame up again. "I am sorry dear. I did not have the strength to last any longer. I did not mean for everyone else to leave."

"Of course they would as you were their host."

"You could have taken my place."

"Father, do not concern yourself. It has been a very long day and I am sure they were all ready to go home anyway, except for maybe Victoria and Mrs. Lambert. I am glad you ended it early, for your sake. You are not looking well. Is there anything I can get for you, poppa?"

Richard smiled at the endearment, as he always did, but nodded his head in the negative. "I am fine. It is nothing some sleep could not cure. You go and enjoy the rest of your evening. I am sure you have plenty to entertain yourself with and if not go sit on the front porch, it is a lovely evening."

Finding herself left to her own devices she used the time to catch up on her correspondences and her journal after which, still not ready to settle down to sleep, she took her father's advice and wandered down to the front porch. A nearly full moon shone brightly in the sky and the salty breeze caressed her skin. The evening was warm enough she didn't need the shawl she had picked up on her way out.

She leaned back and set the rocker in motion letting her mind wonder over the day's events and trying not to dwell on her father's illness. She supposed if she was really honest with herself she was secretly hoping to see Max. She chastised herself for wanting to see him but in the end let her mind dwell on the idea as it was the only thought that kept her from worrying over her father. But these thoughts led her to wonder what was next? Now that the ship was repaired and the cargo would soon be released her father would be ready to resume their journey to Montgomery. It distressed her in ways she hadn't expected. She enjoyed Victoria's friendship but knew it was the blond salvage captain that pulled her most. She supposed she could try to use her father's illness to convince him to stay longer in the hopes she could - what? Convince a sailor he was the marrying kind? And did she really feel so strongly about him?

Max returned to his ship after dinner but tired of fighting a restlessness he couldn't contain found himself walking down Front Street following the same path he had walked every night he was in port for the last two weeks. He turned on Fitzpatrick and slowed as he approached the boardinghouse.

He was a man torn. On one hand he was running away from his feelings just as he had always done. He wouldn't allow himself to get close to anyone after his parents died, except for his mentor and benefactor, Captain Hamilton. When he died, Max's defense was to not feel, trying to protect himself from the inevitable heartbreak by keeping all his relationships at a safe distance. On the other hand, Abby had caught him by surprise. He had been riding the tide of their crossed paths, simply enjoying her company, until the kiss had turned it serious. Now he found himself drawn to her which led him night after night to walk past the boardinghouse and see if the light was still burning in her window, hoping to catch a glimpse of her. The third night he had done this he had learned which room was hers as she happened to lean out the window for some unknown reason as he had neared. He was pretty sure she had not seen him. Last night he had been fortunate enough to find her on the porch. What would tonight bring?

He didn't really expect to see her or her light. It was getting late. A few more strides and he was in line with the front porch. A shadow moved by the door causing a pause in his stride and his heart to jump. Then he heard a familiar feminine voice ask, "Who goes there?" How foolishly brave she was, but oh, how glad he was to see her. He stopped at the bottom of the steps. "It's Max." The shadow moved to the railing and took on the lovely moonlit silhouette of Abigail Bennington and Max's heart jumped again.

Softly she said, "Good evening, Captain Max."

"Good evening to you, Miss Abigail. How is your father?"

"He is resting comfortably, thank you." Abby walked down the porch steps to get closer to Max, unconsciously seeking the comfort of his presence.

She was close enough now he could see the luminescence of her eyes. "It was a good day, wasn't it? I'm glad things worked out for you. Was everything returned in the chest?"

She smiled. "Yes, thank you for helping to see it was returned safely."

"You're welcome." A faint hint of rose water drifted his way stirring the comforting memories of his mother's rose garden. She reminded him of the fragrant smell of the delicate blooms on a warm summer evening. The petal softness of her skin beckoned him to reach out and brush her cheek. He noticed in the moonlight her lips were the same coral colour as his favourite rose growing in the corner of the garden. He was intoxicated by her and his memories. "Is your middle name 'Rose'?" he asked.

She was drowning in the depth of his eyes again but his question finally registered and it was with quiet surprise she nodded, "How did you know?"

"It is the ship's name and it suits you. Would you like to take a walk along the beach?"

Abby hesitated. It was highly improper and likely to have severe consequences but this being the first overture from him in days and being caught up in some strange mood she threw caution and upbringing to the wind and accepted his invitation by holding out her gloveless hand towards him. The warmth of his fingers curled around hers and a strange sensation spread through her viscera.

As they walked down Green Street towards the beach Max asked, "Where do you live in England?"

Abby could hear the faint sounds coming from the bars further down Front Street but on this end it was very quiet and she realized most were probably in bed. Hopefully no one would see them. "Near Southampton. It's a port town on the southern coast of England."

"I am familiar with the place. I was there, once, a long time ago."

Abby was surprised. "How have you been there? Oh that's right; I remember you said you were on a merchant ship as a boy. Strange to think our paths could have crossed all those many years ago."

"Not likely, as I was not allowed ashore."

"Oh, of course, you were only allowed ashore with the captain's permission."

The sound of a bow drawn across the strings of a violin from the piazza of a house just ahead startled them both. Max quickly changed their path to keep them out of sight of Dr. Waterhouse. Upon reaching the beach, they turned south away from the docks headed towards the lighthouse.

Abby asked, "What was it like where you grew up? I still think of New England as colonies, not much more civilized than here."

"It resembles England much closer than it does this place in looks and culture. That's probably why I haven't been back. I like the unstructured freedom I have here."

"I like it too. It is so unlike England. Despite the attempts at civilized behaviour there is a wildness or maybe it is more of a relaxed attitude."

Max looked at her in surprise. He would never have believed an English rose could like this untamed island. It pleased him, very much.

Abby interrupted his thoughts. "Why salvaging? Why not fish for a living? It would seem like a much steadier income."

"I like the adventure of it. Pitting myself against nature and the ocean. Taking back from the sea that which belongs to man."

"What about the money? You cannot tell me money does not figure in to why you prefer salvaging over fishing."

She had him there. "The money helps, not that I've seen much of it lately, but I'm providing a valuable service saving lives and cargo. Thanks to men like Talmage we've had a lot of bad press." He stopped walking and turned to face her. "Having been directly involved yourself, what do you think? Am I a hero same as a marshal or something more akin to a pirate?" Teasing he asked again "Which am I to you?"

She softly but boldly whispered, "Pirate."

"What?" Max couldn't believe after everything between them she would think that.

A soft smile on her face, she said it again, "Pirate. You are trying to steal my heart."

With the waves softly lapping behind her and the moonlight enchanting her features Max realized too late she had turned into a sea siren pulling him to her. He was drawn in by the acceptance in her eyes and the softening of her lips. No longer able to resist he leaned down and claimed the lips that belonged to him. Later he would worry about that thought. For now, he was caught in a swiftly swirling whirlpool of desire that somehow in the space of a heartbeat had grown out of his control.

Instinctively testing the power she had over him, Abby moved her mouth against his closed lips slightly changing the pressure and was gratified to hear his moan. This kiss was so much more than the first.

Max felt true panic building in his chest. This kiss was so much more than the first. He wrenched himself away from her and took a step back, then another, breathing heavily.

Abby was left adrift as Max suddenly broke the contact. When rational thought returned she said, "It is not like this with everyone, is it?"

Max was instantly wary. "How would you know something like that?"

"I have been kissed before you," *and this was different, very different.*

Now he was skeptical. "Really?"

"Mostly on the cheek..."

He was relieved. She was referring to her father. "Not the same."

Feeling compelled to honesty she admitted, "... and once on the lips."

Jealousy and sudden anger took Max by surprise. He was barely aware he asked, "By whom?"

"Who is of no consequence, what matters is the feelings were not the same."

He took another step back and she saw his features closing off to her again. He was shutting down his emotions, distancing himself from her both physically and emotionally. He turned and took a few paces away from her before Abby called out a plea. "Don't!"

He stopped but kept his back to her. "Don't what?"

Taking a wild guess in an attempt to keep him there, "Don't run from your feelings. I am scared of mine too but please do not leave me alone again with all these emotions while you pretend nothing has happened." He didn't move. She was starting to worry he wouldn't return to her.

Max finally relented. He squared his shoulders and turned to face her again. He confessed, "This is different. What that means, I don't have the luxury of finding out. My life doesn't allow for a woman. It is a dangerous life on the reef. I'm out at sea more than I am here. There's no room for a wife."

"You could marry if you wanted to. My father's a merchant. I understand the dangers at sea."

"But he's not out there looking for those dangers, I am. That's where my job is. I will not put another's life and happiness at stake with mine. I can't."

It sounded more to her like a plea for his, rather than for her, needs but she could tell she had pushed him as far as he was willing to go tonight. Without saying another word they fell in step with each other headed back to the boardinghouse, not touching but still connected by the invisible bond of their attraction for each other.

As they approached the boardinghouse Max realized he could still taste her sweetness and suddenly didn't want to end the night with emotions so strained between them so he tried to lighten the mood.

"I forgot to tell you, my crew found Fish this afternoon. He had shut himself up in the Sweat Box. Figured it would be the last place Talmage or his crew would look for him. Guess he was right."

Taking the olive branch for what it was Abby laughed at the thought of Mr. Tish purposely locking himself up right under Talmage's nose. "How very smart of him."

They had reached the porch steps. Max said, "I hired him on."

Abby climbed the three steps to the porch and turned expecting Max to follow behind her. Instead she found him waiting at the bottom to say goodnight. "That was very kind of you, Captain Max."

"Not at all, he's an excellent diver and a good deckhand, not to mention the man knows how to find the fish. All of which is needed on the *Mystic*."

Abby smiled to herself, her earlier question answered concerning Mr. Tish's nickname. "And does he like being called 'Fish'?"

"He asked me to, so I guess so. Good night, Miss Abigail."

"I expect this is more like good-bye Captain Max."

Her words brought him up short, feeling like a blade across his heart. He was going to ask her to explain when the door suddenly opened to reveal Captain Andrews.

Chapter 15

"Do you see them yet?" asked Richard from his prone position on the bed.

Captain Matthew Andrews crossed to the window for the fourth time in twenty minutes to peer out at the darkened street searching for the return of two shadowy figures. As expected he did not see them. Turning back to the room he shook his head in the negative and took a seat on a ladder-back wooden chair stationed next to the opened window so he could hear any sounds carried on the night air.

Richard was losing patience. "What is he thinking keeping her so long?"

Matthew crossed his arms over his chest. "I thought you wanted this when you kept me from going after her." He had seen Abby leave the front porch with Max headed in the direction of the beach from the same window by which he was now stationed having arrived earlier to check on Richard. He was headed out of Richard's room to retrieve her after having explained to Richard what was going on only to be stopped before reaching the door. Richard's only explanation was it would do them good. Captain Andrews failed to understand how sacrificing Abby's reputation could possibly be good for her but did as Richard asked and waited for their return.

"I expected them to take a short walk but this is taking a turn for serious." Thoughtfully Richard continued, "Maybe this is even better than I had hoped." He noticed his friend send him a questioning look and finally realized how strange his behaviour must seem to Matthew. "I have noticed a growing attraction between them since the moment they met. I have asked the opinion of many on the island who have dealt with the young captain and all have high praise of his character. With my heart condition worsening I am anxious to see my daughter is taken care of..." Richard held up his hand to forestall Matthew's protest. "I know you would protect her but you know you cannot offer her the same security as a husband."

Understanding finally dawned on Matthew. "You plan to force them to marry!"

"Well, actually, I had only meant to encourage the courtship to proceed at a more accelerated pace but, yes, I am now thinking if they return and have not suddenly decided to dislike each other an imminent marriage would be satisfactory. Necessary, as it were, with her reputation at stake. Wouldn't you agree?"

"Are you sure he is the one for her? Once you start down this path it will be nearly impossible to reverse if you were to change your mind."

"I am sure of Abby but I am gambling on the strength of Max's affection in order to see my daughter settled." Passing out yesterday had really scared Richard. He now felt an urgent need to have Abby married. "If my ploy doesn't work then Max isn't the one for her and we'll have to set sail as soon as possible."

Matthew turned his ear towards the window to listen. "Shh, I think I hear something." He stood up and peered into the shadowy darkness. He couldn't see them but he heard the distinctive sound of female laughter and then Abby's voice not far distant. "They are returning."

"Would you mind bringing them both to my bedside? Don't let on what we have been discussing."

Matthew left the room to do as he was asked. He didn't agree with Richard's tack but he couldn't say he wouldn't do the same if he were in Richard's position with a daughter he was trying to protect and the fear of time growing short. He paused in the hallway when he heard them at the front porch to give them a few more moments of privacy before opening the door and changing their lives forever.

If the situation had not been so serious, he would have been amused by the look of horror on Abby's face and the guilt that swamped Max's. "Abigail, your father would like to speak to both of you. He is waiting for you in his room." Silently they both walked past him and climbed the stairs, heads hung low, as if going to the executioner.

Abby found her father dressed and pacing the room, looking very grim and still pale. She felt Max step into the room behind her. "Father, please, sit down, do not stress yourself so."

He looked from one to the other of them and said, "Abby, please wait in the hallway, I would like to speak to Captain Eatonton alone."

"Poppa, please let me explain."

Richard cut her off, "Go, and shut the door behind you."

She couldn't remember ever having heard that tone from her father. He hadn't raised his voice but he spoke with absolute finality. She was forced to reluctantly leave the room casting a look of apology to Max as she passed by him. She shut the door and looked around the empty hallway for a chair to sit and wait. Not seeing one she realized it didn't matter she wouldn't be able to sit still anyway, she was too agitated. Instead she crossed her arms around her middle and started pacing. Minutes ticked by. Maybe it was a good sign they weren't yelling at each other.

Whatever had possessed her to walk with him? The excitement of a clandestine encounter, of course. The adventure of doing something so forbidden in England had her dropping her guard and throwing caution to the wind. Miss Winterfeldt warned her she would one day regret her impulsive actions. This looked to be the day. When her father was finished with Max he was sure to have his say with her as well.

As Abby passed by the door for what seemed the hundredth time she overheard her father say, "...will be taken away from you..." She desperately wanted to know what was being said but she hadn't meant to eavesdrop. She quickly moved on and changed her path further from the door. What did her father mean? Was he referring to Max's ship? Could he take it away? She knew her father got his way most of the time in business. She wouldn't be surprised if he was able to somehow find a way to do such a thing but how could he be so cruel as to take Max's ship? And for such a minor indiscretion. It should be her he was punishing, not Max. Her pacing became even more agitated as she allowed her anger to take hold.

The silence in the room, after Abby's departure, became deafening. Richard waited for Max to break it; a negotiating tactic he had found useful many times before.

After waiting for her father to speak Max finally realized he was expected to speak first. "Mr. Bennington, sir, I apologize for suggesting a walk to your daughter alone and after dark. It was very improper and badly done. I promise to take better care to guard against such inappropriate behaviour in the future."

Richard, intentionally showing weakness and playing on his illness, collapsed into a chair in the corner. "I am sure you mean well and would do so. The problem is if even one person witnessed it, her reputation is ruined and odds are someone saw you. Worse than England, gossip spreads quickly on an island and with so few people it wouldn't take long for everyone to know. Abby would be easy to identify with so few females and being new to the island she would become easy prey for the lesser men with no one to protect her." Richard paused for effect, as if he needed the rest, and held up his hand for Max to wait. "I only see two solutions. Marriage..." He looked to see how Max took to the idea. As expected the guilt was washed away with something akin to panic. "...or she will have to leave the island - expediently. Captain Andrews told me just this evening he will be ready to sail in a few days. That should protect her, don't you think?"

"If you think it best sir, but why are you telling me all this?"

"You do care for my daughter, do you not?"

"Yes, but..."

Richard continued with more strength in his voice. "I thought it would cause you some concern to learn she will be taken away from you, removed from your realm, become unreachable as we have no plans to return to this island, as charming as it is."

Max knew what Mr. Bennington was hoping for as soon as he mentioned the word 'marriage' and he automatically had started building a defense against the idea. A defense that crumbled in the wake of Richard's announcement. Even with Abby having said as much earlier, he still had not been prepared to hear it put so bluntly from her father. The thought of Abby sailing away - forever - in just a few days - never to be seen again brought a pain and emptiness so deep it surpassed every loss he had ever felt before now. *How had this happened?* How had he come to care so much about her in such a short time?

Richard watched the emotional waves crossing Max's face. At the opportune moment Richard added his last tactic to seal the deal. "My brother mentioned a nearby plantation owner, in the market for a wife, in his last letter. He thought this gentleman and Abby would suit each other nicely, despite the age difference. I believe I will encourage her to accept him. I so want to see her settled with my health deteriorating as it is. You can understand how a father would want to assure his daughter's wellbeing under such circumstances."

Max had never considered himself a jealous man as he had never experienced it before but here was that emotion overwhelming him for the second time this evening and this time it was strong. So strong he was forced to accept he did not want Abby to be with anyone but him, especially not some stodgy old plantation owner. As a captain he had to make split second gut decisions. It was in his nature. He did so now in deciding to marry her. One look at Mr. Bennington and Max could see he knew he had him. Not seeing any point in voicing the obvious, he gave a single nod in resigned acceptance and left the room.

Abby quickly turned at the sound of the opening door to see Max exit on a determined path down the stairs without even looking in her direction. Anger emanated from him. She looked into her Father's room and cried, "What have you done?" before taking off after Max. She caught up to him as he was opening the front door and laid a hand on his shoulder. "Max?" He was so tense his muscles felt like stone under her hand.

He turned to look at her. There was anger in his eyes. "We're getting married." It was such a statement of finality - like a death sentence. Her chin dropped as well as her hand in shocked reaction. He left. Gathering her wits and her skirt she followed him. From the porch she watched as he disappeared in the night with quick angry strides.

She returned upstairs to confront her father only to find he was settled back into bed and all he would say was, "Not tonight, Abigail," leaving her to pace her room with all her restless thoughts. *Men! Why did they assume they had decided her fate for her and she need not have a say in it?*

The next morning when Abby exited her room she met Mrs. Mallory in the hallway carrying a breakfast tray for her father. "Please, let me take that from you Mrs. Mallory."

"That's all right luv, I don't mind."

"I wish to speak with my father and bringing him food may help."

"A smart lass you are knowing the way to a man's heart is through his stomach."

The ladies smiled at each other as they exchanged the tray. Mrs. Mallory knocked on the bedroom door and when her father beckoned she opened it for Abby then returned to her chores downstairs.

"Good morning poppa," Abby cheerfully greeted her father despite the serious nature of her visit.

"Good morning, daughter." Richard straightened up in the bed to accept the breakfast tray from Abby. She fluffed his pillows behind him and then took a seat in the chair next to his bed. He knew what brought her to him this morning. He had chased her off last night having felt drained after his confrontation with Max. He knew she would not allow him to defer her grievances this morning so he mentally prepared himself as he added preserves to his toast and stirred his tea.

Abby asked, "How are you feeling this morning?"

"Better."

She didn't believe him. The only other time in her life her father had broken his fast in bed he had been under a doctor's care for a fever. He still looked unrested and it worried her.

"And you, sweetheart? How are you this morning?"

"Fine." She really felt fatigued herself after spending the night tossing and turning with all the questions she wanted to ask her father and Max but now faced with the opportunity she didn't know how to broach the subject with her father looking so frail.

"Abigail, how unlike you to not speak your mind. I must look even worse than I feel. Come child." Richard held his hand out to her. Abby leaned forward and slid her hand into his grasp. "You have feelings for him. You cannot deny it. He is a good man and will make you a fine husband. It relieves my mind to know your future is now secure."

And with his last sentence all her protests no longer mattered. She would do this to make her father happy, to ease his worry, and most importantly to safeguard his health. "I do care for him. I hope he cares for me as well."

"He does."

Her father said it with such conviction she felt forced to accept it, but were Max's feelings strong enough to overcome their strained beginnings? When the duchess forced Jason to marry her he rebelled but when Max was forced he accepted it. Each man had something valuable to lose so was it more than the ship that had caused Max to agree? She was pinning her hopes and dreams on it.

Richard picked up a scrap of paper from the table by the bed. "Max sent a message over this morning requesting the wedding be held tomorrow."

Abby's eyes opened wide. "Tomorrow! Did he say why so soon?"

"No. Do you have a reason to postpone it?"

"I could think of a great many but none that couldn't be overcome if it is what you desire as well," said Abby being uncharacteristically submissive.

"Good. Then I will send him a favourable reply and ask that he join us for dinner this evening." Richard felt a little guilty manipulating his daughter but he was sure he was only hastening the inevitable conclusion.

"I believe I will go visit with Victoria this morning. It seems I am in need of a maid of honour and some reinforcements. Will you promise me you will rest today, Poppa?"

"I will. Enjoy your visit and pass along my regards to her parents."

"Certainly." Abby closed the door of her father's room and considered her intentions. They were bold but she deemed it necessary. She stopped by her room to pick up her gloves and parasol and then went downstairs to find Maria. Breakfast was the last thing on her mind.

Maria wondered at her mistress' determined pace. The path they were taking did not lead to the Lambert's residence which she had assumed would be their destination. The next possibility was they were headed to the market for Mrs. Mallory but that didn't seem likely either. Which left the wharf; maybe Abby was running an errand for her father but then Abby stopped at the first pier where the *Mystic* was berthed at the end. Maria watched as Abby lifted her skirt, squared her shoulders and started out across the wooden dock. Maria followed curious as to what could be afoot that would cause her to undertake such a bold visitation.

The morning was comfortably cool and the water on either side of the dock was a clear shade of turquoise. Any other day Abby would have noticed. Today she was focused on her destination and how to accomplish her mission. Her steps brought her to the end of the dock before she had figured out what she intended to say to her future husband. She stood at the threshold of the gangplank and debated between asking permission to board and simply doing so. She did not see anyone on deck and really did not want to speak so loud she would draw unnecessary attention to herself. Maria caught up to her and feeling compelled to make a decision, she opted to board without permission. She traversed the gangplank and upon setting foot on deck Thomas appeared from below.

He took one look at the two of them and turned to call over his shoulder, "Captain, we have guests."

Abby nervously waited for Max to make his appearance while she watched Thomas and Maria greet each other warmly. When Max emerged the anger she saw on his face almost made her want to turn around and run as fast as she could for the boardinghouse.

"Abigail, what are you doing here? Have you lost your head? What if someone sees you?" His face and tone completely changed as he had another thought. "Has something happened to your father?"

"No. Father is fine and supposedly we ruined my reputation last night and now you've dictated we will marry tomorrow so what does it matter if someone sees us? Just like a man, you think because you said we are getting married I'll just fall in line. You haven't given a thought to how I might feel. It probably never even crossed your mind..."

As she spoke, her anger grew and her speech increased in volume and pitch to the point Max grabbed her elbow and led her towards the hatch saying, "Not here." Abby obediently climbed down the ladder and upon reaching the bottom she moved aside to allow him room but was ready to pick up right where she left off.

"It never crossed your mind I could object to the whole idea. I will not be treated as if my feelings and opinions do not matter. This marriage..." Abby found herself effectively silenced by his lips.

Max figured the most expedient way to stop the flow of words and get her to drop her guard was to give her pretty mouth something else to do. Besides he found her righteous anger flushed her face in a very desirable way. When he felt her melt against him he broke the kiss. "That is why I assumed you would agree to marriage."

It took Abby a moment to recover her wits before pushing away from his chest. "You thought I would be agreeable just because I happen to like the way you kiss?"

"You yourself said what we have is special," replied Max.

"No sir, I said the feeling was not the same as with others; besides it was more of a question..."

"It didn't sound like a question."

"... and as I recall after agreeing with me, you said you *would not* consider marriage so you can imagine my surprise when less than twenty minutes later you announce, as you are walking out the door, we *will* be married."

Max asked in a very rational manner, "You are getting exactly what you wished for so why are you not happy?"

He brought Abby's thoughts up short. *Did she wish to be married to Max?* "I never said I wished to be married to you."

"You didn't need to say it to know that's where you were headed."

"Maybe," she conceded. "And you are willing to marry me just so you won't lose something that matters to you?" asked Abby, getting to what really had brought her here.

"Yes," replied Max, unaware she was referring to his ship and not herself. "And to save your reputation, remember?"

"So you believe I owe you my gratitude?"

"That I do and I know the best way you can show it." Max gave her a lascivious grin. She had yet to understand the warning in his smile. He placed his hand behind her neck and pulled her to him before she had a chance to back away. He brought his lips to hers. She resisted at first but as she relaxed he deepened the kiss, teaching her more in the ways of intimacy. He could really get used to this part of being married.

Abby lost all sense of time and place. Her knees weakened and she now depended entirely on him for support. She feared if he let go she would collapse in a puddle on the floor. Thought became impossible. She could only focus on what she was feeling. New sensations flooded her being and she lost herself in them. She didn't even hear Thomas but thankfully Max did.

"Captain?"

Max lifted his head from hers, only breaking the contact of their lips. He held her close shielding her from view. "Yes? What is it Thomas?"

"I tink you better come on deck, sir."

Max spoke low for Abby's ears alone. "I think he's right or the consummation may come before the marriage." He slowly disengaged himself from her except for one hand on her back. He led her to the ladder.

Abby struggled to escape the fog she was in while automatically climbing the ladder. *What kind of magic spell did he weave on her?* She felt as if she would have agreed to anything he had suggested. As it was she figured she had tacitly agreed to their wedding. In all honesty she did want to marry Max. Others had married knowing even less of their spouse with success so why couldn't they make it work? Giving in to the inevitable she turned to ask Max one more question before the rest of the crew reached them. "Why tomorrow?"

Max steadily held eye contact with her. "I don't want to wait."

"You do not want time for all your family and friends to be here?" She realized her *faux pas* the same time he reminded her.

"I don't have any family and my friends are all here. What about you? Do we need to wait for your family?"

She considered it for a moment. "The most important person in my family is my father and he is here. It would take Uncle James and his family at least two months to get here. My father's health will not allow us to wait long so, no, we do not need to wait for any others."

Max cringed inwardly. She confirmed what he had suspected. Her father had much to do with her agreement. He tilted his head in a gesture of consideration. "Is there any other reason you would wish to wait? Abby if you need more time then of course we will wait but I've made my decision and I don't have any reason to wait longer to make it official."

The openness of his expression gave Abby the courage to ask the one question bothering her most. "Last night you said you would not marry. Am I to believe you changed your mind so quickly?"

"You said you understand the dangers I face at sea and I believe you have the strength to withstand the absences and the hardships of being a wrecker's wife."

Abby was taken in by his soft tone and confidence and wanted to believe him until she remembered he was trying to save his ship and he would say anything to do so. But in the end, knowing it was her father's desire to see her married before another episode with his heart prevented it she said, "Tomorrow will be fine. Do you have any preferences for the ceremony?"

"No; whatever you and your father decide will be fine." The crew was now filing up the gangplank and in hopes of saving Abby from their questioning Max ended the interview. "Until tomorrow, Miss Abigail." He lifted her hand to his mouth and placed a kiss on the skin of her wrist above her glove. Abby's heightened senses felt this kiss as deeply as the other and the look in Max's eyes was warm and alluring, a caress all its own.

He didn't break eye contact as he led her to the gangway. In a haze she said goodbye and exited the ship, barely even acknowledging the returning sailors. It took till she reached the end of the dock before she started to feel like herself again. That Max could control her with just a look made her even more nervous about their upcoming marriage but her fate was now sealed. She had made her agreement known to both her father and Max and she would not cry off over something that was probably temporary. Once the newness of their relationship wore off she would feel more like herself around him. He would not always be able to control her so easily.

Regaining her sense of purpose she stepped off the dock and turned right headed towards Whitehead Street. Now that she was reconciled to a wedding on the morrow she headed to the Lambert's to recruit Tria's assistance in the preparations.

Chapter 16

"Max and I are getting married tomorrow." Abby watched as Tria's eyes widened and her mouth dropped open. "I would like for you to be my maid of honour."

Tria was so stunned she didn't know what to react to first. "Maid of honour? Married - to Max! Tomorrow! You want me to be your maid of honour? Of course I will be, but tomorrow? How? I mean, why? How did this come about? Really, Abby, tomorrow?"

Abby couldn't help her growing smile as Tria sputtered. "I am not really sure myself how it happened."

"What do you mean, you're not sure? How in the world does one become engaged and not know how it came about?" Tria was becoming more incredulous by the moment.

"Am I really engaged if I never actually agreed to marry? I suppose not disagreeing in essence is agreeing," mused Abby, teasing Tria with the suspense.

"Abby, please! Tell me the story. I must know."

Abby took a deep breath. "Very well. Max and I took a walk last night after dark along the beach."

"Alone? Why would you do such a thing? Your reputation!" Tria then had another train of thought. "Is that when he asked you? How romantic."

"He did not ask me. He told me we were getting married after talking to my father. It seems father was waiting for our return and sent me from the room. I overheard him threaten to take Max's ship from him. When Max left the room he said we were getting married. I went to see Max this morning expecting him to have reconsidered but instead he seemed almost enthusiastic."

Tria responded to the doubt in Abby's voice. "And why wouldn't he be? You will make a good wife. Why must it be tomorrow?"

Abby gave a graceful shrug. "Max requested it."

"Really? How interesting. Why are you going along with it? What did the two of you do last night to necessitate such speedy nuptials?"

Abby pleaded, "Certainly nothing as impermissible as you are thinking."

"Then why are you blushing so?"

"I am? Well if you must know, we kissed."

Tria pounced on her admission wanting to hear the details. "Really, what was it like?"

Abby was flabbergasted. "Victoria Lambert, do you mean to say you have never been kissed?"

Tria pouted in displeasure. "Don't tease."

Abby couldn't decide if Tria was serious or putting her on to get more details. "Not that I am by any means an expert on the subject but when Max kisses me it is like the rest of the world no longer exists; it is just the two of us and I never want him to stop."

"How many..." Tria was interrupted by her mother inviting them to tea.

Victoria told her mother of the upcoming event but thankfully Mrs. Lambert did not ask anything Abby was uncomfortable answering. If she assumed the haste was due to improper behaviour she did not indicate so, instead their conversation naturally centered on wedding plans.

Tria was very enthusiastic and Abby gratefully let her take the lead. "I suppose you will have to be married in the Custom House. How dreadful we do not have a proper church. Has your father spoken to Judge Webb? I suppose he would perform the ceremony."

"No, I don't believe he has spoken to anyone yet."

"What will you wear?" asked Mrs. Lambert. "Such a shame there isn't time to make a proper wedding dress."

Considering her wardrobe there was really only one choice. "It has to be the rose gown. I received it just before leaving England and have not worn it yet. It is appropriate I suppose as Max was forced to save the dress when he rescued me."

Tria smiled. "It does sound like the perfect dress and it covers the something new." Tria recited the old English poem.

Something old, something new
Something borrowed, something blue
And a silver sixpence in her shoe.

Tria asked, "Do you have something old?"

Abby didn't even have to think about her answer. "Yes, and very sentimental as my mother wore it on her wedding day."

Tria continued. "You need something borrowed and something blue. Can one item serve both purposes?"

They both looked to Mrs. Lambert to answer. "I suppose so but the borrowed item is supposed to be from a happily married woman."

"Well then you still need something borrowed but I have something blue for you." Tria exited the parlour and returned a moment later placing a delicate blue handkerchief with lace edging in front of Abby. "My father gave it to me when I was twelve but I want to give it to you as a wedding gift."

Abby ran her finger over the exquisite lace. "Thank you, Tria."

Mrs. Lambert rose to her feet. "Excuse me dears, I will return in a moment." When she returned to the table she stood beside Abigail. "I consider myself a happily married woman and would be honoured to offer you the loan of this fan which I carried on my wedding day."

Abby gently accepted the slightly yellowed lace and pearl fan. "Thank you, Mrs. Lambert. I will take great care with it."

"You are welcome, dear. And to finish the poem." Mrs. Lambert placed the coin in Abby's other hand.

Abby was touched by their overwhelming support. "You both have been very helpful in making this occasion special, despite its awkward nature. How can I ever repay your kindnesses?"

Mrs. Lambert waved her off. "Nonsense. We haven't done anything extraordinary."

Abby's eyes welled with tears. "Yes you have and I cannot thank you enough."

Finished with tea, Abby decided she needed to return to her father. She thanked Victoria and her mother again for their assistance.

Tria laid a restraining hand on her arm as they reached the door. "Please send word as soon as you know the time and place we should meet you tomorrow or if you are in need of further assistance before then."

"I will." Abby hugged both ladies then she and Maria returned to the boardinghouse.

They found Mrs. Mallory in a flurry of activity. Abby climbed the stairs wondering what all the fuss was about. She knocked on her father's door. Not receiving an answer she knocked again. When she still didn't receive an answer she tried the handle and finding it unlocked she peaked her head around the door. To her surprise the room was empty. *Where could he be?*

Abby left the room and descended the stairs in search of Mrs. Mallory. *What has caused such an uproar, I wonder?* She stopped one of the downstairs maids rushing past with a stack of folded linens. "Is there a special guest arriving to cause such commotion?"

"Why no Miss, everyone is preparing for your wedding reception, of course."

Abby was taken aback. She hadn't considered the ripple affect her impromptu marriage would create. Feeling as if she should be doing something she decided to offer her help to Mrs. Mallory. She asked the maid one more question before letting her proceed. "Do you know where my father went?"

"No miss, I don't."

While Abby was at the Lambert's, Richard quietly left the boardinghouse to make a visit of his own, taking care to avoid Mrs. Mallory's disapproving look. Unlike his daughter, he asked for permission to board when he arrived at the *Mystic.*

Max opted to face Richard on deck, not wanting to meet with him less than five feet from where he had taken advantage of his daughter a short time ago after promising him last night to take care of her reputation. Besides it was now going on noon and too hot and stuffy below deck. Instead he chased his crew off ship so they could have a private conversation. He wondered what brought his soon to be father-in-law to see him. What could be important enough to bring him from his sick bed?

Max greeted Mr. Bennington at the head of the gangway. "Good afternoon, sir. You are looking well." To look at Mr. Bennington now you would not believe anything was wrong with his health. *Was his weakness last night a ruse?* But then Max had witnessed his unconsciousness the first day of the trial; had helped get him back to the boardinghouse and then seen him the next morning back at court, not quite as well as this morning but still almost himself for the rest of the trial. Whatever his illness was the affliction seemed to come and go which would make it conceivable for Mr. Bennington to pretend to feel worse than he did in order to manipulate both Max and his daughter. *Should he confront him with his deception?* No, it was not the reason he had agreed to the marriage and it would only strain their relationship going forward, although it did seem to be a strong factor in his bride's capitulation with the abbreviated engagement. Max would keep in mind the possibility Mr. Bennington was faking his illness the next time he used it to get his way.

"Good afternoon, Captain Max." Richard shook hands with Max and carefully examined his features. He had expected to find Max at least somewhat belligerent towards him for forcing his hand but he appeared to be fully accepting. "I was surprised to receive your note requesting the wedding be held tomorrow. May I ask for your reason?"

"I would think you would be happy with having it so soon."

Richard held up a hand palm outward. "Don't misunderstand; I don't object I was simply wondering why you would not want to wait a week or a month to make plans."

"Time will not make a difference in the outcome and as I told Abby this morning..."

Richard interrupted in surprise. "Abby was here this morning?"

"Yes and for much the same reason you are here. The decision is made; I see no reason to delay the action."

"You are a man of action. I admire that. But you are also a man of haste. You left before we had a chance to discuss the business of marriage."

Max shifted his weight. "What business?"

"Her dowry to start."

Angry pride coloured Max's words. "I don't need her dowry."

"Regardless, you will receive it upon your marriage. It is a sizeable amount. Enough to set you up in business."

Max said tightly, "I have a business."

Richard heeded the warning in Max's tone. Not wanting to anger Max, he made his tone carefully neutral. "Right, ship salvaging. Have you ever wished to do something else?"

Max did his best to reply with less anger. "No. I like the challenge of fighting the weather and I am doing something useful. I am saving people and cargo from the sea." *Why was he justifying himself?*

"A noble occupation to be sure but an extremely dangerous one as well."

Ah, now Max understood Mr. Bennington's concern. "I am well aware of that fact sir. As I said to Abby earlier in the evening yesterday I did not want to tie a wife to my fate but she believed she could handle the uncertainty."

Richard was shocked, although he couldn't decide if he was pleasantly surprised they had already discussed marriage or outraged at Max's disrespect to him. "You proposed marriage with my daughter before our meeting last night?"

Max straightened his spine. "No sir. We were discussing marriage in general."

Richard relaxed. "Of course. So you love what you do and if it will not support my daughter you have her dowry to live on and unlike most of her counterparts she has her own money. A very tidy sum inherited from her mother's side."

"You don't believe I can support a wife?" asked Max.

Richard tried to help Max understand the responsibility he was acquiring. "A wife maybe but the likes of Abby who is used to having certain comforts? I would not know. How much of a living do you make from shipwrecks?"

Max nearly groaned aloud at what he had led himself into. His pride would not let him tell the whole truth but he was compelled to be honest. "I have been able to supply my ship and my crew even though it has been tough at times. All I need is to be first at one of the larger wrecks, to be declared wreck master, and I'll be set."

"What are the odds of accomplishing that?" asked Richard.

"Fair," was all Max was willing to say.

"You have your business and the dowry to start out. Having discovered your island and its unique position in the region I am considering opening an office for my shipping line here. If you find the demands of a wife and your career are not compatible I will name you office manager." Richard could see Max putting together his defenses and not wanting to continue this particular argument in the hot sun, let alone before the wedding, he quickly deflected the conversation to another topic. "Do you have a ring?"

Max had been gathering his arguments to counter Mr. Bennington's proposition and now found himself thrown totally off guard and lost by his question. "A ring?"

"Yes, a wedding band for the ceremony." Richard reached into his breast coat pocket.

Max hated to admit a ring had not crossed his mind. He watched as Richard pulled a handkerchief from his pocket and unfolded it to reveal a gold band.

"I gave this to my wife, Abigail's mother, and thought if you did not have a ring you could give her this one." Max started to protest until Richard added, "I know it would please Abby."

Not having the means to purchase a ring and wanting to please Abby he accepted Richard's offering. Upon closer inspection he noticed the band had intertwining roses engraved on it. How appropriate. "Thank you, Mr.

Bennington."

"Please, call me Richard. Tomorrow you will become family."

The thought gave Max pause. Becoming Abby's husband was daunting enough; he hadn't given any thought to becoming a son-in-law.

Richard used the handkerchief to mop the sweat from his brow. "I must be going. I can feel my strength waning in this heat. I will send a message with the time and place of the ceremony after I consult with Abby, unless you would like to join us for dinner?"

Max did not want to spend his last bachelor evening dining at the boardinghouse with Richard so he gave him an excuse. "I have a lot of duties to attend to before tomorrow besides I have already told Abby whatever you two decide is fine with me."

"Very well then, I will see you on the morrow." Richard tipped his hat to Max. "Good day."

Max watched his progress down the dock and across Front Street as he contemplated their conversation. It was clear Richard did not think highly of wreckers. Most people didn't. If Max was not able to prove himself a worthy provider he had a feeling he was going to find himself highly pressured into the managerial job Richard had mentioned. The rigging line snapped overhead in the wind drawing his gaze upward to the top mast of his ship. *His ship*. Max was not willing to give up what he had achieved. He would just have to make sure he found the wreck that would prove his worth, and he needed to do it soon.

He hadn't realized how tightly he had squeezed his fist until he felt the bite of the ring in his palm. He was getting married tomorrow. It still seemed surreal.

Jonathon walked up to Max. "What has you tied up in knots?"

Max looked to his returning first mate whom he hadn't seen since the case had been won yesterday afternoon. "Where have you been? Wooing Miss Sanchez or hiding from her father?"

Sheepishly Jonathon admitted, "A little of both, I suppose."

"Here, hold onto this for me until tomorrow." Max held his hand towards Jonathon, palm up, revealing the gold band.

Jonathon stared at the ring; his brow creased. "What's this?"

"I need you to stand up as my best man."

Arrested in the motion of taking the ring from Max's hand, Jonathon's head popped up. "What?"

Max gestured with his palm reminding Jonathon to take the ring from him. "Abigail Bennington and I will be married tomorrow. You didn't already have plans, did you?"

"Well, no. I didn't make any plans as I assumed we would be setting sail having been in port for over a week now. How in Hades did you end up a bridegroom today when you were a confirmed bachelor yesterday?"

Max answered in a deadpan manner, "Mr. Bennington is quite persuasive especially when you've compromised his only daughter."

Jonathon was baffled, "I would have thought you would know better than to tumble a lady."

"I didn't tumble her." Max was insulted his friend would leap to that conclusion.

"Then what did you do?"

"We took a walk."

"Just a walk?"

Max shrugged shamefaced. "Alone, after dark."

Jonathon said, "So the English are nearly as strict as the Cubans. How's her father treating you?"

"Welcoming with open arms. Probably because I agreed to marry without a fuss. He offered to set me up in his business."

"Yikes! You didn't take him up on it, did you?"

"No but I think he believes Abigail will bring me to do so eventually."

Jonathon grimaced. "What a difference. Miss Bennington's father is pulling you in while Esperanza's father is doing all he can to push me away and neither one thinks we are worthy as we are."

Chapter 17

November 13, 1828

Abby was standing before her mirror bathed and dressed in the rose gown. She picked up the gold crown from its resting place on the velvet tray. It was carefully polished to a shine the night before by her father who had insisted he be the one to do it. Abby gently held the crown across her open palms and let her thoughts drift. When her father had first mentioned it, she had pictured in her mind something heavy like a royal crown but this was a light tiara with delicate gold filigree in the shape of leaves while emeralds, diamonds and sapphires were set to form flowers. It was the most beautiful headpiece she had ever seen. Her mother had worn this as did her grandmothers. She now felt tied to them in a way she had not before. For a moment she allowed the tears to form in grievance of all she had missed not having her mother. She was glad she had this link to her today when she stood before God and all and pledged her life to a man she barely knew because her father requested it of her. She had no idea how this marriage would work. She had no preparations for it, no examples of marriage in her life to follow except for Elizabeth's. Oh Elizabeth, how much easier this would be if her friend were here to confide in. At least she had Tria but it was not the same for Tria was not any more experienced than she.

Another turn in the direction of her life. She was supposed to be at her Uncle's plantation getting to know his family and instead she was on a tiny island about to marry for something other than love to relieve her ailing father of his concern for her future without him. Without him - she didn't know how to imagine life without him. Her father had always been there like a rock in her foundation she took for granted.

The previous evening her father had sought her out, ostensibly to comfort her, assuming, and rightly so, she would be suffering from nervous tension. She had a feeling it was more to reassure them both they had made the right decision. Abby told him her only concern was having to say goodbye when he left to visit his brother and return to England. He told her not to worry. He had already sent a message to his Liverpool manager advising he would be staying much longer. He was considering opening an office in Key West given its strategic location to the Gulf of Mexico. So he would be returning to the island. Besides, he hoped Abby and Max might go with him to visit her Uncle James.

A knock sounded on the door intruding on her musings. "Who is it?" asked

Abby as she critically reviewed her reflection in the mirror for any signs of the distress she was feeling. "Victoria," came the reply from the other side of the carved panels. Abby gently laid the crown on the dresser and mentally lightened her mood before crossing the room to open the door for her friend. Tria looked lovely this morning in a light dress of pale sea green enhancing the colour of her eyes.

Tria greeted her with a quick hug and then stepped back to look Abby up and down. "Is this the dress you told me about? The one you rescued from the hold? You were right. It was definitely worth it. The dress is perfect for you. Such a wonderful shade of rose." Tria looked back to Abby's face. "What are you going to do with your hair?"

"I have no idea. I am sure Maria will come up with something. She is a wonder at hairdressing. Come, let me show you something." Abby returned to the dresser to pick up the crown and held it out for Tria to see.

"Oh my goodness! I have never seen anything so exquisite. You'll look positively like royalty. You don't think it's too much for a wedding like...." Victoria didn't know how to fix what would have been a crass remark.

Abby understood what she meant and didn't take offense. She had already had the same thought herself and dismissed it. "Probably so but the women of my family have all worn it on their wedding day and this is one tradition I want to keep no matter the circumstances of the day."

"Certainly dear, it is understandable." Tria gave Abby an impulsive hug intuitively knowing she needed the emotional support.

There came a quick knock before the door opened and Maria entered the room. "Good morning Miss Lambert. Miss Abby, are you ready for me to do your hair?"

"Yes please." Abby seated herself at the dressing table and Maria wasted no time getting started. Tria occasionally offered suggestions as Maria pulled the hair from her temples and gathered it at the crown of her head then set about making silky auburn ringlets cascade down her back. She carefully placed the crown to perfection and stepped back to admire her handiwork. Both girls exclaimed how lovely the result was to the point Abby could no longer wait to see for herself. Standing in front of the mirror over the bureau she saw something of her mother's portrait reflected back causing her to grow wistful again. Brushing aside the feeling she turned and smiled at the others. "Thank you Maria. Will you go let Father know I am ready?" Maria bobbed her head and left the room.

Abby held out her hand to Tria, who took it and gently squeezed. "You are a beautiful bride and you will make a fine wife. Max Eatonton is a very lucky man. Although he is a catch himself and the way he dotes on you... I change my mind, you are the lucky one."

"He may have doted before but I do not expect so now that he has been coerced into a marriage not of his choosing."

"Your father may have shortened the courtship but trust me when I say

Max would not be marrying you if he didn't want to no matter what your father said. He has always been his own man and I've seen how he cares for you. Eventually he would have asked and you would be wearing the crown about to walk down the aisle to him even had your father not intervened so try to put aside your nervousness and enjoy the moment. You only have one wedding day."

There came another knock on her door. Tria opened it to admit her father.

Richard stepped into the room and paused at the sight of his beautiful, precious Abigail. His mind slipped back in time to the morning of her birth. He and Anna had not been able to come up with a name they could agree upon for a girl until she arrived. Everyone around them had offered suggestion after suggestion to no avail. When the mid-wife placed the tiny perfect little girl in his arms he was so enraptured he suggested the name, Abigail, meaning 'father's joy'. Anna deemed it perfect. Sometimes it was hard to believe the bundle he once held was now the woman before him. She still enraptured him. He sighed. If only Anna were here to share this moment with him. "It is time Abigail. Are you ready?"

Abby nodded and together with Tria and Maria they descended the stairs to join Mrs. Mallory in the foyer. The whole party then walked to the wharf where they would be taken by long boat to the *Abigail Rose* anchored in the harbour. Abby had been delighted by her father's suggestion to have the wedding on their ship with Captain Andrews officiating. Walking down Front Street on her father's arm, nervousness began to overwhelm her. She tried thinking what Elizabeth might be doing today in England to keep from dwelling on the change her life would take in the next hour.

Abby now stood at the edge of the dock looking down into the long boat. The knot of anxiety just under her diaphragm spiraled upward into a flash of fear. She couldn't breathe. Her father stood next to her. The new first mate of the *Abigail Rose* was assisting Maria into the boat. Tria and Mrs. Mallory were settling on their seats. It was her turn next. She wasn't sure she could do it. She wasn't sure she could get in the boat without getting tangled in her skirts and she definitely wasn't sure she was ready to get married.

Fear turned into panic. Wildly she looked around her. Others were going about their day. A few noticed their well-dressed party and probably wondered at the occasion. The sky was clear, the water was turquoise, the wind gently blew. Everything was normal - except her. She wanted to run but she couldn't run back to girlhood. She couldn't run back in time. She had to face today and then she had to face tomorrow.

Abby closed her eyes and reached in her mind for comfort. Thoughts of Max surfaced of their own accord. She remembered his kiss - and could breathe again. Remembered the feel of his touch, recalled his gentle gestures and the adoration in his eyes and her heartbeat slowed. There was nothing to fear. She could do this. She opened her eyes to see the concern on her father's face. Lifting her head, she breathed deep and gave him a small smile. She could do this. Calmly and gracefully she descended into the boat.

Four crewmen rowed them to the *Abigail Rose*. Another boat was already tied to her side undulating on the water. Abby guessed it to be from the *Mystic* and lifted her gaze to the ship's deck looking for Max. She was disappointed not to see him at the railing. A few minutes later they pulled alongside the hull of the ship. Hook lines were dropped and the crewmen secured the boat then they were hoisted up. As the boat made its slow jerky assent from the water to the ship's deck she tightly gripped her seat and anxiously watched the bulwark growing closer. She needed to see Max. She continued to tell herself she could do this but until she saw his face and found acceptance, and hopefully desire to be her husband, her mantra only served to keep her from jumping out of the boat. She couldn't even contemplate how she would feel or what she would do if his aspect revealed mere resolve or worse - the anger he had felt at the initial idea of marriage.

Suddenly she lost her courage. She closed her eyes as the ship's deck came into view. She prayed with all her heart while her grip on the seat turned white knuckled. The boat stopped its assent and lightly swayed. Those around her began moving preparing to exit the boat. Still she kept her eyes closed, motionless. The boat rocked as two of the crew exited then pulled it closer to the ship.

Her father touched her on the shoulder. "Sweetheart."

She knew he expected her to get up but she remained as she was - waiting for courage, waiting for him.

"Abigail?"

Max's coaxing, uncertain tone had her smiling as she opened her eyes and turned her head towards her betrothed. Her smile broadened as she found the acceptance she needed and then the dimpled smile she craved. Everyone around them faded away as they absorbed each other across the distance between them.

Max held his hand out to her. "Come sweetheart."

Abby moved towards him as if in a dream. She knew others were there to help her cross the divide from the rowboat to the ship but she was only aware of Max's arms; one under her knees and the other supporting her back as he lifted her across the bulwarks. Her arms automatically slipped around his neck and she inhaled the musky scent of ocean, soap and him. She wanted to savor the moment, cradled against his strong chest, the weightlessness of being held, but he let her go. Her feet dropped to the deck and as she let him go awareness of the others around her flooded back. They stepped apart then moved away from the railing so the others could exit the boat. Abby noticed the crewmen assisted the others by holding their arms as they stepped from the boat to the deck. Max must have wanted her in his arms to have removed her from the boat in such a manner.

Hope soared within her.

Abby waited for her father while Max walked towards Captain Andrews standing in front of the master's cabin with Bible in hand and took his place between the captain and Mr. Keats. The crew of both ships fanned out along the railing leaving a wide path for their approach. Mr. and Mrs. Lambert stood off to her left. Mrs. Mallory and Maria moved forward out of the way then turned to watch them. Tria took her place to the right of Captain Andrews.

Richard gently tugged Abby's hand to turn her towards him for a private moment, her back to the assembly. Taking up her other hand he said, "Abigail you are beautiful. Your mother would be so proud of you. I am proud of you."

"Thank you." Abby was perilously close to tears. She didn't say more for fear of losing control of her emotions. She hoped her father understood.

Her father smiled in encouragement and squeezed her cold hands. "You will be fine. Are you ready?"

"Yes." She gave her father a tight smile before turning to face her future.

Richard tucked Abby's hand into the crook of his arm and escorted her, for the last time as simply his daughter. Next time she would be a married woman. In a few short moments he would give her into the care of a young man. Even though he chose this man for her and respected him, Richard still worried whether or not he had made the right decision.

Abby focused on Max. He was wearing the same suit he had worn to court except he had added a handkerchief to the pocket and he was wearing a neck cloth which made him seem uncomfortable. It also made him look like someone else so she focused on his face. He had slicked back his freshly washed hair and now, half dry, some of the curls were returning to their natural shape. He did not appear to be nervous but rather impatient waiting on her to approach and probably impatient for the whole ceremony to be done. Her eyes met his and the look of open adoration helped ease the tension in her belly until she noticed the subtle smoldering change that set her insides aflutter. A slow smile appeared on his face growing broader with every step she took closer to him. She smiled in return and saw his dimples deepen.

Her confidence in their future grew.

Max stood impatiently between Jonathon and Captain Andrews. He wondered what Abby and her father were discussing at the railing. What last words of advice would a father give his daughter? The neck cloth was causing him discomfort and overall he was ready to be done with the ceremony. To distract himself he tried thinking of the evening ahead and then later when they would finally be alone but those thoughts led to other discomforts. He was searching for another train of thought when Abby finally turned to face him.

Earlier he had been focused on getting her safely aboard the ship and had not noticed much beyond her lovely face. He was quite unprepared for the full impact of her beauty. His bride took his breath away. He could hardly believe this vision would become his wife. He could no longer recall a single reason he had had for not getting married. She would be his wife to kiss and hold whenever he wanted and only his after the sun went down. Feeling guilty for his lewd thoughts during a solemn ceremony he tried to focus his attention elsewhere. She was only a few steps away from him when he noticed the crown she wore nestled in her curls. He smiled. He was marrying his very own princess.

The ceremony was a hazy blur for Abby. She responded where required but could not recall any details later except for hearing Max's full name for the first time and one moment of pure clarity when Max slipped the ring on her left hand and she looked down to find her mother's wedding band on her finger with the distinctive rose pattern carved into the band. She recalled her father showing it to her as a child. He told her he had always thought of her mother as a wild Irish rose. She lifted her tear filled eyes to Max's and smiled to let him know she was happy with the ring. She barely heard him whisper, "My Rose Princess."

Abby felt the finality of the wedding when Captain Andrews pronounced them, "man and wife," and then turned them to introduce "Captain and Mrs. Alexander Maximus Eatonton." Not even signing the marriage document felt as final as hearing her new name. It was as if Abigail ceased to exist. Her independence gone. The right to choose her own path now limited to the whims of a husband.

Everyone seemed to rush forward at once to congratulate them. Time blurred for Abby. She kissed and hugged, smiled and nodded, and moved where she was led. Every once in a while she would look up at Max and wonder how was she supposed to be his wife.

After the ceremony they returned to the boardinghouse where Mrs. Mallory had arranged a small outdoor reception. At least it was supposed to have been small. Mrs. Mallory had invited some of Max's friends and those acquainted with Mr. Bennington but as word got around the island many invited themselves bringing food to share. Abby and Richard were both taken aback by the number of people, well over fifty, waiting in the fenced backyard of the boardinghouse for their arrival. The others took it as a normal occurrence on the island.

Abby and Max were trailing behind, not touching, but walking together in a companionable silence. When she noticed the gathered crowd her nervousness from before the ceremony returned. It must have communicated itself to Max as he took her hand and squeezed it in a comforting gesture. He then leaned over to say for her ears only, "Relax this part's supposed to be fun," adding a smile to melt her resistance. It didn't quite work.

They climbed the porch steps. "It would be fun if ours was a normal wedding. I was not prepared to share this with everyone on the island. I am not even comfortable with you yet."

The others had already gone inside so instead of opening the door for Abby, Max pulled her to face him and held both her hands. He smiled again and was pleased Abby was able to return a tremulous smile of her own. "I know this is difficult but we can do it. I'm right here by your side." He saw her eyes drop to his mouth and thought kissing her senseless might not be a bad idea. It certainly had been on his mind since he had lifted her from the boat. Actually truth be told he hadn't stopped thinking about it since their last kiss. Leaning down he brushed his lips to hers.

Abby was touched he took the time to comfort her. When he lifted his head and smiled she couldn't help but return the gesture. Facing him as she was his dimples enticed her and just as she realized she was staring at them he leaned down and kissed her again. It was a very gentle kiss - at first - and then he deepened it. She pressed closer to him wanting more.

Max pulled back before things could get out of control. He would never hear the end of it if he showed up at his wedding party with a noticeable desire to skip to the wedding night. "Are you feeling more comfortable with me now?" His question embarrassed her and the accompanying blush matched her gown and heightened her beauty increasing Max's thankfulness he had been impulsive enough to marry her.

Abby apologized for her thoughtless comment. "Forgive me. I did not consider how it would sound to you. I ..."

Max placed a finger against her lips to silence her. "Shh, I understand what you meant. No apology is necessary. Are you ready now to greet our guests Mrs. Eatonton?" Max found he liked using her married name. He was proud to call her his wife.

Abby took a steadying breath. She tilted her head to the side and looked into her husband's clear blue eyes, absorbing his strength. "It was a momentary weakness. I am ready now." She was starting to believe this marriage would work; that they would get along very well together. He was being very kind, attentive and supportive to her today. If he had any misgivings he was hiding them well.

Max ushered her in the front door and gave her a moment to run upstairs to deposit her reticule and check her appearance. When she returned, he took her hand and together they exited the rear door to the garden heralded by cheers and applause. It took them nearly an hour to greet all of the guests before they were ushered by Mrs. Mallory to a table set up in the shade of some lime trees and given plates of food and cool lemonade to drink. Abby, tiring from the heat and stress, was thankful for the respite. Although she was barely able to touch her food, she drank several glasses of lemonade in deference to the heat.

Max never left her side and it didn't take long for her to relax and even enjoy herself. Everyone was very accepting and not one snide or cynical remark reached her hearing concerning the speed of their nuptials. It was a far cry from what she would have faced had these events transpired in England. Abby was feeling benevolent towards her new island home when suddenly from the edge of the crowd there was heard a cry of "Wreck Ashore!" She felt Max instantly stiffen beside her. "What is it?" They heard the alarm again before he answered her.

Max looked at her with regret clouding his features. "An end to our party, I'm afraid. A ship wreck has been spotted. Let me see if I can find out more details."

Abby followed Max with her eyes as he made his way to the gathering of sailors around the man who had arrived with the news. Tria came to stand next to her for moral support. A moment later many of Max's friends were quickly leaving the yard barely taking the time to send a farewell wave to Mrs. Mallory and Abby. Max and his crew, as one unit, had started to follow suit when Max suddenly stopped and returned to her with a tight look on his face that did not bode well.

"You need to go?" Abby knew it was more of a statement than a question.

"A large ship full of cotton went down near Tavernier Key. The ship is a loss but they need all hands to salvage the cotton. It may take weeks to work the wreck."

Max was looking at her expectantly and Abby realized he was seeking her approval. Although he hadn't asked for her permission he was giving her an opportunity to ask him not to go. Glancing at his crew anxiously waiting behind him she really had no choice, with so many men's livelihoods depending on her answer, what could she do except send him off. She said what she must but he would have to forgive her if her eyes beseeched him otherwise. "I understand. You must go." Almost as an afterthought she added, "Please be careful."

Max hesitated another moment as if assuring himself she was sincere. "I will." He gave her a quick kiss on the cheek and took off running after his crew but in the back of his mind he was thinking it had been a long time since someone had been concerned for his safety. It was nice but it also reminded him of why he had been against the idea of getting married. Now someone else's fate was aligned with his and he felt the burden settle heavily on his shoulders.

Abby felt bereft. In a few short hours her life had become so tangled with his that she felt the loss of his presence. Her father was still here. For the time being she would stay where she was in the boardinghouse. Really not much had changed since she awoke this morning and yet everything had changed. *How dangerous was it to salvage cotton?*

The remaining guests were talking excitedly amongst themselves as they left in groups to spread the word around town of the shipwreck. Everyone's lives were affected. If not directly by loved ones leaving or providing needed services then they would feel the effects later from the resulting income.

Her father moved to Abby's side for support. "Are you alright?"

Abby tried to pull her thoughts away from her new husband and where he was headed. "I am fine. I do not need to worry about him, do I?"

Tria laid a supportive hand on her shoulder. "You needn't worry about Max. He's a good sailor. I've heard many compliment his ability."

"As have I," added her father.

Abby nodded her head in acceptance of their reassurances. Looking for something to take her mind from the situation she said to Tria, "Let us help clean up and Father, please go rest."

Richard didn't want to show his weakness but he knew Abby was right; she didn't need another burden so he agreed to go rest. As he walked to his room, he acknowledged the subtle shift in their relationship as Abby unconsciously slipped into adulthood.

Abby had just started collecting dirty plates from the closest table when Mrs. Mallory came to shoo her away with her lovely Irish brogue. "Now missy der tisn't any need for you to help. Stop before you go soiling tat lovely dress. I've got me staff to take care of this. You run along now and try to enjoy the rest of the day even though your man had to leave." She took the plates out of Abby's hand and didn't budge till Abby turned to leave the yard. A nod in Victoria's direction sent her trailing after Abby.

"What do I do now?" asked Abby at a complete loss.

Tria gave her a mischievous smile. "We could go to the wharf. If we hurry we may be in time to wave his ship off."

Abby wasn't sure she could handle saying goodbye again but agreed to go anyway because the alternative of staying there doing nothing was worse. Reaching Front Street they could see the *Mystic* still at her berth. There was a flurry of activity along the wharf as the ships prepared to leave and a few were already sailing out of the harbour. They hurried down to the pier but once they started walking across the planks Abby's pace slowed not being sure of their reception. Bless her, Tria didn't question the change in pace but simply slowed her stride to match Abby's. They reached the gangplank as Thomas was seen taking what appeared to be the last load of provisions aboard ship. Abby hesitated but Tria, in her usual brazen manner, called out, "Permission to board."

Max looked over the railing at them. Abby couldn't be sure but he didn't appear pleased to see them. Instead of granting permission he walked down the gangplank to them.

"What brings you ladies here? We will be leaving in a moment."

Tria answered for them. "We came to wave you off. A proper send off for our heroes."

Abby felt the need to lighten the mood so she said in a teasing tone to Tria, "Careful dear that is my husband you are flirting with."

"So it is." Tria lifted Abby's left hand. "And with a ring to prove it. I'll just go wait over here then until you're ready to shove off." She walked a little ways down the dock to give Max and Abby some privacy. Catching Billy watching her from the ship's deck she gave him a flirtatious wave.

Max continued the lighthearted tone by teasingly scolding Victoria, "And leave my men alone. They have work to do." He then turned his attention to Abby. "You are a distraction....but I'm glad you came to see us off." Not caring who was there to see he gave her a full, albeit quick, kiss on the lips that left Abby flushed with embarrassment, just the way Max wanted to see her.

Abby looked at him shyly. "I will be waiting for you when you return."

"I'm looking forward to starting our honeymoon so I can kiss you all over."

Abby's blush deepened at his indecent suggestion. He couldn't mean *everywhere*. The wide grin spreading across his face suggested he did. A grin that could make her agree to anything. *What was she going to do with such a handsome husband?* He kissed the back of each of her hands before loping back up the gangplank to the deck.

Tria returned to her side. "Lucky girl."

Max's attitude towards her this morning was not that of a man forced to marry. Abby felt very fortunate he was looking forward to starting their married life. She watched as Max quickly issued orders to his crew, his back tall, head up, shoulders straight, a man confident with himself and his place in the world. She admired that about him and she envied it a little too. He had purpose and meaning. She had yet to find her purpose in the world. She supposed being a wife and eventually a mother should be enough - how wonderful the possibility of motherhood was closer now that she was married - but she wanted to do more. She just didn't know what more could be. But here, on this tiny frontier island, she felt like she had a chance to do more than the role she would have been held to in England.

Jonathon teased Max as he returned to the helm. "You're not running from your wedding night, are you?"

Max gave him a tight smile and under his breath said, "Not hardly." Then he said loudly for the crew to hear, "Prepare to make sail."

Hearing the frustration in Max's voice, Jonathon turned away to hide his smile from Max. "Aye Captain."

Abby and Victoria watched the activity on deck. In no time at all the gangplank was pulled in, the ropes were untied and the ship began to drift away from the pier. Tria waved to the crew but Abby waited until Max glanced over his shoulder, towards her, to offer a shy wave just for him. The girls stood there, silently, side by side, arms linked and watched the ship sail away until it was hardly a speck on the horizon.

Chapter 18

Abby gave up the pretense of sleep long before dawn. She had so many questions running through her mind, rest had been next to impossible. Things she and Max hadn't even discussed yet. *Where would they live? On his ship or in a house? Would they travel for their honeymoon? How long would he be gone?* But it was one thought in particular keeping her awake night after night. *How dangerous was it to salvage cotton?*

She dressed herself in a simple gown not wanting to disturb Maria at such an early hour and wandered downstairs to the dining room where she found Mrs. Mallory breaking her fast. The proprietress greeted her cheerfully. "Good morning Mrs. Eatonton. How are you this morning?"

Apparently everyone else was going to be used to her new name before she ever was. Abby nearly looked over her shoulder for someone behind her before she realized Mrs. Mallory was addressing her. "Good morning Mrs. Mallory. I am fine and yourself?"

"Fit as a fiddle. You are up early. Have trouble sleeping, did you?"

"How did you know?" asked Abby, a little disconcerted.

"You look a little peaked and tis only to be expected having newly acquired a husband only to have him go rushing off to do dangerous work and before you've even properly celebrated your wedding." She briskly cleared away her dishes. "I will bring you some tea and toast directly."

Abby's concerns for Max swelled again with Mrs. Mallory's comment of 'dangerous work'.

She returned with Abby's breakfast tray and setting it down on the table placed the items in front of Abby. "What you need lass is something to occupy your time till your man returns. Is there something useful you like to do? Cooking or baking perhaps?"

"I do not know how to cook or bake."

Mrs. Mallory tried to hide her surprise. "I suppose with your upbringing it wasn't necessary for you to learn but you are a married woman now and there are times when it comes in handy to know such things. It would also keep your mind from your troubles. Would you be interested in learning?"

Abby thought there was some sense in what Mrs. Mallory said and there was only so much reading and writing a person could do to distract oneself from her own thoughts. Here seemed a good solution to her growing problem. "Thank you madam. I believe I will accept your gracious offer."

"Good girl. Join me in the cookhouse when you are done with your breakfast."

A short while later Abby, with her finished breakfast tray in hand, made her way outside to the cookhouse. It was a small building, the size of one room, built in the yard behind the house so the heat from the cooking fire did not warm the main house. Mrs. Mallory handed her an apron and commenced teaching her how to make and knead bread. Abby found nothing to like about baking and was grateful when Mrs. Mallory dismissed her as soon as the bread was in the oven due to concerns Abby still wasn't fully acclimated to the island heat. Even though it wasn't quite mid-morning the cookhouse was nearly sweltering. Mrs. Mallory suggested she rest and return in the afternoon for dinner preparations.

Abby quickly realized cooking was definitely not her forte but she continued with the lessons, mainly because she agreed with Mrs. Mallory. One day it may come in handy. It was a few days later when she discovered something of great interest to her. One of the local fishermen, Captain Graham, came to see Mrs. Mallory with a deep laceration in his hand from a fishing hook.

Mrs. Mallory carefully cleaned and examined the wound. She looked to Abigail and found her not only unaffected by the blood but also interested. "Can you sew?"

Abby had a horrible suspicion. "Tolerably well."

"He needs stitches and my hands aren't steady enough for that kind of work anymore. Dr. Waterhouse sailed to Havana this morning. It's up to you dearie. Can you handle the needle?"

Abby considered her request. She was nervous but willing to try. "I think so."

"Of course ye can. I'll fetch my mending basket." Mrs. Mallory left the room.

Abby smiled weakly at Captain Graham. Seeing her nervousness he sought to reassure her. "I've been stitched before by those less skilled than you and certainly never one so fine to look upon as yourself." He nodded to the brown bottle on the table behind her. "Would you mind fetching that bottle of rum over there? I have a mind to get started on numbing the pain."

He took a few long swigs from the bottle before Mrs. Mallory returned and pulled it from his grasp. "Best take care of your hand before you drink it all." She then grasped his hand firmly and poured some of the rum across his wound. The good Captain let loose a string of curses before the pain subsided. He apologized to them for the wickedness of his tongue. Mrs. Mallory handed him back the bottle then made ready the needle and thread before passing them to Abby.

Mrs. Mallory held the wound closed. Schooling herself Abby took a deep breath and held it as she put the needle to his skin. The first stitch was the hardest. The feel of the needle going through his flesh made her queasy but the more she focused on the task of making small even stitches the less ill she felt. She couldn't look at the Captain. If she saw the pain on his face she didn't think she would be able to continue. It took twelve stitches before Mrs. Mallory declared her she to be done.

Afterwards, Captain Graham nodded in satisfaction and Mrs. Mallory excused herself from the room. Reaction set in and Abby started shaking. She sat down in a chair suddenly unable to support her own weight.

Captain Graham held the bottle of rum to her. "Looks like you need this more now than I do." Abby hesitated. He gestured with the bottle. "It will help."

Abby took a small sip. She felt it burst inside her mouth. She didn't like the taste but then it left a comforting warmth. She took another sip before handing him back the bottle. She did feel better now but suspected it was more the distraction than the alcohol.

Mrs. Mallory returned with a stem of a plant she had cut from her garden. She squeezed the pulp and rubbed it across his wound. Abby bound the Captain's hand with a clean dressing.

When he left, Abby helped Mrs. Mallory clean up while she satisfied her curiosity. "What plant did you use on his wound?"

"Aloe Vera. It comes from Africa. I keep it in my garden for medicinal purposes."

"What is it good for and why did you put it on his hand?"

"'Tis believed to ward off infection in wounds. I also use it to soothe burns and it can be used as a purgative."

Abby was fascinated. "Mrs. Mallory, would you be willing to teach me what you know of healing?"

Mrs. Mallory was flattered by her request. "It would be my pleasure."

Abby spent most of the next two and half weeks learning everything she could from Mrs. Mallory about healing the sick and injured, when she wasn't learning to cook. It succeeded in keeping her occupied during the day and well into the evening making notes of all she had learned. Still the nights were difficult. That was when all the questions and doubts returned to haunt her.

Every day she would find time to walk past the wharves hoping to see his ship only to be disappointed to find it was still absent from its berth. Inquiring about the work the men were doing, she had learned cotton bales weighed three to five hundred pounds each when loaded on a ship. Water-soaked bales of cotton could weigh more than three times greater. She couldn't understand how it was possible to raise something of such great weight from a sunken ship. Her father tried to explain the principles of block and tackle and leverage but she still could not comprehend how it was done. She did understand how the work could be dangerous.

Occasionally a ship reloading with supplies for the wreck site would bring word of the salvage operation. Those families with men working the wreck would swarm the sailors in port with questions of their progress, when they thought the job would be completed and most importantly the health of their loved ones. So far only one serious injury had occurred; a sailor's hand was caught in the lines and badly abraded. Although the sailor was recovering well it heightened the concerns of all involved. The good news was if the weather held fair they expected to be done before the end of three weeks.

Prayers were regularly sent heavenward this would be so. The islanders were pleased to have a visiting preacher for Sunday services who prayed hard and often for those working the wreck.

Everyone was relieved when the wreckers began returning home late one morning eighteen days later having saved nearly all of the cotton. It started a week-long celebration. Cheers went up from the wharf for each returning vessel and the bars were full of wreckers telling their tales of dangers and heroism.

Abby nervously waited for the return of her husband. For three days she kept a vigilant watch on the harbour to no avail. His was one of the last ships to return. Early on the fourth morning Maria brought her the news the *Mystic* had slipped into its berth. Abby donned her second best dress and waited in the parlour as it had the best view of the street.

A few hours after word arrived they had returned, Thomas entered the front door and approached Abby. He was clearly there to tell her something but he kept hesitating so she finally asked him with fear constricting her chest, "Is Captain Max alright?"

"Yes ma'am."

Her relief was so great it nearly overwhelmed her. "Then what is it Thomas?"

"I've come to ask your permission to marry Maria."

Abby had expected this to happen eventually. Still his announcement caught her by surprise today as it was the furthest thought from her mind. She noticed Maria watching from the doorway. "You don't need my permission Thomas. Maria is a free woman and can do as she pleases but I will give you my blessing."

Maria dashed across the room to impulsively hug her. "Thank you Miss Abby." She then turned to Thomas and hand in hand they ran off to make their plans. Abby was left standing in the center of the room jealous of their happiness and disappointed Max had yet to make an appearance but Thomas had had time to find and propose to Maria.

She started pacing the room telling herself he was delayed with ship's business. He was the captain after all. He would have more to do than one of the crew. She sat down on the sofa and tried to find her patience. She honestly did try but a few moments later she rose from the sofa determined to seek out her errant husband. She decided she was going to walk right up to his ship and see for herself what was taking him so long. Gathering her parasol and reticule from her room she descended the stairs considering what she was going to say when she found him. She was mere steps from the front door when it suddenly opened and there, standing on the threshold, was the focus of her thoughts in person.

"Going somewhere?" he asked.

Her heart started beating faster making her feel lightheaded. Max shut the door without taking his eyes from her, then took the few steps necessary to bring him to her. Without warning he scooped her up in his arms and started up the stairs. Abby's arms automatically went around his neck. She didn't know whether to be flattered or to protest. They reached the top of the stairs without her having made a decision. She had expected him to put her down but he carried her straight into her room shutting the door with a competent back kick. He then let her slip to her feet but kept her within his embrace. Her arms rested against his muscular chest, hands on his warm rugged shoulders. His still damp hair curled just above her fingertips. He smelled of sea and soap. Her forehead was at a level with his lips. She tilted her head back to look at his face.

By way of making an excuse for his behaviour he said, "I wanted to give you a proper 'hello'," and brought his lips down to hers.

Abby's eyes closed of their own volition and she let herself respond to this kiss without reservation, having no reason to hold back. This time it was proper for a husband to kiss his wife and there was no one around to observe them. One of Max's hands slid up her back and into her hair lightly holding her head to add just the right angle and pressure to the kiss. There was an urgency she had not felt before and wondered at its cause but her thoughts became distracted as his hand trailed down her neck to her chest. The intimate caress made Abby suddenly pull away from his embrace. They stood for a moment facing each other, breathing hard.

Max was aware of his wife's innocence but he had not expected her to be so untouched. It was unchartered water for him but he was looking forward to exploring its depths... with her.

Abby felt disconcerted by the way Max was looking at her, as if he would devour her. She felt a need to flee from the room, to return to a more public place. "I believe it is time for tea. We should return downstairs."

Max recognized her retreat for what it was and nodded in agreement. "You go ahead. I'll be down in a moment." He needed time to cool his ardor. Abby shut the door behind her. Standing quietly in the middle of her room, he could hear her footsteps receding down the stairs and another door closing further down the hall. The walls of her room were thin and her father slept in the next room. Max hadn't really given any thought to the details of their first night beyond the basic event. He now decided plans were needed. It didn't take long for him to determine what he did want. He found Abby downstairs and excused himself from tea with the promise he would return in time for dinner. He had a lot to do between now and then to prepare a bridal chamber.

Once Max returned to the boardinghouse, the hours until they would be able to retire for the evening stretched endlessly in front of him, until he discovered a way to amuse himself and hopefully add to the success of his plans for the evening. He made a game of finding ways to covertly touch his wife in intimate places: a caress along the back of her neck, running a finger delicately along the inside of her arm, dropping a kiss behind her ear and fortunately being seated next to each other for dinner offered him more temptations. When he couldn't touch her, he would send her smoldering glances when no one else was looking which made her, without fail, drop her eyes and try to hide her blush.

Abby was feeling like stalked prey. Before and during dinner Max was put upon by all those present at the little boardinghouse for details of the recent wreck and extensive salvage operation. Still he somehow managed to send Abby covert glances and administer secret caresses; all of which had her growing ever more nervous as the hour approached when they would retire to her room. She was unable to keep her mind focused on the dinner conversation. Her food was dry and tasteless not that she felt like eating with the butterfly feeling in her stomach. The end of dinner brought some relief to the constant assault on her senses but her nervous anticipation only grew as the clock ticked ever closer to the end of the evening. She was torn between anticipation of finally taking the last step into womanhood and the consternation of relinquishing herself to another.

After dinner her father led the way from the dinner table to the parlour followed by Captain Andrews, Max, Abby and another couple staying at the inn. Talk centered on general topics like the weather. Max and Abby were seated in wing back chairs set next to each other facing the room.

Max was feeling quite pleased with his little game of cat and mouse. Abby had even shyly returned an advance of her own during dinner. He had been caressing her hand under the table and found she squirmed most when he rubbed his thumb across her open palm. After failing to stop him by holding his hand still, she had reversed their roles; caressing him and rubbing her delicate thumb across his work roughened palm. The sensation had nearly made him squirm in his chair. Max was looking forward to taking it to the next level.

Abby's back was to the foyer so she was not able to see Maria drop a satchel by the front door. She did see Max nod to someone behind her but when she looked over her shoulder the foyer was empty. When she looked back at Max, he winked at her and returned his attention to the conversation in the room. She did too. Then she felt his hand slip under her sleeve where it ended at her elbow in loose folds. He ran his fingers along her sensitive inner arm in a light caress that sent chills down her back. To break the contact she pulled her arm to her side but he must have anticipated the move as his hand followed. She shifted away to sit on the front edge of the chair breaking the contact altogether. Her father, noticing her erratic movement, stopped what he was saying to inquire if she was alright which furthered her discomfort. She mumbled something that seemed to satisfy him for he returned to his conversation. She leaned to the side of the chair furthest from Max. Abby didn't think she could stand much more of his teasing. She was trying to keep calm but it was growing harder as the sunlight was disappearing from the parlour window.

A short time later, her father, who still tired easily from his illness, stood up and bid good night to the room in general. He paused at Abby's chair by the doorway to kiss her on the cheek. He looked intently at her and squeezed her hand a moment longer than usual causing Abby some concern. She rose from her chair to wish him goodnight and was pleasantly surprised when he pulled her into his embrace despite the others in the room. In that brief moment she was torn between letting go of him to take the final step into womanhood, becoming a true wife and one day hopefully a mother, or clinging to him and holding onto the safety of girlhood and the life she had always known. Giving herself body and soul into the keeping of her husband was daunting and in her fear of the moment she wanted to hold onto her childhood just a little longer. Her father broke their contact before she consciously made the decision. Not that there really was a decision left to make. Vows had been made. The days of her girlhood were gone, never to be reclaimed. Her future was with the man standing behind her. She only had to be brave enough to grasp it. She stepped away from her father bringing herself next to her husband.

Richard grasped Max's hand. "Take care of my little girl." Then he turned to climb the stairs heading to his room. Abby wondered at her father's choice of words. He had not referred to her as his 'little girl' for longer than she could remember. Max, however, understood the message behind his words loud and clear.

Richard's departure signaled Captain Andrews' as well. After he left, Max and Abby bid the other couple 'good evening'. Abby expected Max to lead her to the stairs but instead he turned towards the front door, opened it, and then leaned down to pick up her bag.

Abby was not able to hide her shocked dismay, "You had Maria pack a bag for me?" She realized now the trap was sprung. The predator had caught his prey for she would not argue with him here in the foyer especially with the other couple in the parlour as witnesses. She would have liked to have been asked but at this point to have at least been told of the plans would have been nice. Accepting her fate would be sealed elsewhere tonight she gathered her courage and walked through the door he held open. Knowing his ship could be the only destination he had in mind she started off in that direction.

Max followed realizing the mood he had tried all evening to create had suddenly vanished like stars in the morning sky. He tried offering Abby his arm and she refused to take it. He then placed his hand on the small of her back only to have her pull away. So they walked the distance to the wharf in silence, not touching, each lost in their own concerns, neither one taking any enjoyment from the spectacular sunset happening in front of them. The orange sphere turned crimson then dropped below the horizon as they reached the gangplank.

Abby knew her anger was unreasonably high. The cause of her emotion she understood. The escalation of that emotion had to be from the constant state of nervous tension she had been subjected to this evening. She knew a husband had the right to make decisions for her without consulting her wishes but for someone who had been used to making most of her own decisions it was a lot harder to accept in reality. Her dreams of a husband had been one who would give her an equal say in their lives. It was distressing to realize she had not married that man.

Knowing she was going to have to make the best of her situation she made a conscious effort to push away the anger as they boarded his ship. Standing on deck under the main mast she kept her back to her husband. The breeze blew gently across her cheek, sea birds flew past the furled sails overhead, the gentle sway of the ship and the waning light of evening made for a romantic setting. She suddenly realized there was an unusual quiet. It took a moment to attribute it to the lack of crew on board. She also noticed a light was burning below deck. She descended the stairs to discover the light was emanating from his cabin. Entering the room she found the oil lamp burning on the desk, his bunk now held two pillows and appeared to have freshly laundered sheets. Max had gone to a lot of effort to set up this scene. It helped soften the anger and soften her heart.

"You set all this up for me?" she asked him in amazement.

Max had stopped a few steps from her waiting for her reaction. At her question he moved another step closer. "For us." He reached out to brush a stray tendril from her face.

"I know not what to do," whispered Abby.

Max smiled and assured her. "You don't need to. Just follow my lead; better yet do whatever you want to do. But first, I am going to keep my promise."

"What promise is that?"

"To kiss you all over."

Abby's eyes widened. He couldn't mean to literally kiss her everywhere. *Could he?* She blushed. The thought was as daunting as it was exciting. Abby took his advice and did what she had wanted to do from the first moment they met. She lifted her right hand to his face and traced her finger along his dimple then watched as his lips descended to hers. She slipped her hand behind his head and let her fingers run through his hair liking the way his curls wrapped around them. She melted into him at the touch of his lips to hers.

Chapter 19

Abby was awakened by seagulls squawking so close she thought they were in her bedroom. She opened her eyes and was further disconcerted to find she was not in her room. A second later memory rushed back of all that had happened since yesterday morning. The anxiety of waiting for Max's return. The joy she felt for Thomas and Maria and the feelings they obviously had for each other. The long wait for Max to come to her and then the uninhibited kiss she had shared with him in her room, followed by hours of anticipation and finally sharing their first night together. She remembered hearing him whisper just before she fell asleep, "Flowers and thorns, you are all mine now. My Rose Princess." Smiling to herself she stretched and felt her leg brush against his. She turned her head to find her husband still sleeping. She watched the rise and fall of his bare chest. Even at rest his body exuded strength. The muscles outlined under his golden skin fascinated her. She turned towards him and lightly ran her hand over the bulges of his upper arm. When her touch didn't disturb him she ran her fingers along his upper chest then down the center to splay her hand across his chiseled abdomen. Looking to his face to make sure he was still sleeping she was disconcerted to discover blue eyes watching her. Blushing, she lifted her hand from his torso only to have it captured in his. She followed her hand with her eyes as he lifted it to his lips and kissed it.

"What a charming way to be awaken, with caresses from my blushing bride."

He then climbed out of the bunk and grabbed his shirt and pants and started dressing with his back towards her. "I'm starving. I'll go see what we have to eat while you dress."

Suddenly left alone in the room, a bewildered Abby climbed out of the bunk and looked in the satchel Maria had packed for her to find a clean dress and chemise. She found a clean cloth, bowl and pitcher with fresh water on a stand in the corner with which to refresh herself. Something else he had done special for her. She slipped into her clothes fastening the back of her dress as far as she could before leaving the cabin. She found Max in the galley slicing mango to add to a platter of banana, bread and cheese for their meal. She had noticed from the porthole it was late morning, not that she needed the visual confirmation. Her stomach was letting her know it was long past time for sustenance. Not able to resist she seized a bite of banana while she waited for Max to finish his task. As soon as he cleaned his hands she presented her back to him and pulled her hair aside. "Would you mind doing the rest of my buttons?"

Max moved closer. She felt his hands grasp the edges of the dress as expected but then felt an unexpected soft kiss placed on the skin above her chemise sending a chill across her back. So far she was enjoying being married and didn't regret her decision one bit.

By afternoon, Abby changed her mind. Being married was exasperating. After their late breakfast Max left her at the boardinghouse saying only that he had some business to do and would be back soon. It was several hours later and she had run out of ways to entertain herself; had grown weary trying to figure out what was keeping him; tired of always waiting for him; frustrated they had yet to discuss anything of importance and feeling very unsettled as to where she would be calling home. All of which had put her in a foul humor.

She was sitting on the front porch vigorously fanning herself against the afternoon's warmth. Her father had left to visit Mr. Lambert after lunch. When he asked her to join him she had turned him down expecting Max to return at any moment. Now she wished she had accepted. A visit with Tria would have been much more enjoyable. Abby was contemplating leaving Max a note and joining her father at the Lambert's for tea when she saw him turning the corner from Front Street. His long strides brought him up to the porch in no time. He wore a boyish grin on his face as he held his hand out to her.

"Abigail, come quickly. I have something to show you."

She stopped fanning herself and considered his request. His good mood was infectious and being a little curious, Abby gave in. "Let me get my hat." She returned a moment later, descended the porch steps and took his proffered arm. "Where are we headed?"

"To the other side of town."

"What do you want to show me?"

"You'll see. It's a surprise."

Abby affected a serious tone. "What if I don't like surprises?"

Max hadn't considered the possibility. His brow furrowed as he tried to decide how to proceed with his plans if she didn't like to be surprised. He looked her way and opened his mouth to try and explain when he noticed the gleam in her eyes and realized she had been teasing him. He responded with a smile and a soundless chuckle, somewhat surprised to discover he enjoyed her teasing.

The exchange left them both feeling light-hearted as they walked hand in hand the rest of the way down Front Street and turned right on Simonton. Abby recognized the house standing on the corner as belonging to the Martin's. Even though it had been dark the night of the ball the facade of the house had been well lit from torches placed in the yard. They continued past the Martin's but as they approached the small foot bridge over the tidal stream Max pulled Abby towards a house that stood on the right in front of the stream. It was a modest two story unpainted clapboard house with what looked to be a walkway built onto the roof. The house appeared to be empty so Abby wasn't sure why Max had stopped there.

"Do you like it?" asked Max.

Abby wasn't sure how to respond. The house was certainly nothing grand. It was very similar to many others but sensing Max had a purpose she said, "It is nice. Do you know the owner?"

"As a matter of fact, I do, and it happens to be available for rent. It will be our home, Abby, at least until I can afford our own land to build our own house."

Abby was momentarily stunned and dismayed that such a momentous decision was made completely without her input. She did realize there probably weren't many vacant houses to choose from but she still would have liked to have been included in the decision. Remembering Mrs. Winterfeldt's admonishment that a wife must defer to her husband, Abby put aside her feelings and reached out a hand to Max trying to inject enthusiasm in her voice. "Show me. I want to see inside."

Max had felt Abby's disappointment even though she tried to hide it. He could only attribute it to the fact this house was probably not as nice as her father's house in England. He hated to have to further disappoint her. "We can't. It is not ours yet. Mr. Simms is willing to hold it for me - for us - until I receive the settlement from the cotton ship."

"But Max, we do not have to wait for a settlement. You have my dowry."

Max's expression tightened. "I will pay for this with the money I have earned. I'll not use yours."

"It is not mine, it is really your money for marrying me, but you could think of it as ours."

"I did not ask to be paid. I didn't marry you for money." Max turned and started walking briskly back the way they had come.

Abby called after him. "It is just the way it is done in England." Max kept walking, back stiff. Abby picked up her skirts and chased after him in as ladylike a manner as she could muster. "Would you stop for a minute and talk to me?"

Max abruptly stopped and turned to her. "Talk about what?"

Abby frantically thought: *What did she want to say? What did she want to ask?* She ended up asking the only question she really needed an answer to, "Why did you marry me?"

Max saw the sincerity in her question but he wasn't ready to admit the truth to himself, much less to her. They stood there staring at each other and when she started to think he wasn't going to answer he finally said, "It was the only thing I could do...," *to keep from losing you.* But he didn't voice the last part. He wasn't ready to give so much of himself away. Considering the conversation over, Max again started walking back to the boardinghouse pondering how he had arrived so excited to share his news and was now walking back feeling miserable.

Abby was sure the rest of his sentence would have been - *to keep from losing my ship.* Feeling disappointed and miserable she followed Max in silence the rest of the way back to the boardinghouse.

When they reached Mrs. Mallory's front porch Max turned to her. "If you don't mind, I'm going to return to the *Mystic*. With the New England fishermen arriving late in the season so they could vote in the presidential election, I've decided to have the crew do some fishing in their absence to bring in some extra funds. We'll set sail now so we'll be on good fishing come dawn. Give your father my regards." Almost as an afterthought he kissed her cheek and then left her standing there.

Abby shut herself in her room and had Maria bring her a dinner tray. She was not ready to face anyone, especially her father. She was feeling ashamed and alone. Her marriage was barely started and it was already strained. From her upstairs bedroom window she glimpsed the *Mystic* between the buildings headed south. She hadn't thought to ask where he was sailing to...just let him go. Let him walk away from her. She should have told him she liked the house. Should have thanked him for finding them a place of their own. If she had been a proper wife that's what she would have done. Not insulted him with money concerns or pressed for an answer she really didn't want to hear. She resolved to make amends as soon as he returned and to try harder to please her husband as a proper wife should.

It was about an hour before dawn, the world still dark so that one's senses were more focused on sound; the lapping of water against the hull, the creaking sounds of the ship as it was rocked by the waves, the light snapping of the rigging in the breeze, the sea birds circling in the air currents. The *Mystic* was anchored just off the reef near Big Pine Key, her crew still asleep below. Max walked the length of his ship to stand at her bow facing eastward with only the fading starlight to guide him. He hadn't bothered to bring a lantern. He knew every square inch of the *Mystic's* deck and his crew was well aware of his intolerance for gear left strewn about the deck.

Propping his booted foot on a neatly coiled rope he leaned his back against the forward mast and took another swallow of hot coffee feeling the heat drift down his throat. It was a nice offset to the coolness of the morning. He relished the chill in the air during this, the coolest hour of the day. Before long the sun would rise and with it would come the customary heat that characterized the tropics. Max leaned his head back against the mast, closed his eyes and waited for sunrise.

His mind was troubled. He had slept little the previous night and finally giving up the pretense he had risen and made coffee before coming up on deck. Although he had every intention of bringing in fish for profit, the truth was he could have sailed out with the morning tide. It had not been necessary to leave yesterday. He was running. Running from his wife. Running from the quickly crumbling defenses he had so carefully built around his heart. Trying to buy some time to think rationally; to try and understand why he had disappointed her - twice already - and why it mattered so much to him. She had tried to hide it but he had noticed the temporary change in her demeanor before she pushed past it. The first time she had been disappointed was when he took her to the ship for their delayed wedding night. She probably assumed their first night together would be spent at the boardinghouse and maybe it was his thoughtful planning that had overcome her objections because she lost her resistance shortly after boarding his ship. Her other disappointment was the house he had found for rent. She probably was comparing it to her father's house and surely found it lacking. Max had dreams of one day being able to build a fine house but first he had to find a wreck to fund those dreams.

Besides his concern for her he was distressed at how quickly it had come to pass that her feelings now directly affected his. Her disappointment was his. Her joy, his. Her worry, his too. It was a part of their marriage he had not anticipated. He had planned to keep her at a distance. Keep the walls he had built to protect his heart in place. Feeling her slip swiftly past his defenses he reacted on blind instinct - he ran.

Max was not aware Jonathon had joined him on deck until he heard him speak from behind. "Looks like we could be fishing for more than just dinner."

Opening his eyes Max saw the sun had begun to make its radiant appearance above the dark water creating a naiant streak of crimson across the sky. The old sailor's adage ran through his mind:

Red sky in morning, sailors take warning.

Red sky at night, sailor's delight.

Jonathon was referring to the strong possibility of a storm later in the day which could mean the possibility of a wrecked ship in need of rescue. Most sails would try to keep a wary distance from any storms, but the *Mystic* was one of a handful of ships that sought them out in the hopes of finding the next pay load. "Wake the men. It's time to fish. Maybe we can get a load into port and get back out before it breaks."

"Aye Captain." Jonathon left to relay his order to the men.

Max pushed away from the mast and downed the rest of his coffee. He rounded up his fishing gear and chose a place at the ship's stern to cast his line. Jonathon joined him while the others took up spots along the port and starboard railings. The men threw occasional boasts and taunts at each other but Max and Jonathon fished in silence for the better part of two hours.

Although they could see the large fish swimming in the clear water around the reef they had little reward to show for their efforts. Even 'Fish' had failed to catch more than one. The mood of the crew now matched that of the overcast skies. The bantering had all but stopped and a sullen silence took its place. Still Max did not call a halt. He still hoped to gain something from the day, although he was thinking of moving to another site. He just hadn't roused himself enough yet to expend the effort. Instead he broached the subject occupying his mind all morning. "What do I do with a wife?"

Jonathon looked to his friend not sure what he meant by his question.

Deciding to tease Max out of his serious mood he asked, "What do you want to do with her?"

Max gave his mate a sarcastic look. "You know that's not what I'm talking about. I mean what do I do with a wife?"

"So you mean what do you do with one when you're not doing that?"

Ignoring Jonathon's amusement Max continued, "You protect her, you provide for her. That's what a husband should do, right? She wants to use her dowry to rent the house and I want to pay for it with my earnings. Is that so wrong?"

"Oh, that's why we are out here fishing. I wondered. You've always been adamant we are salvagers not fishermen."

"Now that I have to provide for a wife, we need the extra income. I can't afford to wait for the next shipwreck."

"So we are losing our primary focus just so you can save your pride."

Max went on the offensive. "Why are you suddenly being so belligerent?"

"Am I? Maybe it's the weather."

"Never bothered you before. What's really on your mind?" He waited while Jonathon baited his hook again and tossed it in the water and waited some more until he had begun to believe Jonathon wasn't going to answer.

"Esperanza's father has refused to allow me to see her again."

"Did he give you a reason?" asked Max.

"Because of my friendship with you."

"Why would our friendship matter to Mr. Sanchez?"

"He heard about you taking advantage of Miss Bennington, your unchaperoned walk prior to your marriage, and decided I couldn't be trusted with his daughter if I am influenced by behaviour such as yours." Jonathon tried to keep his tone even but the truth was he was displeased that Max's actions had cost him his relationship with Esperanza.

"Unbelievable! Mr. Sanchez is holding you accountable for my actions. What are you going to do about it?"

"Nothing. What can I do?"

Behind them the crew had grown more combatant as well, arguing amongst each other loudly enough to cause Max to turn and order, "Enough!"

They all settled into an uneasy silence eventually broken by Jonathon picking up their earlier conversation. "You should use the dowry for the rental. Whose money do you think she is living on at the boardinghouse? Her father is paying the bill so in essence he is supporting your bride. You may not have earned the money with sweat but it is yours just the same."

Jonathon made a reasonable point. Max decided he would take care of the rental as soon as he returned to the island. Meanwhile he would need to move them to some better fishing grounds.

Strong winds heralded the arrival of the storm that afternoon. They had yet to find good fishing so it was with great relief his crew packed away the fishing gear and made ready to sail. They looked forward to pitting themselves against nature and on this trip in particular working off some of the angst they felt towards each other. Max set a course parallel to the reef watching for stranded ships. As the storm intensified this task became much more dangerous. He and his crew were familiar with the waters of the area but still the danger existed they could become caught on the reef. If he sailed too close the waves, now over six feet high, were large enough to drive his ship into the coral and they would be the ones in need of rescue.

Headed south, Max noticed a moving light in the distance on the other side of the reef. Moving closer to investigate, he carefully threaded his way through a break in the reef into the channel. Due to the rain he had to get very close before he was able to identify Captain Talmage's ship anchored in the channel with one of his crewmen waving a lantern from the upper deck.

Fish came to stand at Max's side. "Best move on Cap'n. Nothing to do here."

Heeding the warning behind his words, Max sailed past the *Sinistral* without hailing its captain. Once they were safely out of the channel Max questioned the former *Sinistral* crewman. "Tell me Fish, is Captain Talmage deliberately signaling a ship towards the reef so he can salvage it?"

"Aye, Captain. He usually has a prearranged deal with the other captain."

Max thought there should be a way to keep men like Talmage from being in this business. He had more questions for Fish but they would have to wait. He needed to watch where he was sailing and besides the rain made it difficult to carry on a normal conversation.

Six or seven nautical miles away from Talmage's anchorage they found Captain Pritchard, a friend of Max's, working to loosen a stranded merchant ship. Max's crew was much younger and stronger than Pritchard's so he engaged their help to kedge the ship off the reef.

Max, Thomas and Billy rowed the longboat bringing it alongside the merchant ship *Carolynn*. Her crew lowered the anchor and hawser to them. Thomas and Billy secured the heavy anchor athwart their longboat while Max coiled the hawser line. Rotating turns at the oars they fought against the swelling sea and driving rain to get the anchor out to deeper water. When they reached a distance of Max's satisfaction they turned the boat and Billy and Thomas pushed the anchor off with the hawser line attached. With the anchor planted they rowed back to the *Carolynn* paying out the hawser as they went. The hawser was then secured to the capstan of the *Carolynn* and her captain put crewmen to hauling around it. They strained with all their might but the stranded ship wouldn't budge and then the anchor gave way. Now the crew circled the capstan easily pulling the anchor back to the stranded ship. They lifted the anchor just high enough from the water to get the longboat underneath and the process started all over again.

The seas were growing higher and his men were tiring from their efforts. Max consulted with Captain Pritchard and they agreed with this second attempt they would back the anchor. Max's crew hauled the first anchor out while Pritchard's crew hauled a second anchor beyond them after securing the end of the hawser from the second anchor to the first anchor. The first anchor's hawser was taken back to the *Carolynn*. Max prayed the rising tide would be enough to free the ship. He didn't think they had enough strength left to make a third attempt. The crew aboard the *Carolynn* manned the capstan once again. Their strongest men pushed and struggled with all the strength they had trying to turn the capstan to no avail. Just when all were ready to accept they would have to unload the cargo, a large wave lifted the ship just enough to finally free her of the reef. The cheers of all the men were so loud and heartfelt they could be heard over the sounds of the storm.

Max, Thomas and Billy used what energy they had left to row the longboat back to the *Mystic's* anchorage. The others understood the hard battle they had just waged with the sea and the 'twins' stood ready to help them aboard and to haul up the longboat once they cleared the railing. Max made his way to Jonathon standing at the wheel.

"At least we're not going home empty handed." Jonathon had to shout to be heard over the storm as he relinquished his post to his weary friend.

Max nodded to his first mate in agreement. The fee for their service had been agreed upon between the captains before they started. Their share would not be much but as his friend pointed out it was better than nothing which is what the day's fishing had produced.

Jonathon called out orders to the crew getting them under sail to follow Captain Pritchard who had decided it was best to get the merchant ship back to Key West immediately.

They sailed all night reaching Key West mid-morning. The storm blew itself out along the way. It felt like an eternity to Max. His eyes were scratchy from strain and lack of sleep and he was sure he could drop where he stood and be asleep before his head hit the deck. He had never been so relieved to sail into this harbour.

Chapter 20

After settling business with Captain Pritchard, Max returned to the *Mystic* ready to turn into his bunk. He had only had a few hours of sleep in the last forty-eight hours thanks to marital troubles, a storm and rescuing a stranded ship. Reboarding his ship he scanned the deck to make sure all was taken care of properly before dismissing the crew. He and Jonathon were alone on deck when Max heard his wife ask for permission to board.

Puzzled by her appearance Max nevertheless gave his assent for Abby to board and offered his hand to assist her transition to the ship's deck. "What brings you here?"

"I have been watching for you since yesterday," said Abigail.

"It has been a long trip and I'm tired. I was planning to take a nap." After a pause he added with an irresistible grin and a lift of his eyebrows, "You could join me."

Abby automatically replied, "I don't need a nap I just....Oh" She realized what he was alluding to and blushed deeply not only at the implication but because Mr. Keats was standing close enough to overhear.

Taking advantage of Abby's momentary discomfort Max said, "Wait for me at the boardinghouse. I'll be along after I have had a few hours of sleep."

His request unexpectedly ignited Abby's temper and she responded without thinking. "That is all I have done since the day we married is wait for you!"

Max was shocked by the sudden vehemence from his wife and in his tiredness he was ill equipped to deal with it. Her eyes sparked and her chin was firm. Unconsciously he was aware her beauty was intensified by her anger but he still found himself responding with ire of his own. "You knew that would happen before we married. You said you were used to it with your father and could handle it."

"In point of fact we were discussing the dangers of the sea not my waiting at home. Besides I had my own pursuits in England to keep me busy. On this," she swept her arm to the side indicating the island, "miniscule speck of earth sadly lacking in any kind of society. I have very little to occupy my time, not much to say in letters back home, only one friend to visit and not much point in shopping when the height of fashion here is three years behind London and only a handful of merchants to patron. The highlight of my day is going to the fish market for Mrs. Mallory and even that is nothing more than a few fishermen at the end of a pier displaying their catch, the same choices day after day. I am bloody bored of this place!" As Abby finished her tirade she realized how petulant she sounded. Worse, none of the things she mentioned really bothered her except for the first. If she had something to keep her busy she could get along without the rest. Audibly sucking in her breath and pulling her bottom lip between her teeth, unsure if it would be better to offer an apology or remain silent, she waited for her husband's reaction.

Max was too tired to hold onto his anger. It slipped away from him to be replaced with a mental weariness to match his physical fatigue. "I'm sorry you feel that way. We'll discuss it later Abigail. Right now - please - let me get some sleep." He placed his hand on the small of her back and guided her towards the gangplank. Scanning the pier he did not see anyone waiting for her. "Did you walk here alone?" he asked, his voice soaked in disapproval.

"No, of course not. Maria came with me but she and Thomas left together."

Resigned to his next ordeal Max said, "Come then, I'll walk you back to the boardinghouse."

Abby decided it was best not to provoke him further by insisting his escort wasn't necessary or suggesting she could stay on the ship with him. She knew he would disagree.

They walked to the boardinghouse in silence. Abby observed the droop in his shoulders and the heaviness of his eyes. It seemed to take all his energy to put one foot in front of the other. She was regretting her anger for its own sake but now she also regretted adding more to her husband's burdens. When they came to the porch Max stopped at the bottom as if to leave her. Abby placed a hand on his arm to hold him. "There is no reason you have to walk back to the ship. Come inside. I can get you some food and a bath and you can sleep."

Max shook his head no. "It doesn't seem proper."

Abby smiled at the notion. "What is not proper about it? I am your wife. There is no reason why you should not stay. It is my duty to take care of you."

"I don't have any clothes."

"We can find some here or I can send an errand boy to retrieve yours." She let her hand drift down his arm in a caress. "Please, let me take care of you as a wife should."

The softness in her voice was his undoing. He nodded and together they climbed the stairs to the louvered front doors. He opened them and stood aside for her to enter. Abby summoned the nearest maid and requested food and bath to be sent to her room.

Entering her bedchamber, she gestured towards the desk chair and watched as Max collapsed into it. She knelt in front of him to help pull off his boots. He started to resist but gave in at her insistent look. A knock sounded on the door and Abby opened it to accept a tray of bread, fruit and cheese from the kitchen maid who curtsied and quickly disappeared back down the stairs. Abby closed the door and deposited the tray on the desk in front of her husband. She selected a wedge of cheese for herself and sat on the bed across from him. "I apologize for my behaviour earlier. I should not have lost my temper. It was inexcusable."

Max politely finished chewing a bite of bread before replying, "I'm sorry for losing mine too."

"You only barely lost yours. I am the one who threw a childish fit."

"Under normal circumstances I probably could have given you a run for your money. You're fortunate I didn't have the energy to match you."

"A good thing you did not. We could have really made a scene in front of the whole town. Probably would not have been able to show our faces for days."

"Weeks at least," teased Max.

"Months," said Abby.

They both smiled at their private joke and then fell silent as Max struggled to eat despite his fatigue.

To fill the silence Abby told him some of the island news. "Mrs. Mallory received a letter from her son. She is very excited he plans to come home for Christmas." Max merely nodded. "Oh, Judge Webb has suddenly left the island. He packed up as soon as his first court session was closed. They say he has returned to his family in Florida but no one knows why or for how long. Mr. Whitehead has sent a letter of complaint to Washington."

"Good thing I have an agreement for the *Carolynn*. No telling how long we would have had to wait for the Judge to return if it had been brought to suit," replied Max.

"What is the *Carolynn*?"

"A merchant ship stranded on the reef. We helped another salvage crew work the wreck."

Abby smiled. "So you had a successful trip then? I am glad. I also heard talk of a large group of fishermen arriving this week."

"They would be the New Englanders who stayed home to vote in the Presidential election."

"Why could they not vote here?"

"Only the States can vote. Key West is part of Florida which is only a territory of the United States."

Another knock sounded on the door. This time Abby opened it to allow a tub to be brought in along with all the staff carrying pitchers of hot water to fill it. An extra pitcher was left on the wash stand for rinse water.

Max looked at the dainty size of the tub, hardly big enough for a child, and raised his eyes to Abby. "How am I supposed to get into that?"

Abby knew what he meant. The tub was so small she required Maria's assistance to bathe. She knew what she had to do. She would have to help him. She was a married woman now, she could handle this. Decisively she said, "We will start with your hair. Take your shirt off."

Max said, "We?" He hadn't required help bathing since he wore short pants.

"Yes, we. There is nothing wrong with a wife assisting her husband. Why must you disagree with my every suggestion?"

He had already lost control of his emotions earlier with her. He did not want to lose control physically as well. But then again it could lead to something interesting. He didn't have to hold back anymore. Some of his weariness left him at the thought of allowing this scene to play out. "Just stubborn, I guess." He removed his shirt.

"I am afraid I only have my floral scented soap, unless you want me to borrow my father's."

Not wanting to prolong the situation Max shook his head no. "I believe my masculinity can survive a little floral scent." He dipped his head into the tub to get his hair wet and then leaned forward over the tub so she could soap it. Her fingers running through his hair was soothing in a way he hadn't expected while at the same time as pleasing as expected.

Abby was enjoying the feel of his hair running through her soapy fingers but knowing he was tired she didn't linger as she would have liked. Finishing the task she picked up the porcelain pitcher of rinse water and carefully poured some of it over his head then wrung the excess water from his locks. She took up the soap and washcloth as Max lifted his head, ready to help him finish his bath.

Max couldn't take another second more of the sweet torture of her light touch. Seeing she was prepared to help him wash he nearly bellowed, "Enough." Moderating his tone he said, "I'll wash myself if you please."

"What about your back?"

Max replied impatiently, "I can tend it. Go! Go find me some clothes." He needed to get her out of the room. He could not allow her to continue her sweet ministrations.

Abby replaced the soap and cloth on the wash stand, "As you wish." She left their room and entered her father's to search for some suitable clothes for Max to borrow.

Making the most of the short time he would probably have alone he stripped off the rest of his clothes, stepped into the tub, grabbed the soap and hand cloth from the wash stand and quickly washed away the salt and sweat from his body.

He was in the process of rinsing off when she returned. Shutting the door behind her, she froze at the sight of water rivulets running down his broad shoulders to the muscles of his back and over the rounding of his buttocks. Torn between maidenly shyness and womanly curiosity, she laid the clothes on the bed and picked up the towel. She crossed to his front as he poured the water across his chest. Mesmerized, she watched the water run over the hardened plains of his chest and not being able to resist she laid her splayed hand over his heart feeling his pectoral muscles tense.

Max lowered the pitcher. "May I have the towel, please?"

Abby started at the sound of his voice and the vibrations under her fingertips. She withdrew her hand from his chest and raising her eyes to his opened the towel towards him.

Max briskly dried himself while he watched his wife nervously flit about the room under the pretense of tidying things that were already neat and orderly. He left the towel on the back of the chair and donned a pair of smallclothes then moved to the bed pulling the covers back. He climbed in and pulled a light sheet over his middle.

Despite his weariness he had noticed the circles under her eyes and realized she was nearly as tired as he. Max softly called to her, "Sweetheart, come talk with me until I fall asleep." Abby turned from the dresser and walked to the chair preparing to move it closer to the bed. "I meant come lay here with me. Put your head on the pillow next to mine." She hesitated and he gave her an encouraging smile, "Take your shoes off, get comfortable." He smiled as she obeyed. She removed her shoes and placed them together at the foot of the bed and then stretched out on her back. "Turn to me, sweetheart." He placed his hand on her hip, gently nudging her closer to him as he moved closer to her.

She couldn't help but melt each time he said the endearment. Her father often called her 'sweetheart' but it was just a pet name. It was like a verbal caress when Max said it making her willing to do whatever he asked.

"You didn't sleep well last night?"

"No. I was awakened by the storm winds buffeting the house." The storm moved across the island a few hours after she had fallen asleep. The wind blew so hard it rearranged small items in the room as it rushed through the open window rousing her from her slumber. She was forced to get up and close the shutters and then her worries for Max's safety had not allowed her to go back to sleep. She held vigil at the window even after the storm passed and the sun came up. She nearly dragged poor Maria out of bed to walk with her down to the pier after spotting from between the buildings what she thought might be the *Mystic* returning. She hadn't really expected to be right but once they realized it was the *Mystic* she almost couldn't keep up with Maria who's pace turned brisk with her excitement. Caught up in the comfort of the moment Abby confessed, "and I was worried for you."

Max didn't want her to be concerned about him. "It was a mild storm and we're moving out of the hurricane season, nothing for you to worry about, sweetheart."

Oh, how the endearment sounded so much sweeter when he said it. "Storms have never bothered me before. I guess because this is such a small island they seem stronger. I think I would prefer to be out on the water in it than trapped here."

He ran a finger down her cheek. "Then we have that in common." With only a few hours of sleep herself she could no longer keep her eyes open. Even though it was barely noon Max and Abby drifted off to sleep together.

That evening Abby stood in the parlour of what was now to be her home on the island. Their first home together. She was still a bit overwhelmed by the events of the afternoon. They had awakened from their nap and enjoyed a late lunch together. Then Max had surprised her by saying he had changed his mind about using the dowry to rent the house. She didn't know what had caused the change but she was glad for it. He further surprised her by asking if she wanted to go with him to settle the rental agreement with Mr. Simms. That done they had returned to the boardinghouse to share their news and then, with her father joining them and Mrs. Mallory pressing a set of clean sheets and some candles into Abby's arms with a promise to come help later, they had walked to the new house not wanting to wait another day to start settling in.

Maria was left at the boardinghouse to pack up her belongings. Her father and Max were inspecting the outhouse, cistern and the fireplace in the cook house to make sure all were in proper working order. She was supposed to be headed upstairs to change the sheets on the bed but had paused a moment in the parlour to let it sink in, she now had her own home. Their home - hers and Max's. She was a little nervous about trying to make a home together but excited too and looking around she was full of ideas of how to turn this simple house into a comfortable home.

The house was about six years old, built by a ship's carpenter and sold to Mr.Simm whose family occupied it when they first arrived on the island until they built a larger house on Whitehead Street last year. She had been told the downstairs consisted of four rooms and the upstairs two, all with sparse furnishings.

The front door opened to the parlour. On the left was another room that could be used as an office or a bedroom. It was currently bare of furniture but she walked into it anyway and discovered a cabinet built into the wall cleverly using the space under the staircase. The parlour had a comfortable looking sofa, rocking chair, two small end tables and a pianoforte. From the front door you could walk a straight line to the back door. Max told her the houses were built in this fashion to allow for cross ventilation to help cool them. Behind the parlour was a dining room with doorways to the hallway and the parlour. It held a long table, six chairs and a buffet. Heavy pewter candlesticks stood at either end of the buffet and a simple candelabrum on the table held fresh candles. She checked the drawers of the hutch and discovered silverware, towels and matches. Behind the cabinet doors she found a mismatched set of china dishes. She thought of her hope chest back in England full of so many items she could use now. Dishes, linens, tea service, doilies and so much more. She would have to get her father to send a message home to have it sent on the next ship. Across from the dining room were the stairs and beyond was a room formerly used as an office with a full-sized desk, empty bookcases, and two wooden chairs. Upon inspection the desk drawers were empty as well. None of the rooms had pictures or any other decorations beyond the occasional candle sconce.

Climbing the stairs she found two bedchambers. The small one had a single bed with smaller trundle bed underneath, a wooden chair, and a small dresser. The larger room had a double bed, wardrobe, chest of drawers, washstand and a dressing table with mirror and padded seat. Neither bed had linens. She tested the mattress and found it to be tolerably comfortable with two feather pillows. An empty sconce hung on the wall at the door otherwise the walls were bare. All the windows were bare too. She was glad the neighbors were not close. They would have no privacy tonight while the candles were lit.

Everything had a coating of dust but that would have to wait till later. She used the edge of her skirt to dust a corner of the dressing table to set the clean sheets down. She then set to work turning the mattress over and fluffing the pillows before making the bed. She finished just as she heard the men coming inside. She picked up the pitcher from the wash stand to take downstairs to fill and made a mental note to bring up a candle for the sconce. She then left the room to join the men downstairs.

From the upper hallway there was a door on the front side of the house that opened onto the second floor balcony but she turned towards the stairs instead, leaving the balcony exploration for later. She discovered at the other end of the hall another smaller staircase - more like a ladder - she hadn't noticed before because it had been behind her. It led to a trap door in the ceiling. Curious, she put the pitcher down at the foot of the bottom step to have both hands free to climb. Reaching the top she pushed on the trap door. It opened easily and Abby found herself in the attic as expected. The roof had a steep pitch to it. She could only half stand at the opening but the center of the room was spacious. Looking around she saw some old furniture, a trunk with a broken latch, crates full of discarded items. Things one would expect to find in an attic. Then, behind a partition wall, she found the ladder leading to the trap door in the roof.

She threaded her way through the attic stores to the second ladder and climbed it to reach the roof hatch. Pushing it open she stepped out into the warm salt breeze to a view overlooking the tidal pond behind the house. Her very own highpoint on the island. She looked across the expanse of untamed land to the east before circling the rectangular walkway made of tight fitting deck boards, heavy spindle railing, and scuppers very similar to the deck of a ship. She followed the northern coastline to the front of the house where she could see over the rounded mangrove trees and wavy palms and over many of the other houses and buildings but to her disappointment the warehouses blocked her view of the docks. All she could see was the top mast of one of the larger ships. Judging by its location she thought it might be the *Abigail Rose*. Past the warehouses she could once again follow the coastline all the way to the lighthouse on the southern point.

"Abigail?"

It was Max calling from the other side of the hatch door. Not moving from her spot she answered him, "I am up here."

He came to stand a few feet from her. "Do you like the Widow's Walk?"

"Is that what this is called? What a horrid name!"

"I've also heard it referred to as a Captain's Walk."

"Well then that is what we shall call it. It is my favourite part of the house. The only thing more I could wish for is to be able to see your ship from here."

His eyes left her face to look in the direction of the docks. "You're right. Mr. Greene's warehouse blocks the view. It is too bad." Bringing his gaze back to her he added, "Your father was looking for you. He is ready to go back to the boardinghouse."

"Thank you." He continued to look at her intently making her uncomfortable. "Is there something wrong with my face?"

"No. It's absolutely perfect in the evening light." He leaned down to kiss her.

She pulled back hissing, "Max! Someone could see us."

He followed her retreat answering, "So. Let them."

She had to submit when she was backed into the railing. It was a hard quick kiss that left her thankful for its brevity but also left her wanting more.

Max turned to lead the way back inside and smiled to himself. He was looking forward to their first night alone in their house.

Abby closed the door behind Mrs. Mallory as she left their house with one of her maids and Maria who would spend one more night at the boardinghouse. The three women had arrived just as her father was leaving and the four of them had given the house a quick cleaning recruiting Max's help to move furniture as needed. Mrs. Mallory had also brought them a light dinner and the makings for breakfast and lunch tomorrow. Abby and Max had been overwhelmed by her generosity.

It was now going on nine o'clock and Abby realized she was beyond tired. A glance at her husband confirmed the same. Their nap earlier was too short to make up for the loss of sleep they both had suffered the previous night. By mutual consent they headed upstairs. Abby carried the candle upstairs while Max blew out the ones downstairs.

Abby set the candle on the dressing table and began pulling the pins from her hair.

Max walked into the bedroom to find Abby uncoiling her hair and letting it cascade down her back. She then picked up her ivory handled hairbrush running it from the crown of her head down to the ends falling in a gentle twist nearly to her waist. Her silken curls enticed him. He wanted to know if they felt as soft and luxurious as they appeared in the flickering candlelight. He took the few steps needed to bring him to her and picked up a strand lying across her shoulder. He let it run through his fingers, fascinated to find it was even softer than it looked. Her movements arrested and feeling her gaze he lifted his eyes to her reflection in the mirror. She silently offered him the hairbrush. He took it from her, his hand lightly caressing hers as he did so. Following her lead, he started at her crown and ran gentle sure strokes down to the ends watching the luminescent glow of the silky strands.

Abby drifted in a hypnotic state feeling the glide of the brush and watching

Max in the mirror until her eyelids drooped. When Max noticed he laid the brush down and coaxed her to her feet. Pushing her hair to the front of her shoulder he began unbuttoning her dress. When he finished Abby moved to the bed to pick up her nightgown intending to retreat into the corner of the room, mindful of the uncovered windows, to change. Max tugged the nightgown from her grasp. "You won't be needing this."

Max awakened to an empty room filled with morning light. He dressed quickly and followed the curious sound of muffled hammering. It led him downstairs and out to the cook house where he found Abby perspiring as she worked to remove the outer green husk of a cocoanut by pounding it against the sharp brick edge of the fireplace. Having removed the husk she started on the shell, striking the middle, turning it and striking again until it cracked open and she poured the water in a bowl she had at hand. Max was impressed. "You are quite good at that. I didn't think they had cocoanuts in England."

"We don't. Mrs. Mallory's cook showed me how to open them. It is probably the only thing I learned how to do properly."

She started working on the next one but Max took it from her. "You're too warm. Sit down and rest. I'll open this one. Drink the cocoanut water too." Max was more concerned than he needed to be and on one level he knew he was over-reacting but he kept remembering how scared he had been when she had gotten overheated on their walk to the lighthouse. He didn't want it to happen again.

Abby wanted to object to his cosseting but he had started beating the cocoanut against the bricks and really her arms were tired from working on the first one. She found a heavy spoon and started removing the cocoanut from the shell she had opened while surreptitiously watching her husband and wishing he wasn't wearing such a loose shirt. She would have enjoyed watching his muscles ripple as he wrestled with the fruit.

Her wish was surprisingly granted. After removing the husk, Max made the first strike against the shell with so much force it split halfway. He then tried to pull the shell apart and when it suddenly gave way he was showered with cocoanut water. Abby couldn't help herself, his face was so comical in his shock she burst out laughing. Max removed his wet shirt giving her the view she craved but then he tossed his shirt at her head. "Think that's funny do you?"

Abby pulled the shirt off her face still giggling. "Yes, I do."

"Not so funny when I have to walk through town shirtless. I don't have another clean one here."

Abby instantly sobered. She didn't like the idea of any of the other women eyeing her husband. "I will go wash it out. If I press it between some towels it may dry enough so you can wear it soon. Would you finish removing the cocoanut from the shells?"

When Abby returned to the cook house after cleaning his shirt she found him gathering the fruit onto a plate. Abby removed the cloth from a loaf of bread Mrs. Mallory left for them and pulled off two large pieces to add to the plate. She also added some beef jerky. They carried their makeshift breakfast into the house and set it on the dining table.

Max remembered his manners just in time. He quickly set down the tray so he could pull out the chair for Abby. Once seated, he started to grab a piece of bread when he noticed Abby had bowed her head. He pulled his hand back and bowed his too while Abby said a quick blessing. It was coming back to him now, those long forgotten manners; he waited for her to choose something from their shared platter before he did rather than the all hands in way his crew ate. It had been a long time since he had spent a great amount of time in polite company - that is to say anything longer than an hour - making him feel uncomfortable now at his own table.

Adding to his discomfort, he was sitting there without a shirt. His mother had taught him better - God rest her soul - when he was just a boy. She would be ashamed to see him now but his wife didn't seem to mind. In fact there was anything but disgust on her face every time she looked his way, which was often, until she caught him watching her which sent her eyes to her plate and a delightful stain across her cheeks. Max was no longer feeling mentally uncomfortable. Instead his discomfort became physical and he nearly groaned out loud to realize he would have to wait at least a week before he could do something about it. He had to earn a living which meant leaving her to sail the reefs. And it was getting late. "I have to go. My men are waiting for me."

"I will retrieve your shirt."

While Abby went upstairs, Max carried their dishes out to the cook house. He reentered the back door as Abby reached the bottom of the stairs. They stood mere feet from each other. Abby shook out his shirt and held it out to him. He slipped it on feeling only a slight dampness. It would do. "Thank you."

His smile warmed her heart and she returned it. He brushed a finger along her cheek.

She asked, "How long will you be gone?"

"Probably a week. Not more than two. Will you miss me?" Max didn't know what made him ask her that and what concerned him even more was he held his breath waiting for her reply. Darn it, he was not supposed to become this attached. It would interfere with decisions he had to make as the captain of a wrecking vessel.

"Yes."

She said it with such openness and regarded him expectantly. He tried to regain some emotional distance before giving her the kiss she so obviously was waiting for. He kept it light and simple and quickly moved past her to the front door.

She called after him, "Max, please be careful and come home safe."

That had him stopping at the door and turning back towards her. Dang it all but he liked having someone care about him.

She lightened her tone adding, "Remember our house has a Captain's Walk not a Widow's Walk."

And that had him wanting to sweep her up in his arms and take the stairs two at a time. Reminding himself he had to leave, he teased her in return and with a jaunty salute he pushed through the front door. "Aye, aye Wife."

Abby stood in the doorway, still wearing a half smile, watching him till he disappeared around the corner.

Richard was walking towards the docks on his way to meet with Captain Andrews when he saw his son-in-law headed towards his ship. He was whistling a spirited tune which gave Richard the last assurance he needed, it was time he finished his voyage. Max and Abby were obviously getting along. His daughter would protest his leaving but she would not be devastated by it. He hailed his son-in-law, "Hello Max," as he met up with him at the dock.

Max stopped whistling and automatically stiffened his spine. "Good morning Mr. Bennington."

"Please, call me Richard, we are family now."

It had been so long since he had family one would expect he would be anxious to count himself a member of any family. Having been on his own for so long, he had become very independent and had not intended to marry so he hadn't considered the aspect of gaining a father-in-law. He wasn't sure how he felt about it. "Of course, sir."

"Going to do some fishing?"

"No sir. I'll be sailing the reefs." He would normally have said he was going 'wrecking' but knowing Richard's aversion to his profession he chose to phrase it differently.

"Oh yes, of course. How long do you plan to be gone?"

"At least a week, most likely." Max wondered where his questions were leading.

"In that case it is fortunate our paths crossed this morning."

"And why is that sir?"

"I will be leaving in a day or two to finish my voyage. I need to get the cargo delivered, see to business in Mobile and visit my brother. I will stop by on my return to England, of course."

"Have you told Abigail, yet? She hasn't mentioned it."

"I was going to today."

Max knew Abby would not take her father's leaving lightly. It left him torn between doing what he needed to do and staying to comfort her when she received her father's news. The clear blue sky along the horizon mocked his need to sail. He should stay. He would tell his crew they would wait another day to leave.

Richard continued, "I am glad I had this chance to speak with you. I made a start on laying the groundwork to open a shipping office here and have arranged for docking and warehouse space. When I return in a few months we can discuss it in more detail. I know you are anxious to get to work now."

Max's thoughts of staying abruptly ended. Richard was giving him only a few months to make his salvage business profitable, to secure their future, before he found himself coerced into a desk job by his wife and father-in-law. "Yes sir. The tides wait for no man." He held out his hand to Richard, "Have a safe journey, sir."

Richard shook Max's proffered hand, "Take care of my girl."

"Of course I will." *She's my wife!* Max stood where he was as Richard walked away feeling an unreasonable and impotent rage building the likes of which he had never known. Taking deep breaths he reasoned with himself. He was reading more into Richard's words than the man had intended. Richard may have doubts about his success as a wrecker and it was yet to be seen if he could support his wife but he was not inferring Max *could* not be successful and he certainly was not saying Max *would* not take care of Abby. Scanning the clear horizon again and taking another deep breath he gained enough control over his emotions to continue to his ship and make ready to sail. He needed to find a storm and a wreck, something he could use to work off this angry energy.

He needed a really big storm!

Chapter 21

After waving Max off to sail the reefs with his damp shirt clinging to him, Abby returned to the cookhouse to finish cleaning up their breakfast. It was a simple wooden structure with a door on either end to allow the breeze to pass through. A brick fireplace with a built in oven was on one side of the room; on the other pots, pans, and utensils hung from pegs while shelves held pottery, glass bottles and jars, spices and dried herbs. A worktable occupied the center of the room. Putting the last clean dish away she wiped her hands and debated what to do next. She hadn't thought to ask where he was going nor had he mentioned it so she decided to go up to the Captain's Walk and see if she could catch Max's ship sailing away. Maybe she could at least learn if he was headed towards the Upper Keys or the Dry Tortugas. She grabbed a bonnet on the way up to protect her face from the sun.

Elbows on the railing, Abby braced her chin in her hands and let her thoughts drift back to the night before. Despite their fatigue they had succumbed to a slow and sensual convergence before slumber overtook them. Max had treated her with more care and tenderness than she had imagined a man was capable of showing. He made her feel more than wanted, almost cherished. The feeling was still with her this morning. Although she didn't believe his feelings ran as deep as love there was something there to build their marriage upon. He had shown himself to be considerate of her feelings after the wedding ceremony and every occasion since. It was the reason she was growing to care for him - deeply. Did it also mean he cared for her? He did seem reluctant to leave her giving her hope of his deepening affection. It had been difficult for her to let him go hence the reason she was up here on the roof watching for his sails.

She had been waiting about fifteen minutes and was starting to feel her quest was in vain when her attention was caught by a large brown pelican flying overhead. It circled her a few moments before landing on the railing furthest from her. His neck stretched tall, his bill pointed slightly upwards, he stared at her. She stood there quietly watching the bird while it watched her; amazed it would venture so close. Then suddenly it flapped its wings and took flight headed towards the coastline behind the house. Abby turned back to her vigil of the harbour. A moment later she heard the pelican flying overhead and as she turned to look for it over her left shoulder it returned to its perch on the railing with a nice fish. Pretending not to notice she faced the harbour and watched the bird from the corner of her eye. He tipped his head back and with a few expert tosses lined the fish up to slide right down his gullet. He then spent a moment using his bill to clean his breast feathers before settling down and tucking his neck into his body as if waiting with her. His sleek greyish-brown feathers glistened in the sunlight beckoning her touch. She wanted to know if they would feel wet or oily; curious as to what caused their sheen. His snow white neck had a unique black band just under his head, barely visible from under his bill in his current position and he had more black colouring around his eyes. Quite a dashing fellow as pelicans went.

Expecting to scare him off she said, "Hello there." To her amazement he dipped his bill a little as if in greeting and stayed put so she resumed her watch of the harbour in time to see a ship headed out to the left of the warehouses. Looking closely she could see the distinctive topsail of the *Mystic*. Wanting to share her excitement she turned to the bird. "There he is!" To which the pelican flapped his wings in agreement and then resumed his perch. He was quite a charming fellow as birds went.

She watched the ship sail past the lighthouse and finally out of sight. He would be headed towards the Upper Keys again. Scanning the clear horizon she was happy on one hand he was not in any immediate danger but on the other hand it presented no opportunity for wrecking. What a conundrum to want and not want at the same time.

Her thoughts were disturbed by the pelican suddenly taking flight towards the harbour. He gracefully dropped down to skim the surface of the turquoise water before disappearing from sight behind the warehouse. Deciding she had wasted enough time Abby headed back downstairs to make a list of needs for the house. She wondered what she was going to do with herself when she ran out of these little tasks.

She had just finished making her list when someone knocked on the front door. She opened it to find Maria with two men and a cart holding her trunks. The men hauled her trunks upstairs to the bedroom. Having decided to turn the front room into an office so Maria could have the back room for her bedroom, she negotiated an extra fee to have the men move the office furniture from the back room to the front.

Maria had only a carpetbag containing her few dresses and personal items which she left in the now empty downstairs room Abby declared to be hers. The first room she had ever had all her own. It was a small room, perhaps eight feet squared, but to Maria it felt as large and overwhelming as the empty church she had once visited in Jamaica.

Abby paid the men with her pocket money and waved them away. Turning back in the house she told Maria, "First thing we need to do is find some furniture for your room. You can use the upstairs room until then but the bed is not large enough for you and Thomas after you are married." Maria insisted they could make do but Abby replied, "That will not be necessary."

Abby and Maria were both startled by another knock on the door. Abby was pleased to find her father standing on her front porch. She welcomed him into the parlour where they sat together on the sofa.

"Maria, would you please be so kind as to bring us both some water with lime?" Receiving her nod of assent, Abby turned to her father. "How was your morning?"

"Good. I went to see Captain Andrews and check on the preparations for departure."

Abby felt a sinking feeling in the pit of her stomach. She knew where this conversation was headed. "And when will he be ready to sail?"

"Day after tomorrow." Her father picked up one of her hands giving her warning she would not like what he was about to say. "Sweetheart." He waited till she met his eyes. "I will be sailing with him. It is time for me to go. I have delayed as long as possible but the goods need to be delivered and I have other business to attend to as well in Mobile."

She knew this day was coming but still it caught her by surprise. She thought she had more time to prepare herself. "Are you still planning to visit Uncle James?"

"Yes, of course. I could not come this far and go home without having done so."

Oh my!

It hurt thinking of him leaving her to see her uncle and even more so to contemplate the day he would be returning to England without her. Automatically she said, "I want to go with you."

Richard gave her a sad and reproachful look. "Abigail, your place is here with your husband. I am sure one day you and Max can make the trip to visit them. I will send word on a return ship as soon as I arrive in Mobile and I will write when I get to your uncle's and I will stop here on my return voyage." He tried to lighten her mood. "Chin up, daughter. You knew you would leave my house one day."

She gave him a weak smile. "Yes, but I always pictured it would be some house on the other side of Midanbury not the Atlantic Ocean."

"Life does have a way of redirecting our path. But you are a strong woman and you wanted adventure. I know you will embrace your circumstances and make the best of it and I believe you will find you have all you could ever wish for right here."

"Maybe so, but upon reflection I should have been more specific about the kind of adventure I was seeking."

"You are not the first to have those thoughts, to be sure."

"Not you father."

Richard grudgingly admitted, "A time or two in my distant past."

Father and daughter spent as much time together as possible until the ship was ready to sail Saturday morning. Abby carefully watched her father for any signs he might be too weak to travel. In truth, she was looking for any means to postpone the inevitable. But other than tiring more easily than he used to he did not show any signs of weakness she could use to her advantage. In fact, under Mrs. Mallory's care his health had greatly improved these last few weeks.

Richard insisted on helping Abby find a servant to serve as butler and escort while Max was away. Abby protested at first but in the end gave in to make her father happy. They agreed on Mr. Robert Baxley, a retired butler from New England in his late fifties. A lighthearted jovial man, devoted to his wife. He and his wife had traveled to Key West with their employers every winter for four years. The fourth year they decided they would stay permanently. They had not been blessed with any children but Mr. Baxley assured Richard he would take care of Abby as if she were his own.

Standing on the deck of the *Abigail Rose* Saturday morning she wanted to hug her father but refrained knowing he would not like the public display of affection. "Take care of yourself and be sure to write."

Richard squeezed her hands. "Be careful daughter, while Max is gone. Take Mr. Baxley with you whenever you leave the house. Remember, most of the men on this island do not adhere to the same standards as English gentlemen. They will take advantage of you if you give them an opportunity to do so."

She smiled indulgently. "Yes poppa."

Richard squeezed her hands again, hard. "Oh dear, I did not think it would be this hard to leave you."

Captain Andrews approached them. "Young lady, I'm afraid it is time for you to go ashore."

"Yes sir." She cast her father one last look, then allowed the captain to escort her to the gangway. She whispered to him, "Remember, you promised to keep an eye on his health."

"Aye, miss. Don't you worry about your sire. He has many years left in him." He helped her step onto the gangway. "Take care, lass." She nodded then made her way down to stand on the pier. She waved as they pulled away from the dock, still managing a smile for her father.

She stood there watching her namesake sail away, oblivious to the everyday activity taking place behind her on the pier, until she could no longer discern the men from the ship. Spine stiff and chin lifted she made her way to where Mr. Baxley waited for her in the shade of a palm tree.

She felt the cracks starting in the dam she had built to hold her emotions in check. The closer they got to the house the harder it became to hold herself together. Entering the front door she rushed past Maria without a word. She glimpsed the concern on her young maid's face but if she stopped her flight now she knew she would shatter in front of them. Leaving her two servants to say what they would to each other; she flew up the stairs thankful she didn't trip on her skirts in her haste. She entered her bedroom not a moment too soon. Shutting the door behind her she braced her back against the cool wood as the hot tears she had held at bay for three days could no longer be contained.

Silently they flowed heavy and unstoppable.

This feeling was worse than missing a mother she had never known. And it was so much worse than leaving England and Elizabeth and the nanny who had raised her as she had been the one doing the leaving and had expected to return. Her heart ached and there was no one here who could soothe it. She knew her father would return in a few months' time but her heart wouldn't listen. It constricted to the point she could barely breathe. All she could do was stand there, arms wrapped around her middle, trying desperately not to sob out loud.

When the worst of it had passed and the ache in her chest had somewhat eased she pushed herself away from the door and made her way to the washstand. Soaking a cloth in the basin of water she wrung it out then pressed the cool cloth to her cheek. Seating herself at the dressing table next to the open window she transferred the cloth to her other cheek. She leaned against the back of the chair and let her gaze drift to the horizon. She felt the wetness of her lashes on her cheeks as she closed her eyes and focused on the sounds of the island. Deep cleansing breaths helped to calm her emotions as she listened to the calls of the seabirds flying nearby. She could hear the distant sound of hammer and saws and workers calling out to each other in the process of constructing another building near Front Street. The world continued on oblivious to her turmoil. She could hear the palm fronds rustling outside her window from the sea breeze that flowed across her face drying her tears. She took another deep breath and opened her eyes. Once again feeling in control she turned to her reflection expecting to visibly see the inward damage revealed on her face. Instead only the puffiness surrounding her stormy grey eyes gave any hint of her weeping.

Gathering her strength she washed her face and picked up her list for the house. Her father's news had postponed shopping but the day was young so with Maria and Mr. Baxley in tow she headed to Victoria's on the other side of town in the hopes of joining her for lunch and then together they could work their way through all the shops back to her house. It would not only accomplish something tangible, it would also keep her from dwelling on her situation.

Tria had been more than willing to shop with her and they had taken care of most of the needs on her list. Now she was ready for bed and restless. Feeling the need to put her emotions on paper she pulled out her journal. It helped give her perspective. Next she wrote Elizabeth sharing all the events that had occurred since last she had written. By the time she was done her eyes were moist but the dam of emotions was repaired. She was still heart sore to be sure but she had the strength to be on her own just as her father had said.

Lace curtains billowed in the breeze of the front parlour window. Abby and Tria stood at the front door admiring the changes they had made over the last four days. Mostly small homey touches that made the space feel more comfortable and lived in. The rest of the house had been favoured with similar treatment, all the changes being small and inexpensive with the exception of furniture for Maria's room. Tria had not only joined her for shopping the day her father had left but had made it her mission to help Abby every step of the way so that the days were easy for Abby. A few of the nights she had been exhausted enough to easily fall asleep. It was the other nights that dragged on her soul and left circles under her eyes in the morning.

They scoured Abby's attic and Tria's for furniture and decor with only minor success. Abby had made an offer to Maria to deduct a small amount each week from her pay to reimburse the price of a bed so at the end of a year the furniture would belong to Maria. Abby was pleased to see the joy her offer had brought to Maria's eyes. Unfortunately, the dry goods store did not have furniture in stock and to place an order would take months, so on the advice of Mrs. Mallory they posted an advertisement. By the end of the day they had two offers of furniture for sale from islanders downsizing their households. Abby purchased a double bed and wardrobe that met with Maria's approval.

The curtains were made from remnants bought at a discount from Betsy. The sweet seamstress even offered to help sew them - no charge. So one evening was spent in comfortable companionship as Abby, Betsy, Maria and Tria worked on the curtains. Tria did more to supply the refreshments and entertainment than actually help with the sewing. Abby was amazed at the amount of island gossip Tria, a gently bred lady, was privy to and freely shared with the group. Many of her tales were humorous and some should not have been repeated in public.

And so it was the five days from her father's departure to Max's return flew by in a flurry of activity. Thursday morning, the start of the second week since Max sailed, Abby was in the front room she had turned into an office going over the household accounts when Tria burst in with her maid trailing a few steps behind. Abby had grown accustomed to her friend's bold behaviour but this habit of walking right into her house without knocking might be a problem when Max was home. Perhaps she should say something to Tria now. Knowing she would not get any more done, Abby closed her ledger and looked up expectantly, waiting to learn the reason for the excitement turning Tria's cheeks aglow.

"I have news for you Abby girl! Guess!"

"You are going to Rome?" Abby teased.

"No, you gooseberry! I just saw a certain ship enter the harbour on my way over."

Jonathon asked Max the question that was on the mind of all the crew as they approached the dock. "How long is shore leave this time?"

Max replied to the crew at large, "Twenty-four hours," and received a collective groan in response.

Jonathon, standing at his side, said under his breath, "That long, eh."

Max lowered his voice so only Jonathon could hear. "That long. You know the storms are few this time of year. We have to be out there; ready to be first to arrive if a ship is stranded."

"And what will Mrs. Captain have to say about such a short visit?"

"None of your damn business mate!" growled Max.

Max's tone clearly indicated any mention of Abby was off limits but Jonathan continued to prod him. "If you're so worried about catching the next storm, what are we doing in port at all? With the fish Fish has caught we've got enough stores to stay out another week. Couldn't wait to see her again, could you?"

Jonathon was too close to the truth for comfort. Ever since her father had told him he was leaving Max had felt a burning need to comfort Abby. He had made a change in course just so he could make an overnight run home to check on his wife. He was having problems admitting the real reason to himself, he certainly wasn't going to enlighten his first mate he was now using a woman's feelings to guide his ship. "We've seen nothing but other wrecker's between here and Indian Key. We're headed out to the Marquesas for some breathing room and it only makes sense to stop on the way and resupply."

Jonathon chuckled. "If you say so."

Max thought *...and therein lies the problem of having a best friend for a first mate. Uncontrollable insolence.*

Jonathon changed the subject. "The ship needs an easy dozen crewmen the way we operate. You've got the advantage on the other wreckers being owner and captain. You can and do pay your crew more. While you're here why don't you hire some of the better ones away from them? Then maybe we wouldn't be the walking dead when we do stumble upon a wreck."

Max knew he needed to find more men. He just hadn't made the time to do so and he had been postponing the extra wages. "Six more is not going to happen, my friend. But I will consider adding two, maybe three, more."

Ship secured, Max made ready to leave with the 'twins' in tow to purchase the ship's supplies. Fish would be left on guard overnight.

Jonathon called after him, "Give Abby my best." Max gave his friend a cutting look for his intended jibe. Once he cleared the gangplank Jonathon hollered, "And make some time to find more crew. I'm bloody tired of being shorthanded."

Insolent lubber! One more task to keep him from going straight home. Max bought the ship's stores as quick as possible and left the 'twins' to see they were loaded on the *Mystic*. Next he went to a dock side bar where he thought he would have the most luck finding good sailors. He spent an hour there interviewing potential crewman after making an announcement to the room in general. He told a few of them to show up on the dock in the morning for his final decision but he knew others would probably hear the news and be there too. He should have told Jonathon to narrow it down to a few to save time in the morning.

Finally, with the afternoon shadows lengthening, he turned on Simonton.

Abigail's heart took flight at Tria's news. Max was home! She couldn't send her friend home fast enough so she could prepare for his arrival but good manners prevailed. She served refreshments and tried to focus on whatever it was Tria was saying while breathlessly waiting for Max to show up at any minute even though she knew it would take him time to bring the ship in and secure it. She was so distracted Tria finally gave up her one sided conversation and took her leave. Abby felt a little guilty for her rudeness but couldn't bring herself to halt Tria's departure.

Once she was alone, she raced upstairs to change into a nicer dress and freshen her coiffeur. She kept looking out the window every few minutes expecting to see him walking her way. Finished primping she made her way up to the Captain's Walk to wait for him but the sun's warmth soon forced her back indoors. She began pacing the upper balcony instead. Finally she saw a man headed her way but it didn't take more than a glance to see it was Thomas. The front door opened and Maria went running towards him to be swept up in his arms in the middle of the street. Feeling like a voyeur, Abby retreated inside once again. A few minutes later Maria returned and called to her from the bottom of the stairs.

"Mrs. Abigail, would you mind if I took the afternoon off?"

"No, Maria. That is fine. You go right ahead. Tell Thomas I said hello."

"Yes ma'am."

Alone again and waiting. Abby took her time going down the stairs. All excitement - well not quite all but most of her excitement - drained from her. *How long did it take to secure a ship?* Looking at the clock on the pianoforte she realized it had been well over an hour since Tria's announcement. She looked at her desk but knew it was hopeless to expect her mind to focus on any task. She walked out to the front porch and sat down in the rocker Mr. Baxley had found and cleaned up for her. He actually had found two of them but the second one needed repairs before it could be used. Pushing against the floorboards with her toes she put the chair in motion, crossed her arms over her waist and waited...

As Max approached the house he immediately noticed the difference. It welcomed him with a comfortable looking rocking chair on the front porch and windows open to allow the breeze to pass through with glimpses of lace curtains flirting with the air currents. Max briefly wondered where Abby had gotten them but pushed the concern aside not wanting to spoil his homecoming. He opened the front door expecting to find her waiting on the other side. It only took a few steps in either direction to realize the downstairs was empty. Something was bothering him about the rooms but he didn't stop to puzzle over it in his quest to find Abby. Thinking she must be upstairs he called out as he started up the stairs. "Abigail?"

213

Having chastised herself for being angry at Max's delay Abby decided a good wife, which she aspired to be, would have something ready to eat for her husband rather than sitting on the front porch waiting to fuss over his tardiness. She didn't have much in the way of food stores having taken most of her meals at the boardinghouse or the Lambert's the past week. She had a crock of leftover turtle soup and she supposed she could make some bread.

Until now she had successfully avoided the onerous task of starting a fire. She found the firewood stacked outside the cookhouse. Gathering three logs she neatly stacked them in the fireplace and then looked for kindling. What she found was a basket of cocoanut fibers. It looked as if it would burn well. Deciding to give it a try she pulled the strands apart allowing more air passage and placed it under the logs and some in between. Then she searched for a means to start the fire. Not finding anything she went to the house to retrieve the matchsticks she had found in the dining room buffet. Returning to the cookhouse she struck the match, involuntarily jumping at the large finger long flame it created before dwindling to a more controlled burn, and lit the husk material. She was deeply satisfied with her efforts as she watched the fibers burn and the wood start to catch. She then started gathering what she would need to make the bread.

Halfway up the stairs Max realized it was too quiet. A noise from the backyard had him retracing his steps down the stairs. He left one of the two bags he was carrying in the house and went out the back door and across the small expanse of yard walking quietly up to the open cookhouse door. The sight of Abby, wearing a full apron over her flowered dress intently studying a sheet of paper, made him stand still and watch. A sack of flour on the table next to her, a bowl in front, she attempted to extract flour from the deep sack with a measuring cup but the opening kept getting in her way. Although he thought she moved gracefully this was obviously a task she had rarely, if ever, performed. She lacked the economy of motion that comes with repetition. Finally removing the cup full of flour from the bag she turned it over from above the rim of the bowl. The flour dropped all at once landing with a soft thump and sending a white cloud billowing upward to cover Abby's arms with a fine layer of pulverulence. She made a sound of frustration. Max couldn't contain his amusement.

Hearing Max's soft laugh brought Abby's attention to him and flushed her cheeks with embarrassment. "How long have you been there?"

Max crossed the room coming up behind her to peer over her shoulder. "Not long. What are you making?"

"Bread for our dinner."

The moist heat of the room tightly curled the tendrils of hair around the nape of her kissable neck. Unable to resist he wrapped his arms around her waist and touched his lips to the point where her neck curved into her shoulder.

Abby pulled away from him in modest protest and in the process spilt more flour across the table. "Max!"

Max moved away from her and dropped the bag from his shoulder onto the table beside her.

Curious, Abby asked, "What is in the bag?"

Max reached in and pulled out a dead fish. Abby stared at it as if she had never seen one before in her life. He wondered if maybe she was trying to identify the species since they probably didn't have it in England. "It's a yellowtail snapper."

"Oh." *That doesn't tell me how to cook it.* Abby lifted the tail between two fingers.

"Since you are working on the bread I'll clean the fish - this time."

Abby was relieved, not having the faintest idea how to clean it having avoided that lesson at the boardinghouse. It wasn't because she was squeamish she just had no desire to mess with a dead fish. Now, she was desperately trying to remember what she had learned from Mrs. Mallory's cook about preparing fish. It was frightfully little and she really didn't want to admit it to Max. He took the fish to a table in the yard she had not noticed before to clean it. She moved to the other side of her worktable so she could watch him clean the fish while she finished kneading the bread. She shaped the ball of bread on the bread pan and put it in the oven built into the brick fireplace while Max was cleaning up outside.

Bringing the neatly trimmed fillets into the cookhouse he looked at Abby expectantly. She could no longer avoid it. "I have not the foggiest idea what to do with the fish. Mrs. Mallory's cook showed me once how to pan fry it. Although there is a pan behind you we cannot put it on the fire. The flames are too high."

"Um, what were you planning to make for dinner?"

Abby sheepishly pulled the crock from the shelf behind her. "Leftover turtle soup."

Max was thoughtful for a moment. "We could cut the fish into small pieces and maybe it will cook in the soup as it is heating."

Not having a better idea to offer Abby said, "It is worth a try." She pulled the large kettle from below the worktable and wiped it clean, then poured the soup in while Max cut the fish into smaller pieces and added them to the pot.

It seemed as if they were doing well at pulling together another meal until it started going wrong. The fire was so hot it scorched the soup on the bottom before either of them realized what was wrong. They stirred it more often afterwards but the room was filled with the burnt odor. Abby pulled the bread out of the oven at the appropriate time. The outside was a nice even colour and the fresh baked smell helped to overcome the burnt soup but when she sliced it open it was still uncooked in the middle. Max tried to console her by removing the gluttonous center and leaving only the edges on the plate.

SUSAN BLACKMON

They took their poor meal into the house. Max following behind Abby carrying a tray with the two soup bowls. Passing the back bedroom door something caught his eye. He backed up a step and looked into the room to see furnishings he didn't remember being there before. Continuing to the table he considered if maybe she had moved some of the upstairs furniture downstairs. He joined her at the table but didn't mention the furniture.

After prayers they each cautiously tried a spoonful of soup and both tried unsuccessfully to hide from the other how awful it tasted. The bread wasn't any better. The texture wasn't right leaving Abby to think she must have measured something wrong paying so much attention to what Max was doing and she didn't think she had learned much for the trouble either. Miserable and both unwilling to admit it they suffered through the meal with the aid of lots of water for Abby and ale for Max. There were only two redeeming factors. One, the fish was cooked and two Max had also brought home bananas which they opted to have following their dinner.

When they were finished, Abby suggested Max relax in the parlour while she cleaned up hoping for some time alone but he insisted on helping. They worked in silence until they were almost done when Max tried asking as gently as he knew how, "Do you have plans for any more cooking lessons?"

"No, I do not."

Carefully Max said, "May I suggest you reconsider?"

"No, you may not," retorted Abby. She had spent the entire dinner chastising herself for her inferior cooking skills leaving her unable to deal with his remarks no matter how he meant them. They finished cleaning the dishes and Max banked the fire. They returned to the house and still being early evening they both looked at each other not sure what to do. By unspoken agreement they headed towards the parlour. Max waited for Abby to be seated on the sofa before he chose a chair.

She heard the clock ticking off the seconds in the silence before Max asked, "Has your father left? I didn't see the *Abigail Rose* at the dock."

"Yes, he sailed a few days after you did." Another subject Abby had no wish to discuss tonight. She had been waiting for him to notice the changes to the room. She had seen his eyes looking around but he had yet to mention it. Watching him she noticed his gaze fix on the painting across the room as if he was studying it. She and Tria had discovered it in the Lambert's attic. It was a well done oil of a three-masted brig riding the high waves of a storm. She particularly liked the way the artist had captured the light and dark tones of the sky and water. To distract him from further talk of her father she asked, "Do you like the painting?"

Her question was like setting a spark to dry tender. Max had been trying to hold back his growing anger. She had reacted so testily in the kitchen over her cooking skills he knew any unfavourable mention of the decor would not go well and he didn't want to start a fight tonight over brick-a-brac but he was tallying up a hefty sum with all the items he had seen added to the house downstairs - he couldn't imagine what he would find upstairs - while the cookhouse was empty of food stores. He had left her some money but not enough for all of this. He could only come to one conclusion. Her father had left money for her. He wasn't sure which was worse; that Richard had so little faith he could provide for Abby or that Abby was so spoiled with nice things she felt it necessary to immediately improve the house.

"Where did it come from?" he asked in a deceptively calm tone.

"From the Lambert's attic."

"And the curtains?" he asked in a slightly harder tone.

"The material was remnants Betsy sold to me at a very nice discount. Betsy and Tria helped sew them."

Getting up from his chair Max pointed towards the front door. "What about the rocking chair on the front porch?"

"Actually it's one of a pair Mr. Baxley found and gave to me, I mean us."

He should be grateful she hadn't spent a lot of money but instead he was even more irritated she hadn't. He was still trying to hold onto his anger but the questions came out harsh and fast. "So we're a charity case now? What about the furniture? Who gave you that? Or did you move it from upstairs? I don't remember a full size bed in the second room."

In response Abby became defensive. Getting to her feet she answered him, "I bought them second hand...for Maria."

"Why would Maria need a full size bed?"

"For when she and Thomas are wed."

"And why should we buy them a bed?"

"We are not buying them a bed. I will be deducting it from Maria's wages."

Max actually approved of the idea but he wasn't ready to end the argument. "What else have you been spending money on? It obviously hasn't been used for food."

"I am not going to let you make me feel bad for dressing up this place. You will be gone again in a day or two while I have to live here. And if you do not like it just go on back to your ship now. I do not need you."

"You're behaviour is not what I will tolerate from a wife. I will not have you giving people the idea I can't provide. I issue the orders around here. And I know your father gave you funds before he left but you will not spend it dressing this house. Only what I give you will be spent on our home. Understood?"

Abby was so angry at his egotistical chauvinistic attitude she couldn't speak.

Max took her silence for agreement and continued, "And who the hell is Mr. Baxley?"

It was a question she had been dreading since her father had first made the suggestion. How was she going to explain his employment to Max when he was already so enraged over her expenditures? Going on the offensive she answered him in a condescending manner. "You haven't met Mr. Baxley? He and his wife live a few houses away. They are a very nice elderly couple. But let us go back to how I can and cannot spend my funds. Decorating our home is a 'no' but providing food for the table would be a 'yes'?" At his begrudging nod of agreement she continued, "We have not discussed servants but as I have been paying Maria from my money without your objection I take it you do not mind."

"I do mind but as you need a maid and I can't afford to pay her the situation will have to remain the same."

"If that is the criteria then there should not be a problem."

Feeling as if he was about to step in quicksand he said, "A problem with what?"

"With Mr. Baxley, of course."

Max shook his head in confusion. "Why would there be a problem with our neighbor?"

"My father felt I required a suitable escort while you were out to sea. He hired Mr. Baxley as a butler and to serve as an escort."

Max wanted to protest but her father's reasoning was sound and he was chagrined he had not had the presence of mind to consider the need himself. But then as long as her father had been here there had not been a need and he hadn't found out Richard was leaving until just before he set sail leaving no time to take care of it, if he had thought of it.

Abby wanted to make another point with Max. "For someone who did not want a wife you sure have strong ideas of how you expect me to behave."

"I don't have to want a wife to know everyone expects a wife to be demure, obedient and faithful."

"You should have realized from my behaviour when we first met I would not be that kind of wife. Demure and obedient I am not."

"What about faithful?"

The question threw her off balance. She was a little insulted he would ask so rather than answer she turned the tables on him. "Will you be faithful?"

Max wondered how the hell they had ended up facing each other in the middle of the parlour questioning their fidelity when he had planned to spend the evening taking advantage of it. Trying to get back in that direction he said in what he hoped was a seductive tone, "If you keep me satisfied I will." In the back of his mind he knew it was a terrible thing to have said to her but the lingering anger was clouding his judgment.

She heard the invitation in his voice but she was still too enraged to answer it in kind. "And if I choose not to?"

He hadn't expected to be challenged. Anger flashed through him and he reacted without thinking; feeling a strong need to dominate this woman who challenged his every notion of marriage. "You don't have a choice."

Abby found herself tossed over his shoulder in the same manner as when they first met. The suddenness in which he did so caught her by surprise and the force of her landing on his shoulder momentarily robbed her of breath. He climbed the stairs with her and even though she knew from experience it was useless she still kicked and pounded him on the back in protest. Reaching their room he closed the door and dropped her on the bed. She landed on her back in the middle and immediately turned over to try and climb off the other side but Max pulled her back by her shoulder as he joined her on the bed and used his thigh to anchor her in place. She tried to get up anyway pushing against his chest but he was too heavy to move. "Let me up!"

"No. Not until you admit you need me." Her earlier declaration bothered him more than all of the rest of their argument and he was determined to prove it false before the night was over. His lips met hers in a punishing kiss, one meant to show his dominance over her; manly and primal. Her struggles grew futile as she became drugged by his kiss past the point of caring about their argument. The angry tautness governing her body gave way in the wake of heated desire. She should have been fighting for her rights in the relationship, for her independence, instead she found herself responding to his primitive call despite herself.

She should have been pushing against him, instead her hands glided over his shoulders to pull him closer. She should have been indignant, mad, disgraced but she was melting in his embrace, returning the fire of his kiss. She should have been demanding equality instead of wrapping her arms around his neck. She succumbed when she should have been fighting for her dignity, fighting for the kind of marriage she wanted. But she discovered it was hard to do what she should do when someone was feeding her cravings and she craved his touch.

This was what she had wanted since his first appearance in the cookhouse door. In truth it was what she had waited for all week.

With her surrender his kiss changed from domineering to a greedy demand that found its equal in her. Breaking the kiss Max raised his head to look at her. He opened his mouth to say something but Abby put her fingers against his lips and pulled his head down. She didn't want to argue anymore.

A little while later they both awoke to the sound of the front door being opened and a whispered conversation. Max sat up and was reaching for his pants when Abby recognized the voices. She laid a restraining hand on his arm. "It is only Maria returning with Thomas."

Max laid back down. "Isn't it late for him to be bringing her back? You're not worried about her being compromised?"

"Thomas is a good man."

"I know he is but you still shouldn't allow her to run loose with him."

"He has asked her to marry him."

"He did? When?"

"When you returned from the cotton wreckage a few weeks ago."

"He said nothing to me about it. It explains why he didn't volunteer for watch while we are in port."

They fell into silence for a few moments before Max asked, "When do they plan to have the wedding?"

"Maria has not mentioned it yet. I will ask her tomorrow."

They heard the front door open then close and latch and Thomas' footsteps recede as he left the porch. Maria called up the stairs. "Mrs. Abigail, I have returned."

"Good night Maria."

They heard the maid shut her bedroom door and they lay there side by side in the dark, both awake. Abby guessed it to be somewhere between nine and ten o'clock. "Max?" she whispered.

"Um?"

There were a lot of questions she wanted to ask of him to clarify some of the things he had said earlier but she lost her nerve, not wanting to rekindle the anger tonight. Instead she asked, "When will you be leaving again?"

Max wondered if she was anxious to see him off. After the battle they had had tonight and the barbaric manner in which he had ended it he wouldn't blame her, even though she yielded to his challenge, the result of which was going to make it very hard for him to leave her again, she may still wish to be rid of him. "Tomorrow."

Abby was disappointed but did not want to disturb their unspoken truce by asking him to delay. She knew he felt pressured by her father to succeed. And it was obvious from much of their earlier argument his pride was badly bruised from not being able to provide for her in the custom she was used to. She had been so focused on turning this house into their home she had not thought through how he might react to even the smallest of expenditures. She wondered what he would think of her lavishly decorated bedroom in England. Her lips curved at the image of Max standing in the center of her cream and blue, plush and satin room with his jaw hanging open but her smile faded as she realized if he knew it would only increase his current concerns. She heard the deep and even breathing that told her he had again fallen asleep. It was some time later before she was able to join him.

Early the next morning Max bent over to kiss his sleeping wife. She stirred but did not waken. If only he could return from this trip with a salvage claim he would be able to stay a few days and they would have some time to get to know each other better. Right now he had men at the dock waiting for him to decide who would join his crew.

Chapter 22

Abby watched the pelican settle himself on the end of the railing to wait for the treat he expected from her. It had become a morning ritual to spend some time watching the Island awaken from the Captain's Walk and the same pelican - it had the same band of black around its neck - that had visited her the first time always made an appearance. On the third morning she had brought him some fish she had picked up from the market. She held one up by the tail for his inspection and to her surprise he opened his large bill as if waiting for her to feed him. Gingerly stepping closer she placed the fish at the edge of his bill which he promptly snapped closed. "Oh, my!" Abby snatched her hand back in reaction. He then tilted his head upward and tossed the fish further down his gullet. The bird's antics reminded her of a country squire she once knew who had also been stately but surprisingly funny at times and so she dubbed him Sir Percival, after the gentleman. Percy for short.

As Percy tucked his neck and wings in to roost Abby admired God's great canvas. The morning sky was filled with clouds. Broken brush strokes of cirrus clouds in shades of white and grey started in the west growing thicker and heavier towards the east building to an almost solid cloud cover except for a low horizontal break allowing the rising sun to burst through in a splendor of white gold.

This morning marked five days since she awoke alone to find Max had left without saying a word. She supposed she should have been angry at the barbaric way Max had ended their argument but she found it hard to do so when she had enjoyed the result as much as he did. She was disappointed they had not had time to learn more about each other and how their marriage was going to work. A few hours here and there seemed to only spotlight issues as they occurred with no chance to prevent new ones. Even more disconcerting, she had no idea when he would return. She had been told the wreckers were generally gone for weeks at a time and Christmas was only a week away.

Strange it was mid-December. To her the sunshine and palm trees mocked the date on the calendar declaring it to still be summer. She supposed the changes in seasons on the island were much more subtle than in the higher latitudes. Preparations for the holiday seemed foreign without snow and holly and she couldn't imagine what made up a holiday dinner without a turkey or goose to serve. Homesickness washed over her temporarily drowning her in a tidal wave of emotion. It was the first time since she had left she truly missed England; missed it enough to - almost - wish she were there now, but not quite.

She could not explain what exactly it was about the island that appealed to her. As islands go it was nothing grand or dazzling, just comfortable and accepting. It wasn't old and set but rather new and changing with a wildness about it, an untamed beauty.

It was also isolated, as illustrated by an event earlier in the week - the arrival of mail. A once a month occurrence that infused a new energy in the inhabitants. For a little while the citizens of Key West were once again connected to the rest of the world and momentarily they didn't feel so small and detached.

She hadn't really expected to receive any letters for her as any posts from England would have been sent to her Uncle's plantation where she was expected to be residing and they would not have had enough time yet to be forwarded to Key West, but still she was disappointed. Some contact from loved ones would have helped her loneliness.

Passing by the Custom House she discovered many a gentlemen were gathered on the piazza exchanging information garnered from their own reading interests and Mrs. Mallory's parlour was the scene of ladies studying the latest fashion plates and pouring over magazines until every scrap of news had been absorbed, every tidbit shared once if not multiple times. This lasted for a few days before they were once again shrunk to the watery borders of their island.

Yesterday the focus returned inward once again when one of the wrecking ships returned with injured crew and passengers from a lost ship. The *Magnolia*, sailing from New Orleans, had been caught in a storm in the Gulf. It was pushed off course and suffered damages then had the misfortune to run out of food and water before running aground on the north side of Cudjoe Key while looking for a path through the islands rather than taking the time to sail around. It was a poor decision by the Captain to say the least. Fortunately for the starving crew and passengers they were discovered by a wrecker instead of the Indians known to fish those waters and to be hostile towards shipwreck victims.

The wreckers had to use longboats to reach the stranded ship and finding the crew and passengers in more danger than their vessel they ferried them back to the wrecking ship and brought them to Key West for medical care. Arriving around noon Dr. Waterhouse, Mrs. Mallory and Abby spent the rest of the day treating the nineteen men for starvation and dehydration while the wreckers returned to salvage the stranded ship.

It was after nine last night when Abby and Maria were getting ready to leave the boardinghouse full of patients when three of the wreckers were brought in with injuries sustained while trying to haul the stranded ship to deeper water. None were life threatening, mostly cuts and abrasions, but as she helped tend to the injured sailors she couldn't help but worry about Max.

Her concerns for her husband were still first on her mind this morning as she watched the activity in the harbour.

"Percy, I know I told Max this was a Captain's Walk but it could so easily become a Widow's Walk - my widow's walk." It was silly talking to a pelican but she found some comfort in it. Absentmindedly she tracked the progress of a ship sailing into the harbour. "If only you could fly out there and tell me where he is and if he is alright? I know he is and I am just having foolish thoughts but it would be nice to know for sure. How is a woman supposed to deal with all this waiting and uncertainty?" She glanced at Percy looking for sage advice in his stoic profile. Not finding any she looked back at the ship. "I suppose it is time I headed back to the boardinghouse to help Mrs. Mallory with her patients." Her gaze sharpened. She tried leaning forward in an effort to see more clearly. She recognized those sails. They were his sails. Nearly jumping up and down in excitement she shared the news with Percival. "He is here! He is here!" Naturally, Percy didn't care for the interruption of his peaceful repose. He squawked in protest before flying off but Abby didn't notice as she was already flying towards the roof door, then down the stairs. Unwilling to wait for Max to come to her she decided this time she was going to meet him.

The *Mystic* came to rest gently against the dock as two of her crew jumped the railing to land on the pier and secure the ship. Turning his attention to the deck Max searched for the reason he had returned to berth so soon. Seeing a booted foot protruding from behind the forward hatch his eyebrows knitted and he groaned. The sailor was one of the new men he had hired before he left five days ago. Mike and Flynn were both Irishmen who worked efficiently and were well liked but the first day out the one called Blue, a tall dark haired man, had nearly caused the *Mystic* to be the one in need of rescue from the reef. He misread the sounding line not once, but twice, leading Max to believe they were at a safe depth until he heard the hull brush against the coral. Next, he refused to climb the rigging. Max had disciplined him by cutting his wage and confining him to quarters for the afternoon but that had allowed the man time to drink and from then on he had been either three sheets to the wind or passed out for much of the past four days often to be found sprawled across the upper deck in the way of those working the lines. If he at least had had the decency to pass out in his hammock below deck they may have waited a few more days but as it was Max could not get rid of the sod fast enough.

"Tim!" The 'twins', working in the rigging, satisfactorily snapped their attention towards him. Pointing towards the offending boot he said in a voice ripe with temper, "Grab that good for nothing barrel of bilge water and get him off my ship!"

They replied in unison only too happy to oblige, "Aye, captain." They finished securing the sail they were working on and scrambled to the deck to grab the drunken sailor under the arms and legs and carry him across the gangplank. Max watched them reach the dock and stand in confusion unsure what to do with their burden. Not having any other ideas they stepped away from the gangplank and left him on the dock to sleep off his stupor. They returned to the ship speculating if Blue might roll into the water before he awoke.

They still could use one more crewman so Max would have to send someone to retrieve another man he had interviewed previously and he wished now he had hired. "Billy." He gestured for the youth to come speak with him.

"Captain?"

"Do you know where to find Mr. Buttons?"

"Aye, I believe so."

"Find him and tell him we sail midday if he's still interested."

"Aye Captain." Billy turned and left the ship at a near run hurdling a large crate in his way.

He called after Billy with a grin, "And be quick about it."

Max thought about delaying a day so he could spend the night with Abby but the northeastern sky looked promising and he could feel the change in pressure so he wanted to sail for Looe Key as soon as possible, within the hour if he had his way. They had just come from the Marquesas sailing near where the Spanish treasure fleet sank in 1622. Most of the wreckers preferred the Upper Keys so Max tended to favour the Lower Keys to the Dry Tortugas. He had hoped to get lucky this past week but it was not to be. There was a wreck but darned if Captain Talmage didn't beat him to it and worse, this time Talmage wouldn't accept his help. Then he had the trouble with Blue. So Max decided to drop off his burden and try another direction. Surely the expanse of reef was great enough for him and Talmage to not cross paths but it sure seemed to be a problem lately.

"Mr. Keats, send Buttons to me when he arrives. I'll be working in my quarters."

Jonathon looked up from the rope he was coiling. "Aye, captain."

A short time later Max heard a tentative knock on the door frame of his quarters. Finishing the notation in his ledger he called out, "Enter." He looked up expecting to see the lanky seaman he was hiring; instead he found a smiling beauty standing there. His wife was a vision of auburn hair and sparkling eyes in a yellow frock. Max rose from his chair and gestured for her to step further in the room while he shut the door. Despite the turmoil of his last visit she looked happy to see him. He was surprised to see her. He had not planned on her knowing he had slipped into port. Hesitating, unsure how to greet her he placed his hands lightly on the edge of her shoulders and placed a chaste kiss on her cheek, then quickly stepped back. "Abigail, I wasn't expecting you. How did you know I was here?"

Abby was disappointed by the lack of enthusiasm in his greeting but tried to hide it behind a smile. "I was on the Captain's Walk this morning when I saw your sails and thought I would surprise you."

Max admitted, "Well, you did and it is a good thing too. We were just making a brief stop to exchange crewmen and I wouldn't have been able to make it to see you." Indicating the chair he had vacated, "Would you care to sit?"

"No thank you." Abby was further disappointed to learn they were leaving again. Just to make sure she understood him she asked, "You are headed back out - today?"

"Yes. In an hour or so."

Resigning herself to this news she asked, "You will return for Christmas, won't you? It is just a week away."

Max wouldn't have realized the holiday was upon them if Abby hadn't mentioned it. He had never worried about it before. Most of the men who sailed with him didn't have ties to a home. For them it was another day out on the reef unless one of them happened to recall the date in which case passing around an extra round of rum and sharing childhood stories was all that would mark the occasion. He replied nonchalant, "Of course."

Abby got the feeling he didn't seriously mean it. "Promise me you will be back for Christmas."

Seeing how much it meant to her he said, "I promise."

As they talked unconsciously they had drifted closer to each other. Her stormy grey eyes reflected the turmoil she was feeling. Max could see the loneliness lurking in their depths. Studying her beautiful features, he felt awareness flash between them. It was a simple matter to reach out and touch her arm in comfort, to pull her close and lean in to kiss her but just as their breaths mingled they were interrupted by a knock on the door. Max gave her an apologetic look before saying loud enough to be heard through the door, "Be with you in a minute."

Reluctantly Abby pulled away. "You have work to do. I should be going."

She reached for the door but Max wasn't ready to let her go. "Wait a minute." He took the kiss he had been wanting. Still too quick for Abby's liking but she was relieved at least he had wanted to kiss her. She had been starting to wonder. He then opened the door to let her out.

Abby didn't want to go. She was being excused. *Shouldn't a wife feel more important?* But then she had known from the start the ship surrounding her had more of a claim on her husband than she did. She nodded to Max as she passed out the door, a compressed smile on her lips the most she could offer him. "I will see you in week."

He started to protest but then remembered he had promised her Christmas. *Why had he done that?* If he found a wreck he could be breaking his promise. He would just have to cross that bridge when he came to it. He watched Abby gracefully leave while he allowed Buttons to enter his cabin to sign aboard the *Mystic.*

Abby had brought Maria with her knowing she would want to see Thomas. Reaching the deck she had to disrupt their pleasant reunion which made her feel even more depressed. Together she and Maria left the ship headed for the boardinghouse to help Mrs. Mallory continue caring for the sick and injured. She consoled herself at least this time she knew when he would be back. He had promised her Christmas.

The sky was heavy and threatening when Abby and Maria walked home from Mrs. Mallory's in the late afternoon. By unspoken agreement they quickened their strides in an attempt to reach the house before getting wet. It was not to be. The sky opened up as they turned on Simonton Street. Both ladies lifted their skirts and started running. In no time they were soaked and Abby thought how ridiculous they must look to anyone who happened to see them. The image in her head was so funny she was laughing out loud by the time they climbed the steps to the front porch. Maria looked at her questioningly. As Abby continued to laugh, Maria smiled in confusion. Abby couldn't control herself, it was a release from all the stress and disappointment of the week, she continued till her sides hurt and tears' came to her eyes. Laughing of that nature was contagious and so Maria found herself joining her mistress despite not knowing what Abby found so funny.

When Abby was finally able to catch her breath she released her pinned up hair to squeeze the water from it before entering the house. Finally able to answer Maria's unasked question, Abby said, "I was thinking what a sight we must have made trying to out run the rain." Maria nodded in agreement even though she didn't find it as humorous as Abby. After removing as much water as they could on the porch the ladies entered the house. Abby went upstairs to change into dry clothes and then returned to the front room she had made into an office.

She liked the way this room had turned out best. In the corner, between the front and side windows she placed two comfortable captain's chairs she had found in the attic. Between them was a table just large enough to serve tea. It was covered with a white cloth embroidered with yellow flowers and currently held a celadon vase full of deep purple bougainvillea and palm fronds from the yard. The windows were framed with long jonquil yellow panels. She had placed the heavy dark stained desk in the middle of the room facing the front. Behind it hung a large landscape by a talented artist of an English cottage and the surrounding summer countryside, another contribution from the Lambert's attic. Apparently Mrs. Lambert had a love of paintings. Their home was full of them with a good supply in storage. Abby felt honoured to have been loaned her choice of those not in use and then was told to consider whichever one was her favourite as a wedding gift. She brought home three paintings in all with the cottage being gifted. The sea tossed ship was in the parlour and another landscape of islands and sea hung in the bedroom.

Abby paused to look out the window before sitting at the desk. The rain had lightened and looked to be moving off. She tracked the progress of a leaf as it followed the flow of milky water down the street towards the tidal pond. Max must have been in a hurry to leave knowing the rain was coming. The thought made her feel a little better. It soothed her pride to think he was running towards the weather rather than running away from her. He would be sailing through the storm in hopes of finding a ship in distress. Their misfortune would be his payday. No wonder some who didn't consider the service being provided thought him akin to a pirate.

Turning from the window she walked around the desk and pulled out the chair. She removed ink, quill pen and a few sheets of paper. The sky was brightening with the passing of the storm making it unnecessary to light the oil lamp sitting on the corner. Dipping the pen in ink she started her letter: *Dearest Elizabeth*. She paused to consider what to write her friend.

Max was frustrated. They had left Key West four days ago and raced the storm headed towards Looe Key. As storms went it was a mild one with wave heights less than fifteen feet. He sailed right through to a safe anchorage and waited. The last three days had followed the usual pattern of cruising the stretch of reef from Pine Shoal to Sand Key before returning to their anchorage at Looe Key where they now were. He had seen many ships in the last few days but none in need of his services. He felt wrong wishing for someone else's misfortune but that was what he was doing. He had a deadline in front of him and nothing to show for his efforts. It was December twenty-second. He expected Richard to return by the end of January or early February. Big storms were not common this time of year. In all likelihood he may not find a wreck at all between now and then. On the plus side at least he had not seen Talmage.

His men were gathered on deck finishing a meal and sharing stories. Max had not been paying attention to them. Their talk turned to Christmas and memories of their youth and then to gifts they had given their sweethearts. Max's reverie was disturbed by Billy innocently asking him what he planned to give Abby for Christmas. His men laughed at his surprised look. He hadn't given it any thought not having given a Christmas gift to anyone other than his mother and that had been nothing more than a child's charcoal drawings.

Jonathon tried to impress upon him the importance of his predicament. "Ladies - they set great store on a man's gift and wives - they expect them."

Max was suitable concerned but he was out on a reef, what could he possibly find for a gift here? His crew tried offering helpful suggestions.

Billy said, "You could write a poem about her eyes. I did that for one of my girls once."

Thomas offered to dive for shells or coral or maybe a nice sponge for bathing. Max thought the sponge might be a possibility.

Buttons said, "You ought to buy her some of that scented stuff. Womens like that."

Max discarded the idea. Too expensive and besides he liked the rose water she used now and he knew she had a nearly full bottle.

Flynn said, "Not much to choose from in Key West. Why not sail to

Havana?"

Jonathon perked up. "What a good idea, Flynn. We have just enough time to get there and back. What do you say Captain?"

Max looked at all the eager faces around him. He didn't have a better idea. They would only be losing a day on the reef and the sky was clear. Not much chance of a wreck. "All hands make sail."

A collective cheer sounded from his men.

The sailed all night to arrive in Havana mid-morning. Max didn't know what he was looking for he only hoped he would find it. As they wandered through the street vendors his crew continued to offer suggestions.

"Give her jewelry," said Billy.

"She has a chest full of it, remember?" replied Max. Besides he couldn't even afford paste jewelry.

He was leaning towards a delicate looking shawl a few carts back when he came to a vendor peddling odds and ends and found the perfect gift he had to have for her. He haggled over the price until he felt he had a fair deal including gift wrapping. It was more than he had meant to spend but he didn't care. He was sure it was what he had been looking for.

He rounded up his men intent on getting underway immediately. Sailing through the night again they should reach Key West by late morning.

A few days earlier Abby was shopping with Tria in search of a gift for Max. Although she found several things she could have bought for him it didn't feel right. After all their arguments over money she knew he would appreciate the gesture more if she made him something and there was only one thing she could make without spending any money. There was the gift she had started for her father but she could make it for Max instead. The more she considered her plan the more she liked it. She would have just enough time to get it done before Christmas.

Chapter 23

The *Mystic* sailed into Key West harbour the afternoon of December twenty-fourth, Christmas Eve, a little later than Max had planned. After securing the ship and dismissing his crew for a two day shore leave, Max hurried down the street to the rental house. He couldn't wait to see Abby. She would be happy he kept his promise to be home but to his disappointment he found the house was empty. A thorough search proved no one was home. He could only think of two possibilities; one being the Lamberts and he hated the idea of disturbing them only to learn she wasn't there, the other was the boardinghouse. Often the islanders would gather around Mrs. Mallory's table to share stories after dinner. He imagined it was likely Christmas Eve would be such an occasion as to bring more guests to the inn. Hadn't Abby mentioned something about Mrs. Mallory's son coming home from school for the holiday? Making his decision he covered the distance in no time with the sun setting behind him.

It was a crush at the boardinghouse. It seemed Mrs. Mallory had thrown a party in her son's honour. The downstairs rooms were full to capacity with everyone drinking and talking and having a good time. It took some effort to navigate around the guests but to Max's disappointment his wife was nowhere to be found. He asked one of the maids he recognized from Abby's stay at the boardinghouse if she had seen her but the maid said no. Working his way back to the door he walked the short distance to the Lambert house. To his relief their butler answered his knock. Max could hear voices beyond him, in the dining room where the Lambert's were also entertaining, getting his hopes up. He asked if his wife was present and received a negative reply. He left quickly before he was discovered by Victoria or her parents. He had no reason for it but still he was embarrassed to not know where is wife might be. Trudging back to his own house he struggled to think of any other places to check. Maybe he should have brought Thomas with him instead of leaving him on watch. He might have known where else to look.

Reaching his home again he poured himself a drink from the sideboard in the dining room then settled in to wait in the rocking chair in the parlour where he could see out the front window. He must have fallen asleep for he was startled awake by voices outside. Abby entered the house followed by Maria and the man she had hired as an escort. From the reflected light of the lantern he carried Max could tell he was much older than expected. Old enough to be their father which gave Max some comfort. Abby gave a satisfying squeal of excitement when she saw him and rushed to greet him as he stood up from the chair. She wrapped her arms around his neck hugging him. "You made it!" Stepping back she asked, "How long have you been waiting? Are you hungry? I think Mrs. Baxley put aside some bread and cheese for a snack. Mr. Baxley, would you be so kind as to light some candles?"

When she took a breath, Max asked, "Where have you been?" He noticed it was quarter past seven by the clock on the pianoforte.

Mr. Baxley crossed the room to light the candles. Maria still stood by the door.

Catching the angry tone behind his question Abby cautiously replied, "Taking care of a sick mother and her family."

"You made me promise to return the least you could do is be here waiting for me."

Abby was amazed after years of keeping her temper under control, it slipped so easily with her husband. "All I have done since we have been married is wait for you!"

Mr. Baxley mumbled something about getting his wife to make dinner and hastily retreated out the front door. Maria crossed to the back door taking the lantern with her presumably to start a fire in the kitchen. "I had no idea if, much less when, you would arrive and the family needed my assistance. Mrs. Mallory was not available."

And there was Princess Thorn. "Why must it be you? Aren't there other women who could take care of them? What about Victoria? She's not married."

Abby gave a short laugh. "Can you seriously see Tria taking care of anyone other than herself?" It wasn't that Victoria didn't care about others she just wasn't the nurturing type.

"All right not her but surely there is someone else."

"The others all have families of their own to look after."

"You have a husband."

"Who was not here when I was asked to help."

They stared at each other. Max gave in. She was right and he knew he was being unreasonable. It was the long voyage to Havana and then to Key West with very little sleep combined with his disappointment causing him to lose his temper. Changing subjects he asked, "What's for dinner or have you eaten already?"

Taking the olive branch Abby replied, "I have not. I will see what Mrs. Baxley has made for dinner."

"Who is that?" Max asked, the edge returning to his voice.

"Our cook,." Abby braced herself for more of his anger.

"I can't afford a cook." Max's anger rekindled. *Now there was a third servant.*

"I can." She was getting tired of having this discussion.

Max clenched his teeth. "I thought we discussed this."

"We did. You said if the help was needed you did not have a problem with my paying their wages."

He recalled saying that in regards to the butler/escort which he saw the need for but a cook was taking it too far in his opinion. "Why don't you just learn how to cook? If you don't cook and clean, what do you do with your day?"

Abby had no desire to cook so she went on the offensive. "What does it matter to you? You are never here anyway so why do you care what I do?"

"Because you are my wife!" He knew he was being autocratic but he really didn't have a better argument handy.

She said it quietly, her anger losing its steam in the wake of hurt feelings. "Most days I am your wife in name only." She wanted to go back to the way it felt to be with him before they had married when they seemed to understand each other.

Max saw the wounded look on her face but still he said, "I can't be here and salvage ships. You know that."

"Yes, of course." He didn't understand. It wasn't the physical absence she missed but the emotional absence and she was not prepared to explain it to him tonight. She dropped her eyes to the floor and stepped aside intending to retreat upstairs for a moment.

The defeat in her posture was his undoing. He didn't want to fight. Not anymore than she probably did. He stopped her escape and pulled her into his embrace tucking her head under his chin. He held her a moment before saying, "I'm sorry Abigail." He brought his hands to either side of her head so he could gently tilt her face towards his. "You are my Rose Princess. I am at your service until day after tomorrow. I promise not to cause anymore fuss between us. We will enjoy the holiday together."

His pledge made Abby melt. She hadn't even realized she was crying until he wiped a tear away with his thumb. Max leaned his head down and gave her a quick kiss that held the promise of more to come later then he smiled and that smile could make her promise him anything. "Oh Max. I am sorry too. I seem to lose my temper so easily around you. I promise to try harder to control it."

He heard sounds coming from the cookhouse. "Why don't you go see what's for dinner, let the others know the coast is clear to come back. Oh, and ask Maria if she would like to walk with me to invite Thomas to join us for dinner."

Dinner was a lively affair with Thomas, Maria and Mr. and Mrs. Baxley joining them for a simple fish dinner followed by pleasant conversation over wine and spirits. As the evening waned Max could barely keep his eyes open after sailing two days straight to get home in time. Abby was enjoying herself so much she hated for it to end but all too soon the Baxley's declared it was time to go home and excused themselves. Thomas bid Maria goodnight at the door and returned to the *Mystic*.

Max had learned from the conversation at dinner how his wife was spending her time caring for the sick and injured and integrating into the island society. When he discarded his personal feelings he was quite proud of the way she had learned healing skills and was taking care of others. But still it went against his notions of what was proper for her to work outside their home.

Abby lay wide awake beside her sleeping husband. They had had an enjoyable evening despite their earlier argument but then maybe it was because they were not alone. Otherwise they seemed to only get along when they were being intimate. Abby was starting to wonder. *Is this all we have?* It was a long time before she drifted off to sleep.

She awoke Christmas morning to find Max watching her with a schoolboy grin on his face and the weight of a small package wrapped in white paper with a red ribbon on her chest. "What is this?"

"A gift for my beautiful wife. Open it." He couldn't wait any longer.

Abby picked up the package then worked herself into a sitting position while Max impatiently waited. She undid the bow and let the ribbon fall to her lap then carefully unwrapped the paper and laid it aside to later be smoothed out and saved for future use. In her hands was a beautiful wooden music box with a carved rose, larger than her palm, covering the top. She ran her fingers over the carving feeling the ridges of the smooth wood before opening the box. Inside under glass she could see the delicate mechanics of the musical workings.

"You have to turn the handle and wind it up."

"I know. I have one back home my father gave me." She turned the handle and waited for the notes to start. The tinkling tones of 'Greensleeves' filled the room. It was one of her favourites. She smiled at Max. "Thank you. It is beautiful. Your gift is in the top drawer." She indicated the dresser behind him.

Max was disappointed. He was so sure he had found something she didn't already have but worse was her telling remark that she still considered England her home. He opened the drawer and pulled out a package wrapped in plain brown paper. He turned with a smile to hide his feelings from Abby and returned to sit beside her on the bed. Unwrapping the paper, he revealed a navy, cable knit, heavy sweater.

Nervously awaiting his reaction Abby explained, "I made it for you from yarn I already had. I know you will never be able to wear it here but maybe if we visit my uncle during the winter you might need it."

"You would be surprised how cold fifty degrees can feel once you've acclimated to this place. It will come in handy over the next couple of months and it means a lot to me that you made it. I should have made you something."

"No, no. I love the music box. It is beautiful." Since yesterday's high was seventy-five she thought he was just trying to humor her about being able to wear the sweater, still she said, "Try it on." Max obliged slipping the sweater over his head but it was soon very clear it was too small. "Oh no! I started out making it for my father. When I redid it I forgot to allow for your broader shoulders and chest."

"It's alright Abby. You can fix it later."

Abby's brow creased as she frowned. "Unfortunately I cannot. There is no more yarn. I used it all." She was so disappointed she felt like burying her head in the pillow and crying.

Wanting to ease her disappointment Max tried to lighten her mood. "Then I shall just have to shrink to fit it."

Abby quickly responded, "Oh, no you won't!" When Max gave her a questioning look she sheepishly replied, "I like you just the way you are," which earned her a generous kiss. At its end Abby said, "We should get dressed. A visiting minister is holding services at the Custom House this morning. We will need to hurry to get seats and we are invited to dinner afterwards at the Lambert's.

Max was feeling like a fish out of water. The lavishness of the Lambert's home always made him uncomfortable. Adding to his discomfort, dinner included two other gentlemen lawyers, Mr. Cathcart and Mr. Jenkins, who had traveled extensively. Conversation around the table was centered on activities of the more affluent society and foreign places leaving little for him to contribute to the conversation. Abigail, on the other hand, was holding her own leaving Max to wonder if she would be able to handle life on a remote island. Would the lack of social amenities along with the other hardships eventually cause her to hate this place he called home? It was a disturbing thought. And if she hated the place would she not eventually hate him for keeping her there?

After dinner the men left the women for brandy and cigars in Mr. Lambert's office. The room had wall to wall bookcases many of which were legal tomes. A massive wooden desk was centered in the room with a leather sofa on one side and two leather armchairs facing the desk which Mr. Lambert pulled away to form more of a triangular sitting area. Max chose a chair and the other gentlemen the sofa. Mr. Lambert offered a box of cigars to his guests and then poured brandy into crystal tumblers. Max accepted and enjoyed both. Conversation swirled around him mostly to do with court business of which the other three shared in common leaving him to sink deeper into his depressing thoughts until Mr. Lambert interrupted them. "You've been quiet this evening Captain Eatonton. I apologize if we are boring you with our talk of shop."

"Not at all, sir. I have other concerns weighing on my mind."

"Salvage business I presume. Captain Talmage is not causing more trouble for you, is he?"

"No more than usual. I have been trying to avoid crossing paths with him."

"Just as well you do. There is a lot of talk he is not operating above board but nothing can be proven in court. Many would like to make a case against him but so far he has been very careful."

"Just what is he supposedly guilty of?" asked Mr. Cathcart.

"It has been suggested he is making deals with captains to intentionally wreck ships allowing Talmage to not only know where the wreck will occur but getting their cooperation for high salvage fees ahead of time thereby swindling the owners and the underwriters. So far none of the cases have been brought to court due to the lack of evidence and the length of time it would take to do so in St. Augustine but now that a trial can be held here all that is needed is a case to be filed with a good witness and he could be brought to justice."

This gave Max an idea. "What kind of witness?"

Mr. Lambert said, "One of his crew to testify to the planning..."

Max interrupted him, "That won't happen."

"One of his crew helped in the Bennington case."

"Yes, but the rest of his crew are loyal and cut from the same cloth as it were as their captain."

Mr. Cathcart said, "Then you would need a witness from the crew of the wrecked ship or someone else who is aware of their plan."

Max doubted anyone involved would be willing to come forward. "What if another captain witnessed the intentional wreck, would that be sufficient?"

Mr. Jenkins replied thoughtfully, "I believe so, if the captain's integrity could not be questioned and it was clear the ship was wrecked intentionally, then yes, such a witness would be beneficial. What are you thinking?"

"Just that I should keep an eye on his activities whenever I run into Talmage such as a few weeks ago I found him anchored in an unusual place at dusk and displaying what appeared to be a signal light. Mr. Tish, his former crewman, suggested I keep moving and not stop to investigate."

Mr. Cathcart was clearly interested. "Captain Talmage brought in a questionable wreck a few weeks ago. The owner contacted me seeking advice on the claim. It sounds like Mr. Tish could provide some testimony to the Captain's activities."

Max was a little concerned he may have involved Fish in another court matter but it couldn't be helped now, "I'll ask him."

Mr. Cathcart said, "No need. I'll contact him myself. Thank you."

Mr. Jenkins mentioned another case that may serve as precedence for Mr. Cathcart and so Max relapsed to his own thoughts now swirling around Talmage and his activities. He knew the man could be underhanded but he had not considered the possibility Talmage could be arranging intentional wrecks. It was too unethical for Max to have ever conceived of the idea but it certainly explained why Talmage was bringing in more wrecks than any of the rest of them.

Meanwhile in the parlour, Mrs. Lambert asked, "Abigail, how are you getting along with your husband?"

"Well enough I suppose."

Mrs. Lambert displayed a secretive smile. "I remember having many fights as a newlywed, but the making up was always enjoyable."

"Mother!" Tria was shocked her mother would say something so bold.

"Hush. Abigail does not have a mother around to discuss this with and you'll be married soon yourself. It wouldn't hurt to understand what comes with wedlock."

Abby was thinking Tria came by her bold behaviour naturally. "We are arguing of trivial matters. Is it normal for newlyweds to disagree? I am afraid it may be worse for us because of our circumstances."

Mrs. Lambert reassured her. "No dear. It is quite normal. It is the usual outcome of trying to find the balance between your needs and his until you find what works for both of you. Only beware, no marriage ever is or could be equal. The woman always gives up more of herself, not just in the bedroom."

Abby's cheeks bloomed in embarrassment at her mention of the bedroom. She was thankful Mrs. Lambert moved onto discussing plans for New Years.

Max and Abby left the Lambert's in time to watch the sun set over the shoreline to their left as they walked home. The breeze had a chill causing Abby to pull her shawl tighter. Max put his arm around her for added warmth. "That's a winter wind blowing. I doubt it will reach sixty degrees tomorrow." They fell into silence each wrapped up in their own thoughts. Max was considering taking action to bring down Talmage while Abby was reviewing their arguments to date in the hopes of reassuring herself their marriage was normal.

The next morning Max tried to leave quietly not wanting to disturb Abby's slumber or face her continued requests he stay home longer. She asked him to delay his departure last night before going to bed and he was sure she would again this morning. He nearly made it to the door when she stirred awake.

Abby smiled drowsily at him. "Time for you to leave, already?" She brought herself to a sitting position one foot tucked underneath her bottom, the other calf, uncovered by her nightgown, dangled off the bed. "How long will you be gone?"

Bruskly he said, "I don't know." Then, in a more soothing tone wanting to placate her, "I promise as soon as I find a wreck, I will stay home for a whole week."

"It would mean a lot to me. Can I have a kiss goodbye?" Max returned to her bedside and leaned over to give her a kiss full of longing and regret. She hadn't intended to ask again, had in fact reminded herself over and over not to ask. With her father gone, her need for him was strong; for his companionship and for emotional strength. She laid a hand on his arm in a pleading gesture. "Please stay one more day. Max, you are the captain. You can decide to stay if you want to."

Max's anger flashed as quickly as St. Elmo's fire. "Your father took that decision away from me. Let me go Abby. I have work to do." He strode from the room without looking back. He hadn't wanted to leave like this. If only she had stayed asleep he could have left without the hurt and anger burning between them.

Abby clasped her trembling hands together in her lap. It was her own fault. She knew what the answer would be before she asked the question and still she had asked it. Sitting on the bed just as he had left her she listened to his footsteps, each one another wound to her emotions, down the stairs, out the front door, across the porch and down the steps to the limestone walk where they mercifully became muffled. The emptiness of the room overcame her and once again she found herself weeping. The need to cleanse her spirit with tears was too strong to be denied. *How long could they go on like this? How long before he got tired of her trying to cling to him and how long could she handle the emotional hunger? What if they never found a way to love each other?*

Abby allowed herself a few minutes to indulge in self-pity then she steeled her spine, got up, washed her face and dressed. There had to be some kind of volunteer work she could do on this island besides care for the sick and injured. If not, she would start one, there had to be many needs to be filled. She was not going to sit around this house feeling sorry for herself.

Walking towards the ship, his anger having a chance to cool, Max knew he should go back and apologize. If he went back he probably would end up agreeing to stay another day or two and if he missed finding a wreck first he would find himself permanently stuck behind a desk in her father's offices. The idea of shuffling papers was enough to keep him walking towards his ship. She would understand when she stopped to think about it and if not he would make it up to her when he returned. Surely he could find a ship this time and be able to stay home long enough to give them the time they needed to understand each other better. It wasn't as if he didn't want to stay with her. He could think of lots of ways to enjoy another day with Abby.

Walking up the gangplank Max found his crew at ease around the deck. Unreasonably irritated he barked out orders sending them all satisfyingly scurrying. He overheard Billy warning the new crewman the Captain was in a temper and best to follow orders quickly but his tempers never lasted long. Max supposed it was true. He approached the helm where Jonathon was standing with a knowing look on his face. Not wanting to discuss his morning Max tried to avoid it by saying, "Mr. Keats, ready the ship. We sail now."

Jonathon forwarded the order to the crew but then turned back to his friend. "Another disagreement with the wife? Do you think you intentionally pick a fight with her to make it easier to leave?"

Max refused to respond to Jonathon's baiting but he contemplated the possibility his friend might be right. They argued every time he was home but not always when he was leaving. Still it was something to be considered. He could be unconsciously creating reasons to argue.

Jonathon took Max's silence as acceptance. "You should stay home and work it out with her. She deserves more from you."

Max's anger flared again. "Not you to! You of all people know how important it is we find a wreck and the only way to do that is to be out on the reefs."

Jonathon casually replied, "Then bring her along."

"Absolutely not! Bring a woman on a shipful of men, have you gone daft?" Max walked away from Jonathan to visually check the ship's readiness to sail.

Jonathon spoke to his retreating back, "That's just an excuse. You know you have a good trustworthy crew." Max continued his work, trying to ignore Jonathon who was following him. "You would be able to spend time together. She could help cook."

That made Max stop and turn. "You don't want her to cook." Max smiled, remembering the meals she had tried to prepare and failed. "But she can open a cocoanut."

"Bring her along, she might surprise you."

Max decided it was time to end the conversation. "No. She would be a distraction for all of us. A woman does not belong on a wrecking ship." Jonathon started to say more but Max cut him off with a raised hand. "End of discussion. Don't you have work to do?"

Recognizing defeat Jonathon changed the subject. "Where are we headed this time?"

"Alligator Reef."

Jonathon was surprised. "I thought we were trying to avoid Talmage? You know that's his reef of choice."

"Aye, we were. Now we're not"

"Why is that?"

"I'll explain later." Max yelled to the crew at large, "Weigh anchor!"

Abby was having tea at Tria's on a bright January afternoon. It had been some time since Abby had been free to indulge in an afternoon visit. When she wasn't helping the sick and injured she was volunteering to teach reading, writing and arithmetic to the few children on the island and to some of the adults brave enough to want to learn. Abby was also working on finding support to build a petition to have the law abolished. All of which kept her very busy.

Tria greeted her warmly. They joined Mrs. Lambert in the parlour. Once the maid had left, Mrs. Lambert served tea. Abby was thinking how nice it was to relax. She had missed this lately.

Tria said, "I have not seen the *Mystic* in a while. How long has Captain Max been gone?"

Abby grimaced. "Nearly three weeks. I had thought he would have been home days ago."

Mrs. Lambert handed Abby a cup of tea. "Brace up dear. I'm sure it has nothing to do with you."

Tria agreed and tried to cheer her friend. "I'm sure it is his work that keeps him. Why in the world would he stay away from such a beautiful bride?"

Abby sipped her tea and nodded her head to acknowledge the compliment. She was embarrassed her insecurity was so obvious to her friends. She often wondered at night if their fighting wasn't the reason he stayed away so long.

Mrs. Lambert said, "You are doing the right thing, keeping busy."

Tria frowned. "But please not so busy you couldn't find more time to visit."

"Have I neglected you so much, Tria?"

"Yes, you have and life on this island has been quite boring because of it."

"Well then, I shall have to make it up to you." Abby considered what she could offer her friend. Struck by inspiration she smiled broadly towards Victoria. "I know, I shall enliven your world by throwing a dinner party three days hence, Friday evening. Whom shall I invite besides you and you, Mrs. Lambert, and of course Mr. Lambert?" She considered her options. "I should keep it small. The Messrs. Whitehead, perhaps?"

Mrs. Lambert replied, "Thank you dear but Mr. Lambert and I have other obligations."

Abby nodded. "Of course. It is short notice after all."

Victoria said, "William Whitehead, of course, but his brother, John, is currently visiting Washington. How many guests were you thinking to invite?"

Abby considered her dining area. "I have room for six guests but I was thinking only four to keep it simple, so two others. Betsy should be one. Is there a gentleman of interest to her?"

Tria frowned at Abby. "I don't know and by that reasoning are you thinking Mr. Whitehead is of interest to me?"

"Actually, I had not considered it but why not? He is of similar age, handsome, educated and of some influence in the island politics. Quite a catch for any lady."

Tria countered with, "Staid and boring and he likes traipsing around the island jungle."

"He did it to draw his map; now that it is almost done he most likely will not be out so much."

Tria waved aside Abby's defense. "Still there is no excitement to be found in his demeanor and he probably plans to live here the rest of his life."

Mrs. Lambert said, "I would disagree with your reasoning. Excitement is not a good quality in a husband."

Tria and her mother had had this conversation often and she did not want to continue it again in front of her friend so she tried a diversionary tactic. "I believe Stephen Mallory is still in town on winter break."

Abby thought Mr. Mallory a good choice. "Well that will keep the party all of one age group, does it not? Or would it give the impression of matchmaking if all the guests are single? Should I be concerned?"

Mrs. Lambert said, "It cannot be helped unless you invite another older couple. There is only one other married couple I know of your age. They have several very young children making it difficult for them to attend an evening dinner. The only problem you face is by inviting the island's two most eligible young ladies you will have hordes of men of every age wishing for an invite. There will be envy for the ones who do get invited. And I would not suggest making a habit of this kind of party or you may incite some violence."

Tria grimaced. "Oh mother, sometimes you only think of the worst that can happen."

Mrs. Lambert admonished her daughter. "Dear, it would be wise of you to take more time to consider your actions as often you are too wayward and headstrong for your own good."

Abby decided to interrupt before this conversation grew more uncomfortable for everyone. "What do you think I should plan for the menu?" It worked like a charm. Mother and daughter instantly responded with helpful suggestions.

When tea was done Abby excused herself to go home and write invitations and to go over her plans with Mrs. Baxley.

Max was leaning over the bulwark staring out at the eastern horizon deep in thought. They were anchored for the night a few hours sail from Key West. They had not run across Talmage. Max had intended to stay on the reef a few more weeks in the hopes of finding him or a ship but alas a split in the mainsail they were unable to repair on the ship was forcing him home early after three weeks out. If the wind was favourable they should make port in the morning.

With too much time to think on the reef his thoughts, as usual, strayed to his wife and their strained marriage. He was sure it was mostly because his feelings of frustration continued to ride him hard. He had yet to find a wreck, much less find one first. Her father could return in just a few weeks and he had nothing to show for his efforts. He carried that failure home with him and allowed it to colour his interactions with Abby. When he was on the reef he felt the need to be home and when he was home he needed to be on the reef which constantly left him feeling frustrated. What would happen when her father returned and he refused to take his company job? Besides her dissatisfaction with their marriage what if she decided she could no longer handle living on an isolated island? She clearly deserved and expected more than he was able to give her. If he refused her father would she in turn refuse him? The thoughts circled round and round in his head and kept leading back to the certainty he had to find a wreck that would bring in enough to put aside some of the issues and give him time to work on the others.

He also knew his crew was tired of his surliness which at this point had nothing to do with anger and everything to do with thwarted passion. It was a darn good thing they were headed to port. He often found himself dwelling on her image in the daytime. His dreams had become sheer torture. Many times he was up pacing the deck long before first watch. He had told Jonathon she would be a distraction aboard ship but he never took into account she could become a distraction to him even when she wasn't on board. She was in his soul and he didn't deserve her.

Friday morning Abby was on her way to the fish market with Maria to purchase food for her dinner party that evening. She had hoped Max would come home in time but scanning the harbour again, she still did not see his ship. A new arrival, the *Southern Belle*, was docked at the wharf in the *Mystic's* usual place. Giving up the idea of Max presiding at the head of the table as wishful thinking she purposefully made her way to the end of the pier over the turtle kraals to select her fish. She hired a page to have them delivered to Mrs. Baxley and then made the return walk down the pier while making a mental checklist of all the things she would need to do today. She stepped down from the wooden pier and turned left, headed towards home when she heard a male voice call her name over the crowd.

"Miss Bennington!"

Chapter 24

January 9th, 1829

Max stepped ashore for the first time in three weeks. So many ships were in port there was no space at the wharf. He was forced to anchor the *Mystic* in the harbour. He and most of his crew rowed ashore in the longboat with the damaged sail. They came ashore next to Mr. Browne's wharf at the north end of Front Street. Leaving Billy to secure the boat, the other crewmen were in a jovial mood and ready to inflict themselves on the closest bar. Max had intended to walk with Thomas to the sail maker to commission the sail repair and then onto the rental house in the hopes of spending an enjoyable afternoon with his wife.

In the space of a heartbeat his world turned upside down. He was casually observing the bustling scene in front of him - sailors, passengers, vendors, shop keepers all going about their business walking to and from the wharf - when the passing of a cart briefly parted the crowd allowing him to see a scene unfolding further down the street past the last wharf. Max gestured for Thomas to go on to the sail maker without him. He then slowly walked down the street as he witnessed his wife warmly greeting a man, a rich gentleman judging by his appearance, he had never seen before but with whom Abby was obviously well acquainted. They were facing each other, the man and woman, their profile to Max. Maria was standing a few yards beyond them. Max paused under a palm tree to watch them converse for a few more minutes before Abby linked her arm in the gentleman's and they turned away from him walking further up Front Street. Max followed behind and watched them turn on Fitzpatrick Street headed to the boardinghouse.

He turned back, his mind spinning with all the possible scenarios of how Abby knew the gentleman. Maybe he was a friend of her father's or someone Victoria was seeing. Maybe he was one of her kin from Alabama. Trying to believe anything but the worst he found himself in a bar ordering a pint of courage before heading home to confront her when she returned. Rational thought would argue she was only directing the gentleman to the hotel. His wife would never betray her vows. Even if she entered the hotel he knew from experience Mrs. Mallory would do her best to maintain propriety. The problem lay in that Max was currently unable to maintain rational thought.

"Miss Bennington!"

Abby quickly searched the men in front of her for the familiar voice. Seeing him standing still a few yards in front of her Abby whispered on an incredulous breath, "Jason."

"Miss Bennington, is it really you?"

Abby was having trouble believing, strolling towards her, was none other than Lord Jason Malwbry who seemed to be just as surprised to see her. He clasped her hands as she offered him a curtsey. "Lord Malwbry, as I live and breathe, what brings you to this island?"

"You, actually."

Abby blushed profusely at once flattered and yet feeling guilty by his declaration. Mindful of those around her she turned her back to the dock in an attempt to hide her blush from others nearby. Jason stepped to the side in order to continue facing her.

"I have chased you across two oceans and am quite shocked to find you within five minutes of debarking not that I had expected to have any trouble finding you on such a small island it is just I was sure you would no longer be here."

"You really just arrived?"

"Stepped off the gangway of the *Southern Belle* only moments ago recently departed from Mobile." Jason gestured to the ship behind him she had noticed earlier. It was still being unloaded adding credence to his declaration.

"Mobile? You really were following me. How did you know to look for me here?"

"At your relatives' direction."

"You met my Aunt Virginia and Uncle James? I would love to hear more about them but I am in a dreadful hurry this morning. Would you like to come for dinner tonight? I am hosting a small dinner party and there is plenty of room for one more."

"I would be delighted to attend."

"You must be staying at the boardinghouse."

"Right you are. I am told it is the only accommodations so you must be staying there as well."

"Not anymore. We have a house on the other end of town. I will walk you to the boardinghouse and introduce you to Mrs. Mallory and I can point out our house from just beyond so you will know where you are going later this evening."

"Excellent." Jason offered her his arm and they strolled to the hotel. As they walked Abby asked him about her family. "Are my aunt and uncle well? Did you meet my cousins?"

"Yes. They seemed to be enjoying good health. Of course, they were very disappointed by the delay in meeting you. You know they asked me all about you."

"You were kind, I hope."

"No reason to fear otherwise. I will have you know they generously welcomed me into their home." He didn't tell her they only welcomed him after he told them he was her fiancé and he had hoped to surprise her for

Christmas. "Although I only put them out for one night choosing to leave promptly the following morning to return to the coast after they explained what had happened to you."

Reaching the boardinghouse she continued walking past it and pointed to the rental house on the other side of the pond. In jest Jason asked, "Must I traverse the pond in order to get there?"

Abby laughed. "Heavens no, you will walk back the way we came. Follow Front Street to the end and turn left on Simonton."

"Walk?"

"I know, I thought it strange at first too but I have only seen one buggy on this island and as you can see it is not far."

Mrs. Mallory had gone out and so Abby left Jason in the capable hands of one of the maids. Stepping down from the boardinghouse porch she made an impulsive decision to visit Tria but not far down Whitehead Street she was stopped by Dr. Waterhouse, the postmaster, hailing her from his doorway. "Mrs. Eatonton! Mrs. Eatonton! I have some mail for you, just arrived today on the *Southern Belle*." Eagerly she made her way to his porch to retrieve the letters. She hoped one would be from her father. Dr. Waterhouse handed her five letters in all; one from her father, one from Mrs. Winterfeldt and three from Elizabeth. Changing course again, she hurried home, Maria barely able to keep up, tightly clutching her letters as if afraid the wind would rob her of them. She couldn't wait to reach the solitude of the Captain's walk to read them. Not only was it the first letter from her father but also the first letters to reach her from England. Party preparations would just have to wait.

Max was raising his third pint of ale when he saw Abby, trailed by Maria, walking past the window at such a brisk pace she was nearly running. His head swiveled following her progress. He had no idea what she was up to but she did at least seem to be headed home and by herself. He debated the wisdom of following her or rounding up his crew and leaving port. Practical matters like not having a main sail prevented the second but really the overriding factor was, weather he deserved her or not, she was his wife and he wanted to know why she was warmly greeting a stranger in front of the whole town. Putting down his nearly full tankard he left money for the barkeep and headed after his wife.

Abby was called to duty as soon as she entered the house forcing the letters to wait until much later. After calming Mrs. Baxley's concerns and setting tasks for Mr. Baxley and Maria, Abby went to work wiping the plates and silverware and setting the table. Hearing the front door open she walked to the end of the table to peer down the hall. She was pleasantly surprised to find her husband standing in the opening. Her fondest wish for this party had just been granted, not to mention she was simply happy to have him back home. Three surprises in one day. The tides were being good to her. She laid the plate and towel on the table and rushed to embrace her husband then kiss him. Her impassioned greeting helped reassure Max a little but he did not fully return her embrace despite his wife's exuberance.

"Oh Max, I am so thankful you have come home today."

"Really? What is special about today?"

"I am hosting - well actually *we* are hosting a dinner party tonight. I had so hoped you would be here and here you are." Impulsively she kissed him again.

"What is the occasion?" he asked thinking of the stranger she met earlier.

"It started as a way to get Tria out of her doldrums but it worked for me as well. I have actually become very excited about it."

Max asked in a deadly calm voice, "It wouldn't have anything to do with the gentleman you met with in town?"

Abby was so excited to have Max home she wasn't paying much attention to the tone of his voice. "Lord Malwbry? No, he is not the reason I have looked forward to this evening, although I did invite him to join us. Just arriving in town it seemed the proper thing to do and he has met my aunt and uncle and I so want to learn what they are like. My father's point of view would be biased as it is his brother."

"Who is this Lord Malwbry?"

"Jason Malwbry." She hesitated suddenly realizing acquainting her husband with the full truth may do more harm than good for all involved. "He will be the future Duke of Rothebury. We come from the same village in England. I have known him most of my life."

Max was surprised to get the truth, at least most of it. He heard the telltale hesitation and wondered at it. He didn't think she was lying to him but she had definitely chosen not to reveal something of their history. Letting that go for now he resigned himself to playing host for the evening. Too late to run back to the ship. "Who else have you invited?"

"Tria, of course, and Betsy Wheeler. William Whitehead had to decline and Stephen Mallory left this morning headed back to school. Being too late to invite anyone else without seeming like a second fiddle invitation, it was going to be just us three ladies until you and Ja... Lord Malwbry sailed into port."

Her slip told Max she was on a first name basis with this Lord. There was no way he was going back to his ship now. In fact, it looked as though he needed some reinforcements. "Would you mind if Mr. Keats joined us?"

Abby brightened. "What an excellent idea, Max! Do you think he would?"

"Absolutely." It didn't matter what plans Jonathon had he was going to be their guest tonight. Max would order him to if necessary. "I'll go personally invite him."

Mrs. Mallory saw her latest guest in the foyer ready to step out for the evening. She hurried to greet him. "You must be Lord Malwbry. I am Mrs. Mallory, the proprietress of this establishment. If there is anything I can do for you to make your stay more enjoyable please let me know. Have you had your supper, milord? We have a wonderful turtle soup tonight."

"Thank you, madam, pleased to make your acquaintance but I was just on my way to dinner with the Bennington's."

"Pardon?"

"Miss Abigail Bennington. She invited me this afternoon."

"Oh. Perhaps you're not aware having just arrived. She is Mrs. Eatonton now. She and her husband," Mrs. Mallory emphasized husband, clearly disapproving of the situation, "live on the other side of town."

Jason kept his face from showing his disappointment at the astonishing news Abigail had a husband. Her aunt and uncle had not mentioned it and he had assumed during their earlier conversation that 'we' and 'our' referred to Abby and her father. A husband had never crossed his mind. It had only been a few months. Mrs. Mallory hadn't mentioned her father. Jason wondered where he was. Had something happened to him forcing her to marry? It was not a question he wanted to ask Mrs. Mallory, although she could probably answer his query. He had the feeling Mrs. Mallory was very protective of Abby and may not let him pass if she continued to question his intentions. "Yes Madam. Mrs. Eatonton pointed her residence out to me this afternoon, as well. I am a friend of the family from England."

Forced to accept that nothing untoward was going on Mrs. Mallory replied. "Well then enjoy your evening, Lord Malwbry.

Jason stepped from the porch relieved to have survived the interview but feeling keenly disappointed, after finally finding Abigail, to learn his quest was for naught. She was effectively out of his reach...unless...she was in need of rescuing. He would see for himself she was in a good marriage before cutting his losses and heading home.

Abby greeted Victoria from the staircase, leaning over the railing she said, "Heavens, is it that late already or are you early?" She stepped into the hallway fastening her other earring then opened her arms to greet her friend with an embrace. Tria was wearing a silk gown the colour of pale blue forget-me-nots that enhanced her dark features.

"I am unfashionably early. I was simply too impatient to wait any longer." Grasping Abby's hands Tria held them out to admire her dress. "You look beautiful. That shade of green reminds me of the shallows around the islands in the bright afternoon sunlight and it is perfect for you."

Abby's smile broadened and her cheeks flushed at the sincere compliment from her friend. "Thank you. Your dress is also the perfect colour for you. You look splendid."

Tria smiled broadly, "I know."

It was said so matter of fact Abby couldn't help but laugh. "You minx. Come sit down." Abby directed Tria towards the sofa in the parlour. "I have a surprise for you."

"Oh I love surprises! Tell me."

"Besides Betsy and Mr. Keats I have invited someone else. A friend of mine from England has arrived this morning, Lord Jason Malwbry." Abby hesitated for effect seeing the excitement build in Tria's eyes before adding with emphasis on his title, "The future Duke of Rothebury." Abby's smile broadened at the widening of surprise in her friend's eyes.

"A future duke! If I recall correctly, is this not the same Lord Jason you were avoiding a marriage proposal from when you left England?"

Max was about to descend the stairs to join the ladies when he overheard Victoria. He didn't condone eavesdropping but he couldn't bring himself to make his presence known without first hearing Abby's reply.

"Your memory is much too good. He never actually proposed and when I left he was interested in Lady Torrington."

"Then what is he doing here, now?"

Abby prevaricated. "We did not have time to discuss it earlier."

"He will be here shortly. Maybe I will ask him."

"Victoria! You wouldn't dare!" The idea scared Abby quite a bit since Jason told her she was the reason he was here, not that it had been hard to figure out, but the last thing she needed was for her husband to find out.

Tria was suddenly worried about proper etiquette. "How do I address a future duke? I would not want to make a bad impression."

"Simple. Either Lord Malwbry or milord."

Max had heard enough - there was no way he would be addressing the interloper as *my lord* in his own home - and yet not enough. He wanted to know more about Abby and this Englishman. On the other hand he was afraid he would find out something he would rather not know. Deciding it was time to make his presence known Max started down the stairs.

They both heard Max's tread on the steps and Abby gave Tria a meaningful look while continuing their conversation. "Unless he gives you leave to use his first name in which case you should say Lord Jason."

Max entered the room. "Victoria. What a pleasure to see you again and may I say you are looking lovely this evening."

Max took a seat in the chair on the opposite side of the sofa from where Abby was sitting. She wondered if he had done so on purpose. She also felt slighted. He had neglected to compliment her this evening. Not even before she came downstairs. Trying not to read too much into his actions she focused on her duties as hostess. "Pardon my manners, Tria. Would you care for something to drink? Wine or perhaps some punch?"

"Punch please."

"Max, your usual ale?" At his nod Abby signaled Mrs. Baxley.

Minutes later there was another knock at the door. Mr. Baxley opened it to reveal Betsy escorted by Jonathon Keats. Abby thought she was clever to have suggested Jonathon escort Betsy to dinner but Max had warned her Jonathon wasn't interested. He and Betsy had walked that road once before and nothing came of it, besides Jonathon was in love with Esperanza. But Abby wasn't ready to give up the idea. It wouldn't be the first time an old flame was rekindled or new circumstances changed old results. Jonathon and Betsy joined the group in the parlour and talk centered on the mundane happenings around town while they waited for the final guest to arrive.

Jason approached the house of average size for the island but less than a cottage by his family's standards. Lanterns lit the front porch revealing a cozy domestic scene of curtains and rocking chairs suggesting a happy couple spending evenings together in pleasant conversations. The image created an aching empty place in his soul for what could have been his if he had not been so stubborn. Pushing the unpleasant thought aside Jason raised his hand to knock on the door when he was arrested by the sound of laughter from the occupants inside the house. Jason felt a strange feeling of insecurity began to build. Reigning in that emotion as well he knocked on the door.

An elderly gentleman opened it and rightly assuming him to be a butler Jason gave him his name upon which the butler welcomed him inside. Jason stepped into the foyer/parlour and faced the group of strangers. He glanced past the others before locking gazes with Abby as if she were a lifeline and he about to drown.

Abby stepped forward to greet him. "Lord Malwbry how good of you to come. May I introduce your host, Captain Max Eatonton?"

Jason extended his hand to the man he would have had no trouble identifying as her husband. The captain made clear his claim on Abby without uttering a word. "Pleased to make your acquaintance, Captain Eatonton."

Max replied, "Likewise, Lord Malwbry." He thought Jason to be nothing more than a fop who had a passing interest in his wife and nothing better to do with his time than to chase her around the globe in a futile quest. He tried to convey his opinion in his firm but brief handshake. At least it was a futile quest for her hand in marriage. Max was afraid her heart may be another matter. He had not seen Abby so open and lighthearted since their picnic lunch on Flamingo Key, two and half months ago. He hadn't considered until now they had not had a pleasurable outing since then. If only he could find a wreck to bring home enough earnings for him to spend more time with her. Then he could take her on another 'adventure' as she calls it.

Abby noted Jason was immaculately attired as always in a snowy white cravat, black waistcoat with threads of red, green and blue, dark jacket and dark trousers fastened under his highly polished square toed shoes. It was quite a contrast to Max and Jonathon's open white shirts, buff breeches and high boots. Jason may cut a dashing figure but Abby found her husband to be more masculine and appealing, at least to her. Abby pulled herself away from her musings to introduce Jason to the other guests.

Jason greeted Miss Betsy Wheeler, a modest seamstress wearing a stylish lavender gown, Mr. Jonathon Keats, clearly ready at the slightest nod to stand with the Captain against him and finally Miss Victoria Lambert of the

Charleston Lamberts, a lovely dark haired woman. Jason gave a bow to Miss Wheeler and shook Mr. Keats' hand but he took Miss Lambert's gloved hand and gave her a deeper bow. This dark haired creature had captured his attention like no other especially when she withdrew her hand mid-bow with a feigned aloofness. The others were openly curious about him but he could tell Miss Lambert was more than curious even though she tried to hide it with disinterest.

"Lord Malwbry, please have a seat." Abby had noticed Jason's attention favoured Tria. It shouldn't have surprised her, Tria was a very lovely woman, but still it had caught her off guard. It was a little disconcerting to think she might be vain enough to be jealous of his attention straying elsewhere after sailing the Atlantic and Gulf in pursuit of her when she did not return his sentiment. Realizing the room had settled into an uncomfortable silence, Abby sought to end it with mundane conversation. "Lord Malwbry how was your voyage? No storms I hope."

"Only a few mild ones."

"And how were your parents when you left?"

"Much the same thank you for asking. I notice your father is absent. Nothing untoward has happened to him, I hope."

"Oh no, he is well. As a matter of fact you probably crossed paths with him. He left just over a month ago to continue on to his brother's. A letter from him telling me he arrived safely in Mobile came on your ship."

"Indeed. Our coaches probably travelled right past each other without notice."

Searching for something to redirect the conversation, Max's eyes came to rest on the pianoforte across the room. He asked Abby, "Do you play?"

Puzzled Abby asked, "To what do you refer, sir?"

He gestured towards the instrument behind her. Turning her head to look Abby grimaced. "No. That is not a talent I was able to acquire much less master."

Jason nodded. "I would have to agree. You are much better suited for dancing to music than making music."

Victoria was going to say she played very well but hesitated long enough she missed her opportunity. She was growing jealous of Abby's history with Lord Jason and wanted to turn his attention towards her but did not want to be obvious in doing so.

Surprised and embarrassed Abby turned to Jason. "When did you ever hear me play?"

"It was a long time ago. I believe it was your friend Mrs. Elizabeth Kendall's debutante ball. You and Marc Danvers and a few others were gathered around her grand piano in the parlour entertaining each other with much hilarity, if I recall."

Blushing Abby recalled the evening and couldn't help the fond smile. "I do not recall your presence."

"No you would not have. I remained in the doorway not wanting to intrude on your coterie."

Their whole conversation was making Max very ill at ease. He had intended to take the focus off Jason. It was very irritating to have instead put a magnifying glass on the history Jason and Abby shared. He was greatly relieved when Mr. Baxley stepped into the doorway and announced dinner was ready to be served.

Max seated Abby at the foot of the table while Jonathon seated Betsy on one side and Jason did the honours for Victoria on the other. Max took his seat at the head of the table feeling only slightly less uncomfortable than he had at the Lambert's Christmas dinner. With a hinted gesture from Abby he raised his glass in a toast. "To friendship, old and new." He realized afterwards he probably should have toasted his wife instead. At least then his toast would have rang true. He had no intentions of ever calling Lord Fop a friend.

As dinner progressed Max contributed little to the conversation. He barely listened to Abby and Jason discuss people they knew in common in England as well as her aunt and uncle but they must have talked of other things too because he was aware of the others contributing to the conversation. He watched his wife talking animatedly with her guests. She fairly sparkled at the other end of the table and it stabbed him in the gut. He had not brought that light to her eyes. She didn't belong with him. She belonged with a Duke visiting foreign lands and surrounded by life's luxuries. He had forever taken her away from the advantages of wealth she was discussing with their guest.

Their house had not bothered him before. He didn't need those trappings but looking at it now through the eyes of an English aristocrat he saw all that was lacking. Abby knew those kinds of luxuries. He hadn't considered what all she had given up. How could someone like her, used to all the finer things in life, handle a place like Key West with its lack of society and all the daily hardships of living here not to mention a husband with a dangerous occupation? The answer was she couldn't. Twice she had railed about always waiting on him and one of their first fights she had said she was 'bloody bored' in her adorable English accent. How would she manage years on this island when she was probably used to nights at the theater and balls every weekend.

Pushing the food around his plate he was feeling inadequate as a husband. He couldn't give her what she was accustomed to and worse he had tied her fate to his. Something he had never intended to do to a woman. He had acted on impulse and didn't stop to reason it out; hadn't allowed himself the time to reconsider. He had married in haste, selfishly wanting to hold onto something that never should have been his. He was beginning to believe their marriage was a mistake.

Wrapped up in his own thoughts Max hadn't noticed Tria's interest in Jason. He only noticed the way Abby and Jason had a lot to talk about while Abby had hardly said three words to him. Although to be fair he hadn't said much to her or anyone else.

Abby was proud of the way her dinner was progressing. All her guests were engaged in the conversation and she had received the answers she sought from Jason. Everything was going smoothly except for one detail. She noticed how well Jason and Tria were getting along and she was jealous. Not jealous she had lost Jason's affections but like Thomas and Maria it came easily for them while she and Max were struggling to get along.

Thinking of him naturally drew her gaze to her husband only to find he was staring at his plate. She realized he had not contributed much to the conversation all evening. Letting the discourse continue without her Abby wondered what had Max so preoccupied. Maybe he was angry with her. She did spring this dinner on him as soon as he walked in the door. She couldn't help but think he was unhappy with her and their marriage. They had been at odds with each other a lot lately. Was he thinking about her? Was he wishing he was on his ship sailing into a storm rather than hosting a dinner party? Or worse, was he wishing he had never married her? Her thoughts made her frown. The bloom was definitely off the rose, so to speak - if it had ever really been there to begin with.

Max looked up to find his wife looking at him, her brow furrowed. She was probably not happy with him for being such a poor host. As his eyes met hers, her expression turned questioning. He became aware of a silence in the room. Looking around he found the others watching him except for Jason who was focused on Abby.

From a distance Abby heard her name being called bringing her attention back to the others gathered around the table. Peripherally she noticed Jason was looking at her expectantly and she realized he must have asked her a question. "Pardon?" Abby dragged her gaze from her husband to meet Jason's query.

All the guests realized something was going on between Max and Abby. Jason was seriously starting to question their relationship. He had intended to ask Abby her opinion relative to the conversation but seeing the frown she directed towards her sullen husband instead he asked, "Is there something between you two I should be concerned about?"

Varying levels of shock emanated from those around the table at Jason's boldness in asking such a question, except for Victoria who was shocked and disappointed because Jason still seemed to hold a *tendré* for Abigail.

Abby knew that wasn't the original question he had asked of her. She quietly answered, "No." Her gaze was immediately drawn back to Max who was now frowning at her in return. The table remained quiet and realizing Jason was still waiting she looked him in the eye and firmly added, "No, of course not. What would make you ask such a thing?"

Jason looked from Max to Abby and shrugged. "I felt it my duty in your father's absence to assure your well-being."

Max had had the feeling from the start he was on trial with Jason but had tried to shrug it off. He was no longer in doubt. This intruder considered himself to be a self-appointed guardian of his wife. It was more than he could stand to take from Lord Fop. "My wife is no concern of yours."

Jason responded, "And you sir, do not deserve her."

After spending most of the evening questioning his marriage and his own self-worth in his own mind Max struggled not to reveal how close to the mark Jason's barb had struck.

Not wanting the situation to get worse Abby intervened telling her husband, "I am sure Lord Malwbry meant no disrespect to you, sir." Turning to Jason she laid a hand on his arm earning her another cold stare from her husband. "Lord Malwbry, thank you for your solicitude but I am well and you have no reason to be concerned for my safety. My husband is a very honourable gentleman."

Jason accepted the truth in her eyes. Whatever was going on between them it was not abusive. Abby was not afraid of her husband. "Very well."

For moments the only sound heard was the occasional clink of silverware against ceramic plate as the other guests made a pretense of continuing with dinner in the ensuing silence.

For Abby's sake, Max made an effort to pay attention to their guests. "Miss Wheeler, have you heard from your mother recently?" He caught the look of gratitude his wife sent his way.

Understanding Max's intent Betsy played along. "Yes, I received a letter in this month's mail. She is doing well and says she may come for a visit in the spring."

"I look forward to meeting her," said Max.

Noticing that everyone was done eating Abby stood to bring an end to dinner. The gentlemen rose to their feet in respect. "We should adjourn to the parlour for drinks."

Max circled the table to pull away Abby's chair and escort her to the front room. Jason escorted Victoria while Jonathon and Betsy followed in last.

Jonathon had had enough high society for one evening. He looked to Betsy and seeing the same sentiments reflected in her face announced to the room in general. "Mrs. Eatonton, thank you for dinner. It's getting late and if you don't mind, Miss Wheeler and I are going to call it an evening."

Abby understood his real reasons for leaving and couldn't blame them for not wanting to risk subjecting themselves to more discomfort.

Jonathon turned to Victoria. "Miss Lambert, may I offer you an escort home?"

Max said, "An excellent idea."

Victoria had other plans for getting home. She demurred. "Thank you kindly Mr. Keats but my home is out of your way and besides you have Miss Wheeler to see to whereas Lord Malwbry is headed in the same direction."

Both Max and Jonathon offered protest, after all this man was a stranger to them and both counted Victoria as a friend. Abby intervened. "She will be fine.

Lord Malwbry is an honourable gentleman and she has her maid for chaperone."

Nodding to Victoria, Jonathon said, "As you wish. Good evening Miss Lambert, Lord Malwbry. Thank you for your hospitality Captain and Mrs. Eatonton." Jonathon bowed as he exited the front door in an obvious hurry to escape their company.

Betsy bid them good evening as she followed him through the open doorway.

Max caught the louvered door as it swung shut keeping it from banging against the door frame before facing the remaining company in his front room.

Victoria wanted to prolong her contact with Lord Jason. She was well aware his pursuit of Abby had brought him here and with Abby married he may leave suddenly not having any other reason to stay on the island. She wanted to guarantee herself one more day in his company so she asked the others in what she hoped was her most appealing voice, "Why don't the four of us go on an outing tomorrow?"

Max didn't know what Victoria was up to but his first instinct was to run. "I'm afraid I can't." Jonathon was not going to like what he said next. "I was thinking of keel hauling the ship tomorrow." Heaven knew he would prefer the brutal laborious task over spending a day in the company of Lord Fop.

Abby frowned at him. "Must you do it tomorrow? You just came home."

Max looked to his wife. "It is long overdue."

Tria called him out. "You're just making an excuse to avoid something that might turn out to be fun and what is Abby to think - that you don't want to spend time with her? I am sure you could put it off awhile longer."

"If Captain Eatonton has work to do I'm sure I can escort you ladies to some kind of entertainment," said Jason.

Max was caught. He really didn't want his wife spending any more time with Jason, especially not without him. "All right, I'll postpone the keel haul. What did you have in mind Miss Lambert?"

Tria couldn't help the smile that spread across her face. "Well, I'm not sure." Turning to Lord Malwbry she suggested, "Having just arrived today we could show you the town."

Max nearly laughed out loud. "And what do you propose to do after those five minutes? Besides he's already seen most of the town just walking from the boardinghouse to here."

Jason asked, "Do any of you ride?"

Max thought this was getting more ridiculous by the moment. "Sorry mate, we don't have the horses or the pasture for that pastime." '

Victoria said, "We could go for a sail."

Jason grimaced. "After sailing for the better part of three months, I have no desire to step foot on a boat so soon, luv."

Resigning himself to the inevitable Max said, "Well there are really only two points of interest on the island; the lighthouse or the salt ponds."

"The salt ponds sound interesting," said Jason, his curiosity piqued.

Not having been there yet, Abby was of course interested. Max didn't even have to ask her to know she would be in agreement.

Victoria could only wince at the idea of trudging through the jungle growth in the heat to look at a brackish pond but she would go along to be with Jason. "Salt ponds it is then."

He should have stuck to keel hauling the ship. Max doubted Lord Fop would be up to swinging a machete to clear the path to the pond which would leave him doing all the hard work. He asked anyway. "Malwbry, don't suppose you have clothes for clearing underbrush with you?"

"I am afraid I do not."

"I'll loan you some. Be back in a minute."

Abby asked, "Max, you do not think the heat will be too much for Lord Malwbry to be doing hard physical labor before he is acclimated?"

"Nonsense. It's not as warm as it was when you arrived." Besides he wanted to bring the future Duke to his level, test him in the hopes of besting him.

Max left the room to retrieve the clothes. Abby excused herself to take care of a quick task leaving Jason and Victoria momentarily alone. Her eyes were captured in the warmth of his gaze and she knew she was done for.

Victoria had started out the evening trying to keep at least a figurative distance from this man. It had seemed the prudent thing to do since she did not fully understand Abby's relationship with him, much less how he felt about Abby. During dinner, she had observed them and found only a casual interaction allowing her to unconsciously loosen the hold on her own feelings. She became aware of her folly when Jason had confronted Abby at dinner. She had felt physically stabbed by jealousy and disappointment thinking Jason had to still have feelings for Abby to have so boldly questioned her relationship with Max. Quickly gathering herself together Victoria had tried to return to the aloofness she had begun the evening with but it disintegrated under his warm gaze as easily as ocean foam overcome by the next larger wave. Jason had easily accepted Abby's reassurances and promptly returned his attention to Victoria. Not with words or touch, it was more his energy she felt focused on her and it was exciting. She wanted to prolong the experience for as long as possible which led to the idea of an excursion.

Jason moved to Victoria's side and lifted her gloved hand to his lips. "Alone at last," he whispered and kissed the back of her knuckles, his eyes never leaving hers. His lips lingered. A shiver raced down her spine, her mid-section tightened and her palms grew moist. *Was he flirting with her simply because she was available?* She hoped not. Her attraction to him was too strong for simple flirtation. She considered herself skilled in the art but under his gaze she was unable to think clearly. There had been many questions on her mind during dinner she would have asked if they had been alone. Now that opportunity presented itself her mind was blank. She was focused on the warmth his fingers transmitted through her glove. He continued to hold her hand and stare into her eyes and she could read them now. He wanted to kiss her. Her breathing shallowed and her lips grew dry. She unconsciously moistened them. He broke eye contact, dropping his gaze to her lips. She dropped her eyes to his lips as well. Simultaneously they leaned towards each other. A step was needed to bring them closer together. She waited, breathless. Just as she felt him lift his foot to do so they heard Max descend the stairs. Jason stepped away from her, letting go of her hand with a gentle squeeze of her fingers before returning to the place where Max had left him. Victoria's cheeks burned in embarrassment. She turned her back to the room pretending interest in the oil painting. *How had she fallen so quickly?*

Max returned to find Abby absent from the room. He handed the clothes to Jason and after settling the details for tomorrow shook his hand bidding him a good evening. He then watched Jason walk towards the door and stop in front of his wife as she appeared in the doorway of the office. After retrieving her maid from the kitchen, Victoria approached Max and thanked him for agreeing to the outing. He barely paid attention to her as he watched his wife pass a note to Jason. He was frustrated he could not hear her conversation over Victoria's speech. It bothered him not knowing what her note was about.

Abby couldn't help but be aware of Max's heavy glare as she handed Jason the note she had written to Mrs. Mallory requesting a picnic lunch for tomorrow's outing but she did her best to ignore it. Next she handed Jason a lantern. "We do not have the luxury of street lights. It is awful dark out there."

Jason accepted her offering. "Thank you. I will see you in the morning Mrs. Eatonton."

Max and Victoria walked over to them. Abby kissed her friend goodnight and Max shut the door as Jason assisted Victoria down the front steps. Returning to the parlour Max said, "Why don't you head on upstairs. Tomorrow will be a long day for you."

"And for you."

"Yes, but I am more accustomed to it than you are."

Abby wanted to disagree but didn't think it was worth the fight. She picked up a candlestick from the table and walked up the stairs alone.

Mr. and Mrs. Baxley stepped into the room to tell him the kitchen was cleaned up and they were heading home. Max thanked them for their services and followed them out the door then took a seat in one of the rocking chairs. He wasn't ready to face Abby alone. He wanted time to think about all that had happened today and try to gain some perspective.

Abby had pocketed her letters from Elizabeth and Miss Winterfeldt when she went into the office to write the note to Mrs. Mallory intending to read at least one of them before bed. She had only been able to spare a few moments earlier in the day to read her father's brief letter informing her of his arrival in Mobile. She set the candle down on the dressing table and pulled the letters from her pocket but instead of sitting down to read she left them next to the candle and made her way to the balcony. She stepped out into the fresh salty air, inhaling its healing balm. Her emotions were still in turmoil from dinner. She walked to the railing and wrapped her arms around her midsection. Leaning against a column she considered Max's behaviour this evening.

He had been distant from her the moment he walked in the door. Thinking back to their conversation when he first arrived she realized he had seen her and Jason in town. He could have seen them walking to the boardinghouse but judging by his actions she was more inclined to think he had witnessed their greeting. So was his coldness due to jealousy or anger? He hardly spoke to her as they were getting ready for dinner. He complimented Victoria's attire but not her own. He was nearly hostile to Jason when he greeted him, sullen all during the meal and except for questioning if she played the pianoforte he hardly spoke to her at all. It was Victoria's pleading, not her own, that had him capitulating to the outing, there was that cold look when she handed Jason the note and now he was clearly giving her time to get to bed before him. She did not see jealousy in his actions. He seemed angry with her and if he was angry, how was she going to deal with him when he did come upstairs?

Abby stirred from her reverie at the creaking sound of the rocking chair on the porch below her. Max must be outside as well. Something they shared in common but were not sharing with each other. It struck her as ironic they were so alike and yet unable to get along with each other. Stranger still was a truth she had discovered tonight. She had noticed the changes in Jason. He was more his own man now. He wasn't living the life of his mother's choosing. The changes in him may have made a difference for them in July but now.... now it didn't matter. It only highlighted how much she cared for Max. And, maybe, she was growing to love her husband. Despite their fights she would rather be with him than anyone else. She didn't care why he had agreed to go tomorrow. She was only happy that he had. She would have another day with him. She wished he wanted to spend the day with her too.

A soft tap on the door frame had her heart soaring in the hope it was Max. She was disappointed to find Maria standing there offering to help her undress. Resigned she preceded her maid into the bed chamber and allowed her to undo the buttons down the back of her dress.

Max heard the creak of the wood over his head as Abby left the balcony. He wondered what thoughts were weighing on her mind. *Was she wishing she had married Jason?* Max had little to show for his efforts since their marriage and storm season was many months away which greatly limited what he could provide before her father returned. He understood a little better now her father's concerns over his lack of income. Abby was used to having money. He was not going to be able to hold on to her without it. He had resented her father for putting pressure on him thinking he was overprotecting a spoiled daughter. The truth was Max and this island would probably not hold her attention for long. She was used to so much more. He would have to earn the money and the chances that wrecking would provide it were slim. Fishing would barely keep them in this house and there in was the limit of his skills. He didn't know anything about running an office. Even if he did take her father up on his offer what were the chances he would succeed? She should have married someone like Lord Fop. He should never have allowed Richard to coerce him into marriage. *What had the man been thinking?* Surely he could have allowed their transgression to slip by unnoticed. Marriage had not been absolutely necessary to save her reputation. Of course it hadn't. Max could have let her leave. Why had Richard not insisted on her leaving? Why had he so readily accepted their marriage knowing Max could not afford her? Was it to ensure there was someone he could trust here to run his shipping office? Did Richard sacrifice his daughter for his company? No. Richard loved his daughter. He may consider it a benefit to have Max head an office on the island but it would not have been his primary motive. His illness was the only logical reason left.

Why did Abby agree? Because she wasn't really given a choice by either one of them.

Abigail.

She didn't seem to resent her life here. In fact she was more involved in the island than he was. She didn't even need him really. She had money from her father to live on, the sick to care for and friends to keep her company. So maybe he was being overly pessimistic about her not being able to live here but he still couldn't provide a living for her like a husband should and if they continued to live on her father's money wouldn't she lose respect for him? Of course she would. He would lose respect for himself. There was only one benefit of marriage he currently had to offer her and although they both seemed to enjoy it, he knew it was not enough to build a marriage.

Tired of his morose thoughts and realizing the house had been quiet for some time, Max decided it was time to head to bed. He checked the downstairs and kitchen to make sure all the candles had been extinguished and then made his way upstairs in the dark. He paused inside the bedroom door. He wondered if Abby was sleeping yet. She lay with her back towards him. He could barely hear her breathing. Still not sure if she was awake or not, he quietly removed his clothes before slipping into bed beside her. He lay on his back looking at the ceiling. He wanted to hold her. If she was awake would she reject him? He was no longer sure of his reception with her. If she was asleep would she know it was him? He was not brave enough to find out the answer to either of those questions tonight.

Abby felt the bed dip as her husband joined her. Not sure what kind of reception he would give her she remained as she was, hugging her side of the bed. She did not want to further irritate him if he was truly angry with her. She didn't think she could bear his rejection tonight, not after realizing her feelings for him were deepening. Just the thought he might reject her was devastating enough; she did not want to experience the reality. It was a long time before she relaxed enough to fall asleep.

Chapter 25

Abby awoke at dawn and turned over to find she was alone in the bedroom. She chose a simple muslin day dress she could don herself and sturdy boots that would survive the rough walk to the salt ponds. They weren't expecting Jason and Tria for a few hours so taking advantage of her time Abby picked up the letters she had put aside last night and made her way to the Captain's Walk. The trap door was already open and suspecting why she nearly changed her mind. Taking a breath to fortify her resolve she climbed the steps. Her head cleared the hatch to find Max facing east with his back towards her. The sky beyond him changing colours with the rising sun while overhead the night sky was fading to a pearl grey. Without saying a word Max turned and offered a hand to assist her to the deck. She accepted placing her hand in his palm. His warm fingers curled around hers then threaded between them once she was standing beside him. They silently stood next to each other, hands entwined, watching the grey gradually lighten and the melding colours of saffron, apricot and salmon near the horizon bleach out as the edge of the sun made its appearance. Afraid to ruin the moment they both remained silent until the light of morning touched them.

Using their clasped hands Max coaxed Abby to face him. He wanted to know what she was feeling. He was hoping to read the answers in her eyes. Instead he found questions behind her soft dove grey irises. He didn't know what the questions were nor did he want to ask. Talking seemed to get them in trouble. He looked for signs of rebuff or rejection and was relieved to find none. Her lips parted as if to say something. He pressed the index finger of his free hand against them to stop her words from breaking the moment. Finding her lips smooth and soft, her breath warm and moist beneath his calloused touch, he couldn't stop his head's descent any more than he could stop the tides. His hand dropped down, index finger and thumb gently lifting her chin while the other fingers caressed her throat. His smallest finger rested at the base of her neck against her clavicle. He could feel her pulse beating like the wings of a butterfly. As his head descended he saw her eyes close, her lashes lightly flutter against her cheeks. He pressed his lips to hers and held. Nothing more, just a moment's touch before lifting his head just enough to break the contact. He felt her disappointment as keenly as his own and so he gave them both what they wanted. He returned his lips to hers, giving her more. When he broke the contact again she parted her lips in protest and he returned invading the warmth of her mouth, delving deeper, taking more, slowly devouring her. He brought both hands to her face, tilting her head to a better angle, holding her close as if she might flee. He felt her hands go around his waist and up to his shoulder blades pressing him closer. He couldn't get enough of her. He slid his hands over her shoulders and down her back pulling her closer to him.

If not for Maria's call from below he might well have ravished his wife right there on the roof of their house. Breaking the kiss he watched Abby's eyes slowly open and look straight into his soul before blinking and returning her to herself. She took a deep breath and then took his breath away with an angelic smile and an impish, "Good morning Captain." He couldn't help himself. He kissed her again.

This time they both heard Maria's call. "Mrs. Abby, are you up there?"

Pulling away from Max's kiss she answered, "Yes, Maria, I will be right down."

Her husband had not loosened his hold so she took a step away from him causing his hands to brush across her hips.

"What's that?" he asked feeling the paper in her dress pocket.

"Letters from home." She felt Max immediately tense and then he released her. The tender moment they had just shared vanished in the space of a heartbeat. Not sure why letters had caused such a reaction she nevertheless sought to reassure him. "They are from Elizabeth and Miss Winterfeldt. I had intended to take a moment to read them up here."

Max backed away. He smiled at her, in a distant friendly way, as he moved to the hatch stairs. "And so you shall. I'll see what Maria needs and leave you to read in peace."

She watched as Max disappeared into the house thoroughly bewildered by his actions. How did he manage the lightening transition from intoxicating kiss to a cool smile while she felt bewildered and bereft? What had caused the change? Surely he didn't begrudge her a few letters from a childhood friend and a nanny. And why had he held her hand and kissed her in the first place after keeping his distance last night? She was at a loss to explain his behaviour.

Removing the letters from her pocket she lifted the wax seal of Miss Winterfeldt's letter first.

Sussex, England 18th September, 1828

My dearest Abigail,

I do not know what I would have done if not for your friend, Mrs. Kendall. No sooner had you left did she offer me the post of nanny for her impending family. Of course, I most graciously accepted. It will not be the same as my dream of caring for your children but it nicely resolved my current employment concerns.

As the pending arrival of the Kendall offspring is many months away, I am free to do as I please in the interim. Thanks to your father's generosity I have been with my sister these past three weeks since you left and plan to stay until the Kendall birth calls me away. We are having a grand time together taking day trips as my sister's health allows and generally acting as carefree as our girlhood.

I do miss you and your youthful exuberance. I hope your journey has been pleasant and this missive finds you safe in the household of your uncle. Please thank your father again on my behalf for the wonderful gift he has given me.

With love,
Mildred Winterfeldt

She would have to write her father and let him know what he had done for her nanny. Abby was happy for her.

Next were three letters from Bethy. Finding the one with the oldest date, she eagerly broke the wax wafer with the Kendall crest impression.

Midanbury, England 2nd de Septembre

Mon Amie,

What am I to do without you? You only left yesterday and already I feel the abyss of your absence. I have cried many tears to the point Avery has insisted I must stop for the sake of the baby. Meanwhile, you are probably having a grand adventure sailing the high seas and not thinking at all of me.

You will be happy to know as soon as your carriage was out of sight I offered employment to Miss Winterfeldt. She is a jewel and I am most fortunate you have let her go at such an opportune moment. She will be a grand addition to our household and I know our child will receive the best of care. She seemed just as grateful to receive the offer. What a blessing for us both.

Please write often. I am looking forward to your letters to keep me entertained during my upcoming lying-in. Your return cannot come soon enough for me. I miss you my friend. Your teacup awaits you.

Au revoir,
Elizabeth

Abby had to wipe away the tears pooling in her eyes so she could read her next letter.

Midanbury, England 13th October, 1828

Dearest Abigail,

Where are you today I wonder? I picture you sitting on a veranda in Jamaica surrounded by tropical plants and exotic flowers sipping tea. Life here is more mundane. Only two news items you would find of interest. Marcus Danvers has safely married his love. He assures me Mary has forgiven you for causing such a ruckus with the gossips before your departure. The other bit is quite shocking. It seems Lord Jason has suddenly departed for parts unknown. The Duchess has had a fit of vapors and not been seen in weeks. Speculation abounds as to his whereabouts but I have it on good authority he is crossing the Atlantic in pursuit of a damsel. As my letter was posted much later, I believe you may already be aware of these events. Who would have guessed he had such gumption? There may be something worth having there after all. Should I begin addressing you as Lady Abby?

As for me, my waistline is no more. The sickness has finally passed but I remain peakish. I am assured this is normal and I should be satisfied to sit all day with my feet upon a stool doing needlework. Alas, I am not. Where is my friend to visit and comfort me but across the ocean in a warm climate while I pull my shawl a little tighter against the chilly draft. The only thing that makes this bearable is I can feel the babe move sometimes.

I eagerly await the post every day for your letters. I miss you dearly.

Devotedly yours,
  Elizabeth

Abby smiled. She was in Jamaica when Bethy penned her letter albeit sequestered in a hotel room instead of on a veranda and she now knew Jason had followed her before reading her letter just as Bethy had predicted. If they had not been shipwrecked she may very well have consented to be Lady Jason. Amazing.

Abby reached up and felt her lips. The feel of his kisses still lingered. She did not regret marrying Max. She had faith somehow they would find happiness with each other.

Midanbury, England 29th November, 1828

My dear friend,

I received your letters today. Bless you. You have given me a distraction. I helped Avery draft the petition to Parliament urging the emancipation of slaves in all of the British colonies. We have spent evenings strategizing which Lords would be most likely to help our cause. Avery has persuaded several key figures to present the petition and feels confident the measure will be favourably received.

Abby could hardly wait to share this news with Maria.

I am enjoying the little season as I will be lying-in for much of the regular season. Avery keeps a close eye on me and allows only one dance per ball but I make the most of it. I am growing more excited as the months progress for the arrival of our child. I only wish you were here to share it with us.

Your devoted friend,
Elizabeth

p.s. Hope you are enjoying flirting with your Captain Adonis but please do not fall in love with him. I could not bear for you to live so far away.

Of course Abby had mailed many letters detailing her relationship with Max. Poor Elizabeth. She must have been devastated to learn of her marriage. Today was the tenth of January. Bethy's last letter was dated six weeks ago. Abby had already been a bride of two weeks by then. Their letters probably crossed each other on the ocean.

Abby wished there was not so long a delay in responses for she could sure use some friendly advice today. Max's constantly changing emotions were baffling her. It was like he had built a wall and sometimes he was outside it with her and other times he was locked tight within. She was never allowed inside. If she could just find her way through those barriers maybe their marriage would have a chance.

The rumbling of her stomach reminded her of the need for food before their hike. She made her way to the kitchen and found Max working on a cocoanut while Mrs. Baxley pulled a perfectly done loaf of bread out of the oven. Mr. Baxley and Maria joined them at the table in the dining room for breakfast. Conversation was minimal. Max was congenial, if quiet, with the others but towards her he was withdrawn.

Max was afraid to look at his wife. Their earlier kiss had driven home a truth. His wife had the power to destroy him emotionally if he didn't keep her at arm's length. He had felt his heart opening to her this morning and just as he had almost forgotten the lessons of his past she uttered a single word to remind him. *Home.* 'Letters from home,' she had said, home referring to England not here with him. It may be asking a lot, too soon, for her to consider 'home' to be with him but it was how he felt. If he wasn't her 'home' then he couldn't open his heart to her. He wouldn't risk more heartache for anything less from her. Another unfortunate truth he discovered this morning, the walls around his heart were harder to reinforce once penetrated than they were to build. Today he would need to keep an emotional distance between them while he tried to do just that and at the same time not give Lord Fop any reason to further question their marriage.

Victoria was dismayed upon opening the door to find a very different Lord Malwbry. The elegant Englishman of yesterday now looked like every other sailor on the island dressed as he was in a loose fitting white shirt and tan breeches borrowed from Max. Victoria didn't like the outfit but the man who bore them was still immensely appealing. Sleep had not cured her of the infatuation. Jason didn't seem to be fond of the clothes either. He looked very uncomfortable, as if he felt undressed in public. She smiled in sympathy. "Good morning Lord Malwbry."

"Please, call me Jason. How are you this morning Miss Lambert?"

She answered with a smile in her voice. "And you may call me Victoria, if you please. I am very well, thank you. Is that a picnic lunch from Mrs. Mallory?" Tria gestured to the basket hanging from his arm.

"Yes it is. Abigail thought of it last night, clever girl. Are you ready to go?"

Tria leaned inside the door to retrieve her parasol and call her maid to join them before saying, "I am now." She smiled at Jason as they walked side by side towards Max and Abby's, followed by her maid. His compliment of Abby stung her vanity a little but as it was deserved Tria brushed aside her pettiness. "Have you travelled much, Lord Jason?"

"A little around Europe. This is by far the furthest I have been from home."

"And how does our island compare to your side of the world?"

Looking at her expectant face he said the first word that came to mind. "Lovely."

Tria blushed. The look in his eyes told her he wasn't describing the area around them. Normally, easy flirtatious banter came naturally to her, but with this man she found herself for the first time in her life at a loss for words. She ducked her head to hide the bloom in her cheeks and tried to think of something to say.

They walked towards the wharves in silence for a moment before Jason asked her, "How long have you known Captain Eatonton?"

Recalling Jason's bold questioning of Abby last evening, Tria guessed his reason for asking her about Max. She was disappointed and perhaps a little jealous Jason was thinking of Abby but seeking to put his mind at ease she said, "Long enough to know you have no cause for worry. Max is a good man; one of the best on this island. Any woman would be lucky to have him."

She paused for a moment giving Jason concerns that Victoria may have had feelings for the Captain.

"They were attracted to each other from the first. Max typically went out of his way to avoid romantic involvements until he met Abby. I believe they love each other, they just haven't discovered it for themselves yet. Abby's father may have pushed them to marry but given time I am sure they would have ended up together anyway."

Jason felt the sting of wounded pride. Mr. Bennington may not have denied him to court his daughter but he certainly had not been overly encouraging and had led Jason to believe it was Abby's choice. So why then had he forced his daughter to marry the Captain? Did Mr. Bennington consider him such a fine husband? More likely, despite Victoria's ringing praises, the Captain must have taken advantage of Abby. "Why did Mr. Bennington insist on such speedy nuptials?"

The tone in Jason's voice and the continued concern for Abby was giving Tria doubts she had correctly interpreted his earlier meaning. Maybe he really had been referring to the island as 'lovely'. Turning on Simonton Street, their destination only a few hundred feet ahead, she carefully answered his question in an effort to protect her friends and for her own selfish reason. The walk along the beach that precipitated Max and Abby's wedding would certainly lead to a strained relationship between Max and Jason and probably ruin what could be her only chance to spend a day in Jason's company. "Her father took ill while he was here. It was serious enough he wanted to ensure Abby's future. He also saw what everyone else could see; they were attracted to each other. Maybe even knowing his daughter better than anyone else he knew she loved Max. I do know he questioned many of the islander's as to Max's character before allowing her to marry him."

"How was Mr. Bennington's health when he left? Was it the reason for his departure?"

"I don't believe so. He seemed well enough and Abby has not mentioned any concerns to me. I assumed he left to visit his brother as that was his original destination."

After breakfast, Max and Abby waited for their guests in the parlour. Abby took a seat in the rocking chair facing the front window and watched Max pace the room. He was obviously not looking forward to the day's outing and his feelings were draining any enthusiasm she might have had leaving them both miserable.

Max stopped in front of the window, "They're here. What is Malwbry carrying?" As the pair moved closer Max was able to identify the item at the same time his wife confirmed it.

"Most likely a picnic basket from Mrs. Mallory. I sent her a note requesting it."

Max turned to his wife, relieved at last to know the contents of the note she had passed to Jason last night but still he needed to disabuse her of the notion today would be a romantic outing. "You do realize there will not be a makeshift table and chairs today?"

Max's tone offended her but not wanting to argue she replied in an even tone, "Of course. A blanket on the ground will suffice."

"There most likely won't be any clear ground for laying out a blanket. The hammock is overgrown with trees and brush. The ground will either be too rough or too wet. It would make for a most uncomfortable picnic. Besides I will need Malwbry's help to clear the path which would leave you ladies carrying the basket several miles over rough terrain."

"Fine, you have made your point. We will leave the basket and eat when we return," conceded Abby.

Max said, "However, we should bring water. I believe I saw some canteens on the shelf in the kitchen. I'll greet our guests while you go fill them."

His orders grated on her nerves. She was not one of his crew to be ordered about but she held her tongue and left to do his bidding. Fighting with her husband when guests were about to arrive on their doorstep could only do more harm than good.

Max listened to Abby's retreating footsteps before going to open the door to their guests. Determined to at least be civil today he stepped out to greet them. "Here Malwbry let me take that for you." Max held out his hand to take the lunch hamper. "I'm afraid we'll be leaving this behind for later." Max held the door for Jason and Victoria to precede him into the house. They turned to him expectantly in the parlour. Max crossed the room and set the basket on the dining room table. He then turned back to his guests. "Please, have a seat."

Jason and Tria both sat on the couch keeping a respectable distance between them. For a moment silence reigned. Finally Tria asked, "Where is Abby?" at the same time Abby reentered the house from the backyard.

"Good morning." Abby held three canteens filled with water. She looked to Max. "Are we ready?"

"I believe so." Leading the way out to the front porch Max leaned down and picked up the gloves and machetes he had left on one of the rockers. He handed a set to Jason before walking down the steps to the street. Max led the way around the house to the Simonton Road footbridge that crossed the entrance of the tidal pond behind their house and then across the cleared expanse beyond. They walked in pairs with Max and Abby leading the way followed by Tria in a yellow day dress and Jason wearing the borrowed clothes from Max. Tria's maid chose to stay behind with Maria.

Abby cast a sideways look at her husband. He was courteous to her but continued to be withdrawn having said barely a dozen words to her all morning. She could hear Jason and Tria talking animatedly behind them. Jason was currently describing Midanbury and bringing to mind images that gave Abby a momentary wave of homesickness. She didn't want to feel melancholy today. The sky was a cheerful shade of blue, the weather was comfortable, she had her husband by her side and she was off on a small adventure. Choosing to be joyful she opened herself to the wonder around her. The birds and butterflies, the flowers, the caressing breeze were a far cry from the frigid cold of January in England.

Jason asked the group in general, "Is it not warm for this time of year?"

Max replied, "No, it's about right - seventy degrees or so."

Jason eyebrows rose. "Only seventy? I would have thought it was closer to ninety."

Victoria said, "It is the tropical moisture making it feel warmer. It takes some time to acclimate to it."

Now that they were outside the town small trees and bushes became more prevalent. Ahead of them lay a canopy forest called a hammock. Max led them to an old path grown over from disuse. He turned to the man behind him having waited for this chance to best Lord Fop. He was confident he could easily out work a soft aristocrat. "Malwbry, want to give me a hand with this?" Max gestured towards the undergrowth on the pathway.

Abby gave Max a stern look. "Lord Malwbry."

Max gave her a direct look in return. "We're not in England - titles don't mean much here."

Abby would have argued but Jason came up to take her place next to Max. She handed each of them a canteen keeping one for herself and Tria to share then fell back to Tria's side while the men worked together to clear the path. It didn't take long for Abby and Tria to realize there was a silent contest going on between them. Knowing it was useless to diffuse the situation they let them work out their aggressions on the innocent vegetation.

Abby linked her arm with her friend and leaned a little closer. "You and Jason seem to be getting along very well."

Victoria gave a wry smile. "I suppose."

"You are not getting along?"

"We are. It's just..." Tria wasn't sure she should say more but seeing Abby's concern she admitted, "He has been concerned for you."

Abby smiled. "That is touching."

"Yes it is except..."

"Except it makes you wonder how much he cares for me."

Victoria nodded. "He followed you here from England."

"Maybe so but he was never interested in me the way he is in you."

Max expected to easily outstrip Jason in clearing the path to the ponds but much to his surprise and aggravation Lord Fop was more useful than he appeared. He seemed to easily keep pace with him and so they reached the salt ponds in no time.

The trees and brush suddenly opened to an expanse of open ground with large puddles of water as the tide was currently out. A white heron, disturbed by the noise, took flight. Jason had expected a pond of water rimmed in salt crystals. The muddy limestone was a bit of a disappointment.

When they turned around the ladies were several lengths behind them. Standing there catching their breath and drinking the cool water from the canteens Max viewed their handiwork and realized in his single-mindedness to outdo Jason he had neglected to mention the hazards of the area. Several distinctive plants stood on Jason's side of the pathway. "Malwbry, you'll want to step this way." He cupped his hands and called out. "Abigail, Victoria stay to this side of the path and hurry."

Picking up their skirts the ladies moved to Max's side of the path and quickened their pace. Coming up to the men Abby looked to Max. She had heard the concern in his voice when he called to them. "What is it?"

"Poisonwood." Max nodded to the waist high trees with spotted leaves.

"Several of them on his side." Max looked intently towards Abby. "Do you know a treatment? Did Mrs. Mallory teach you anything that would help if Malwbry has come in contact with it?"

Closing her eyes Abby tried to remember what Mrs. Mallory had told her. They had treated a case of the painful rash on Mr. Barnum, Mr. Whitehead's assistant, weeks ago. Her eyelids flew open as memory returned. "Gumbo limbo. We need to rub the oily bark over his exposed skin and then cover it to protect it from the sun."

Max looked at the surrounding trees for the telltale peeling bark but to no avail. "There should be one nearby."

Abby nodded in agreement. Max went to look for the bark while Abby moved towards Jason. "Let me see your arms."

Jason held them out in front for her inspection. "I do not feel anything."

"You may not even if you did come in contact with the plant. Mrs. Mallory said the rash could show days later. Turn them over."

Jason did as she directed while Tria wiped his brow with her handkerchief.

Abby finished her inspection. "I do not see any sap but I think we should assume the worse and treat your exposed skin."

Abby tore off a strip of her chemise to use as a bandage. Tria did likewise so there would be enough to cover both of his arms. While they waited for Max to return Abby moved around Jason to get a glimpse of the pond. "This is what we came to see?"

Jason grinned at her. "It would seem so. A bit disappointing, is it not?"

Abby moved past the brush to step out onto the dried pond bed for a better view. She could imagine at high tide it wouldn't look much different from the tidal pond behind their house except there was more vegetation. She didn't know what she had expected but she had to agree with Jason. It was disappointing. She returned to Jason and Tria in time to see Max making his way back to them.

Abby started to reach for the bark he was carrying when Max stopped her. "No sense all of us getting sticky. Just tell me what to do with these."

"Rub the oily side of the bark over his skin."

Max did as she directed. He had to admit he was proud of Abby's knowledge of healing.

Jason turned a skeptical look at Abby. "Are you sure this is necessary?"

"Trust me, you do not want to risk getting the rash."

Max finished his task and discarded the bark. He then went to the pond to try scouring the residue from his hands while Tria and Abby wrapped Jason's arms with the torn fabric.

Jason gave them a deprecating smile. "Is this the Key West version of 'tar and feather'?"

Both ladies smiled at him.

Over Jason's shoulder Abby noticed Max was standing still at the pond's edge looking towards the sky. She looked up from where she stood but couldn't see much over the tree line so she made her way to his side. Looking up she only saw clear sky. "What is it, Max?"

"Can you feel it?"

Abby shook her head no. "Feel what?"

"The drop in pressure. There's a storm brewing."

Abby looked again at the clear sky all around but didn't doubt him. After all, he chased storms for a living. "Time to go back?"

Max nodded in agreement.

They started the return trip to the house at a much quicker pace. Not just because the way was already cleared but because Max was in a hurry to return to his ship. Not even halfway through the hammock, when he had turned for the third time to see how far behind the others were following, Abby decided she needed to set him free. She called out loudly. "Max wait."

He waited for them to get closer. "Something wrong?"

Abby put her hand on his forearm. "Yes. Tria and I cannot keep up with your pace and you are going to wear Jason out. He is not acclimated yet."

Max released a frustrated sigh. "All right, I'll slow down."

She smiled at him. "Thank you for the offer but I was going to suggest you go on without us. You are obviously impatient to get to your ship. We will be fine. It is not like some wild animal is going to attack us and we cannot get lost following the path."

Max looked at his wife. She understood and accepted his needs and was willing to let him go. She was amazing. He looked to Victoria then Jason standing there in his ridiculous arm bandages. Twenty-four hours ago it would have been unthinkable to leave Abby with Lord Fop but here he was considering just that and finding himself willing to do so. Working side by side for the better part of a morning in hard labor had changed his opinion of the man. It also helped it was obvious Jason was taken with Victoria.

"Lord Malwbry." He waited till Jason took his eyes off Victoria and looked him in the eye. "Take care my wife gets home safely."

Jason could not believe he had heard him correctly. After all the animosity between them, Max was going to leave Abby behind, entrusted to his care. He didn't understand the reason for Max's hurry but he did understand the significance of the trust Max was placing in him. "You have my word."

Max nodded to Jason. He kissed Abby on the cheek and whispered, "I'll return as soon as I can." He took off running while they trailed behind. All too soon, he disappeared from her sight.

They returned to the house much quicker than the walk out thanks to the cleared path. Abby had only one destination in mind but didn't want to be rude to her guests. "Would you care to climb up to the Captain's Walk with me?"

Tria immediately agreed. "I would love to."

Jason said, "Certainly"

Standing at the railing Tria commented, "It is too bad you can't see the wharf."

"I know but this time the dock was full. The *Mystic* is anchored in the harbour. You can just barely see her over that building." Abby stretched to look where the *Mystic* had been this morning only to find she was already gone. Scanning the ships under sail she found her headed east. "There she is." Abby pointed towards the distant sails. "I am sure the men were ready to leave as soon as Max returned." In the far distance there seemed to be a bank of clouds on the eastern horizon and her worry began all over again. Putting a smile on her face, Abby turned to her guests and asked, "Shall we have our lunch now?"

Jason gestured to his outstretched arms. "How long must I be like this?"

"I think we can clean you up now, but you should stay indoors the rest of the day. If we missed any the sunlight will make it worse." Abby left to retrieve a basin, soap, water and some towels.

She returned to the dining room table and deposited the supplies.

Victoria said, "Let me do this."

Abby happily relinquished the task. She instead unpacked the picnic basket and started setting out their lunch. Her thoughts were preoccupied as always with Max. Once Jason was relatively free of the sticky tree sap they ate their lunch. Jason and Tria's flirtation was wearing on Abby. She was much relieved when shortly after lunch they decided to leave her company.

Tria said, "You're sure you don't mind? If you need company, we'll stay."

Abby kissed her cheek. "No, I will be fine. I promise. Enjoy your day."

The storm broke that afternoon never reaching Key West but word made its way to them some of the other Keys had been hit hard causing several wrecks. Abby could only continue to pray often for Max's safety and that of his crew.

Chapter 26

Captain Talmage and his crew were making their usual morning run from Pickles Reef to Alligator Reef in search of wrecks. The morning was pleasant with a clear sky. Disappointing for his line of work. Needing to refill their water casks he was now headed for Long Key. Off his port side he watched a merchant ship sail past. Obviously a vessel not familiar with these waters as she was closer to the reef than was wise.

A couple of hours later, having filled their water casks and their stomachs, Talmage and his crew were relaxing when the weather began to change. The storm was headed towards them from the southwest. Thinking of the merchant ship and her faulty course Talmage decided to follow after her. Instinct told him she was going to find herself on a reef and in need of his assistance. Grinning to himself he yelled to his crew, "On your feet you scalawags. We've got work to do."

"Sail ho!"

Max scanned the stormy reef in the direction Thomas indicated. It took a moment before he could make out the ship in the distance, too close to the shallows. It appeared to be in trouble. Max's hopes began to soar. Finally, a ship in need of rescue and no other sails on the horizon. If the Captain accepted their help he would finally be wreck master. With any luck they could even save this ship without assistance increasing their reward. But now was not the time to consider money. He had a job to do. Max called out orders to change sails and sent Billy to take soundings. They could not afford to get caught on the reef.

The storm reached them several hours ago, shortly after leaving Key West. The first few hours had been only a mild drizzle leaving them to watch ships sail safely past in the distance. Then the rain intensified into a true storm pelting them with cold water drops and buffeting the hull with ever increasing white capped waves. The storm pushed them forward as they worked their way northeast but still was not strong enough to give Max hope of finding a wreck. Keeping a safe distance from the reef they continued onward. Max was planning to anchor on the lee side of Marathon Key, not far away, when Thomas spotted the stranded ship on Washerwoman Shoal. The two-masted schooner with fore-and-aft sails flew the distress signal flags N and C. Max was confident his services would be welcomed.

Quickly he called out sail changes, correcting their course towards the stranded ship. The storm conditions continued to strengthen. The wind was increasing at their backs and gusting at intervals. It brought with it cloudbursts of rain making his job of maneuvering the ship even more difficult and dangerous. Sail changes had to be quick and precise. He was fortunate to have a crew worthy of the challenge. A lull in the wind gave Max a moment to scan the horizon around them. He discovered a disturbing sight; one he had missed earlier. Another ship headed their way close-hauled with a flag Max didn't want to see. "Oh hell, Talmage is headed this way."

Jonathon had been working near the helm and paused to follow Max's gaze. "You don't think this is one of his conspiracies, do you?"

Looking towards the reef, Max reassessed the stranded ship and the eagerness of the crew to accept their help. It seemed likely it could be one of Talmage's schemes. The storm was bad but not severe enough to have caused an experienced crew to be stranded so high on the shoals with a portion of her underwater hull exposed. "It looks to be the way of it."

Jonathon's lips compressed. "Either way, conspiracy or not, this is our wreck to claim and Talmage is not going to like it. He's going to sail hard to make sure it doesn't happen."

"You're right." Talmage was closer to the wreck but they had the wind advantage. Max called out to the crew, he hoped loud enough to be heard over the storm, "Mates we're going to have to work fast to beat Talmage. Billy, take soundings every few minutes from the reef side."

"Aye, Captain." Billy ran to his station and dropped the sounding line overboard to check the depth of the water.

Max called out more sail adjustments. The men quickly followed his orders. They all kept a weather eye on Talmage.

Billy called out the depth. "Ten fathoms by the deep, sir."

Max glanced toward the *Sinistral*. Talmage was almost to the wreck. He was dousing sail and would be casting anchor soon. In another moment they could be the same distance as the *Sinistral* from the stranded ship, unfortunately they were too close to maintain their speed. He had to slow the ship. They still had a chance to beat Talmage but if the wind changed direction now....

"Seven fathoms by the deep, sir."

Max called out, "Prepare to douse sail."

Billy shouted over the rain, "Six fathoms by the mark, Captain."

"Douse the mainsail."

The crew did so and the ship slowed. Max called out, "Depth?"

Billy answered, "Aye. Six and one quarter fathoms, sir.

As they moved closer in Max doused more sail and the ship began to rock in the waves rather than skimming over them. It was a delicate process to get close to a stranded ship without running into it or getting your own ship stranded.

They were pulling close to the merchant ship maybe a cable length distant. It was breached sideways on the reef and listing portside towards them. Max could see the crew working the capstan, the captain directing his men in one last attempt to save their ship.

"Three and half fathoms, sir"

The *Mystic's* draft was just under two fathoms. They were as close as he dared to take his ship. Max shouted to the crew, "Cast anchor!" then in a lower voice, "we row from here."

Jonathon yelled to the twins before moving to Max's side to exchange positions at the helm, "Ready the long boat. Hurry men!" Talmage's crew already had their longboat in the water with six men at the oars while Talmage issued orders.

Jonathon encouraged his friend, "As long as the wind doesn't change you can still get there first."

Max nodded in agreement. The longboat was ready. He loped across the deck to where it waited calling out to his men, "Thomas, Tims, Mike, Flynn you're with me."

"Aye," echoed as the men answered him.

Talmage's crew was making good distance for pulling against the wind. Max, Thomas and the Tims fell quickly into a familiar and comfortable rowing rhythm from long experience with each other. Max was well pleased when Mike and Flynn matched them with ease allowing them to move rapidly over the stormy waves with the added assist of the current. They caught up to Talmage halfway to the stranded ship. Max could almost see the frustration on his face. Of an accord, they all pulled harder on the oars and began to out distance Talmage who they could hear over the sound of the storm tormenting his men to go faster. They reached the ship with time to spare.

Max called out to the crew of the merchant ship, "Permission to come aboard."

"State your business."

"We're offering our assistance in relieving you from the reef." Max waited impatiently for an answer as he watched Talmage getting closer.

"Permission granted." A rope ladder was dropped for him. Leaving the rest of his men in the longboat to discourage Talmage from boarding the ship as well, Max carefully made the climb up the side of the rocking ship to the main deck and was warmly greeted by the captain.

Jonathon Keats watched through the spyglass a quarter hour later as Max climbed back down the ladder into the longboat. He was confronted by Talmage who had maneuvered his longboat alongside Thomas to wait for Max's return. Even from this distance he could tell they were arguing. It continued for several minutes before two men from each boat boarded the stranded vessel and the boats separated to return to their respective ships. Max left Thomas and Tim Sudduth behind with Talmage's two men to start unloading the hull.

Despite the pouring rain the crew gathered round the returning men as they gained the deck anxious to hear what Max had to say. "She's ours boys! Gather the gear. We've got work to do."

As the others rushed off to ready for the rescue Max and Jonathon went below deck, out of the storm, where Max gave him more details. "Captain Howe of the *Merry Merchant* has agreed to terms. So far they are not taking on water but that could change. She's riding hard and we'll have to drag her off the reef. He claims a series of large waves overtook them and left them stranded. He seemed sincere but I'm still not certain if this was nature or deliberate. They are carrying mostly finished goods; cloth, dyes, crates of china, cookware, flatware, casks of whale oil. The good news is it's all small enough we could unload it without assistance. The bad news is we don't have enough room to take it all aboard the *Mystic."*

"Meaning we will have to accept his help" Jonathon said, referring to Talmage, "What did you argue over?"

Max grimaced. "He insinuated, no actually he outright said, I couldn't handle this salvage and I should let him be wreck master, among other things."

"What an arse. Did you offer him a consortship?"

Max wasn't against entering a consortship to get help if needed but he would have preferred it to be with any wrecker other than Talmage. "Yes. As you said we don't have a choice. We can't do this one alone and I was afraid if I put him off and then asked later he would trap me into agreeing to an unacceptable percentage of the salvage."

"I'm sure you're right. Did he accept it?"

Max smiled. "He didn't want to but he did. Now, I need to get back before he takes over the operation."

The men returned topside where all hands were prepared to do their best to get the *Merry Merchant* back under her own sail. As they rowed back to the stranded ship, Max assigned Billy and Buttons to measure the depth all around the stranded ship. The rest would work on unloading the cargo and manning the pumps if needed. Upon boarding the ship Max was satisfied to see his crew promptly working in a coordinated effort. Talmage and his crew even did as asked, albeit less efficiently. They worked to remove the heaviest of cargo first in the hopes only partially unloading the ship would be required. It was an arduous task to move cargo in the midst of a gale into longboats, then row the loaded boats out to their ships, hoist the cargo aboard and return for more. Wind, rain and clothes plastered to the skin made it uncomfortable, while the rolling ship and high waves made it difficult and dangerous. It was not a job for the faint at heart.

Billy and Buttons returned from sounding the ship. After passing their findings to Max they joined the rest of the men hauling cargo. Sometime later they were working to load the longboats for the second time when the wind suddenly shifted from the southwest to blow from the northwest. Previously blowing parallel to the ship it was now blowing across the beam pushing her further on her port side. A noise overhead had Max looking up to find the mainsail unfurling. It would have to be secured to keep from catching the wind and pushing the ship over into the waves. He caught Billy as he was passing, the closest man available, "I need you to secure that sail."

"Aye, captain."

Billy climbed the mast and out on the footrope and began securing the sail. Max became distracted by an argument between Talmage and one of the Tims. He hurried over to find out what it was about.

Out of the corner of his eye Max saw the sail suddenly catch and fill with wind. All on board were forced to find purchase as the ship rolled over. Some failed and slid down the deck into the bulwarks. Horror filled Max as he saw Billy fall from the rigging into the crashing waves.

Max let go of his hold on a belaying pin and slid down the deck then hurtled himself over the side vaguely aware Thomas had followed suit from further down the ship. Fortunately, he dove into a cresting wave and surfaced in the lull. Quickly he turned around and started swimming towards the ship and where he thought Billy might have landed. A few yards from the ship he searched the surface but could not find his young crewman.

The storm had churned the coral beds turning the water chalky with debris. Thomas breached the surfaced nearby, took a breath, and dove under. Max did likewise. It was nearly impossible to see under the surface. The crashing waves caused lots of air bubbles and the stormy skies further limited visibility. He followed the pull of the water swimming parallel to the hull until he was forced to surface for air. It was taking too long to find Billy. Max was growing fearful of pending doom. Thomas came up beside him and shook his head. They both went under again swimming with the current and past the ship. It seemed like they searched for an hour. In reality it was just over five minutes before Thomas brought Billy's limp body to the surface. The men on board threw them a rope to tie around Billy's chest so they could hoist his limp body up while Max and Thomas wearily climbed up the ladder. The Tims assisted them onto the deck.

Max looked up to find Mike and Flynn securing the sail. The waves helped to right the ship a bit but it still lay at an extreme angle. Max had to see to Billy before he could deal with that problem. Someone had laid the young sailor on the deck and Buttons was with him feeling his head. He looked up as Max crouched next to him. Buttons mutely shook his head in the negative. Max's chest tightened. Buttons pulled his hand from Billy's head. There was blood on his fingers. Max's stomach clenched.

Buttons said, "Sorry captain. Best I can figure he must have fallen in between the waves when the water was low and hit his head on the coral. He never came up for air."

Max wanted to lash out at something to relieve his self-directed anger. It was his fault. He should have sent up one of the more experienced men but guilt would have to be put aside for later. Now he had men from three ships waiting for his direction. Looking at Billy's still face he stood up then looked to the men around him. "Anyone else hurt?" Murmurs came back to him of nothing more than bruises. "Thomas, Buttons you take care of Billy. See he gets back to the *Mystic*. The rest of my crew is going to haul the anchor out on the starboard side and pull the ship upright. The rest of you keep loading Talmage's longboat with the cargo on deck until we get the ship righted."

As the men scattered to follow his orders, Max turned to face the sea and ran a hand over his face. He was finding it hard to accept he had lost one of his own.

One of the Tims came up to him with news.

"Captain, something happened when the ship rolled. She's taking on water."

Max nodded. "It was only a matter of time."

Talmage chose that moment to make a nuisance of himself. "You've got more than you can handle whelp; losing a man, ship sideways, hull breach. Why don't you admit when you're down and turn this operation over to me?"

Max looked at him with fire burning in his eyes. "Take orders from me or get off this ship." Max said it with such intensity Talmage backed up and walked away without a word. Max turned to Tim. "Was anyone harmed below deck?"

"Neigh, 'cepting Flynn who bruised his leg landing on a crate."

Max was glad to hear it. "See if you can find the hole. Hopefully it is small enough to patch."

"Aye, sir." Tim turned and disappeared down the hatch.

Max considered his next move. The current wind direction would help them pull the ship off the reef plus the tide was rising. For once the intensity of the storm could work in his favour keeping the waves high enough to help lift the ship. Situated as they were on the edge of the reef, deeper water wasn't far away. Once they righted the ship and lightened some more of the cargo he would try towing the stranded ship off the reef. It should work.

Max called a halt to the unloading after the third load. Talmage, of course, questioned his decision but Max did not want to risk losing the advantage of high tide. The ship was now sitting upright and the pumps were keeping up with the incoming water from the hole punctured in the side of the ship when it rolled, presumably caused by the coral.

The *Mystic* and *Sinistral* were positioned off the stern of the *Merry Merchant* with tow lines in place. Talmage waited for Max's signal to hoist sail. Checking with Jonathon that all was ready he signaled the *Sinistral*. Sails were hoisted and filled. Both ships strained forward against the tow line. For a moment Max despaired he had miscalculated but then the ship moved. She caught hard again for a moment before completely clearing the reef.

Unknown to Max, Captain Howe had ordered his men to release the anchor prior to the arrival of the wreckers with the intention of using his quarter boat to haul it out to deeper water in the hopes of pulling them off the reef. Unfortunately the chain parted dropping the anchor in the water on the port side. When the ship rolled it landed on the anchor staving a hole in the hull and wedging the anchor in the coral. The hole, when found, could have been temporarily patched but in a continuation of improbable misfortune as they freed the ship from the reef they pulled the hull across the anchor where it caught in the same hole turning it into a long gash.

As Max and Talmage towed his ship out to deeper water, Captain Howe was informed by one of his hands the ship was taking on more water than she could pump. Leaving his first mate in charge of the deck Captain Howe went below decks to investigate. He found a dire situation in the pump room. The water was coming in faster than the pumps could handle and rising at an alarming rate. Then, as if they needed anything else to go wrong, one of the pumps failed. The ship's carpenter was called down to investigate in the hopes of repairing it. The gear was underwater and after several attempts to try and find the problem without success the captain was forced to give the order. "Abandon ship."

Clear of the reef, Max signaled Talmage to drop his tow line, then looked back at the merchant ship to check their progress. He discovered men scrambling across the deck in a rush and then he saw two quarter boats being lowered followed by Captain Howe signaling for his attention. It appeared they were abandoning ship. Max ordered his crew to douse the sails and cast anchor, then ordered his longboat lowered to help rescue the merchant's crew. Max sailed over in the longboat to find out what had happened, although it was becoming obvious the ship was indeed sinking.

Captain Howe met him on deck. "I'm afraid we have another more serious problem. The ship caught on something as we came off the reef. We now have a larger hole. The pumps weren't able to keep up even before one of them failed. Now it is hopeless."

"How much is flooded?"

"I'm sure most of the hold by now."

Max looked around assessing the situation. *What more could go wrong with this operation?* He ran to the bow of the ship and signaled to his ship to undo the tow lines. Then he turned back to the captain. "Do we need more boats to get everyone off the ship?" Captain Howe looked around but didn't answer him. Max firmly asked him, "Captain Howe, how many souls on board?"

Captain Howe answered in a distracted tone. "Thirty-eight including myself."

Max hurried to the bulwarks and leaned over to count the number of men in the three boats. Subtracting his crewmen from the total there were thirty-six from this ship. Max turned to Captain Howe. "You are missing a man." Max scanned the rigging and the open deck. Captain Howe didn't respond. "Captain Howe! Someone's missing. You need to help me search the ship." Max was relieved when the captain finally responded. Both men went below decks. Max had to prod Howe to find lanterns. They started their search on the lowest deck before it could fill with water. Max called out, "Ahoy, anyone down here?"

They cleared the bottom deck and started on the next when Jonathon appeared to help. "Thomas is on deck too."

Max was relieved to see him. "Good, we may need him to search the flooded hold, although I hope not." They continued making a meticulous search until they heard Captain Howe call out. They found him leaning over an unconscious boy and mumbling to himself. Max pushed him out of the way and lifted the boy over his shoulders. With a look and a nod he instructed Jonathon to ensure the captain followed. Reaching the deck he gave the lad over to Thomas to get him into the boat, followed by Jonathon. He then started down the ladder leaving the captain of the ship to be last to leave but only after making sure Captain Howe was going to follow him.

Max was glad to climb aboard the *Mystic*, until he remembered Billy lay below deck. He needed to take care of Billy. That was now a higher priority than the sinking ship. Also, his ship was heavy with thirty-eight men. They were crowded below deck, out of the weather, except for a few with a superstition about being in the same space as a dead sailor. They would have to sail to Key West for now. Afterwards they would return to retrieve cargo from the underwater wreck. He was not looking forward to the travail. Behind him Talmage climbed aboard to speak with him.

"You cockard barnacle...," began Talmage.

Max nearly laughed thinking he had forced the captain past calling him 'whelp' and 'landlubber'.

"....now we have to pull the cargo out of Davey Jones' locker. I told ye it should have all been unloaded. You can't get this salvage right to save your own arse. I'm taking over."

Max saw red. "The hell you will Talmage. Not only am I master of that wreck," Max pointed towards the sinking ship, "I am also Captain of this ship and unless you want me to dispute your claim and tie this salvage up in court you are going to leave my ship taking half of these displaced sailors over to yours. Furthermore, your part in this venture has come to an end. Our agreement was your assistance to remove the ship from the reef. Done. I will seek out others to help with the wreck. You are going to follow me to Key West tonight and in the morning you will unload the cargo from your ship to Mr. Greene's warehouse. Furthermore, you will not speak to me again unless I seek you out. Understood?"

Talmage was forced to acknowledge he was facing a man of considerable character. He had thought if he pushed Max, he would break but he was finding it only made him more determined. The last thing he wanted was to end up back in Judge Webb's courtroom. Besides, it actually was a good thing the whelp didn't want his help. He had an appointment to keep tomorrow. Talmage rounded up as many displaced crewmen as his boat could hold and returned to the *Sinistral*.

Max called Jonathon over. "Round up some men and rope and an empty barrel with a water-tight seal and quickly get over to the ship. Tie a rope to the ship and to the barrel long enough to allow the barrel to float on the surface. We need a marker to find her again when we return tomorrow."

"Aye. Good idea." Jonathon headed off to do his bidding.

As the sun set behind the storm the *Merry Merchant* slipped silently below the water's surface unnoticed by man with only a barrel to mark its resting place. The *Mystic* and *Sinistral* were several miles away headed towards Key West harbour.

The storm blew itself out overnight much to the relief of all.

Chapter 27

Abby shut the door behind Jason and Tria after sharing another meal together. Abby appreciated they were trying to keep her company while Max was gone but their happiness was vexing her. She was going to have to think of a way to dissuade them. She couldn't handle sitting through another meal with them cooing at each other. It wasn't that she begrudged them their good fortune it was just hard to bear with her own estrangement weighing so heavy on her.

Abby said goodnight to Maria and climbed the stairs. She hesitated at the landing, not really ready for bed. Instead she picked up a shawl from her room and climbed the stairs to the Captain's Walk. Clearing the hatch she walked to the railing to stare out at the harbour. There were many ships anchored tonight, their lamp lights like fallen stars on the dark water. She breathed deeply of the salty air, filling her lungs while wishing she could clear her mind. Her worry was growing stronger. She had never given much credence to the notion of women's intuition but now she was changing her mind. All day she had the nagging feeling something was wrong. She wondered for at least the hundredth time where he was and if he was injured.

She wanted to look for him. She wanted the answers to her questions before they drove her insane. *Why couldn't she look for him?* Just because the woman always waited at home before didn't mean she had to now. This was 1829 after all. Some women were learning how to be independent. Why not find a ship to take her out in search of them? If there really was a serious injury she could be of some help. Why not, indeed! Having made up her mind to charter a boat in the morning she left the Walk to try and get some sleep.

Abby left the house early, by herself, even more determined than the night before to find Max. She left before Maria awoke leaving her a note on the table. Hurrying down the street in the early morning light she tried to hold her nervousness at bay. She hoped to find a fishing smack sailing in the right direction. The closer she got to the docks the more she began to question her idea and all that was wrong with it. The area was busy with all sorts of men going about their business. Realizing she would be foolish to continue, Abby was going to turn around and then she froze in place.

A man rounded the corner from Front Street and all her anxiety vanished in an instant. She could only stare, motionless in amazement, as she watched him walking towards her. She wanted to run into his embrace, assure herself of his safety and then she wanted to beat him with her reticule for making her worry so... but of course a lady couldn't behave so, especially not in public.

Max stopped short a good yard from his wife, he was surprised to see her. She should still be sleeping; instead she was standing in front of him in a simple blue dress with a smart little hat atop her glossy tresses. The luminescent grey of her irises reminded him of passing storm clouds touched by the sun. She was beautiful and refreshing after the ordeal he had been through and it frightened him how much he felt for her right now in this moment. The town around them ceased to exist as they focused on each other.

Part of him wanted to catch her up and swing her around while the other part urged him to keep her at arm's length. His heart freshly wounded from Billy, he chose safety.

In a voice stripped of emotion Max asked, "Where are you headed this early?"

Abby was disappointed to see his eyes become shuttered; the wall between them still firmly in place. He asked the question as if speaking to anyone of his acquaintance. She thought they had made some progress. His whispered words before he left had given her hope. Praying total honesty would make a difference she said, "I was going to look for you."

He frowned, "How did you know I was back?"

"I did not. I was going to find a captain to take me out to the reef to look for you."

His eyes flared with anger born from concern, "Abigail, what were you thinking? Thank goodness I'm here. Such an idea was fraught with danger." He grasped her arm and turned her back towards the house. He set a brisk pace.

"I was so worried about you I was past rational thinking. Did you find a wreck?"

He only nodded.

"Is the crew safe?"

She felt his grip tighten infinitesimally on her arm but he didn't answer. She pulled to a stop, turning towards him. "Max, who is hurt? I should go to him. I could tend his injuries." Then she saw the pain in his eyes. The hurt he was trying to hide not only from the world but from himself. She waited for him to answer. He couldn't hold her gaze. She waited patiently. He dropped her arm and looked off to the coastline before finally answering in a dead voice.

"We lost Billy."

Abby had not expected the finality in his answer. Her breath caught and held as she felt the reality of his loss hit her in the gut. Poor Billy. He was so young and such a happy person. He worshipped Max and would have done anything he asked of him. No wonder Max was so upset. Not only because Billy was a favored crewmen but also because it was Max's responsibility to keep his crew safe. He was probably overwhelmed with guilt. The rest of this conversation would wait till they reached the house. Silently she turned and began walking again. He fell into step beside her without saying another word.

Max led the way up the steps of the porch and held the door for her. He followed her inside and when she turned to face him she saw his closed expression. He needed to talk but she had no idea how to get him to do so. He stepped closer to her and her heart began to race. His anger was palpable. She felt the restrained violence in him and was afraid. Not afraid for herself, his anger was directed inward; rather she feared how the violence could eat at his soul. He took her hand and led her towards the stairs. She followed without question all the way to their room where he shut the door. She started to say something then but he wouldn't let her. With controlled motions he removed her hat carefully laying the headpiece on the table. He then released her hair, letting it fall in soft waves down her back before gliding his fingers through it. His movements were governed and methodical.

He didn't want to talk. The anger and guilt were tearing him apart inside. He was losing control of the emotions swamping him. What he needed most right now only she could give him; a few moments of blessed release from the reality of yesterday's tragedy. He needed her and that in itself was also difficult to bear. He didn't want to need anyone. He tilted her face for his kiss. It wasn't gentle but she didn't seem to mind. And it was not enough. He pulled her tightly to him, buried his face in her neck and inhaled the scent of roses. It was not enough.

At the first touch of his hands Abby understood he needed her. He needed what only she could give him. She wanted to give him so much more but for now she willing gave him all he asked of her. She turned her back to him. Moving her hair aside, she offered him the buttons of her dress. She felt his hands tremble as he undid them.

Abby thought Max was sleeping. The mid-day sun spilled across the floor as she got up and dressed as quietly as she could and made her way downstairs. She was hungry and it was the Baxley's day off. Abby's note on the table had been turned over and in Maria's careful handwriting she left a note of her own telling Abby she would spend the day visiting friends. Accepting the fact she would have to scrounge something for them to eat Abby started for the back door when a knock on the front door had her turning around. She had a good idea who she would find on the other side.

Jason and Tria had made it their mission to cheer Abby but she suspected it was really an excuse for them to be together. Today they had decided to bring her lunch. She opened the door to find Jason carrying a basket of food from the Lambert's cook while Tria breezed past her. "Cheers, luv. What a beautiful day it is, don't you think? Jason would you be a dear and set the basket on the buffet in the dining room?"

Abby would be grateful they had solved the problem of food except their company was the last thing she and Max needed. "Tria, please lower your voice. Max is home. He is sleeping upstairs."

"No he's not," said Max from the staircase. The three of them waited, a frozen tableau, until Max appeared in the room.

Jason nodded to him. "Good to see you again, Captain."

Max returned his nod. "Malwbry." To Victoria he said, "Did I hear you mention food? I would love some." He was hungry and he wasn't keen on finding out what his wife had in mind for lunch. He would willingly suffer their company for some good food.

Not much later he was thinking they couldn't finish this meal fast enough. He wasn't sure he could take much more of their whispered lover's conversation or his wife's alternately contrite and sympathetic looks.

Abby was thinking Max looked like a caged animal desperate for a way out. Afraid he was going to run and she wouldn't see him again for weeks on end she realized she must get rid of their guests. Abby gave Tria a silent pleading look and a nod towards the door. Relief washed over her when understanding dawned in her friend's eyes.

Abby made eye contact with Max willing him to stay as Tria said to Jason, "We need to go." Both ladies stood forcing the men to their feet. Abby led them to the door.

Tria whispered to Abby as she passed, *"Bonne chance, mon amie."*

Abby couldn't help but remember the last time a friend had spoken to her in French. Elizabeth had wished her good voyage. It could be debated whether or not her voyage was good. They had shipwrecked but without the wreck she would not be married to Max. But was their marriage a good thing for her? She shut the door behind them then turned to her husband and found herself again facing his emotional wall. At the moment, she was not at all sure her marriage was a blessing.

To fill the silence she said the first thing that came to mind. "They have visited every day to keep me company. They mean well but their simpatico is easier to take in small doses." Max didn't respond and he still looked like he was fighting not to leave. "I have been so worried about you."

Gruffly Max said, "You needn't be. I can take care of myself."

She understood. He didn't want her sympathy but it was so hard not to give it. She walked past him, holding her arms around herself. She stopped in front of the painting of the ship. "Billy was a good boy - a good man. He..."

"Stop. Don't."

Abby compressed her lips. She turned to face him and tried a different tack. "Did you run into Talmage again?"

"Yes."

Blast his short answers. "Was he wreck master?"

Her question reminded him of his blame in Billy's death. "Abigail, I don't want to discuss it."

She walked towards him. "Please talk to me, Max. Tell me what happened."

He turned towards the door. She rushed to block his path. Quietly she said, "Please."

Max looked down into her face. Her imploring and sincerity had him admitting, "I was wreck master. It's my fault he's gone."

"I am sure there was nothing you could do..."

He coldly interrupted her. "You're wrong. I should not have asked him to fix the sail. He would still be here if I had asked someone more experienced or taken care of it myself."

Abby reached her hand towards his face but he pulled away. He couldn't accept her comfort. He didn't deserve it. But it was more than that. Everyone he ever cared about - his parents, Captain Nate, Billy - he lost them. In some twisted way he thought if he didn't care for her, he couldn't lose her. "I have to go."

Taken aback Abby asked, "Where?"

"To bury Billy."

The cemetery was located on the beach south of the settlement. Abby thought it made a nice final resting place. The graveside service was simple with many sailors in attendance. Billy had been well liked by all who knew him. Abby stood beside her disconsolate husband. Jason and Tria were on her other side having learned of the tragedy from others after leaving their house. Max officiated since there was no clergyman on the island at the moment, even though it was Sunday. At the conclusion of the service Max rounded up his crew and sent them to the ship then returned to his wife's side. "Malwbry, will you see my wife home, again?"

Abby couldn't believe what she was hearing. "Max, what is going on? Why are you not staying?"

"There is still more work to be done at the wreck."

Abby threw pride to the wind and pleaded. "Then take me with you. I will not be a burden."

"No."

She started to protest.

He cut her off. "No, absolutely not. Go home, Abigail."

And with that he turned and left her standing on the beach embarrassed, forlorn and heartbroken.

Max recruited the help of two friends to finish the salvage. They both owned their own fishing smacks and were glad for the extra work. It was early evening when they finally found the barrel marking the sunken ship. They would have to wait till morning to start work. The smacks were tied up to his ship while his friends and their crew spent the evening with his crew eating, drinking, talking and mostly remembering Billy.

Max joined them for a few hours until the need for solitude pulled him to his cabin below deck. Besides his grief for Billy he also had a nagging guilt over the way he had left Abby. He was haunted by the hurt look on her face just before he left. He still firmly believed she shouldn't be here. He should have tried to let her down gently but with all the emotions he was feeling in the moment there hadn't been any room left for tenderness.

Thankfully the weather and the waves remained calm. In the morning Max, Thomas, and three divers from the fishing crews dove down to the wreck nearly sixty feet below. Their misfortune continued. Max would have groaned if he hadn't been underwater holding his breath. The ship was laying starboard side up on a downward slope. If it had been sitting upright they would have been able to pull the goods out of the hatch. Now they would first have to make a hole in the side of the ship. On the other hand once they did so they would have direct access to the hold. His other concern was the ship could shift and sink deeper while they were working inside, but as his mother used to say 'no sense borrowing trouble' so he put the concern aside.

They had to resurface for tools, then went down in shifts using axes and saws to work their way into the hold. It was hard work underwater. While the divers opened the hull the men on the ship set up block and tackle with a large net at the end of a rope pulley. They would load the cargo in the net and the men on his ship would haul it up. Once they gained access the operation went much faster than Max anticipated. By the end of the day they had unloaded most of the cargo.

Max was feeling pretty good about their progress as he rested for a moment holding onto a longboat. Pretty good until he noticed Thomas and the others surfacing in a hurry.

Thomas called out to Max, "Dye in the water."

Max had heard of divers suffering blindness from dyes. Not wanting to take a chance he called a halt to the operation until tomorrow after they made another hole in the hull to allow the water to flow through. He hoped the dye would clear overnight.

They were able to finish the next day without further incident retrieving all the cargo and the ship's more valuable equipment. They were sailing towards Key West at the end of the day much to Max's relief.

Wednesday morning Abby and Maria walked to the General Mercantile to do some shopping. Abby's list included flour, ink and fresh vegetables if they were available. Passing through the doors of the store she was surprised to find Max standing at the counter. She stood there in the doorway staring at him until Max and the clerk both looked her way. She thought she saw a flash of guilt cross his face but it could have been her imagination. He left the clerk to walk towards her.

"Good morning, Abby."

She hadn't expected any physical contact, after all they were in public, but she would have liked a little more warmth in his greeting. "Good morning, Max. Did you finish working the wreck?"

"We did. The men are unloading the salvage now." He omitted telling her he had been in port since late last night. He hoped she would think they had just arrived.

"Good, then you can keep your promise now."

Max was at a loss. "What promise?"

"You promised to stay with me a week after you found a wreck."

Fool that he was he had made her the promise in a weak moment. He pulled her away from the doorway as another customer entered. He looked meaningfully at Maria who took the hint and wandered over to the bolts of cloth on the other side of the store. "I'm not staying. We are unloading the cargo, resupplying the ship and headed out again today."

"Max, why?" Abby looked around the store and lowered her voice to a harsh whisper. "Why are you going back out?"

"There are other wrecks in the Upper Reefs in need of more help."

"Let someone else go."

He didn't have to leave. Part of him acknowledged the truth. He was starting a fight to make it easier... easier to leave, easier to pretend he didn't care for her. "And then there is the matter of your father expecting me to show some earnings while he's gone or he has threatened to put me behind a desk."

She continued their whispered argument trying not to attract the attention of the clerk and customers. "He would not do that. Besides you have earned money."

"Not enough. Not nearly enough."

Frustrated Abby asked, "What would be enough for you?"

"Don't you mean for him? What would be enough for him? Or for you?"

"No, I mean what would be enough for you?"

"Before you, I only needed enough to keep my ship and my crew going. Now I'm supposed to earn enough to keep you in a nice house and in the style you're accustomed to, whatever that means, besides clothes and servants and...things," he said with disgust.

"I do not *need* any of it. Yes, I have always had them but if it came right down to it I could live with less. If it bothers you so much we will get rid of all of it."

Derisively he said, "You have no idea how to survive without someone else taking care of your clothes or cooking for you. You've probably never once taken out your own chamber pot."

"Ah," Abby's mouth formed a perfect 'O' she was shocked he would dare mention something so indelicate in a public place.

Max turned on his heel and walked out the door.

Abby was stunned. She didn't know where it had all went so wrong. But she did know one thing; she wasn't going to let him go that easy. Not this time. This time she was going to be brave enough to ask for what she wanted...what she needed. But first she had to catch up to him.

Pushing her way through the heavy front door she found Max several strides down the street headed towards the wharf. She called to him from the top of the steps.

"Max, wait."

He hesitated but kept walking so she lifted her skirts with both hands and ran down the steps then tried to catch up to him while attempting to maintain a ladylike pace.

"Max, stop."

He continued walking as if she wasn't making a fool of herself. "I will follow you all the way to the ship if I have to. Stop running."

That made him stop and turn. "I'm not running." He didn't move.

"Yes, you are." She continued walking towards him. "Running from your emotions." She was almost in front of him. "Running from us." Standing in front of him now she said in a softer voice, "You are still running from me same as you were in the beginning."

"I have work to do Abby. I don't have time for your female imaginings."

"You are brave enough to face storm and sea, why are you not brave enough to face your feelings? If you would just put half as much effort into salvaging this relationship as you do in salvaging ships I believe we could have something wonderful. Something more than either of us could imagine."

Max, desperate to escape, looked her straight in the eye. "I never said I loved you, Abby."

Stunned, she watched him walk away.

"No, you did not," she whispered. *You love your ship.*

The rest of the day was a blur for Abby. She knew she went back to the store, bought the needed items, returned home and somehow made it through the rest of the day but she could not recall the details. Now she was halfway through a miserable night alone feeling like she had lost more than she could withstand losing.

From the moment of her wedding she had maintained a tiny hope they could fall in love. Now hope was gone. Twice this week he had unkindly pushed her away. She wasn't sure if Max still held any affection for her at all.

Unfortunately she discovered her feelings had grown stronger. The moment he said he didn't love her was when she knew without a doubt she loved him.

What a cruel twist of fate.

Thursday, January 15th

Maria was worried about her mistress. She and the Captain were obviously not getting along but it must have been a serious fight this time. She heard Abby pacing the floor most of the night and she was usually downstairs long before now, it being half past nine. Maybe she had finally fallen asleep. Maria greeted Mrs. Baxley who had arrived to cook breakfast. The two women went out to the kitchen together.

Mrs. Baxley gathered the items she needed for making bread and asked Maria, "How is Mrs. Eatonton this morning?"

"Not well, I think. She didn't sleep last night." They had already talked yesterday of what Maria had witnessed in the store. Mrs. Baxley believed it to be a lover's quarrel and nothing to worry about but Maria could not imagine fighting so with her Thomas.

"Oh dear. I completely forgot we are out of salt. I have enough for this morning's bread but later would you mind going back to town to buy some more? I would send Mr. Baxley but his gout is bothering him something fierce."

Maria looked at the empty sack of salt in Mrs. Baxley's hand. "I don't mind. Early in the day I should not have any trouble going alone."

Maria made her way safely past the wharves and bars of Front Street and into the mercantile to buy the salt. She returned to the street, walking with her head down so as to not make eye contact with the men around her. She passed a few store fronts before coming up behind two men in suits walking slow and talking. She had just decided to go around them when she heard Captain Max's name mentioned in a very threatening manner. The man on the right she had seen before but she couldn't remember from where just now. She was sure it would come to her later. The other man was a stranger to her. Keeping her head down she followed them. They were talking low so she did not hear everything but enough to know Captain Max needed to know what they were planning.

The stranger said, "Alligator reef. How will I know where that is?"

The other man handed him a piece of paper. "Why can't ......meet......say.... wrecked?"

The stranger said, "... can't fake damage .... passes by.... reef .... patrolled by others."

"Fine. You get him to wreck.... I'm on the scene. .... wouldn't want anyone else.... first again. What's the name of the ship?"

Stranger said, "*Anna Rose*. .....Monday next. The ship will stop here first. .....not worried...... weather's clear?"

They had reached the corner where Maria had to turn to go home. She debated following them further but just then the other man glanced over his shoulder so she turned away.

Tria had heard the gossip of Max and Abby arguing in the street yesterday. She thought her friend might need a sympathetic shoulder to lean on so at a reasonable hour of the morning she had the butler send a message to Jason informing him of the change in their plans and then left with her maid to visit her friend. Unknowingly she passed Maria as the maid entered the mercantile. Arriving at Abby's home Mrs. Baxley directed Tria to the Captain's Walk.

Percy flew off at the sound of someone climbing the ladder below the open hatch. Abby turned to see Tria's glistening chestnut head appear. She held out her hand to assist her friend over the edge of the opening. A tricky maneuver with long skirts.

Tria couldn't help but notice the sadness in Abby's eyes. For someone who was normally cheerful, it was a stark difference. Looking closer she saw telltale signs of crying. "Abby, what is the matter?"

Abby tried to shrug her off. She hadn't spoken of her marriage troubles to Tria but today she was too emotional to hide it from her any longer.

Tria gave her a stern look. "You know I won't give up asking until you tell me."

Abby gave her a watery smile as the tears started to well again. She worked to control her emotions before plaintively saying, "I love Max."

Tria waited but Abby didn't say more. "Well of course you do but why are you crying?"

Abby didn't understand her friend's calm acceptance of what for her had been a shattering revelation. "He does not love me."

Tria grinned. "Of course he does. What would make you think he doesn't?"

Percy chose that moment to startle Tria by swooping over her head in protest. "Oh!" She instinctively ducked down and twisted sideways to keep her eye on him. Up close and personal pelicans were quite intimidating. "What is wrong with your pet?"

Abby smiled at Tria's discomfort. "You are standing where he likes to perch."

"Well by all means, let me get out of his way." Tria moved to the other side of Abby.

Abby picked up their conversation. "He said he did not."

Tria gave her a confused look.

"He said he does not love me. In the middle of the street, no less, and he has been avoiding me."

Percy finally settled on the railing leaving them to finish their exchange.

Tria had never known Max to lie. "What exactly did he say?"

Abby thought back to the conversation and what she had said and then his response. "I never said 'I loved you', Abby."

Tria was relieved but kept her voice level. "He hasn't said 'I love you', has he?"

Abby shook her head in despair. "No"

Tria looked her in the eye. "But he also hasn't said 'I don't love you'."

Abby looked at her with guarded hope.

"He can't say it because he does love you. He just hasn't admitted it to himself yet. Apparently you just realized how you feel." Abby nodded. "Sometimes it takes men longer, especially when they have no intention of falling in love in the first place. They fight against it. You just have to show him it's not a bad thing."

"I tried to tell him…"

Tria interrupted her. "I said show him. Reasoning isn't going to work. But first you have another problem."

"I do?"

"Part of Max's problem is he didn't get to complete the courting ritual."

"What do you mean?"

"First there's interest - you both felt it - then there is the chase and then the prize of winning your hand in marriage."

"I do not understand. He won my hand. We are married."

Tria shook her head. "No. He didn't win your hand. You were handed to him with a take her or she'll go to someone else threat."

"Worse. He had to accept me or lose his ship."

Tria didn't believe that was the case but she didn't want to get off point. "Regardless, he may have chosen to marry you but he didn't chase you and he didn't chase you because he didn't make the decision to choose you and therefore to chase you."

Abby shook her head in confusion. "Tria, you are going in circles!"

"You have to make him want to be married to you by getting him to chase you."

"How am I supposed to get him to chase me?"

Tria said, "By playing hard to get."

"How do I play hard to get when we are already married?"

"By ignoring him. Make him work for your attention, withhold your affections. Desire is a very strong motivator."

"And how can I do any of this when he is away from home or avoiding me?"

Tria's brow furrowed. "Um, that is a problem."

They were interrupted by Maria's call from the bottom of the stairs. "Mrs. Abby will you come down from there, I have something I need to tell you."

Tria asked, "Why doesn't she come up here?"

Abby replied, "I tried to get her to when we first moved in but she is afraid of heights." Abby maneuvered onto the stairs. "Coming Maria." At the bottom she turned to her distraught maid. "What is it Maria? Has something happened?"

Maria was so upset she spoke rapidly; her island accent thickened making it difficult for Abby to understand her. "No, nothing bad. At least not yet. I heard men talking in town. They are going to do something bad. Somehow the Captain is involved. I heard them say his name."

Tria stepped off the ladder behind Abby. "Who were the men?"

"I didn't know one of them but the other was the man from the shipwreck."

Tria looked to Abby for enlightenment. Abby asked Maria, "Our shipwreck?"

"Yes. The other captain. The one who took your chest."

Abby's concern heightened as she realized who Maria was indicating. "Captain Talmage?" Maria nodded. Abby was now a little alarmed. "Did he see you?"

Maria nervously answered. "Maybe. I'm not sure. He looked behind him just before I turned the corner but I am just a maid. He probably didn't pay me any attention."

Abby considered what they should do. "We cannot trust that he did not notice you. Maria, right now while it is fresh in your mind we should write down everything you can remember hearing." Victoria and Maria followed Abby to the office downstairs. She sat down at the desk and took out a fresh piece of paper and dipped the pen in ink, poised to write. "Now Maria, start at the beginning. What was the first thing you heard?"

"I don't know which one but one of them said, 'Will Captain Eatonton be a problem again?' Then the stranger wanted to know how to find Alligator reef. The captain wanted to know why they had to wreck the ship, why not just meet. The stranger said they had to damage the ship in case someone passes by 'cause the reefs are always..." Maria paused to think "I don't remember the word he used."

Abby said, "You are doing fine, Maria. What else?"

"Talmage told him not to wreck the ship till he was there. Then he asked him the name of the ship. The stranger said it was the *Anna Rose*."

Abby looked at Maria. "You are sure he said '*Anna Rose*'?" Maria nodded her head yes. Abby asked, "Did he say anything else?"

"The stranger said, 'they would stop here first' and 'Monday next' and he asked Captain Talmage if he was worried about clear weather but I didn't hear him answer. That's all I heard ma'am."

Tria asked, "Maria, what did the stranger look like?"

"Dark haired, lanky, taller than the Captain. Oh and he was missing part of his thumb," Maria held up her right hand, "on this hand."

Tria nodded her approval. "Excellent observation, Maria."

Abby read over what she had written then looked to Tria. "We should take this to the marshal, right away."

Tria shook her head. "He won't believe us. It will be our word against Captain Talmage and I hate to say this but we are only women, our word does not count for much. He won't be able to do anything about it, anyway. The crime hasn't happened and he doesn't have jurisdiction over the reefs."

Abby saw her point. "It is too bad Max has left. He would want to know about this."

Tria was surprised Abby was unaware of her husband's proximity. "He hasn't left yet. I saw his ship tied at the dock on the way over here."

Abby thought he had left yesterday. Finding out he hadn't turned her sorrow into anger. She had hoped her plea would matter, that with time to think about it things might be different when he returned but apparently it was not to be if he would rather spend the night on his ship when he could have been with her. She knew her place - his ship, then her.

Tria was sure if Jason were here he would suggest they do something reasonable, like going to the marshal anyway, but Tria had another agenda in mind. Her smile spread. The more she thought about it the more she liked her idea. "This is the answer to your problem, Abby."

Abby looked at her questioningly.

"You need Max to stop ignoring you and Max needs to know what Talmage is planning. Do something bold, Abby. Go to him."

"I could not." He was angry with her for attempting the same thing a few days ago. What kind of reception would he give her if she angered him again for the same reason? He didn't want to spend the night at home after the first time. Would he kick her off the ship?

Still they had to do something about Talmage. If she couldn't go to the sheriff or the marshal she would have to go to Max. Was it worth the risk of another rejection?

Chapter 28

"Go to him," encouraged Victoria. "Get yourself on his ship, preferably for a few days and then play hard to get. You need to hold yourself aloof. You are simply there to share information, not yourself. Show no emotional interest on your part. Then, and you will know when, give him a look but make it quick so he wonders if he saw it at all."

Abby shook her head. "I do not think I could do that. I wear my emotions on my sleeve. Besides he got really angry the last time I was determined to go after him."

Sagely, Tria said, "This time you have a practical reason, not just an emotional one. Men really don't like emotions. They're complicated and they get in the way."

Abby thought there was some sense in what Tria said and besides she didn't have a better idea. "All right, Maria and I will go to his ship and tell Max but I still think we need to tell the marshal too." Abby stood up from the desk, holding the paper. "Let me retrieve my hat and gloves and we will leave directly."

They promptly left the house, Tria's maid included, and walked two by two down Simonton Street. As they approached Front Street Abby was dismayed to see Captain Talmage standing on the corner, as if waiting for them. She found it amazing on an island so small she hadn't seen him since the court hearing. Praying his appearance was simply a coincidence she tried to act natural; tried not to betray her knowledge of how underhanded this man could operate.

Talmage bowed to them. "Good morning ladies. Lovely day for a walk isn't it?"

Outwardly he projected a gentlemanly demeanor but Abby sensed an underlying malevolence. She hoped it was only the product of her fear and not an indication of his intentions.

Abby was trying to gather her wits to respond when Victoria replied in a carefree manner exaggerating her southern accent. "Why it certainly is, Captain Talmage. Don't we have such lovely tropical weather in the middle of winter? Why back in Charleston I would be shivering in front of the fireplace this time of year instead of enjoying the sunshine and I do so love a warm afternoon stroll. You have a nice day now, Captain Talmage."

Tria nudged Abby who finally found her voice to echo, "Good day, Captain."

Abby saw Talmage sharpen his gaze on Maria standing behind her before they started walking again but he didn't react. If he remembered seeing Maria earlier this morning there was no telling what he might do. They would have to take extra precautions to stay safe.

Tria and Abby tried to sound like they were having a normal conversation with each other as they continued walking towards the wharf. They had passed a few buildings when Maria nervously whispered, "I think he is following us." Tria stopped them in front of the next store window and pretended to point out something of interest to Abby while they were really watching Talmage's reflection in the glass. He was on the other side of the street and had stopped also ostensibly to speak with a sailor.

Tria said, "If Talmage is suspicious maybe it's best if we wait till he's gone for you to go to Max. Let's go into the mercantile and see what he does."

They walked past the next few buildings bringing them past the last warehouse on the other side of the street and finally allowing a view of the dock where Max was usually anchored. Abby discretely looked over and to her dismay discovered the *Mystic* was pulling away from the dock. "Oh no!" Even if she ran now she would not be able to catch him. Abby whispered to Tria, "We have a problem. Max is leaving. We will have to come up with another plan."

They entered the general store and gathered around a front table holding sewing notions where they had a clear view of the street but to an onlooker they appeared to be shopping. The *Mystic* had cleared the dock now, Talmage was casually strolling past the last warehouse and the marshal could be seen coming out of one of the warehouses behind him. The two men stopped to speak to each other.

Tria said, "Now what do we do?"

Abby was working on an idea. "You are sure the marshal would not believe us?"

Tria didn't even hesitate. "I'm sure. Even if he did he is not going to do anything on hearsay."

A fishing smack lay at anchor near the beach beyond the Sweat Box. Recognizing the captain, Abby grabbed Tria's arm and pulled her from the store. "I have a plan."

The ladies left the store *en masse*. Abby intended to make her way directly to the beach to speak to the captain without delay not wanting to risk losing this opportunity. Spying one of Mrs. Mallory's errand boys she changed tactics. Calling him over, she gave him a message for the captain along with a coin. Then as an afterthought she asked to borrow his hat which he generously loaned to her - for the price of another coin - before running off. *Smart lad.* She held the hat out of sight and resumed walking. "We need to see Betsy." Abby refused to tell Tria anything more until they were safely in the seamstress' home.

Betsy greeted them in her front parlour. "What a nice surprise to see you. Welcome."

Abby quickly greeted her friend then asked, "Do you have any ready-made clothes appropriate for a cabin-boy of my size?"

Betsy looked at her questioningly. "I might. I'll go look." A moment later she came back with a shirt, trousers and socks. "Will this do?"

"Yes." Elated, Abby took the clothes from her and rushed to the changing screen set up in the corner of the room used for fittings. She was thankful today her dress buttoned down the front. Not only did it make undressing quicker, as she was in a hurry with no time to spare, but she had a feeling it would come in handy later.

Guessing Abby would be wearing long ones, Betsy held up a pair of short pantaloons. "Will you be needing these as well?"

Abby looked up then reached for the underwear. "Yes, thank you."

As she changed she told them her plan. "Captain Graham owns the smack down by the beach. I sent him a message to not leave until I speak to him of an urgent matter. I stitched up his hand a while back and I am hoping he will still feel grateful enough to take me out to Max's ship. To get past Talmage, I am going to dress as a cabin boy and sneak out the back way to meet Captain Graham. Meanwhile, Betsy, will you help us by leaving with the others so Talmage sees four women leave here?" Betsy nodded in agreement. "That should keep me safe. Maria, I do not think it wise for both of us to try and get to the ship. I fear Talmage may suspect you overheard him so I want you to stay with Tria until I return."

Tria couldn't find any fault with the plan. In fact she was excited as it would most likely mean Max and Abby would be stuck with each other's company for a while. "Sounds good to me. Just be careful getting to the ship. What will you do if Captain Graham won't help?"

Abby emerged from the screen. "I guess I will have to make my way to your house. What do you think? It will not pass a close inspection since I did not bind my chest and I will have to wear my own shoes but will it work from a distance?"

Tria looked her over critically as Abby turned. The shirt was a grey tunic with a string closure at the neck. The short pants revealed her shapely calf muscles. "Your profile gives you away but otherwise, from a distance, you should be fine."

Betsy excused herself and left the room while Abby sat down to put on the socks and her boots.

Maria asked, "What about your hair?"

Abby's hair was in a bun at the base of her neck. She pulled it free and then secured it in a knot on top of her head before putting on the wide brimmed sailor's hat she borrowed from the errand boy. "Well?"

Victoria said, "It will have to do."

Betsy returned with a drawstring sack. "To put your dress and undergarments in and I added some other items you may need." She handed it to Abby then picked up her discarded dress and carefully folded it up. Abby passed the bag to Maria who held it open for Betsy to place the clothes inside.

Abby took Maria's account from her reticule and tucked it into her corset then added the reticule to the sack.

Maria returned the sack to Abby. "Take care, Mrs. Abby. Tell Thomas I'll be safe."

"I will." She turned to Tria. "I hope you are right." Both knew Abby was referring to Tria's earlier advice concerning Max.

"I am. Trust me. Now hurry, a smack is going to have a hard time catching Max's clipper."

Abby hugged each of her friends before leaving out the back door. She walked behind two more houses headed further away from town before crossing Front Street hoping to be far enough away to make it difficult for Talmage to identify her. She circled around behind the abandoned Navy barracks and approached Captain Graham from the opposite direction of the general store. She hadn't seen Talmage but still her heart beat fast in nervousness. She walked up to the captain who was still standing on shore looking around him, presumably for her. "Captain Graham, do you remember me?"

The Captain was startled to realize the approaching boy was not a 'he'. He peered closely at her face. "Mrs. Eatonton? Whatever are you doing in that getup?"

"Captain, I need your help to get to my husband's ship." She nodded her head in the direction of the *Mystic*. She dared not point it out in case Talmage or one of his men could see her. "I can explain on the way but please, I need your help now."

Captain Graham confirmed it was her husband's ship she indicated.

"It is urgent I speak with him immediately. He will not return for weeks. Please. Help me. I helped you with your hand."

"Aye you did lass and a fine job of it too. You're not doing something for which I'll regret helping you?"

Abby shook her head. "Absolutely not, sir."

Captain Graham said, "Very well then, his is a faster ship. I don't know how we'll catch him but hurry miss, into the boat, and we'll give it a try. I'm sorry you'll have to get your feet wet. I'm not a young man who can carry a lady."

Happy she had gotten her way Abby sprinted towards the row boat with two crewmen already aboard waiting to take them out to his ship. She wasn't concerned about getting her shoes wet. Even if he could have carried her it would have ruined her disguise and turning him down would have involved more explanations.

They quickly covered the short distance to the smack. Captain Graham barked out orders as they transferred to his ship. The boat was pulled in quickly. All sails were hoisted and they were underway in no time. Max was halfway across the harbour now. It was going to be hard to catch him - or so she thought. Since they were approaching from behind a signal flag indicating they wanted to talk was not enough. Captain Graham hailed the ship with a trumpet. His amplified voice had Abby looking to shore in fear the sound would alert Talmage. At least the *Mystic* responded. Her sails were immediately doused.

They reached the *Mystic's* port side to be greeted by Jonathon Keats leaning over the bulwarks. Upon seeing Abby's face, he dropped the ladder without question. As she nimbly climbed up the rope rungs, one of the crewmen tossed her clothes bag to Jonathon. Abby was looking down when Max leaned over from a few yards away. "What's this? We may need a cabin boy but I didn't ask for one."

Hearing the humor in his voice, Abby looked up at him in surprise. Max could not believe his eyes and was immediately enraged.

"Abigail?!"

Reaching the top she was emboldened by her unrestrictive clothing to put one leg over the railing. No one came forward to help her. All were immobilized by the rarely heard tone from their Captain.

Max was still reeling from the fact his wife had waylaid his ship when her exposed leg appeared in front of him at eye level followed by her *derrière* as she straddled the railing further suspending all reasonable thought. His crew was waiting to see how he was going to handle the situation. When Abby struggled to get her other leg over he finally returned to his senses and came to her rescue, his face a dark thundercloud of emotion. "What are you doing here and why are you dressed like that?"

Abby disregarded his questions. "I need to speak with you."

"Speak and then you're going back on that boat and back to shore where you belong."

She continued as if he hadn't spoken. "Mr. Keats and Thomas should probably hear as well and do you not think I have inconvenienced Captain Graham long enough. Let him go."

Jonathon, taking advantage of the situation, didn't give Max an opportunity to negate her. He leaned over the rail and thanked Captain Graham for his service and waved him off.

Max clenched his jaw as he addressed his first mate. "I'll deal with you later." He placed a hand in the center of Abby's back and urged her towards the ladder.

Abby pretended there was no anger in his gesture and said over her shoulder "Mr. Keats, Thomas you need to hear what I have to say." The two men followed them.

Max was forced to accept this rather than argue with her in front of the crew. "Buttons, you have the helm. Guide her out of the harbour but leave the sails doused."

Abby froze on the first rung of the ladder. "No! You mustn't let him think something's wrong."

"Who?" asked Max.

"Talmage. You must not do anything suspicious."

Max saw the genuine concern on her face. There was more going on here than Max understood but with Talmage involved he did as she asked. "Belay that order, Buttons." He would not trust anyone other than himself to take his ship past the reefs under sail. This conversation would have to wait. He pointed to the open hatch. "Wait for me down there." Abby opened her mouth to protest so he added, "Don't argue, just go."

Needing his cooperation later she did as he asked now.

Max returned to the helm and resumed their course out of the harbour all the while wondering what Talmage could have done to make Abby waylay his ship in disguise.

Abby paced the deck below Max waiting for his return and praying for the words to convince him of Talmage's threat, words that would allow her to stay onboard and for the courage to find love.

Once they cleared the reefs Max turned the helm over to Buttons and signaled Thomas and Jonathon to go with him below decks. The four of them gathered around the table in the main cabin. Max entered last., looking from Jonathon to Abby he said, "That is the last time you two will undermine my authority in front of the crew." Jonathon started to protest but Max cut him off. "You know what you did and I don't care why." Turning to Abby he said, "Now what is this all about?"

"Maria overheard Talmage and another man planning to wreck a ship on purpose." Seeing Thomas' immediate concerns for his beloved she added for his benefit, "I sent Maria to stay with Miss Lambert. She wanted me to assure you she was safe."

Thomas asked, "Did Talmage see her listening?"

"She wasn't sure but judging from his actions later I believe he may have."

Max said, "Start at the beginning, Abby. What exactly did she hear?"

Abby reached for the paper in her bodice causing all eyes to follow her hand much to her chagrin. Max felt the pull of desire thinking of what lay beneath but pushed it aside. Then, seeing the others had been drawn likewise he cleared his throat dragging their focus to him instead. Abby unfolded the paper and laid it on the table. "I wrote it down so as not to forget the details."

Max picked it up and read it out loud for all of them. Abby filled in the details she had not written. Finishing he asked Thomas and Jonathon about the description of the stranger. "Do either of you recognize him?" Both shook their heads no. Returning to Abby he asked, "What happened then?"

"We debated what to do with the information. Tria was certain the marshal would not help. She saw your ship on the way to our house and suggested we tell you. On the way to the wharf we met Captain Talmage. We wanted him to believe we didn't know anything so we pretended to be shopping. He followed us. At the mercantile we saw you leaving so we went to Betsy's where I got this disguise to get past Talmage. Betsy went with the others to Tria's house so Talmage would still see four women. Meanwhile Captain Graham brought me here."

Max reasoned, "Abby is right. If Talmage doesn't suspect anything we have to act as normal as possible to keep it that way. If he is suspicious we should still act as normal as possible to keep him from worrying about what our actions might be."

Jonathon added, "So we can't return Mrs. Eatonton to the island." He had suggested before Max should allow Abby to spend time on the ship and now circumstances had brought that to pass.

Max gave Jonathon a sour look. "You don't have to look so smug."

Thomas said, "What if he does suspect we know?"

Jonathon said, "It would seem as if Talmage suspected Maria had overheard him and told Mrs. Eatonton which puts both ladies in danger and by extension Victoria and her maid."

Abby grew concerned. "Oh my, I had not thought about them. You do not think he would truly do them harm, do you?"

Max added, "Betsy is the one I'm worried most about. If Maria and Miss Lambert went straight to Miss Lambert's home they should be safe enough. Talmage will be leaving port to get ahead of his prey so the chance they could come to harm isn't likely. If he does anything, he would most likely watch for Betsy to leave Victoria's assuming he believes Betsy to have been you," Max indicated Abby, "which does put Betsy in some danger. He would want to know how much you really know. Hopefully, seeing it is Betsy instead of you, he would not have to question her to piece together that you are on this ship, even if he missed seeing Captain Graham ferry a boy to me. And if he knows you are on this ship, he would assume we are aware of his plans."

Abby asked, "Do you think we could cause enough concern he would change his plans?"

Max considered for a moment before replying. "No. He's arrogant enough to think he could stop our interference. Besides it probably isn't easy to find ships and captains to fall in with his schemes and the more people involved the more difficult it is to change plans."

Thomas said, "We know what he is planning to do. How can we stop him?"

"We don't." They all looked at Max in surprise.

Jonathon said, "We can't just let him get away with it."

Thomas wanted to bring Talmage down before he harmed anyone. "Why can't we tell the marshal?"

Max said, "Tell him what? That we heard second - in our case third hand - Talmage was *going* to do something wrong? It won't work for us anymore than for the women."

Abby said, "Could you not stop the wreck from happening?"

Max said, "We could but he would only do it again. Same if we intervene or beat him to it." Max recalled what the lawyers had told him. "We need to witness the crime. A reliable witness in court can put an end to his misdeeds."

Thomas asked, "How are you going to do that when there is no place to hide? If we can see him, he can see us."

Max said, "Talmage should sail by first. My bet is he will return to his usual anchorage and his normal routine. We'll watch for the *Anna Rose* then follow a few miles off her starboard, just close enough to keep her in sight which should keep us out of sight of Talmage who should be ahead of her. When she changes direction to head into the reef we'll hang back long enough for them to believe the coast is clear. When we do approach hopefully they will be too busy to notice."

Jonathon asked, "If we lay in wait how would we explain it in court? Wouldn't a judge question our motives?"

Max said, "I don't know. We'll have to deal with that when the time comes."

Abby said, "There is something else you should know. He has targeted one of my father's ships."

Max looked at her in surprise. "How do you know it is one of his? There are hundreds of British merchant ships sailing these waters and you don't seem to be the kind of girl who would keep up with the names of all your father's vessels."

"You are right. I know the names of precisely two of his ships. The two he is most proud of; my namesake and the very first one he commissioned to be built according to his wishes. It bears the name of my mother." And then Max understood.

In unison they said, "The *Anna Rose*."

Abby nodded.

Max grew hopeful Abby had knowledge that could make their quarry easier to find. "Do you remember what the ship looks like?"

Abby nodded. "Yes, a painting of it hangs in the library of our home."

Max pushed aside the usual annoyance he felt for the reference to her home in England. "Do you remember how many masts she has?"

Abby focused on the image in her mind. "Three, yes definitely three." Following Tria's advice Abby tried to answer him without emotion but it was hard when he was so focused on her and her answers.

Max continued to question her on the details of the ship. 'What type of sails? Square or fore-n-aft?"

"Square except for the first one"

"White sails?"

"Yes."

"Can you tell us the sail-plan?"

"I don't think so." Abby was not at all confident she could recall how many sails much less how they were laid out nor did she know the sail terms used to describe them. "But I might be able to draw a picture."

"Do you know the captain?"

"Not now. It was Captain Andrews till he was reassigned to the *Abigail Rose*. I don't know any of the other captains in my father's employ."

"Too bad. I would have liked to know what kind of man we were dealing with. Maria said she heard Monday next. I would take that to mean eleven days from now but to be safe I think we should be vigilant this Monday as well. For now we sail for Looe Key. Mr. Keats, relieve Buttons from the helm."

Understanding they were both being dismissed, Thomas and Jonathon headed topside leaving Max and Abby alone.

"You'll have to stay below deck. You can't go around dressed like that in front of the men."

"I have my dress."

"And you can't be seen on deck in a dress until we are clear of the area. So like it or not you must stay out of sight for now."

"Max, I know you do not want me here."

"It's not a matter of wanting you here. It's not safe for you and I don't believe a woman belongs on a wrecking ship." He saw the gathering storm in her eyes and had no idea how to handle it but then it suddenly dissipated leaving him confused.

Abby reined in her emotions knowing they would gain her nothing. Lightly she asked him, "You do not believe women can be sailors?"

"No, I don't."

Teasingly she said, "Then how do you explain Anne Bonney, Mary Read, Grace O'Malley, Jane de Belleville?"

"They were pirates."

Abby said, "Still, they were women and I am sure there have been other women who were not pirates."

Max wasn't going to continue this senseless discourse. "Just stay down here."

Abby watched him climb the ladder leaving her alone. She looked around the room for something to do. The neatly kept main room and galley offered no suggestions. She wandered into Max's cabin. His room was neat and tidy as well with the berth made up. Spying the crate of books she recalled the book of poetry she had not been able to bring herself to read the night she spent on board after the shipwreck. Picking up the book she climbed on the berth to take advantage of the daylight streaming through the open port window and the slight breeze that freshened the stagnant air.

She briefly considered changing back into her dress but the boy's clothes, being much lighter, were more comfortable and she was enjoying the freedom from her layers of clothing. She propped her back against the wall and opened the book skipping the dedication on the front page as it would only make her long for what she didn't have with Max. It did, however, bring a smile to her face as she recalled her mistaken belief it had been written by a wife Max never had.

It wasn't long before she realized she was hungry. It was now late afternoon and she had missed lunch. Climbing off the berth she made her way to the galley to search for something to tide her over until supper. She finally found a tin of crackers which she opened and stuffed one in her mouth and took out two more before replacing the lid. She was in the process of replacing it on the shelf when Thomas, who had quietly descended the ladder, caught her.

"What are you getting into Missy?" asked Thomas while affecting a stern disposition.

Startled, Abby spun around, her mouth full, she tried to finish chewing quickly to answer him.

Thomas waited patiently, suppressing a grin.

Defensively, Abby said, "I was hungry."

"Well then, you can help me prepare supper and we will eat that much faster."

Abby grimaced. "I do not mind helping but be warned I am not much of a hand at cooking."

"Not to worry, just do as I say and you'll not have a problem." First he lit the stove then pulled a pot down from its hook and put it on the stove. "Tonight we have conch chowder." He then retrieved a mallet and tray and walked over to the table where he had deposited a bowl of fresh conch meat upon entered the cabin. He showed Abby how to pound the meat then returned to the galley to start the water heating to make a broth and gathered the vegetables from the hold. Abby's arms ached when she was done with the tenderizing. Thomas then handed her a knife to dice the meat while he prepared the vegetables. They worked in companionable silence except for the occasional direction from Thomas. When they were done he added it to the pot then added seasonings with the occasional request for her to retrieve ingredients.

Although half the size of her outdoor kitchen, the galley was well stocked. Neat and compact, it was carefully designed to make use of every inch of available space including the area between the ribs of the ship and overhead. Thomas was a competent cook and a good teacher. Abby found it easy to work with him. The simmering broth soon filled the room with its rich aroma making Abby's stomach grumble. It was hard to wait until it was ready but the first taste made up for the suffering.

The crew ate in shifts. Max, Buttons and the Tims arrived for the first sitting filling up the table. Max gave her a disapproving look. She assumed it was because she was still wearing boy's clothing. She had expected to eat with her husband but had not considered there would not be room for her at the table. Thomas, Mike, Flynn and Mr. Keats would make up the second sitting and would again fill the table not that it mattered. She would not dine with the men unless her husband was present. Resigning herself to eating alone she was not willing to wait until the others had finished. She filled a bowl and took it to Max's cabin to eat at his desk. She listened to the men in the other room talk of various subjects in comfortable camaraderie. They ate quickly with the second group sitting down to eat long before she had finished her meal. Afterwards she helped Flynn, as it was his turn, to take all the dishes to the scullery for cleaning. She let him do the washing while she offered to dry. She then sent him topside while she put everything back in its place.

Abby watched the sun set from a port hole until it was dark enough to make her appearance less noticeable. She ventured topside in need of fresh air.

The wind was brisk blowing her hair about her face. Max was calling out orders to the men, changing the sails as they crossed into the channel to anchor off Looe Key for the night. Abby found a place against the bulwarks out of the way of the crew. She covertly watched Max but was careful to not let him see, following Tria's advice to ignore him.

Max found his attention kept wandering to his wife's profile. The oversized shirt should have disguised her figure but the wind molded it tightly to her chest recalling to his mind details he was better off not thinking of just now. He knew having her on the ship in close proximity was going to test his ability to keep her at a distance.

Following their usual pattern, after the ship was secured the men gathered on deck to share drink and talk and sometimes gamble. It was no place for a woman but before Max could send Abby below decks Jonathon invited her to join them for music and singing. Thomas had one of the conch shells he had harvested their dinner from and a wooden drum, Flynn retrieved some spoons from the galley, Tim Sudduth played a guitar he won in a poker game with a Spaniard and Jonathon played a harmonica. They sang a wrecker's song for her and together the makeshift band produced a lively sound if not a harmonious one. Abby seemed to enjoy their efforts as she clapped in time to the music.

Not much later, Abby could barely keep her eyes open. The sleepless night combined with the excitement of the day had taken their toll. She excused herself from the group thanking them for their lofty entertainment. Continuing with her plan to ignore Max as much as possible Abby walked past him without a word. She felt his eyes upon her as she passed but when she turned to descend the ladder she found him conversing with Mr. Keats.

Max told Jonathon he would be taking first watch tonight just to be sure Talmage didn't make a late run. They both knew he was really trying to keep his distance from Abby but pretended otherwise. Max rested his forearms on the bulwarks while he let his thoughts wander over all that had happened today. He was confident their plan would work. He expected to see Talmage headed towards Alligator Reef tomorrow having not seen him today. Max would feel better once Talmage passed them and hopefully he would notice they were following their normal pattern. He felt guilty having to keep Abby restricted below deck until Talmage passed but there was no help for it. Once they knew for certain Talmage was headed towards Indian Key and Alligator Reef he planned to return Abby to Key West.

What Max failed to consider was in the three days they would wait for Talmage to pass, Abby would manage to find her way into the workings of his crew.

When Max finally decided to turn in just after midnight he quietly approached his berth not wanting to disturb Abby. He judged her to be asleep by her even breathing and was relieved to find she was lying on her side facing the bulkhead and had left him plenty of room. Lying down on his side with his back to her, he quickly fell asleep.

Abby tensed at the feel of Max climbing into the berth. As she listened to Max's deep and even breathing she congratulated herself on convincing him she was asleep having decided earlier the alternative would not help her campaign to win his heart. She was surprised it didn't take long for her to fall asleep.

Chapter 29

Abby awoke to the strong aroma of coffee and found she was alone in the berth. By the time she donned her boy clothes and made an appearance in the main room the ship was again under sail headed southwest patrolling the reef down to the Sambos near the entrance of Key West harbour. Thomas was working on making breakfast and enthusiastically accepted her help. Partaking of the meal occurred in the same fashion as the previous supper except Abby ate her meal last at the table. She again helped with the cleanup, this time with Buttons. They finished the task just as the ship came about and once again headed northeast returning to the point of their anchorage.

Having nothing else to occupy her below deck, Abby made her first appearance of the day above deck. Max was at the bow discussing something with Buttons. One of the Tim's had the helm. Mr. Keats was hunched over a sail affecting repairs. Wanting something to do Abby joined Mr. Keats taking a crossed leg seated position on the deck next to him thereby making herself invisible to any ship passing by in the hopes Max would not object to her presence. "Good morning Mr. Keats."

"Good morning Mrs. Eatonton."

"Please, call me Abby. May I have your leave to call you Jonathon?"

"As you wish, Mrs. Abby." He barely lifted his head from the careful work he was doing to repair a tear to one of the reinforced holes through which the lines run.

"Is that something you could teach me? I have a wish to be useful."

Jonathon considered her request. "Are you handy with a needle?"

"Captain Graham would attest that I am the handiest he has ever seen."

Jonathon's curiosity was piqued. "When did he have cause to witness your skills?"

"When he needed me to stitch his palm back together after having it sliced open by a fishing hook."

Jonathon grimaced at the painful thought of what the captain must have suffered from such an incident while his respect for Abby grew. "You'll do. He handed her a needle and thread covered in beeswax and pointed to another tear in the same sail. He showed her the technique for repairing the tear which she intuitively picked up. They worked in silence for a few moments.

She covertly watched Max as she worked. He had noticed her but had not gainsaid her presence. He was instructing Tim at the helm and she noticed how he felt at home on the sea. Watching him from her location on the deck she realized his demeanor was completely different, more relaxed. He belonged here and it showed. This was the man she had first been attracted to only now, loving him as she did, the attraction was tenfold. She lowered her head to her task lest he catch her watching him.

Jonathon noticed her need for a distraction and thought to take advantage of a rare opportunity for him to get some insight to his own problem. "What is the best way to a woman's heart?"

Abby looked to Jonathon's face in surprise. "Why do you ask?"

"There's a girl... I'm having trouble..." Jonathon struggled for a manly way to state his problem.

Abby took pity on him. "Max mentioned you were interested in a Cuban girl."

Jonathon nodded, "Esperanza Sanchez."

His face lit up at the mere mention of her name leading Abby to conclude it was more than mere interest on his part. "And you are having trouble courting her."

"Yes. Her family is very strict. Her father has become unreasonable and she won't disobey him." They continued to work as they talked.

Abby asked, "Have you met her father?"

"Not directly."

"So you have been seeing her without his approval?" Jonathon gave a sheepish not. "Instead of working around her father you need to work with him. Meet him on his terms. It may sound funny but you should court her father. Once you have him on your side courting her will be much easier."

"Her father does not speak English."

"And you have not bothered to learn their language or their customs. It shows a lack of interest in her family so they would not consider your intentions to be honourable. Show her father you are serious. To him it probably seems as if you are trying to steal his daughter and you have to admit the current public perception of salvagers does not help your image. From what I have seen, Cubans are hardworking people. If you put in the effort to take the relationship seriously they will respect you for it. Do you know anyone other than her who can teach you the language? Definitely not female unless maybe her mother."

"No. Her friends have not been welcoming."

Abby nodded. "Of course not. You are trying to take one of their own." Abby's face brightened as she was struck with an idea. "Max needs another cabin boy, does he not?"

Jonathon was at a loss as to how a cabin boy was relevant to his problem. "Yes."

"Maybe you can lean him towards a Cuban boy who could teach you the language."

Jonathon nodded. "What a great idea!"

"When was the last time you saw her?"

Jonathon grimaced. "Not since before your marriage. Her father forbid it because of...," Jonathon broke off afraid of offending Abby by reminding her of her own conduct.

"Because…" Abby prompted and then patiently waited for him to continue.

"He heard about you and Max out late and unchaperoned before your marriage and he was afraid I would treat his daughter the same."

"Did you condone our behaviour?"

"No."

"Then you will have to make him aware of that and besides we are married now, maybe it will help."

Jonathon considered her words. "Maybe it will. Thank you. You've given me back some hope."

Abby smiled at him. "You are welcome."

They continued to work together silently, each wrapped in their own thoughts. Abby was struck by the novelty of her unladylike situation. Here she was sitting cross-legged, in trousers, on the deck of a ship, giving advice to a man, learning manual labor and relishing every minute of the freedom it afforded her. Men had no idea how hard it was to wear a skirt - literally and figuratively.

Max was impressed. Abby was being helpful and staying out of sight. He was relaxing his opinion and starting to think it might not be as bad as he thought having a woman on board, until he caught sight of the genuine smile she sent in Jonathon's direction. It had been months since he had seen that look on her face directed towards him. The beauty of it constricted his breathing and had him staring at her like a love sick fool. It took Thomas' call of 'Sail ho' to break the spell. Taking up the spyglass he peered at the ship passing by only to be disappointed once again it was not either of the ships they were seeking.

They sailed past their anchorage until they came in line with Bahia Honda Key whereupon Max reversed their course once again returning to their anchorage off Looe Key. On the return run, Fish dropped a hook overboard to troll for dinner. It wasn't long before a four foot cobia was on the line. Abby watched in amazement as he carefully worked the line to bring the fish in. Max had the sails luffed to slow the ship while Thomas helped Fish pull it onboard. It was large enough to feed them all.

Thomas grinned as he approached Abby with a wicked looking knife. "You clean."

Abby looked at him in horror. "I do not know how."

Thomas insisted she take the knife from him. "I'll teach you."

They approached the men attempting to hold the still writhing fish. Thomas plunged his knife into the head of their dinner ending the battle. The men resumed their duties while she and Thomas cleaned the fish on deck and washed the remains overboard. They took the fillets to the galley where they were seared in a pan and served with a spicy mango glaze. Abby enjoyed the flaky white fish with its mild buttery flavor. The only mar to the meal was she again ate alone.

Twice during the afternoon sails were spotted but still no Talmage. Abby spent the afternoon learning how to tie knots from Fish in the shade of a spare sail Max had ordered set up for her. Some of the other crew had taken the longboat and sailed over to a nearby key to resupply the fresh water. It was one of only a few keys where fresh water could be obtained.

This seemed to be the pattern of a wrecker's day. Patrol the reef in the morning while the afternoon was spent doing ship's maintenance and recreational activities. She asked Fish for confirmation. "Is this all you do? Play and wait for the next wreck?"

"Yes mum. Unless a storm brews up then it's all hands to sail."

She had pictured Max working much harder than this while he had been away from her. Though she supposed when they did work it was with great effort.

Over the course of the remaining day and the next, Abby had many lessons. She tried her hand at braiding rope and helped Mike with dressing down the sails which was treating old sails with oil or wax to renew them. Thomas showed her how to make noise with a conch shell. She discovered that Buttons, in his spare time, liked to carve intricate buttons from buttonwood thoroughly explaining how he had gotten his moniker. He generously offered to make her a set with the *Mystic* carved on them. During these lessons she often found herself giving advice on love to many while wishing she could ask them for the same.

She had been studiously ignoring Max in the hopes of bringing him to her but there seemed to be no change in his demeanor. They were still avoiding each other by day and each night was the same as the first. She still wore the shirt and pantaloons procured from Betsy and although Max had said nothing more whenever she chanced to be near him she could tell he still disapproved but was forced to accept the situation.

Max's normally even keel was greatly disturbed. At first it irritatingly seemed as if everywhere he turned he would find his wife engaged with one of his crew talking, laughing, learning. Now he found himself looking for her whenever she wasn't near. He wished he could have returned his unwanted passenger to harbour. It was the interminable waiting that could get under one's skin. He couldn't admit it was jealousy for every smile she gave his crew while none came his way.

Tired of the pent up tension her presence was causing, Max sought out his diver. "Let's go Thomas. Time for another swim."

Thomas grinned. "Are you challenging me again?"

"Yes, I am."

Thomas shook his head. "You trying to impress your woman? No good. You know I beat you every time."

Max ignored his goading.

They both removed their shirts and boots then stood facing each other. The rest of the crew getting wind of the game afoot gathered round. Jonathon tossed a lead weight overboard. Thomas and Max watched its trajectory then, at a nod from Jonathon, they both ran to the bulwarks, leaped to the railing and dove in the water in simultaneous motion.

Abby had been watching the proceedings with curiosity from the other side of the ship until they dove off the railing. Curiosity fled, replaced by fear of sharks and coral. She pushed her way through the other crewmen to reach the bulwark from which Max had disappeared. She leaned over to see the two men going deeper under the water. Thomas was easy to see. His skin contrasted well with the sand and coral. Max was next to him. They swam through an abundance of small fish. She did not see any large enough to bring them harm. She turned to Jonathon, "How deep is the water?"

Jonathon saw the fear in her eyes. "Not deep. Maybe six fathoms. Don't fret they've both worked wrecks much deeper."

His words did not soothe her. She turned back to the water and watched as they kicked off the sandy bottom between the coral to return to air. Breaking the surface they both shook their heads clearing the water from their faces. Thomas held the weight aloft and the men cheered.

Thomas looked to Max, "I told you it was no good."

Max saw Abby at the railing. He wasn't going to give up so easy. "I propose a new game. From here we dive down, touch bottom just below that large elkhorn coral and race back to the surface. On my mark..." They both took a few deep breaths before Max signaled to dive.

It was close but Thomas won again. Then Max challenged him to see who could stay down the longest. Abby's nerves stretched taught as she watched the two men go down again and sit on the bottom for what seemed to her an eternity. She continually scanned the area for sharks and waited. She nearly smiled to see Max give way to the surface followed by Thomas. Not wanting to encourage them anymore she turned and chased the men away from the scene. "Enough of this." Knowing Jonathon would keep watch she retreated below decks. She was relieved to hear the contestants climbing the rope to reboard the ship.

Back on deck Thomas turned to Max, "I told you it would not impress your lady."

Jonathon shook his head at them. "Oh it made an impression. Scared the wits out of her. She chased the men away to put an end to the game."

Max felt remorse for causing Abby unnecessary fear but did not regret his actions. Much of his tension was now replaced with rushing adrenaline making him feel better. Besides it proved his point to Jonathon. If she couldn't handle a little sport she would not be able to watch them work a wreck.

Sunday, January 17th

After anchoring from the morning's run on the reef, Abby was leaning on the railing watching a pod of porpoises playing nearby. No longer able to resist, Max wanted one of her smiles directed at him. He approached her with spyglass in hand. After scanning along the horizon for sails he leaned over the railing as well. Indicating the frolicking mammals he said, "Looks like fun, doesn't it?" He was disappointed when she didn't look at him, only nodded her head in agreement.

Abby was trying to figure out what she should do next. Finally, he had sought her out. She tried to recall Tria's instructions but she was so giddy it was difficult to think. Wanting to keep him guessing she decided to act friendly and to keep the exchange light which meant ignoring the excitement flowing through her veins just from his nearness. Tria said to frustrate him with desire but for the life of her she didn't know how to do that so she settled on treating him like any of the other men. Turning to her husband she decided to question his wrecking experiences. "What was the most unusual wreck found in the keys?"

Max basked in the curious smile she bestowed on him before bringing his mind around to the question. A strange question but he played along wanting more of her company. "That would probably be the *Spermo*. In 1827 she ran aground on Alligator Reef. I wasn't involved in the salvage but I was on the dock when they opened a bundle wrapped in many layers of cloth. It smelled awful. Someone with a stronger stomach than I unwrapped it to expose a human skeleton. It was later determined to be an Egyptian mummy but it smelled so bad they had to burn it and the wrecker got nothing for his troubles.

"Did you know several reefs are named for wrecks that have occurred upon them? The U.S. anti-piracy schooner *Alligator* wrecked on that same reef in 1822 giving it its name." He was gratified when his knowledge earned him another of her coveted smile.

"No, I was not aware of that. What was the most dangerous wreck you've worked?"

"Probably the cotton ship right after we were married. Getting caught under a 1600 pound bale of water logged cotton could kill a man."

His answer startled Abby and brought to mind all her worried prayers those weeks he was gone. "And what was the worst wreck?"

"For me personally, it was the last one, losing Billy, but for the Keys I would have to say the Spanish brig *Guerrero*, because the cargo was not goods but over five hundred African slaves. Just over a year ago, December 1827, she grounded in the upper keys along with a British man-of-war that had been chasing her. Five wreckers were involved in salvaging both wrecks. The British ship was pulled off the reef. Some of the slaves drowned in the initial wreck of the brig. Three hundred slaves ended up in Cuba because two of the wrecking vessels were overtaken by the Spaniards. The *Surprize* brought a hundred and twenty slaves, some of them children, to Key West where they were housed in the Sweat Box in terrible, cramped conditions."

Abby was horrified, "I can imagine. There is hardly enough space in the building for ten men to sleep."

Max nodded in agreement, "Six more died. Attempts were made by a few on the island to free them while others wanted to steal them for personal gain. A rumor reached Key West that a Cuban group was planning to retrieve them so cannons were placed in the streets for defense. Some of the citizens were concerned for the slaves and did their best to take care of them. Needless to say it was a stressful three months for the prisoners and for the Marshal before they were finally transported to St. Augustine last March."

"Where are they now, the ones who were transferred to St. Augustine?"

Max shook his head. "I don't know. They may still be there. Last I heard the President had been petitioned because the slaves were in a legal limbo. The laws governing the illegal slave trade did not apply to them as they were here by shipwreck."

Their conversation was interrupted by Fish asking Abby if she was ready for her rope lesson. Considering how chaffed her hands were from all she had done over the last few days she would have liked to decline but she needed to put some distance between her and Max and the emotionally charged conversation they were having. Abby followed Fish to her place in the shade of the sail. Besides she wanted to show Max she could be useful.

Max watched her leave with mixed emotions. He was attempting to sort them out when a call from above interrupted.

"Sail ho."

Max automatically raised his spyglass and scanned the horizon in the direction one of the twins indicated. Finding his target, his attention focused when it proved to be Talmage. This being Sunday he hoped they would find the *Anna Rose* sailing past tomorrow. After the conversation he just had with Abby the thought came with a small pang of regret that her sojourn on his ship may soon come to an end. He was surprised how quickly he had grown used to her presence. She was fitting in well on the ship. So far, he was the only being distracted from his duty.

By now the whole crew was aware of their mission. They gave a jubilant shout at his announcement the sails belonged to Talmage. He searched the deck for Abby wanting to share the moment with her only to see her head disappear below decks. The next time he saw her she was wearing her dress. It was not the improvement he had hoped. While certain areas of her person were more covered, as was his reason for wanting her to change, other aspects were now more enhanced recalling to his mind the activities of married life he much enjoyed and had been denying himself for far too long. Abby walked past him seemingly unaware of his attention. Max did his best to behave likewise.

He failed.

He wanted her attention. He wanted her smiles, her secrets, her laughter and her affection. The aloofness she gave him was maddening. The woman was slipping under his guard. He desperately tried to recall why it was a good idea to keep her at a distance because all he wanted was to get her close, preferable in private. But then, there was precious little privacy on a ship.

He spent the night on deck dozing fitfully rather than put himself through the torture of lying next to her again, wanting her when she showed no indication of wanting him.

Monday morning they sailed down to the Sambos and anchored in the hopes of better catching the *Anna Rose*. Several hands kept a constant vigilant watch rotating as each would tire of the task. But all was for naught. The day faded without sign of their prey. Max contemplated sailing into Key West for news of the ship but not wanting to take the risk of alerting Talmage's cronies of his interest he decided against it. They would now have to wait another week. Max decided to remain anchored overnight with the intention of returning to Looe Key the following morning.

Again, Max made up a pallet on deck after his watch rather than disturb Abby. Several of his men were asleep in hammocks strung from the rigging but sleep eluded him. He gazed at the stars while thoughts of Abby kept circling in his mind.

He should take her back to Key West. It was his intention from the first. She was after all a distraction. But he was hesitating. He told himself it was because her return may alert Talmage and could somehow put her in danger but the truth was much harder for him to acknowledge.

He wanted her close.

But she was holding him at a distance.

She had been emotionally aloof ever since she boarded the ship. At first, he had attributed it to the seriousness of the situation that brought her to him but as the days passed he realized there was something else going on between them. She never sought him out and some days it even seemed as if she was avoiding him. Why? What had he done to cause her withdrawal?

The answer struck him like lightening. He had done the same to her. From the very beginning he had withheld himself from her to protect his heart from pain. Her aloofness was hurting him. His must have hurt her in the same way; to the point she was now the one trying to protect her heart.

He thought back to the beginning, before their marriage, and how open she had been with him. Doing something fun certainly helped keep their interaction lighthearted but even so he felt the emotional connection with her. After they were married it was still there despite the strain between them. But like an untended fire, the flames had gone out leaving smoldering ashes.

Could he rekindle her emotions? How?

The answer was simple. He needed her to interact with him the way she did at the beginning. Maybe he needed to woo his own wife. To salvage his relationship he would have to use some romance which meant allowing her past his defenses.

Could he risk his heart?

How could he not?

The deterioration of their relationship would be worse than if he lost her. Loving her was no longer a choice but a necessity.

Max fell asleep contemplating ideas to win over his wife's affection.

Chapter 30

While enjoying his morning coffee and watching the sunrise Max thought of something that would please Abby as well as the rest of his crew. It would give them all a well-deserved respite from the stress of constant vigilance. He deemed the risk of the *Anna Rose* running past them today to be negligible allowing them time for a detour. Max took the helm when they set sail waiting to reveal his surprise until they were closer to the area.

He hoped his idea would bring about the desired change to their marital relationship. When Abby appeared above decks after cleaning up breakfast Max pointed to their destination, "Look. Do you recognize it?"

Abby looked to where he indicated then returned her gaze to his, a brilliant excited smile across her face just for his pleasure. "Flamingo Key."

Max's heart took a leap. So far, his plan was working better than expected. "Aye, it is. Would you care for a bath?"

Abby's excitement grew thickening her English accent and spearing Max's chest with pleasure. "Oh! I would dearly love one. My clothes could stand a washing too. But what would I wear back?"

Max laughed, enjoying her practical nature. "I will loan you something of mine. Hurry and gather your things, your transport awaits."

Max laid out his plan for Jonathon. "Abby and I will go ashore alone. When we return you and all of the men can enjoy your liberty for as long as you like today."

Jonathon nodded in whole-hearted agreement, "Aye, Captain." He then turned and sought out Thomas.

Max rowed Abby to the little island in the longboat while unbeknownst to them Thomas and Jonathon made further preparations for the afternoon.

Abby was so excited she couldn't contain herself. As Max rowed she looked all around admiring the azure sky, the clear water and colourful fish under the boat, the *Mystic* growing distant as Max pulled away with sure strokes of the oars. Her dancing eyes alighted on his face and found an answering smile from him. She felt as giddy as a school girl on Christmas morn and then suddenly as nervous as the day he returned from the cotton ship. It had been a long time since she had felt all of his charm focused on her.

The boat ran up on the shore. Max stowed the oars then cleared the side, landing in the water. He reached for her. She put her arms around his neck while holding her sack filled with their clean clothes. He scooped her up and carried her to dry ground. Her breath grew faint to be in such close proximity, cradled in his arms. Her mouth grew dry considering what may happen next. He put her on her feet and then pulled the boat higher aground before leading the way inland.

Reaching the pond, Max gestured her ahead of him. "Go ahead and take your bath. I'll stand lookout." He turned his back on her. The last thing Abby had expected was for him to act so... so gentlemanly. Disappointed, she pulled her clothes off with jerky movements of frustration. She had thought they were finally connecting. Entering the water she was determined to enjoy the blissful bath despite her irritation. She found some soap aboard ship and made good use of it, washing first herself and then both her outfits. She emerged from the water and sunned herself for a moment while hanging her wet clothes to dry on the vegetation before donning her borrowed clothes from Max. She was hopelessly swimming in his shirt and pants being larger than the ones from Betsy. She called to Max to let him know she was finished. He appeared from a short distance away. He eyed her attire but said nothing. When Abby started towards the bushes to give him the same privacy, he said, "Stay here. There may be snakes about."

Abby froze where she was unsure if she should keep her back to him which could be considered impolite or turn around which could be presuming too much. "Hang it all!" she muttered to herself and turned around to find him still undressing. "Max Eatonton just what are you playing at?"

"Not playing at all although I had hoped you would ask me to join you. I did not want to presume too much." His shirt and shoes were off and he was reaching for the closure on his pants. He wondered if she would turn around.

Abby couldn't believe they had been at such cross purposes. "I expected you to join me. You are my husband. I was starting to believe you didn't want me anymore the way you kept pushing me away." Looking at him now, completely undressed, there was no doubt he wanted her at least in one way. He turned and walked into the water. She contemplated following him but he sensed it. "No sense getting wet all over again. I'll be done in a wink and we can go back to the ship and discuss this rationally."

Abby didn't want to wait. She wanted to run into his arms this minute but she shook the thought from her head and turned her back on him the better to regain her composure. She tormented herself with thoughts of what could have happened if she had invited him to join her. She listened to the sounds of the water as he washed himself and his clothes. She heard the splash of water from each footstep and his light tread upon the shore. Out of the corner of her eye she saw him do the same as her, hanging his wet clothes on nearby branches and pulling on dry clothes. She startled at the feel of his hand on her shoulder. "Are you ready to leave?"

Mutely Abby nodded her agreement. He was acting so matter of fact she started to fear she had overplayed her hand and was now quite embarrassed by her admission. Maybe he didn't feel the same way she did. They gathered their wet clothes and walked back to the longboat in silence. The silence continued all the way back to the ship. Jonathon assisted Abby over the railing before moving aside to allow Max to board.

Thomas said, "I left some food in the galley for you when you get hungry." Then he dropped over the side, sliding down a rope and into the boat. The men loaded several crates containing rum, cigars and the makings of their supper before they all piled in leaving the ship empty save for Max and Abby.

She looked to her husband waiting for an indication of what he would do next. Butterflies of nervousness nearly made her sick to her stomach.

Max asked, "Are you hungry?"

Abby convulsively swallowed. "No." She sucked her bottom lip in and clenched it between her teeth. And waited.

Max saw her nervousness, felt her anxiety. It mirrored his own. He had caught a glimpse of her as she entered the pool earlier and it had shattered his defenses. He wanted her; body, heart, mind and soul. He not only wanted to be with her in the physical sense but he wanted to be joined to her spiritually as well. Her aloofness of the last few days had finally made him understand what he had been denying her, what he had been denying them both. She wanted to share his life and he now knew he wanted to share hers.

He took the two steps needed to bring them together. His right hand went under her still damp hair while the thumb caressed her soft cheek and he tilted her head to the proper angle. His left hand circled her waist bringing her flush with his torso as his head descended. Their lips met and opened and finding the same desire within each other the kiss took on a life of its own. He kissed her until the world faded away and desire swelled to overwhelming need.

Neither of them heard the crew's cheer from the boat.

Several minutes later, surfacing for breath, Max said, "I have missed kissing you." He didn't give her a chance to respond.

Much later they sat across from each other at the table. They couldn't help smiling at each other as they shared the food Thomas had left them.

Abby asked, "Did you always want to be a captain?"

Max thought back to his boyhood. "From the time I boarded this ship I did but I don't recall before then what I wanted to be when I grew up. What about you? Did you have any dreams?"

Abby fed him a piece of fruit. "I wanted to join a ballet."

"Really?"

Abby's mouth quirked, "Until I tried to stand on my toes. And decided it was too painful. Next I think I wanted to be a gypsy. Then I wanted to be the Queen but there are rules about that. Then I wanted to run away with the circus but in the end I never wanted to do anything that would take me away from my father. Until you."

"You really wanted to marry me?" Max was nervous waiting for her answer.

"Yes. I was so enamoured by you. Even though you were coerced and upset about it I went along." She paused for courage then laid her heart on the table. "I overheard my father threaten to take the ship away from you. I know how much this ship means to you and I am sorry he did that."

Max shook his head in wonder. "You were mistaken. It wasn't the ship; it was you he threatened to take away."

Abby was incredulous. "You wanted to marry me from the first?" All this time she had been wrong. He wanted her from the beginning.

"Yes, you silly girl." He stood up, leaned over the table and kissed her lips, tasting the lingering orange juice.

Abigail's heart swelled with joy. She could no longer hold back the words. She looked up at her husband's face hovering over hers. "I love you."

He smiled his boyishly dimpled smile that always took her breath away, "I love you too, Abigail." He had been sitting across from her in order to see her lovely face but no longer able to withstand the table between them he moved around to her side and pulled her into his arms. He couldn't help repeating his declaration before kissing her again. "I love you."

Abby allowed herself to melt into his embrace and drown in his kiss. She felt engulfed with the emotions flowing between them. It was all she had dreamed it would be and more.

When Max finally pulled away from her he led her up to the main deck to sit on the hatch where she could nestle between his thighs and lean back against him. His arms circled around her, holding her secure in his warmth. Silently they watched the birds flying over the trees in the distance and enjoyed the late afternoon sun and the coolness of the salty breeze.

Abby grew thoughtful. "I still know so little about you. I do not even know your birthday."

"November twenty-eighth."

"You let me miss your birthday? Why did you not tell me?"

"If you recall, I was busy working a cotton salvage at the time."

"Oh yes."

When she didn't offer, Max realized he was going to have to ask, "And when is yours?"

Abby gave a self-deprecating laugh in embarrassment. "July fifteenth."

"I will have to think of something special to celebrate it."

"Max, can I ask you something?"

Hearing the serious tone, he shifted so he could see her face. "Always."

"Why were you fighting your feelings?"

He shifted again, resting his chin against her head and was silent for so long she began to wonder if he would answer her.

"I have lost so many in my life I cared about. On some level I knew losing you would be devastating and I wanted to believe if I didn't let myself care then I couldn't get hurt. Only I've learned it doesn't work that way."

"Is that why you kept pushing me away?"

His arms tightened their hold. "It was. I was trying to protect my heart. But

I have discovered loving is worth the risk, because of you."

"Can I tell you something without you getting angry?"

He pressed a kiss to the side of her head. "I promise to try not to get angry."

"Our marriage so far has made me feel...,"

Abby hesitated, "restrained."

"Hindered?" Max asked at the same time.

Abby said, "No. Restrained. I wanted a husband who would let me have a say in things that affect my life, like deciding where we should live. I hoped for someone who would make plans with me rather than forcing me to find out in the moment that decisions had already been made for me."

Understanding dawned on Max. It explained her anger and disappointment towards the rental house and the packed bag waiting by the door. "I will keep that in mind, going forward. I'm so used to being the one in charge I didn't realize I was taking something away from you."

Abby felt the need to explain. "It is just that I have been allowed to make my own decisions for a long time now. I do not think I could give it up."

Max nodded. "I can appreciate how you feel and I'll do my best to consult with you on anything that does not involve this ship."

She leaned back and smiled. "Thank you." Remembering his word, she frowned. "Have you felt hindered by our marriage?" Max's head rubbed against the side of hers as he nodded.

"I've had to consider you and your father in every move I've made. Plus when I am away, I feel guilty for being out on the reef instead of with you. When I am home, I feel out of place, like I don't belong and I worry about to not being on the reef earning money."

"Those are things we'll have to find a way to work through, together. But I promise to be more sensitive to your needs."

"And I as well." He lifted her hand to his lips pressing a promise kiss on her wedding band. "Abby, would you want me to work for you father, behind a desk, home every night?" He held his breath waiting for her answer having just given her the power to make his life miserable.

Abby recalled his vehemence in the mercantile when he had told her about her father's alternative to put him in an office. "Only if it was what you wanted too." Her answer earned her another kiss. "Max." She hesitated to ask her question. The answer meant too much. Taking a leap of faith in him she said, "Healing people brings me such joy and purpose. Would you mind so much if I continued doing so? It may mean sometimes I am not at home when you are or I could be called away from you but it gives me something to do when you are not at home and it satisfies my need to be useful. I am not one of those wives who can sit contentedly at home waiting for her husband to return."

"I can see where waiting at home alone for me is a problem but what about when we have children? Would they not be enough to content you to stay home?"

Abby's smile turned soft at the thought of children. She wanted them with all her heart. A little boy, just like Max, with curly golden hair. "They would be enough for me and maybe by then there will be others on the island to tend to the sick and injured. But if not, if I am needed, Max I would have to offer help. I could not turn my back on others."

Max sighed, "I know. We'll find a way to make it work for our family."

Abby kissed him. "Thank you for understanding."

Abby nestled into his back again.

After fighting with himself for several moments, Max couldn't put it aside. He could no longer pretend he didn't want to know. He finally asked her the question that had plagued him for some time, "Have you ever kissed Lord Fop?" When she turned her head to look at him in confusion he added, "You said you had kissed others that night on the beach. I want to know if he was your first kiss?"

It was the first Abby had heard his nickname for Jason so it took a moment to figure out who he was referring to then the indignity of the question struck her. She didn't want to answer him at all but he kept pressing her. She stood up and moved away from him. "No, and that is all I am going to say."

Max stood as well and moved towards her. "No, you have never kissed him or no, he wasn't your first?" Abby stepped backwards then turned and playfully moved away from him. Max gave chase as she circled around the deck.

Moving faster she said over her shoulder, "You asked if he was my first."

"Then you have kissed him?"

Abby picked up her skirts to move faster away from him.

Max called after her, "Now who's running Princess Thorn?"

She tossed him a falsely irritated look over her shoulder.

Max changed direction to cut her off on the other side of the mast. Catching her by surprise he swung her up in his arms. She let out a squeal of laughter then kissed his dimpled smile. Max pulled back. "You didn't answer the question."

"I am not going to dignify that question with an answer."

"Then I shall ask another."

She kissed him deeply in the hopes of kissing him senseless before he could think of any more embarrassing questions. The sound of the returning crew brought an end to their play. Max gently let her feet slip to the deck and released her from his embrace.

That evening the men settled on the deck with their instruments playing lively music. Abby tapped her toes as she leaned against Max as he leaned against the helm. A waxing moon shone overhead and the sky was clear. The ship rocked gently against her anchor. The men were passing around another bottle of rum. When it came to Abby she had intended to hand it off to Max but feeling the urge to be adventuresome she took a healthy swig and sputtered much to the delight of the crew. She laughed at herself as she wiped her mouth and passed the bottle to Max then looked over her shoulder to see his reaction in the hopes she had not displeased him. She was relieved to find acceptance in his eyes. She sputtered less with each successive round of the bottle. The rum warmed her insides and mellowed her mind.

The men started a hauntingly sweet melody. Max pushed away from the helm and held out his hand to her. "Dance with me."

It was as much a command as it was a request. She wasn't sure how she wanted to respond at first so she offered a feeble protest, "There is not enough room."

He countered with, "There's plenty of room."

She understood his meaning. They would not be doing a ballroom cotillion nor even a formal waltz but more like two lovers close together moving in rhythm. She tried to hide how the idea affected her from the watchful eyes of the crew. Shyly she accepted his hand and was pulled into his arms. He tucked her head under his chin and she melted in his embrace, her left hand in his right, she was vaguely aware he was caressing her wedding ring. He had finally opened his heart to her. She felt as if she had finally come home. In his arms, was where she wanted to spend the rest of her life. She snuggled closer into the nape of his neck and closed her eyes. Time seemed to drift away.

The rum, the swaying ship and the music combined to make her drowsy. As if from a distance she heard Max whisper, "I love you." Then she felt as if she were floating.

Max lifted his sleepy wife off her feet. He ignored the snickers of the men as he turned to take her to his cabin. Reaching the hatch Max said, "Sweetheart, hold on tight." Her arms tightened around his neck and warmth spread through his chest from the feelings she evoked.

Abby's last coherent thought was, "A perfect day," which she happened to whisper in her husband's ear as he carried her to bed.

Chapter 31

Over the course of the next five days, the pattern was much the same as the first four with the exception of Max and Abby's behaviour towards each other. Every free moment was spent in each other's company. Talking out past hurts, learning new things about each other, or doing what lovers do in those moments of privacy. It was an idyllic time for both of them but as always happens time brings an end sooner than one would wish and all too soon it was Monday again.

They arrived at the Sambo reefs before dawn on January 26th and again set up watch for the *Anna Rose*. Max and Abby stood together at the railing enjoying the colours of sunrise play across the sky. It looked to be another beautiful day.

As the last star faded in the morning light Max said, "My mother used to tell me a story about the seashells. Would you like to hear it?"

Abby tucked her arm into his and leaned closer, "Yes." She had been right before, what she and Max shared now was so much more than she had dreamed it could be. He was everything she had ever wanted in a husband and so much more. She felt truly blessed.

Max kissed the top of Abby's head and shifted her back to his chest, embracing her. He had never felt joy like he did now with her in his arms. He felt the kind of love that could last a lifetime. A reciprocal bond between them more precious than any treasure on earth and he thanked God for blessing him with her. He held her a little tighter then shared his most treasured childhood memory with her.

"A short time after God had created the world the angels of heaven, having heard so much about it, wanted to see for themselves the wonder of it, so they poked holes in the floor of heaven to view his creation. The pieces of heaven fell to Earth. The bits that fell on land disappeared, absorbed by the ground, but where they fell in the oceans they became sea shells. Some are black as night, others as white as the clouds, but many have the colours of the sunrise and the sunset. When God saw what the angels had done he chose as their punishment the responsibility of always watching over us. We see those holes as heavenly stars."

Abby leaned her head back to look at him, "That is a sweet story but what about the blue sky? I have never seen a blue shell."

"Ah, my ever sensible Abby. The blue ones cannot be seen because the water is blue." Wistfully Max added, "She told me that story shortly before she died. As a boy I often hoped she was looking down from one of those stars and watching over me. I needed to believe distance did not matter when it came to a mother's love."

Abby smiled in wonderment. "I am married to a romantic."

Max hid his blush by kissing her nose. Although he wanted to protest her declaration, he found it mattered more that he not disappoint her.

The *Mystic's* watch paid off a quarter of an hour later when a ship was spotted flying a British flag fitting the description Abby had given them. Max handed Abby the spyglass to confirm.

She carefully studied the ship under full sail a few miles away before turning to Max. "It looks like her."

Max smiled and called to the crew, "Crowd on sail, weigh anchor." They were in the wake of the *Anna Rose* in no time. Having the faster ship, Max occasionally had to luff the sail to keep their distance. Spirits rode high on the *Mystic* in the excitement of the chase. As they neared Alligator Reef Jonathon kept watch from high in the rigging looking for any sign the *Anna Rose* was slowing or turning. When it came he called down to Max who brought the ship to a halt.

Abby looked to Max.

He answered the question in her eyes. "Now we wait."

The crew remained on deck ready for Max's next command and grew impatient at the delay. Abby felt their restlessness and started to say something to Max but then held her tongue. He was Captain and although she was his wife it was not her place to question him on this ship.

Max noticed her reticence and although on a ship it was the way it should be and had to be with his crew and even his best friend with his wife he wanted something different. He wanted to know what she was thinking. "What is it Abby?"

Abby quietly asked him, "How long do you intend to wait?"

Max replied, "Till the timing feels right. We have no way to know for sure what is going on. Now tell me what you are really thinking."

Not wanting to overstep her bounds she searched his eyes for confirmation he was indeed asking for her thoughts. When he raised his eyebrows in encouragement she said, "How do you plan to get aboard the ship? Talmage will try to stop you."

"I know. We'll probably have to fight our way on board."

"And what if the whole crew of the *Anna Rose* is behind him?"

"I'll cross that bridge when I get there."

His lack of concern frustrated her. "I could go with you. I am the owner's daughter. They would have to let me on board."

Max would not allow her anywhere near such possible danger. "No they don't and even if they did what would it accomplish other than giving them another hostage? No, you're not going," said Max, with all the firmness he could muster. To placate her, he added, "I won't be able to focus on what I need to do if I am worried about you."

Abby smiled to herself. His protective attitude was not without its charm.

Just over a half hour later Max set them underway again. They easily found the wreck. The *Sinistral* was anchored on the far side off the stern of the *Anna Rose*. They anchored the *Mystic* within a hundred yards. As he had hoped their approach had gone unnoticed until they were upon them. Max sent Abby below deck beforehand not wanting Talmage to see her. He ordered Jonathon, Thomas, Mike, Flynn and the twins to ready the longboat while the rest of the crew cast anchor.

Max took a moment to go below deck. Abby waited for him beyond the view of the hatch. He passed her to retrieve his gun from his chest. She anxiously watched his movements. Returning to the main room he stood in front of her and placed his hands on either side of her face tilting it up for his kiss.

"Will you be all right here by yourself?"

Abby nodded. "Max, please be careful. We have just discovered our love. I expect a lifetime to enjoy it."

"I will."

She watched him retreat up the stairs.

On the way over to the *Anna Rose*, Max instructed his men once they boarded the ship to look for the man Maria had described while he intended to meet with the captain. They were all preparing for battle sure that Talmage would try to stop them from boarding.

Talmage had his hands full dealing with the crew of the *Anna Rose*. They were not willing to take orders from any man other than their captain, who was currently being detained in his stateroom by Santos, no matter how much Talmage threatened them. His partner, Mr. Cornell, had overtaken the ship with help from some men they had bribed and hid aboard in the dead of night for that purpose. Now seeing Eatonton on the way he cursed violently. He knew the maid had overheard his plans.

Desperate to regain control of the situation Talmage pulled aside two of his men and instructed them to row over to the *Mystic* without being seen and bring back the female on board. Next Talmage had Leo grab the first mate of the *Anna Rose* and hold a knife to his throat in order to gain control of the rest of the crew. Sending Leo and his hostage out of sight he then intercepted Max at the bulwarks.

As expected, Talmage greeted Max and his crew with hostility and threats. Max pushed the older, heavier man aside so he and his crew could board the ship. All rested on them finding the stranger on board. Max strode forward looking about and Talmage scrambled to get in front of Max lest he find Leo. The rest of Max's crew fanned out behind him searching for their target. "You don't have permission to be aboard."

Max ignored Talmage and announced to the rest of the men, "I want to meet with the Captain of this vessel."

Talmage said, "He's not on deck at the moment. Nor does it matter. He has already accepted my help and I am refusing to enter a consortship with you."

Mr. Cornell returned to the deck at that moment to find his plan had gone awry and that buffoon Talmage was talking to another ship captain and vigorously waving him towards them. Stepping into the scene Talmage said, "This here is Captain Cornell. Isn't it true you have already contracted with me to help free your ship?"

Max held out his hand to the tall dark stranger he doubted was any ship's captain much less the captain of this one. "Is that true Captain Cornell?"

Cornell automatically reached out to shake Max's hand revealing his missing thumb. "What Captain Talmage said is true and as the wreck is not severe and the weather is fair I believe only his services will be required."

Max said, "I agree. Good luck in your endeavors sir. We will push off." He turned and scanned the deck, mentally accounting for all of his men. He couldn't help but feel the malice that permeated the ship and the desperate look of her crew scattered about and frozen as if lost. Max walked slowly trying to buy some time as he considered his options. He approached Thomas who turned and walked with him towards the railing. Thomas reported in a whisper what a crewman had risked telling him. "The captain has been taken hostage. The crew's hand is stayed by one of their own being held at knife point on the other side of the cabin behind us."

Quickly Max formulated a plan. Nearing the railing Jonathon and Flynn were also within hearing distance. He gave his orders quickly not wanting Talmage to realize a plan was afoot. "I'll distract Talmage." He looked to Thomas being the largest and most muscular. "Take care of the hostage. Rest of you look around for weapons."

Max was counting on a well-orchestrated attack with no planning and counting on men he didn't know to back them up. He also had no idea how he was going to distract Talmage. At least the number of men was in his favour provided Thomas could relieve their worry over their mate. The only thing that really bothered him was where was all of Talmage's crew? He only knew the whereabouts of four of them; the two holding the crewman and the captain hostage and the two flanking Talmage. There were at least five missing. He supposed they must be below decks and therefore of concern but he hoped at least one or two were still aboard the *Sinistral.*

A nod from Max and it all happened quickly.

Talmage, seeing Thomas making his way around the cabin, asked, "Where is your man headed?"

Max turned towards Talmage. "Nowhere you need to be worried about." Not coming up with any further ideas to distract him Max rushed Talmage. He swung with all his might connecting solidly with the man's jaw. Talmage went down but only for a moment. As he gained his feet he rammed Max in the gut doubling Max over at the same time a bullet went flying by his head. Cornell held a smoking pistol. Darned if Max didn't owe Talmage thanks for causing the bullet to miss its mark.

Tim Grantham took the pistol from Mr. Cornell as he was desperately trying to reload it. Mike and Flynn pulled Talmage from Max while at the same time Thomas, sneaking up from behind, struck Leo on the back of the head rendering him unconscious. The crewman of the *Anna Rose*, now freed from his captor, rushed forward with his fellow ship mates and joined in the fray. With the odds three to one Talmage, Cornell and their men were soon lined up against the bulwarks and held at knife and gun point. The true captain was freed by his crewmen and joined them on deck with two more of Talmage's men in tow.

Captain Smithe wholeheartedly thanked Max clasping him on the back with one hand while shaking his hand with the other. "Sir, I owe you an utmost debt of gratitude for saving my ship."

Abby knelt on the bunk watching Max and his crew row to the *Anna Rose*. She hated being confined below deck. She thought Max was overreacting. Even if Talmage saw her on this ship what could he do about it? The men were now climbing aboard the *Anna Rose*. She saw Max push his way past Talmage and the other's climb aboard after him. It was another moment before she noticed the boat with two men making their way from the bow of the *Anna Rose* to her. Max's crew was too busy to notice them. She only had minutes to figure out what to do before they would be upon her.

Abby scrambled off the bunk and nearly flew to the upper deck. First she pulled up the rope ladder then she looked for weapons. Heavy coils of rope would not do. Even if she could lift them she didn't want to give them rope. Hurrying back down the hatch she surveyed the main room and then searched Max's cabin, ransacking his chest, hoping to find a gun. She did not. A quick glance out the porthole told her she was out of time. Returning to the main room she desperately looked for any kind of weapon. Nothing. She raced around the table to the galley and found a large carving knife and a basket of potatoes. It would have to do. She dropped the knife in the basket and it was only by sheer will she managed to climb the ladder with her burden. By the time she made it back to the railing the men had reached the ship. Setting the basket at her feet she struck the knife into the wood of the deck so it would be ready for her to grab quickly.

She recognized the marauders. Amos Hardy, one of Talmage's crewmen, and Sam Carter, the former first mate of the *Abigail Rose*. The same man who had attacked her outside the bar when she first arrived. Fear raced down her spine. Pushing it aside she started throwing potatoes at the men. A few of her missiles hit their target but did nothing to stop them. Much to her dismay they had brought their own rope and grappling hook. Abby darted out of the way as Carter's first toss flew past her shoulder. He pulled it back to catch on the railing. Abby quickly released it and tossed it down at them aiming for his head. Unfortunately she missed. She threw more tubers as Carter coiled the rope for another toss. This time when it anchored he quickly pulled the rope taught so she was unable to dislodge it. Carter began climbing the rope. Abby dumped the rest of her armaments on his head to no avail. She picked up the knife and started sawing on the rope. Carter reached her before she had made much progress. He snatched her hand with the knife and somehow managed to fling the knife harmlessly into the water.

Abby twisted her arm free and unable to stop them from boarding she fled the deck to lock herself in the Captain's cabin. She climbed across the bunk to the port window hoping to see help on the way. It was not to be. She turned looking around the room for a weapon of any kind when the door crashed open under Carter's booted foot. Amos stood just behind him. She tried to fight off the two men but she was no match. She was captured and gagged before she ever thought to scream for help. Amos bound her hands while she faced Carter who was holding her arms immobile. The look in his eyes as he stared at her heaving bosom offended her. His words frightened her.

Carter licked his lips. "As soon as the Captain's done with his business you and I are going to have that fun I promised."

Abby now understood in a way she had not before what he meant to do and it chilled her blood. She struggled harder but only managed to make Carter smile wider.

Amos finished his task then Carter picked her up and carried her to the deck. He placed her on her feet again while he climbed over the bulwarks onto the rope ladder. Amos pushed her forward and then lifted her as Carter pulled her over his shoulder. She didn't dare move now while he descended the ladder not wanting to fall in the water bound as she was. Carter settled her on the middle seat of the jollyboat while he sat behind her and Amos sat in front.

When they started out both men were rowing. Carter kept up his commentary of what he planned to do to her later. As he grew bolder his words grew more graphic painting a picture in her mind she couldn't escape. Abby struggled with the bonds around her wrists until Carter placed a knife to her back and told her to be still. She obeyed for a moment trying to find a way out of her situation. She looked hopefully to the *Anna Rose* but did not see anyone on board looking in her direction.

Santos pricked her with the tip of the blade. "Don't go gettin' any ideas you'll find help there. They look to be busy with their own matters. Maybe I'll have time to get started with you before Talmage returns to the *Sinistral*."

None on board the *Anna Rose* noticed the jollyboat returning from the *Mystic* until Talmage pointed it out. "Not time to celebrate yet Eatonton. This ain't over." Talmage nodded in the direction of the jollyboat. "Look ye over that side. I've found meself a prize and I think it's going to be worth you letting me and my men go."

Max itched to wipe the sneer off Talmage's face with his fist but looking to where Talmage indicated the thought fled as all the blood drained from Max's face. He felt fear like he never had before. Two of Talmage's men were in the boat with Abby in between them. Her hands were bound behind her back and she was gagged. One held a knife to her spine.

Max's men having seen it too immediately and without orders released Talmage's men who wasted no time stripping them of their weapons.

Talmage walked up to Max. "Take your men and leave now and I'll think about sending her back unharmed." He grinned showing his yellowed teeth. "Well almost unharmed."

Abby grew angry. She was not going to let this man assault her nor was she going to let him use her to control Max. Reacting on instinct alone in one fluid motion she pulled away from the knife, stood up, took as deep a breath as the gag would allow, bent her knees and pushed herself up as she leaned sideways. It worked. She landed in the water and immediately sank below the surface.

She tried kicking her way back up but her skirt hindered her efforts and she still couldn't free her arms. The desperate reality of her situation registered in her soul. She prayed for her life as she sank further, drifting down, watching the boat, fearful rescue might come from her captors. She tried to make peace with her fate while she struggled not to swallow the water that seeped in around her gag.

She had told Max to be safe, fearful for his life. Funny she was the one in mortal danger. Colorful fish swam all around her and there was more colour in the coral below. It was quiet and tranquil here under the waves. She stopped kicking and just drifted...until she saw the shark on the bottom. Desperately she started kicking her feet again.

Above the surface, Carter yelled, "What the hell!" as he watched her go overboard. Not anticipating her actions, he reached for her too late.

Amos dropped the oars and grabbed both sides of the boat as it rocked in the aftermath of her shifting weight.

"Amos, go after her!"

"I ain't going after her. You go. I can't swim."

Max's wrath exploded at Talmage's veiled threat to Abby. He turned and would have attacked Talmage again if he hadn't heard the splash of something falling into the water and the arguing from the men in the jollyboat. With sickening dread he raced to the side to find Abby still bound and gagged sinking to the bottom of shark infested waters about three fathoms deep. He climbed the bulwarks and dove off the ship praying he would not go so deep as to strike the reef but thinking in a perverse way if he did at least they would die together today.

Abby's valiant act changed the tide of fortune. Jonathon Keats and Captain Smithe were quickly able to subdue Talmage and his men again.

As Max kicked for the surface he saw a man diving through the water. He knew it would be Thomas even before he saw his dark skin. He was thankful to have his friend's help. Surely one of them could reach her in time. Max broke the surface then started swimming towards the place where he saw Abby going down. Thomas breached the water several yards from him as they both took in air and continued to swim towards her.

All the while Max prayed they were not too late. He made every deal with God he could think of to save Abby's life despite knowing God did not work that way. He had just begun to discover the joy to be found in opening his heart. Surely she would not be taken away from him so soon. One lesson he had learned from the last few days, sharing their love was worth whatever the cost. He would never again push her away for fear of losing her. Of course that was provided he didn't lose her now.

Max swam harder than he ever had in his life. He surfaced for breath one last time then dove down towards Abby. For the first time ever he was ahead of Thomas.

Abby's relief was so great when she finally noticed Max swimming towards her she choked on the sea water filling her mouth. She struggled even harder to free her hands from the rope afraid Max would not be able to get her to the surface in time.

Max reached Abby before she touched bottom. He swam underneath her and then pushed for the surface with all his might. Abby struggled to keep calm. She focused on the water's surface and the sky above willing herself not to run out of air or swallow more water.

Reaching the surface Max quickly untied the cloth around her mouth while supporting her above water. As she coughed and sputtered, he rained kisses over her face thankful she was alive and reassuring himself he had not lost her.

Tears of release from the fear she had felt for the last half hour streamed down her face. Finally able to catch her breath she said, "Max, my arms."

He turned her around in the water and undid the binding. She turned back to him and wrapped one arm around his neck while she used the other to keep her above water.

Max drew her face to his and kissed her full on the mouth even though he knew others were watching. They nearly went under again. Pulling back Max asked her, "Are you alright?"

Abby brushed the hair away from her face. "I am now."

As soon as he knew Max would save Abby, Thomas turned and started swimming towards the two men in the jollyboat. They were arguing over what they should do next and did not see his approach underwater. When Max and Abby surfaced, the scoundrels decided to row towards the *Sinistral* but it was too late. Thomas had already reached them. Coming up from underneath he surfaced on the far side of the boat, grabbed the edge and pulled it down towards the water with all his might. The men were caught unawares. The sudden shift of the boat unbalanced them and they fell towards Thomas further helping him to capsize the boat. The men landed in the water on either side of him while Carter's knife drifted harmlessly down to the coral bed below. Not being good swimmers both men struggled and floundered in the water.

Thomas pushed the boat ahead of him towards Max and Abby. Once it was safely out of reach of the men, he righted the boat and retrieved the oars. One was floating loose but he had to fight Carter for the other. A battle he easily won by pushing the rogue underwater. Returning to the jollyboat he climbed aboard then rowed it the rest of the distance to his companions. He reached down for Abby who grabbed his muscular arm with both hands. Thomas pulled her aboard then they both gave aid to Max.

Max's only concern was getting Abby to safety. They left Carter and Amos to swim as best they could to the *Sinistral* while Max and Thomas rowed to the *Mystic*. For now, it would have to be punishment enough for her kidnappers. Max climbed aboard first and then assisted Abby. Not wanting to take any chances of losing her again he retrieved a musket he kept hidden on board, loaded it and handed it to her. "If anyone approaches this ship who shouldn't, shoot first and ask questions later." He kissed her and then dropped back into the jollyboat.

Max and Thomas returned to the *Anna Rose* to find Talmage, Cornell and their men rounded up, hands tied and secured below deck with two guards. Meanwhile a man from the *Sinistral* rowed out and fished Carter and Amos out of the water. Max was too busy to do anything about it. The crew of the *Mystic* rowed out the anchor and hawser while the men of the *Anna Rose* hauled round the capstan and pulled the ship off the reef on the first try. A check of the hold found no serious damage.

Max sought out Captain Smithe. "Your ship appears unharmed. Will you be returning to Key West or continuing on your original course?"

Jonathon approached them but politely waited for the captain to answer.

"To be sure, we have deadlines to meet, but alas it will be a trip back to Key West to turn our prisoners over to the authorities. What do I owe you, my good man, for saving my ship?"

"Nothing."

"Nothing?" asked an incredulous Captain Smithe.

Max confirmed. "Nothing. It doesn't seem right to collect money since this ship is owned by my father-in-law."

"Your wife, the one they tried to take, she is Mr. Bennington's daughter?"

"That would be so."

"I wonder if he knows how lucky he is to have you for a son-in-law." Captain Smithe held out his hand to Max. "You have my gratitude, Captain Eatonton."

Max shook the captain's hand and as he walked away Max turned to Jonathon. "I would say that was a job well done."

Jonathon said, "Almost well done."

Max was puzzled, "What do you mean?"

Jonathon indicated the waters where the *Sinistral* was no longer anchored. "Some were able to get away."

"It could not be helped." Max moved to the side to get a better view of the water to the south. Jonathon followed. There was no ship in sight. "We did our job saving this ship and we did not have the men to spare for a pursuit. I had hoped there were not enough crew aboard to get her under sail. Carter must have taken control of the ship."

Jonathon nodded. "That was my guess as well. One or two of the crew were already on board. Amos and Carter were picked up. Four could be enough to get her underway."

They checked the other directions and still found no sign of the fugitives.

Max said, "I would bet they are headed for Cuba and if they're smart they'll stay there to avoid facing charges. Round up our crew. We return to the *Mystic*."

Abby welcomed the crew aboard thanking each one for their help in saving her father's ship. Max boarded last. He walked towards his wife and suddenly was awash in all the emotions he felt for her. He had come so close today to losing the woman he loved, his soul mate, the one who made his life worth living. He could no longer imagine life without her. He now understood love was worth the risk and he was profoundly thankful he had not lost her today. Although if he had he would not have regretted a single moment of loving her, only the time he had wasted in fighting it. Unable to resist touching her, he caressed her cheek and rejoiced in the love she returned to him. Her smile conveyed her joy for his safe return.

Abby's spirits lightened and joy took wing in her heart. They were both safe and in love. Max had proved his love over and over today from asking for her thoughts to saving her from the depths. She had a lot to be thankful for. Even though danger would come again, it was the nature of his business, she would have to trust in the Lord and face it one day at a time but her reward was in moments like these when all was right with her world. She said the only thing her husband couldn't already see in her eyes. "Take me home."

Max thought those were the best words he had ever heard. 'Home' for her was now with him. He knew she would always consider England home as well but it would no longer have the power to bother him. "As you wish, Princess Rose."

"I am no princess," Abby lovingly teased in reply.

Max reached for her hand and lifted it to his lips to bestow an intimate caress.

She enjoyed his teasing but she loved being openly loved by him.

He whispered for her ears only, "You will always be my princess."

Epilogue

January 26, 1829

On the way back to Key West they came upon the *Sinistral* being boarded by the U.S. Revenue Marine Cutter *Marion*. Max pulled the *Mystic* alongside the cutter and relayed the afternoon's events to Captain John Jackson. Captain Smithe had also brought the *Anna Rose* to anchor nearby. Captain Jackson rowed out to the *Anna Rose* to collaborate the story then returned to the *Sinistral* and had Carter and Amos taken into custody. Jonathon piloted the *Sinistral* to Key West with the help of three crewmen from the *Anna Rose*. Marshal Wilson was summoned upon their arrival to escort Talmage, Cornell, Carter and the other crewmen involved to the Sweat Box until Judge Webb could hear their case.

Max and Abby were happy to be home after their adventures of the day saving the *Anna Rose*. Max intended to stay the whole week as promised. That night they celebrated their love and pledged to always be devoted to each other.

The next morning in the dining room as they waited for breakfast, Max opened the subject of where they should live. "I have enough money coming to buy land and build a home of our own." This time he wanted to make sure Abby had a say in the decision. "Some of the wreckers are talking of starting a settlement on Indian Key. It is ideally situated so I could do a morning patrol of the reefs and return home to you in the afternoon. It has fresh water, plenty of work for me and would probably be in need of your healing skills. On the other hand a new settlement is more vulnerable to an Indian attack and offers even less socializing than we have here. What do you think?"

Abby was thrilled Max was keeping his promise of allowing her a say in their lives. "I am happy living in Key West but having you home more is a strong inducement. Which one would be your preference?"

Mrs. Bailey entered the room with their meal.

Max said, "How about on the count of three we both say our choice and see if we agree?"

Abby nodded in agreement. Max counted to three. Mrs. Bailey smiled in amusement.

Abby said, "Indian Key," thinking Max would like to try someplace new.

Max said, "Indian Key," thinking Abby would want him home more often.

Max nodded his head and in a resigned tone said, "Indian Key it is then."

Mrs. Bailey shook her head at the young couple. "Why is it neither one of you look happy with your decision?"

Max and Abby looked at each other perplexed.

"Maybe you need to talk this one out some more." Mrs. Bailey smiled and left the room.

Abby said, "I thought it was what you wanted?"

With a self-deprecating chuckle, Max said, "And I thought it was what you wanted."

Abby saw the humor in the situation and smiled. "So in trying to please each other we almost made us both unhappy."

Max picked up her hand. "It would seem so. At least we have our answer. We both really want to stay here in Key West."

Before Max left to sail the reefs again they purchased a lot on Whitehead Street and started making plans for their home. As they stood in the center of their plot of land and looked out to sea Abby said, "Promise me one thing?"

"Anything, love."

"Our home must have a Captain's Walk with a copula."

Two weddings took place before Max sailed again. Thomas and Maria were married Friday afternoon aboard the *Mystic* under sail in the Strait. As captain, Max said the words that bound them to each other forever. The following day Max and Abby attended Jason and Victoria's wedding. Mrs. Lambert, despite her concerns her daughter would 'marry in haste and repent in leisure,' did her best to put together a beautiful ceremony. Max and Abby were honoured to act as witnesses at the request of the bride and groom. Tria made a beautiful bride wearing a borrowed crown of emeralds and sapphires. Jason proved to be a devoted husband. Abby was happy for them and was sure they would do well with each other.

On Monday, Jason and his bride sailed for England. Tria could hardly contain her excitement as she waved to them from the ship's rail. She was finally getting her wish to travel the world. Abby would have been devastated by the loss of her friend if not for the support of her loving husband.

Max returned to the reef two days later with the promise to return in three weeks to spend another week at home making Jonathon interim captain in his absence. A gesture which confirmed to Abby she was indeed first in his heart and the ship was second. She missed him the moment he left and counted the days to his return.

February 12, 1829

Abby was too impatient to wait at the end of the dock. She had been watching for the *Abigail Rose's* arrival for days now. This morning she nearly jumped for joy to find it gliding into the harbour. As soon as the gangway was in place she made an unladylike dash to the ship's deck not even bothering to ask for permission to board. Finding her father emerging from the companionway she smiled broadly in her excitement while carefully studying his features. She was pleased to find him looking well. He engulfed her in a big hug. It was so uncharacteristic of him to display affection in public, she knew he had missed her. Pulling away, Abigail asked, "Are you ready to go ashore?"

"Lead the way daughter."

They both nodded a greeting to Captain Andrews but didn't stop to talk. Instead they made their way off the ship and upon reaching the landing Richard tucked her arm in his and they walked down the dock and towards her rental house. "Where is your husband?"

"He is sailing the reefs. I expect him home sometime next week."

Richard noticed the cheerful way she spoke and was pleased. "All is well with you and Max?"

Abby smiled. "Wonderful and I forgive you."

Puzzled Richard asked, "Forgive me? For what, pray tell?"

With mock irritation, she said, "For the underhanded way you forced our marriage."

Sheepishly he said, "I only hurried along the inevitable for the sake of my health."

"Justify it as you will, you still meddled."

"Would you have preferred I had not?"

Abby considered it for a second before saying, "No."

They entered the house and Abby showed him to the room downstairs. "Maria will stay upstairs while you are here. I did not want to unnecessarily strain your heart with the stairs."

Richard patted his daughter's hand. "How very thoughtful of you." He looked with pride at the woman his daughter had become. She had purpose and love in her life and she was happy. He could not ask for more - except maybe for grandchildren.

"Come into the parlour and relax. I will bring you something to drink and we can catch up on the news. I have so much to share with you."

Abby made them some tea and then asked, "How are Uncle James and Aunt Virginia?"

"They are in good health. I enjoyed our visit. His plantation is large and profitable although I knew that from his exports. Their eldest son Robert has been accepted to West Point. They are very proud of him."

"As they should be. I understand it to be a highly esteemed Military Academy."

"They insist I convey their best wishes to you and Max on your wedding and for you to know you always have an open invitation to visit."

Abby smiled. "How thoughtful. I would love to visit them. I will have to see that Max finds a way to make time for such a trip. Perhaps mid-summer. I am not looking forward to experiencing how severe the heat can get."

Richard knew it wasn't likely Max would travel in the middle of storm season but he would let Max work it out with Abby. Richard changed the subject. "I was surprised to learn I had crossed paths with Lord Malwbry. Having followed you from England how did he take the news of your marriage?"

"Quite well, actually, after he made peace with Max. He was married here two weeks ago."

Her father choked on his tea. "Eh gad, the boy moves fast. Whom did he marry?"

Abby smiled in anticipation of her father's reaction. "Victoria Lambert."

"Are you serious? And you are happy about this?"

Abby nodded.

"Incredible."

When her father chuckled and then started laughing Abby asked, "What is so funny?"

"I was thinking of how the Duchess was going to react to her new daughter-in-law."

The image evoked in her mind, of the Duchess' face the first time Tria defied her, had Abby joining in his laughter. When she could catch her breath she added, "Tria will keep them from getting too stuffy over there."

When they sobered she told him of the house she and Max planned to build then she told of the ordeal with the *Anna Rose,* although she left out the part she had played in difference to his heart condition. He had just missed seeing Talmage, Cornell, Leo, Santos and Carter being shipped off to St. Augustine in bonds having been found guilty of their crimes. Max and his friends were happy they no longer had to share the reef with the likes of Talmage.

She also chose not to mention a duel of three days ago between Mr. Hawkins and Mr. McRea. She did not want her father to unnecessarily worry for her safety on the island.

After tea they strolled down Front Street. Many of the islanders greeted her father like an old friend, happy he had returned. Nearing Clinton Place they were intercepted by Dr. Waterhouse waving an envelope.

"Mrs. Eatonton. I have a letter for you from England." He handed Abby the letter. "Mr. Bennington, how nice to see you safely returned. How are you sir?"

Abby knew from the handwriting it was from Elizabeth. She hoped Dr. Waterhouse wasn't feeling talkative. She was impatient to know the letter's contents. It had been over six months since she left England.

Her father shook the doctor's hand. "I am well, and you, good sir?"

"Fine, fine. I suppose your daughter has filled you in on our bit of excitement."

"Yes, she has told me all the details of Talmage's scheme and his arrest and trial. I am very fortunate to have such a resourceful daughter and son-in-law."

Dr. Waterhouse said, "Yes, very fortunate indeed sir, but I am referring to the duel of the other evening."

Abby grimaced.

Mr. Bennington looked from his daughter to the doctor. "No sir, I do not believe she has gotten to that particular news item yet."

"Oh! I shall rectify her oversight immediately. We had a dispute of such intense proportions a few nights ago as to deem it necessary for the two parties to meet in the street to find a resolution."

Richard gave Abby a reproachful look but said nothing.

Dr. Waterhouse continued without notice, "It seems as though two former friends, a Captain Hawkins and Mr. McRea, separated by past differences found themselves on opposing sides in Judge Webb's court. Deciding to make peace in order to refrain from unduly affecting their case Hawkins invited McRea to dinner Sunday at Mrs. Mallory's Hotel. All seemed to be forgiven and congenial until Hawkins discovered McRea exiting the window of his wife's bedroom later that evening. A shot was fired but missed. Hawkins demanded his satisfaction and on Monday morning four more shots were fired. The first three did little damage to either party but Hawkin's fourth wounded McRea and ended the contest. He recovers in his bed as we speak."

Mr. Bennington said, "Am I to believe dueling is a rare event here as to create such stimulated recital?"

Dr. Waterhouse grinned like a school boy, "Indeed, it is our first!" Seeing Marshal Wilson approaching he excused himself to deliver an important correspondence.

Richard cast Abby a reproving look. "Nothing else of interest you said. Sweetheart, I am not an invalid. I wish you would quit treating me as if I was or I may decide to return to England after all."

"Yes Pop..." Abby suddenly realized what her father was inferring. "You are planning to stay here? How can you? I mean I am delighted but what about your business?"

"I believe an office here on this island is a good idea and since Max does not have an interest in running it I have decided I will. With my brother and my daughter on this side of the Atlantic, business is the only remaining tie to England and it will be easy enough to put a junior officer in charge of the Southampton office. Family is more important. Now what does Elizabeth have to say? I know you are anxious to hear her news."

Abby touched her father's arm. She knew he would not appreciate a more demonstrative gesture in the middle of the street. She couldn't help her joyous smile. "That is wonderful news Poppa." She turned her attention to the letter, breaking the wax seal and quickly unfolding the parchment she scanned the contents. "Elizabeth gave birth to a healthy boy! They named him Jeremy Lawrence Kendall."

Early the next morning Abby was enjoying the sunrise from the Captain's

Walk and counting her blessings when she finally recognized the signs she had been ignoring for weeks now. She wrapped her arms around her torso, hugging herself, holding the joy close to her heart. She was going to have a baby! What a grand adventure motherhood was going to be. Looking back to July it was amazing how one event led to all the others. How running from becoming a duchess had led her to a tiny island she called 'home', to a man that was her ideal husband and now when July had held no promise; when indeed she had been jealous of her friend's joy, now her one last wish, her biggest dream was coming true. She hoped Max would return early. She was going to have a hard time keeping the news to herself. *How was she going to explain to everyone the silly grin on her face until his return?*

Read on to catch an exclusive sneak peek of

Love Again

the next installment of the Key West series.

LOVE AGAIN

Key West, Florida Spring 1831

It wasn't supposed to be like this....

The knock on the front door distracted Betsy Wheeler from her melancholy. The petite, twenty-six year old, widowed seamstress laid the shirt she was hemming on the table and left her workroom. She crossed the front room of her small home and seamstress shop. It was Saturday, whoever it was had probably come for a social visit. Betsy didn't really feel like trading pleasantries this morning. Maybe she could feign a headache and send her guest on their way.

Betsy ran her hands over her black hair smoothing it towards her chignon before opening the front door to find her friend Abigail Eatonton holding her wiggling eighteen month old daughter, Emily Rose, and escorted by her servant, Mr. Bailey, who tipped his hat in greeting to Betsy. Emily's enchanting smile as she reached her arms out towards Betsy had her changing her mind about the headache and opening her door wide in welcome. Betsy took Emily from her mother and turned to lead the way to her sitting room, then waited for Abby to join her. Mr. Bailey confirmed with his mistress he should return in an hour before retreating down the street.

Betsy noticed the tiredness lurking behind her friend's soft smile and dove grey eyes.

"Abby, would you like some tea or lemon water?"

Abby gracefully seated herself on the sofa. "Tea, please, if it would not be too much trouble."

"No trouble at all." Betsy looked a little closer at Abby's face and added, "Would you like some soda crackers as well?"

Abby grimaced, "Is it that obvious? I thought I was hiding it well."

Betsy transferred Emily to her mother's lap. "We have been friends for too long for me not to notice you are feeling unwell but do not distress yourself over others, most would never suspect."

Abby gave her a weak smile as she tried to contain the toddler. Emily wanted to get down and walk but Abby did not have the energy for chasing her around the room trying to keep her out of trouble. Scissors, pins and needles were too easy for her to find in the seamstress' home.

Betsy quickly exited the back of the house to the outdoor kitchen. She made two cups of tea from the teakettle she kept warm on the wood stove. She added another piece of wood to the stove's fire and refilled the teakettle from the bucket of water she had drawn earlier in the morning from the cistern and replaced the kettle on the back burner. She then added the teacups, a tin of soda crackers and a biscuit for Emily to a tray and carried it back to the sitting room.

Setting the tray down on an end table next to Abby, Betsy took the squirming baby from her. Abby wasn't the only one who was tired. Betsy picked up a large button from a container in her workroom and handed it to Emily to play with then sat down on the ladder-back chair on the other side of the end table and unconsciously began rocking to soothe her to sleep.

"Unless I miss my guess, you are expecting again."

Abby's smile brightened her becoming face. "I am. Max and I are trying not to get too excited so early when so much could go wrong but we can't seem to help it. Neither of us had siblings and we do not want Emily to be an only child."

Betsy inhaled the delicate scent of babyhood still clinging to the child in her arms. It immediately brought a return of her melancholy mood. "I am sure all will go well for you. Are you praying for a son?"

"I am sure Max is but healthy is all that matters to me."

Betsy tried to paste a smile on her face and be a good hostess. "I suppose your condition has changed your plans to visit England this summer."

Abby stopped nibbling on her cracker to answer, "Unfortunately it does and I was looking forward to seeing my friends again, especially Elizabeth and Victoria."

"Have you received any letters from Victoria?"

"Not any recently and the last one was so brief as to be a waste of good paper but then I am not surprised. Tria is not one to sit still long enough to hold a pen to parchment." Abby noticed her sleeping daughter and smiled a sigh of relief. "You have the touch with her. It usually takes me an hour to get her to settle down for a nap."

Betsy looked down at Emily's sweet face and felt the longing in her heart. She would have loved being a mother. She felt her heart constrict. Her emotions were too close to the surface today.

Gently Abby asked, "Betsy, what is it? You seem so somber today."

The concern in Abby's tone was her undoing. Betsy's eyes welled up. Someone to care about her was what she missed most living alone. It had been five years since her husband had passed away and some days, like today, the loneliness became unbearable. She quickly wiped away the unexpected tear as it slipped down her cheek.

As Betsy's silence continued, Abby said, "I am sorry, forgive me for intruding. If you would rather be alone, we could leave."

Betsy swallowed back her tears and looked at Abby. She saw only concern on her friends face, no discomfort towards her weakness and Betsy felt the need to share her feelings swelling in her breast. She had held the grief inside for too long. "No. Please. Stay." After a pause she added, "Today would have been our eighth anniversary."

Abby's tiredness fled in the wake of concern for Betsy. They had known each other for three years now and Betsy had yet to share anything of her past. All Abby knew was she had become widowed after moving to the island. She felt her friend's need to share her story and sought out a way to help her start. "What brought you to Key West?"

"Ben, my husband, he was a tailor. We had been married about a year when he heard about the new settlement here. I think it was the adventure that lured him. I hated leaving all of my family in New York, we both came from large families, but I would have followed him anywhere. As long as we were together I thought I could handle anything. He built this house for us and was going to open a shop in town. He left me for a few weeks while he went to Mobile to buy fabric and notions." Once started with her story, Betsy found she couldn't stop. She shared it all with Abby. "He returned with Yellow Fever. Actually, it was Max who took him there and brought him home. Ben nearly didn't survive the return voyage and Max and Thomas had to carry him home. I nursed him night and day for almost a week with Mrs. Mallory's help but it was not to be. He died still apologizing on his last breath for leaving me here alone so far from my family and not enough money to return to them. He had spent almost all of our money to setup the shop."

Abby said nothing, just waited for Betsy to continue sensing there was more to her story. She watched the emotionally deep pain intensify on Betsy's face and the tears released unheeded, and perhaps unknown, as finally Betsy continued. Abby handed her the handkerchief from her sleeve. Betsy reflexively accepted it. Her eyes returned to the sleeping child in her arms.

"After he passed the only way I found to go on was focusing on the tiny baby growing inside me. I still had a part of him. When I lost the baby shortly afterwards I was devastated all over again. It took quite a while before I was ready to face the world again. If not for Mrs. Mallory's support I don't think I could have done it.

Needing to support myself I hung up my shingle and started sewing. With so many men and so few women there was an abundance of work to keep me busy and enough money to keep me going but never enough to get back to New York. Eventually I quit trying and accepted that this would be my home." Having reached the end of her story Betsy became aware of her tears and dried her eyes with the embroidered linen in her hand.

"What about your family? Couldn't they have sent you money?"

Betsy shook her head. "My parent's had all my younger brothers and sisters to support."

"Were you afraid to stay here by yourself with all the men on this island and so few women?"

"I think there were only four of us women then to over a hundred men, but no, I wasn't afraid. He would never admit it but I believe Max and his crew put out the word I was under their protection."

Abby smiled. It sounded like something her husband would do. "Have you ever considered remarrying? Max mentioned you and Jonathon had once...," she faltered not knowing the exact nature of their relationship.

"After a year of mourning, Jonathon and I had dinner together at the boardinghouse a few times but I wasn't ready to let go of the past and we became friends instead and then he fell in love with Esperanza Sanchez."

Abby gently probed, "And now? Are you ready to move on?"

Betsy considered before answering. "Maybe. Ben is still in my heart but if the right person came along, someone I could at least care for a little I think I could be ready to consider marriage if for nothing else than to put an end to the loneliness."

New York City, New York, Spring 1831

It wasn't supposed to be like this....

Theodore Whitmore reminded his young son for the third time, as gently as his frustration would allow, to stop playing with the spindle top and find his missing shoes. They were late leaving the house - again. Theodore had a noon deadline to meet at the newspaper and he could not be late to work. It was mornings like this he missed his wife the most. He was having a hard time finding the patience to deal with his five year old son. He watched as the child half-heartedly searched for his shoes only to be distracted by a wooden boat he found in a corner of the sitting room. Theodore closed his eyes and breathed deeply to control the building anger. Feeling a little calmer he walked over to his son and crouched down to his height. Taking the boat away from him he asked again, "Henry, where did you take off your shoes?"

Henry scrunched up his face as if thinking real hard. Theodore sighed. The rational approach was not going to work. Taking Henry by the hand, Theodore walked him room to room visually searching the floors and asking each time, "Did you leave them in here?" Each time Henry shook his head 'no'. Where in heaven's name could he have hidden them?

Margaret would have known where to find them. Of course, if Margaret were still alive he would have been headed to the office by now and she would be taking care of their son. A sudden unbidden memory flashed before him of his wife standing on the doorstep holding their baby boy on her hip while teaching him to wave goodbye to Theodore as he walked away headed to the office. Theodore's throat tightened and his step faltered. He missed her so. It had only been a few months but it felt like years since he had last seen her face or held her to him. They both missed her. Henry still cried for her at bedtime although it was occurring with less frequency.

Theodore brushed his hand over Henry's blond head. It was hard some days raising his son by himself but he refused to take the easy way out and turn him over to his crotchety old aunt. The only relative either of them had left. Reaching the nursery, Theodore realized this should have been the first place he looked. The shoes were laying haphazard on the floor at the end of the bed as if having been kicked off in a hurry. He would have thought five years old was old enough to responsibly be able to manage a pair of shoes but apparently he was wrong. Sitting his son on his bed, he put the leather shoes on his feet and buckled them rather than wait the countless minutes it would have taken Henry to do it. Taking the trusting little hand in his big one, Theodore waited for Henry to hop off the bed and together they returned downstairs.

They both put on light coats to ward off the chill of the early spring morning air and then proceeded to walk the three blocks to his Aunt Agatha's house where he would leave Henry in her care while he worked. The arrangement had been made out of desperation in those first few weeks after Margaret's passing and now, although he would prefer to leave his son with someone younger and more congenial, his aunt would take it as a betrayal and so the situation remained status quo. Theodore hugged his son goodbye, and gave his aunt a perfunctory kiss on the cheek then continued the additional eight blocks to the office of the New York Weekly.

It was now half past nine and he had a lot to do to meet his deadline. He stopped in the doorway of the office of his editor and friend, Bob Jenkins. "Good morning, Bob."

The middle aged man looked up from the typeset he was reviewing. "Good morning, Teddy." He waved his hand towards him. "Come on in we need to talk."

"I know, I'm late and you need my story on your desk by noon. I promise I'll have it done."

"It's not about being late or your deadline. Come, have a seat."

Theodore stepped into the cluttered office. He moved some books out of the chair in front of Bob's desk and took a seat. "What is it?"

"I've got an assignment for you. I've been thinking of a way to increase our subscriptions. My sources tell me there is more unrest with the Florida Indians and there is talk of another treaty. I want you to go down there and get a good feel for the situation. If there is a treaty, I want you to be an eyewitness to the event."

"Bob, you know I can't do that. I have my son to consider. I can't leave him for that long."

"Take him with you. The paper will pay the hotel room and for someone to stay with him while you're out in the field."

"It's not possible. Florida is hardly settled. Where would we even stay? It's not as if there are hotels everywhere. Besides it would require travelling in the areas of unrest. I would not intentionally take my son into a hostile area with the potential to break out in war at any moment."

Bob shook his head, "You are exaggerating the situation. There is still peace with the Indians and if they are negotiating war is not on their minds. Besides, I want you to set up base in Key West where you can move between the west and east sides of Florida. Monitor the situation from both sides and send in regular updates."

"Humph, you would not be so eager to send a reporter if there was not a strong possibility of conflict. It is a generous offer but you will have to give it to someone else. My son is suffering enough without his mother. I don't want to take him from the only home he has ever known to live in a hotel on some backwater island."

"A home as full of memories for him as it is for you. A change of scenery will do you both good and Key West is a booming place. Maybe you'll find a secondary story there too."

Theodore stood up, placed his hands on the edge of the desk and leaned towards Bob to make his point. "I can't and won't leave my son to the care of strangers at the drop of a hat and I won't leave him here with my dragon of an aunt. The answer is no."

"I knew you would feel that way so I arranged for my niece to accompany you as his caregiver. You have no objections to her, I assume." Bob had the confident smile of someone about to win his argument. "You could really make a name for yourself as a top reporter in this city."

He really knew how to push Theodore's buttons playing on his deepest desire for his career and knowing he would have no objection to his niece, Mary. She had watched Henry often as a baby whenever he and Margaret went out for the evening.

Bob added, "It will be good for both you and Henry to put some distance to this town and that house full of memories. Some new experiences are just what the doctor ordered." He opened his desk drawer and took out an envelope dropping it on the desk in front of Theodore. "Here is an advance on the travel expenses. Can you be ready to leave by the end of the week?"

Theodore stood up straight with his arms crossed over his chest and in the sternest voice he could muster said, "The answer is still no."

ABOUT THE AUTHOR

Susan Blackmon has enjoyed reading historical novels all her life. With a talent for writing it was only natural for her to try her hand at creating one of her own. All that was missing was inspiration. An unexpected cruise ship detour to Key West and a few history tours later, Max and Abby's story began.

When Susan isn't working full-time and writing part-time, she enjoys being with her family, hiking waterfalls, reading and scrapbooking.

Visit http://susanblackmonauthor.weebly.com to learn more about her books or to find your favorite way to connect via social media.

Made in the USA
San Bernardino, CA
02 January 2014